THE HEIRESS *of* WATER

D1502592

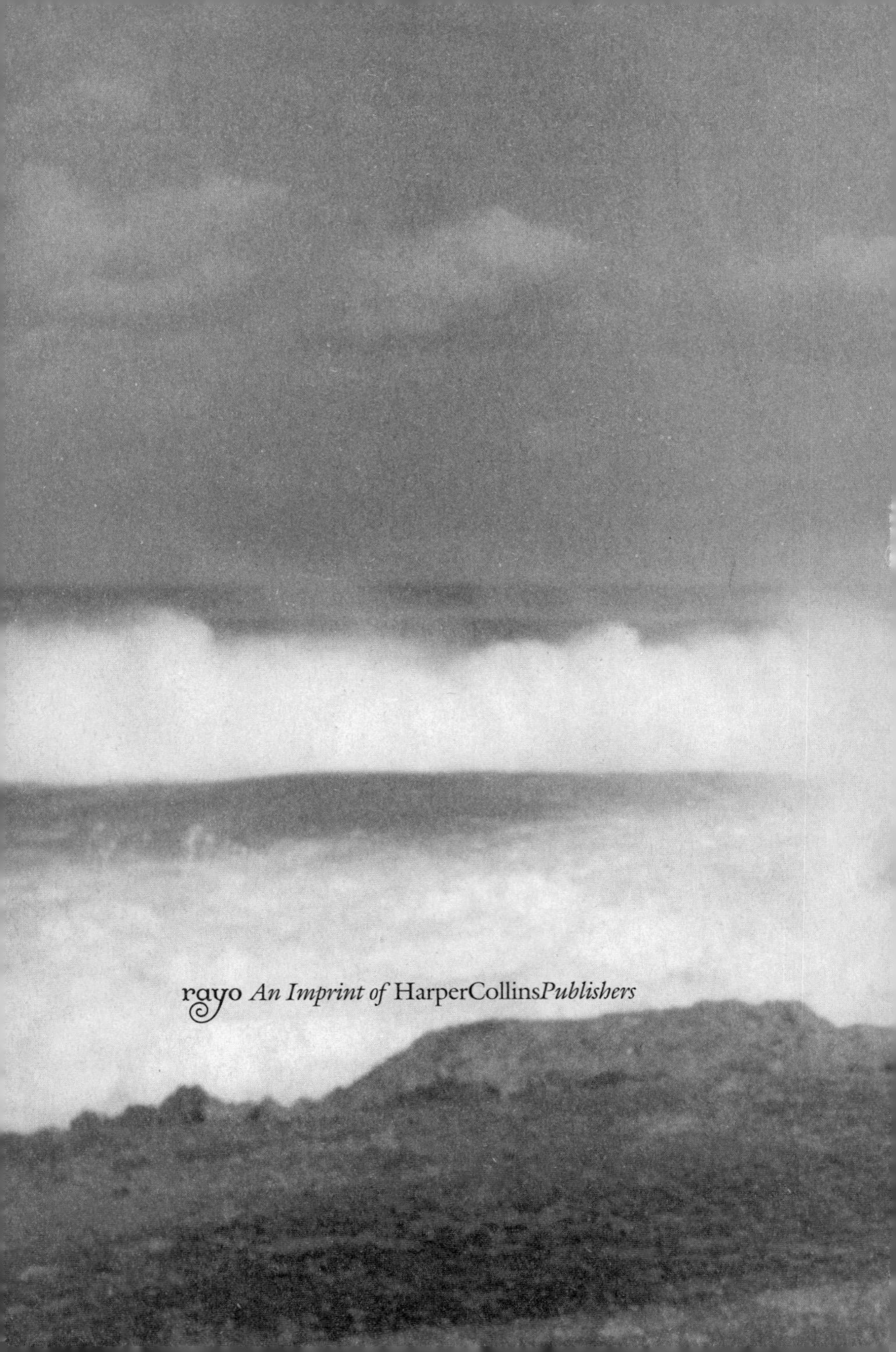

rayo *An Imprint of* HarperCollins*Publishers*

THE HEIRESS *of* WATER

A NOVEL

Sandra Rodriguez Barron

FIRST EDITION

Book design by SHUBHANI SARKAR
Photograph on title, part-opening, and chapter-opening pages © 2006 by Shubhani Sarkar

Library of Congress Cataloging-in-Publication Data has been applied for.

ISBN-10: 0-06-114281-6   ISBN-13: 978-0-06-114281-9

06 07 08 09 10 RRD/DIX 10 9 8 7 6 5 4 3 2 1

ACKNOWLEDGMENTS

I wish to thank my husband, Bob Barron, who gifted me with several invaluable commodities: time to write, a writer's sanctuary in our home, instant readership, and great in-house editing. Thank you, Bob, for all your love and support.

I wish to thank the bookends of my life—my father, Juan A. Rodriguez, who taught me to love reading, and my mother, Yolanda del Cid de Rodriguez, whose job it was to make sure that this passion didn't render me completely antisocial.

When the student is ready, the master will appear. And indeed, they did. A million thanks to John Dufresne for his superb coaching and infinite patience; to James W. Hall and Meri-Jane Rochelson for their editorial advice; and to the faculty and students at FIU who shaped my writing and made the MFA experience one of the highlights of my life.

For consultation on the scientific and medical aspects of the book, I would like to thank Dr. José H. Leal and the staff at the Bailey-Matthews Shell Museum in Sanibel, Florida, and Dr. Jeffrey L. Horstmyer, chief of neurology at Mercy Hospital in Miami, for taking the time to speak with me. I also wish to acknowledge my reliance on the cone shells and conotoxins Web site maintained by Dr. Bruce Livett at the University of Melbourne, Australia. Any fabrications in these areas are my own and certainly not attributable to these sources.

I also wish to thank my aunt and uncle, Ana and Perry Pederson, for fond (and useful) memories aboard their sailboats, and for advising me on matters involving sailing off the New England coast.

For the final phase of this journey, I wish to thank my agent, Julie Castiglia, who found the perfect home for my manuscript. Special thanks to René Alegria and the dream team at Rayo, and especially my editor, Melinda Moore. Seeing all of you transform my manuscript into this beautiful book has been like watching a couturier dress a bride. I am amazed and grateful.

To friends and family members who encouraged me to write and for those who offered editorial and publishing advice, thank you.

A NOTE TO THE READER

The tropical oceans contain over five hundred different species of cone snails. *Conus* prey upon other marine organisms by firing venoms that can induce paralysis or death in seconds. Some species are so lethal that they can kill a human adult in a matter of hours.

In recent years, scientists have discovered that cone venom has extraordinary pharmacological qualities. Each species of cone snail contains an arsenal of peptides (small protein fragments) that exhibit powerful, highly selective activity on nerves. By blocking the passage of electrically charged particles in and out of cells, the toxins effectively shut down messages between the brain and muscles. Recently, the FDA approved a laboratory-made equivalent of the compound found in the venom of the Australian *Conus magus,* a painkiller a hundred to a thousand times more powerful than morphine. Equally as important is its staying power: since it's not a narcotic, the body can't develop immunity to its effects. Other cone toxin combinations are being studied to address more elusive conditions such as mental illness, neurodegenerative diseases, and traumatic head injury.

The development of cone venom as medicine is clearly in its infancy and faces many obstacles. For starters, some venom combinations have plagued trial subjects with adverse side effects. The risks in introducing cone venom into subjects who have suffered a head trauma has made experimentation in this area exceedingly difficult. Still, several biopharmaceutical companies around the world have fast-tracked their plans to decode the healing potential of *Conus* toxins.

In addition to their vast promise as a source of new drugs, cones are valued by collectors for their beautiful, elaborately patterned shells.

Three species described in this novel—*Conus furiosus, Conus exelmaris,* and *Hexaplex bulbosa*—are fictional.

I SHALL THROW AWAY THIS THING THAT I have found as one throws away a cigarette stub. This seashell has *served* me, suggesting by turns what I am, what I know, and what I do not know. . . . Just as Hamlet, picking up a skull in the rich earth and bringing it close to his living face, finds a gruesome image of himself . . . this little, hollow, spiral-shaped calcareous body summons up a number of thoughts, all inconclusive. . . .

PAUL VALÉRY, *Sea Shells*

part ONE

EL SALVADOR, 1981

Alma Borrero Winters believed that everything in life begins and ends with the ocean. "The ocean is the expression of God on earth," she told her daughter, as she pushed open a set of wrought-iron gates. She shaded her eyes and strode onto Negrarena, a desolate expanse of black sand that spilled into the Pacific Ocean in the distance. She turned and clasped Monica's small hand. "Take a deep breath. Go on, smell it. Breathe deep."

Monica happily obeyed, filling her lungs with the rich smells of the sea. "Something's different today."

"You can smell that?"

Monica nodded.

"The currents are combing over the fields of seaweed from the west," Alma said, turning to look down at Monica. "I'm impressed."

They walked in silence, their rubber sandals slapping at their heels. When they were halfway across the expanse of sand, Alma noticed that Monica was trying to conceal something in one of her hands, and Alma leaned back to see what it was. Monica veered away but her mother grabbed hold of her arm. "What are you hiding?"

Monica handed over a small "in memoriam" card. They had been distributed at her grandfather's *novenario,* the nine Catholic masses of mourning, now a full month past. On one side of the card was a pale, pastel-colored image of a bearded deity sitting on a cloud suspended by winged cherubs. On the flip side of the card was a black-and-white photo of Alma's father and a short biography of his life.

Adolfo Borrero had died peacefully of a heart attack, and hundreds of people had attended the vigil for the repose of his soul—family, friends, the elite of Salvadoran society, domestic staff and workers from the Borrero plantations and from Borr-Lac, their dairy plant. All nine of his masses at La Divina Providencia parish had been filled well beyond the grand church's capacity with mourners and the curious. On several occasions, Monica had heard people comment that her grandfather would have made a great president. "He would have cleaned out the communists once and for all," an elderly man lamented as he stood in front of the coffin. Alma's response had been, "Then El Salvador must be pretty desperate for a hero."

Everything Alma despised about the society she had been born into was somehow contained in the traditional prayer cards that her mother had dutifully ordered for the service. Monica, on the other hand, treasured them with equal ferocity. "I know you miss Abuelo," Alma said. "But don't reduce your memories of him—or your vision of God—to this ridiculous card," she said, holding it up.

"Everyone else does," Monica protested, her face reddening as she turned away from her mother. "And nobody else believes in all that crazy ocean stuff but you."

Alma opened her eyes wide. "And *you.*"

Monica shrugged.

Alma flicked the face of the card with two fingers. "This depiction of God sitting on a cloud, bearing a striking resemblance to Santa Claus, is an insult to your intelligence." And with that she ripped the card in half, then turned it sideways and tore it again. "God is so much more than this silly illustration." Alma held up the scraps. "Think of it, Monica. How can infinity have a form? And to give him a *human* form, of all ridiculous things." She lowered her voice to a whisper, which annoyed Monica, since they were completely alone on a private beach surrounded by a thousand acres of farmland. "God has no memory, no shape, no conscience. . . . He just *is*." Alma lifted her eyelids, revealing a pair of black irises reflective and impenetrable as polished granite. She placed one hand under her daughter's chin, swiveling Monica's face toward the expanse of water.

"He just is. Like the ocean just is," Monica parroted, rolling her eyes and imitating her mother's overly dramatic whisper.

"Good," Alma said, giving Monica's ponytail a tug. Since neither of them had pockets, Alma stuffed the scraps of the prayer card into the left triangle of her striped-blue-and-green Brazilian bikini top. Monica experienced a vague discomfort at the idea that both her late grandfather and the Almighty Father were inside her mother's swimwear.

On this particular day, Alma and Monica had chosen to walk on the rugged side of the coast. Their starting point—the sprawling Borrero retreat named Villa Caracol—was halfway between the placid, smooth black-sand beaches of the northern coast and the pockmarked moonscape of the southern coast. The beach and the thousand acres of farmland that surrounded it was collectively known as Negrarena. Most of the Borreros and their guests invariably favored the smooth beach, but the south was a special place for Alma and Monica to explore. It was a beachcomber's dream, with its lava-rock tide pools teeming with marine life. Monica was glad to shift the subject away from religion. Growing excited as she eyed a nearby tide-pool, she said, "Mami, I can name *all* the creatures in the tide pool."

They crouched down together.

Monica began. "*Moluscos.* Common names . . . *concha de abanico . . . casco de burro . . . almeja piedra . . . ostra común . . .* All of these are bivalves," she said, accustomed to switching without awareness between Spanish and English like her parents. "*Bi,*" she explained, "because their shells have two halves." She held up two small fingers to illustrate the concept. She continued to show off, recalling the exact varieties of two lonely strands of seaweed; the species of starfish, sea urchins, barnacles, and crabs. Only once did Alma have to mouth a name to help her out. When Monica finished, Alma clapped. "*¡Excelente!*"

Monica concluded, in the manner of a miniature research assistant, by asserting that this particular tide pool didn't contain anything out of the ordinary, a circumstance that she was expected to report to her mother. "Nothing unusual," she said. "But one day, we'll find the *Conus furiosus,* even if it's the last one in the world. We'll find it, Mami, you'll see."

The idea of finding a living specimen of the rare—perhaps extinct—Central American *Conus* species elicited a slow, dreamy grin from Alma. Her fingers made their way into Monica's hair, tugging at the elastic band and unleashing a cascade of black coils, a miniversion of her own. "If you see a cone shell, do not touch it, Monica, no exceptions. The venom of some cones could stop your heart in less time than it takes to realize what stung you. And even a sting from one of the milder ones can really hurt."

"But, but, what if . . . ?"

Alma put one hand up. "Don't play the hero. If you see something that might be a *furiosus,* you come to find me."

Monica gazed into the tide pool and imagined the *Conus*

furiosus, or "cone of fury." The few remaining indigenous people in El Salvador had described it as a cone-shaped seashell the length of an adult's index finger that could be polished to show its chestnut base and its blood-colored splashes around the tip. Alma often referred to the eighty-year-old specimen in their glass display case as her "Ferrari." It had been added to the family collection back in the days when Monica's great-grandfather, Dr. Reinaldo Mármol, used the venom as a painkiller for his patients. In those days, many of the *Indios* distrusted modern pharmaceuticals, preferring the natural medicines that they had been using for centuries. Monica had heard her mother lecture on the subject at universities in the United States and Europe, reading from the yellowed pages of great-grandfather Mármol's medical journal. On the last page of the journal, the doctor concluded that, indeed, the *Conus furiosus* venom had extraordinary potential to alleviate pain. He also documented that some older Indians had witnessed other, more fantastic uses, such as the improvement of vision and a reduction of the symptoms of dementia; although of these he seemed a bit more skeptical.

The *Conus furiosus* species had been elusive even in the time of Monica's great-granddaddy, and although their empty casings still occasionally washed up onshore, not a single live one had been found in over fifty years. The reason, as in many cases of extinction, was unknown, but most likely had something to do with a change in their habitat. Alma had been told by local fisheries and by environmental experts that in all likelihood the species had completely vanished, yet she remained undeterred in her determination to find a live one.

About a quarter mile into their walk they came upon an enormous and conspicuous mass, unmoving in the shallow surf. They rushed toward it, kicking up sea foam and water. It was a sea turtle, the size of an overturned oil barrel.

"Is it going to lay eggs?" Monica asked excitedly.

"It's dead, sweetie." Alma walked around it and ran her fingers over the flat, salt-dried eyes of the turtle while Monica stood back and held her nose.

"*Uyyy* . . . Mami, get away from it," she begged in a nasal voice.

"What kind of turtle is it, *mija*?" Alma quizzed her daughter.

"Olive ridley," Monica said coolly.

"Nope. Too big."

Monica smiled and rolled up her eyes, suddenly forgetting about the odor seeping from the carcass. "It's a green sea turtle, only it's the black variety."

"Exactly. You can tell because it has a single set of scales in front of the eyes. Other turtles have two."

They both crouched down and examined the turtle's face. "Do you think she . . . ," Monica began.

As a passing wave lifted the turtle, Alma slid both hands under the carapace and managed to flip it over onto its back. "It's a *he*," she corrected, pointing at the turtle's middle. "See how his belly plate curves in? The concave shape allows him to mount the female's carapace during mating without sliding off."

Monica peered in and nodded, running her finger over the slick, rocklike surface of the turtle's belly before her mother returned it to its former upright position. "Do you think he has that sad face because he knew he was dying?"

Her mother shook her head. "Animals aren't sad about dying, ever. They know, somewhere in their tiny brains, that to live, eat, and die is a privilege. Their will is to simply participate in nature's design. And that, my dear, is the simplest, most basic wisdom there is in the universe." She pointed at the sky. "See those birds? They're going to pick the flesh off this turtle. The tide will return what's left to the sea, and the marine life will finish it off."

Monica looked at the turtle's opaque eyes and thought of her grandfather. "What will happen to Abuelo, then?"

"The worms and mites will eat him until he's nothing but a pile of salt. Then, the salt will drain into the ground and the rain will wash him back into the ocean. His minerals will be recycled into something else—perhaps a mango on land."

Monica giggled, tickled by the absurdity of hundreds of people mourning a man who was now a tropical fruit, happily gorging on sunshine and rainwater, dangling in the wind high above the red-barrel-tiled houses of San Salvador.

"Have no doubt that your beloved Abuelo will participate again," Alma assured her. "Hopefully he'll be a far humbler creature the next time around." She lovingly stroked the ridges of the dead turtle's shell. "The ocean's job is to repossess matter that is no longer functional. It's the sea, and its ability to turn itself into rain, that scrubs the whole world clean." Alma gave the turtle a great push with one foot, and it rose with the surf and hovered a few seconds before rolling back toward them. They both shrieked and ran in opposite directions. A burst of stench followed Monica until she gagged. She turned her face away and filled her lungs with fresh, salty air and ran back toward her mother. Alma turned, leaned over, and Monica hopped onto her back, wrapping her bony legs around her mother's waist. She curled her toes up in delight at their little adventure and peered over her mother's shoulder as Alma finished the job of sending the noble beast's carcass off to reconfiguration as a brand-new turtle or a grandfather or a mango. At one point during their walk, Monica said something that made them both laugh. It was then that Monica recognized, for the first time in her life, the subtle yet extraordinary phenomenon that was her mother's soul. Bewildered, Monica looked from her mother to the water and back: unbelievably, the sound that had burst from Alma's insides was identical to the music that water makes as it folds onto itself.

FOUR YEARS LATER, when Monica was twelve, a visit to Negrarena marked her passage into womanhood. Unlike her friends' mothers, who were squeamish about the subject, Alma had explained menstruation with the same scientific detachment with which she explained the feeding habits of jellyfish. Fascinated by this new development in her life, Monica frolicked in the water and imagined herself as pretty and shapely as her famously beautiful mother. She was trying to dwell in these pleasant thoughts and not look up toward the beach, where a man who was not her father was rubbing suntan oil across her mother's shoulders.

Monica kept half of her face submerged in the water like an alligator, her big green eyes, inherited from her American father, fixed on the horizon. She was fighting the current, which seemed intent on turning her body around to face the beach. Monica looked up in time to see her mother untie her bikini straps and allow Maximiliano Campos full access to her curved, smooth back.

Max was a tall, bearded man with unusual, pumpkin-colored eyes and pockmarks on his temples. He was a country doctor, a leader of El Salvador's communist revolution, and Alma's oldest friend. Max's mother had been Alma's beloved nanny, and the two had arrived at the Borrero estate when Alma was a newborn and Max was two. Alma told Monica that Abuelo had forbidden her to remain friends with Max in the years after her debut—her *quinceañera*. Eventually, she had defied her parents by rekindling her friendship with Max, and the relationship had been a source of tension for as long as Monica could remember. If only Monica's father knew how much time Alma and Max had been spending together over the last six months . . . he would probably spend more time with his wife and less time chasing news stories.

Monica got out of the water and walked over to the blanket. Sensing that her presence would help neutralize the atmosphere, she asked Max to move over. She placed herself between them, curling up against her mother. It worked, because Max looked annoyed and sat back. As if in protest, he began to talk about politics. His monologues about communism were always met with respectful silence. Alma usually kept her eyes fixed on her beloved sea and just listened.

Max dug his fingers through the sand and pulled up a broken oyster shell. He held it up to the sun, turning it slightly to let its pearly interior catch the light. "Alma, why do you want to find the *Conus furiosus* so badly?"

Alma was still lying on her stomach. She raised her face, squinted, and shook her head a little. "It's my calling, Max. You know that."

Max crossed his arms across his bare, hairless chest. "Since you have all the money you could ever want, Alma, what about contributing the fruit of your efforts to the poor people of this country?"

"First of all, I'm not rich, my parents are. And secondly, I study and protect the marine environment, Max. That's my contribution to society."

Max slowly shook his head. "To love nature is a luxury, Alma. When people are starving, they don't give a crap about nature."

"True . . . ," Alma said. "And when the politicians fix the economy, then our unspoiled natural resources will be waiting. Until then, I'll be one of its keepers."

"Look at me, Alma." He raised a finger as he spoke. "Let's say you find one of those cones. You copy the molecular structure in a lab. You turn it over to the international medical community for further study. The world will have a better painkiller, and you would have made a contribution to medicine. Wonderful." He folded his hands on his lap. "The rich get richer and things stay the same around here."

"Okay, get to the point, Max."

Max tugged at his chin hair. "Then develop this drug locally. I can help you when it comes time to test it. You can still unveil it to the world, market it internationally, but use the profits to help the poor right here in El Salvador."

"That sounds awfully entrepreneurial."

Max shrugged. "As long as it goes to help the poor . . ." He pulled a bottle of Pilsener beer out of a burlap bag. He opened it and took a swig. "Aw, hell. The *furiosus* might be nothing but a fantasy."

Alma tied her bikini straps and sat up. Monica saw Max's eyes on Alma's breasts as she reached up to release her ponytail. "That cone isn't a fantasy, it's just rare. It'll allow itself to be found by someone worthy," she said. She opened a bottle of beer and poured most of it in her hair without taking a drink.

"Then become worthy, Alma," Max said.

"I *am* worthy," she said, giving Max a hard look. "I'm not insensitive to what's going on in this country. It breaks my heart."

"Then come to a meeting with me," he begged, taking her hand. "Let's do great things together, Alma. You and I are a rare union of the warring sides of this country." He put his hands together. "We are what joins the rich and the poor, like—"

"Like the two halves of a bivalve," Monica piped in.

Alma laughed. Max nodded. "Yes, something like that."

"But, Mom," Monica protested, "going to a meeting is dangerous."

"Being a Borrero is dangerous," Max said, giving her an acid look. "Why do you think you live behind an electrified fence in the city?" He pointed to the land behind them. "Beyond those hills the campesinos fill their empty bellies with the scent of

meat roasting in your kitchen, hating each one of you for your comforts."

"Max, *por favor*," Alma said. "Don't frighten her."

"I can get every fisherman from here to Panama to look for that creature in their nets," Max said softly. "If you can make it lucrative for them to look."

In the distance, a wave rose and bashed itself against the shore. Alma waited until it stretched out across the sand in an exhausted hiss before speaking. "You inspire me," she said softly.

As Monica looked out to the vast field of dancing silver light, she caught the first glimpse of where this was headed, and how deep and sharp the fall ahead. Years later, she would pinpoint the shock wave of consequences that followed back to this moment, to this casual conversation that sent her whole family, and life forever after, into a sick and dizzying spin. Max somehow managed to pervert Alma's compass, and in the weeks that followed, her true north—the sea—became inverted in the direction of the land.

TWO MONTHS LATER, a fisherman with a sharp eye sent word that he had found an unusual cone shell in his shrimp net. Alma jumped into her Land Rover and headed to the small fishing port at La Libertad, refusing to take Monica despite a teary tantrum.

Monica and her father began to worry as the days passed and no one had heard from Alma. The fisherman said that he had given her the cone and that she had left with it in a dishpan, clearly excited.

Four days later, Maximiliano Campos's scorched body washed up onshore. The three bullet holes in his head had been washed clean by salt water.

Monica stayed home from school while they awaited news.

She convinced her father to let her wait for Alma at Negrarena, in the company of her grandmother and a trusted servant. Abuela spent the days under the spell of prescription tranquilizers, while Monica paced the shore from dawn to dusk, scanning the horizon with her mother's binoculars. Every floating palm branch or mass of seaweed made her heart jump to her throat. She survived by retreating into a girlish fantasy world in which she was a beautiful mermaid, a girl wonder with gills who could slip down into the ocean's recesses and find her mother. She could keep her safe in the silent depths for years if need be. They would return to land only when all the violence and death in El Salvador had stopped. Monica would rise up from the sea, her heavy fish tail peeling off in great rubbery chunks to reveal a glorious set of legs. Together, she and her mother would walk up to Caracol and wait for her father. Bruce and Alma would reconcile and have another baby. A boy. An infant who would cement her parents' marriage together like, as Monica had previously illustrated, the two halves of a bivalve.

Weeks passed, and Monica kept up her faithful watch as long as she was allowed to stay at Negrarena. Two months later, Bruce Winters announced that he was moving home to the States with his daughter. Alma had simply vanished.

chapter 2 THE GENTLEMAN

CONNECTICUT, 2000

The first time Will Lucero entered her office, Monica Winters thought he was another one of life's subtle but irritating road signs. She suspected he might be the pawn of a maternal voice that, as she approached thirty, frequently tapped her on the shoulder and whispered, *We all know you're with the wrong man, dear. Look. Here comes an attractive man. Go on, talk to him. Maybe he's the one.*

When Monica looked up from her work in response to a knock on the side of her metal file cabinet, she immediately sensed that Will Lucero was here to somehow challenge the status quo. When she saw the flash of a gold wedding band a second later, she realized that it was not the meddling Mother Spirit that had made her shift uncomfortably at the sight of that handsome face, but rather, the man-on-a-mission focus in his shiny, dark eyes. He had premature salt-and-pepper hair cut close to the head, olive skin, and faint crow's-feet that gave him the look of someone who either laughed a lot or spent a lot of time squinting at the sun.

"You Monica Winters?"

15

She nodded and stood.

Will introduced himself and moved aside to allow a tiny woman in her sixties to step into the office. "Sylvia Montenegro," she said with a slight Spanish accent. "I'm Will's mother-in-law."

"How can I help you?" Monica gestured toward a pair of chairs in front of her desk.

Will pulled out a chair for the woman and made sure she was comfortably seated before he sat down himself. He leaned back, placed an index finger at his temple, like an interviewer. "The entire physical-therapy staff in this hospital comes to you for massages." He pressed one foot against her desk as he tipped his chair back. "It's my wife's thirtieth birthday next week."

"I don't take new clients," Monica said apologetically. "I give massages at home—for my family, coworkers, and a few close friends."

Will pushed back on his chair a little more. "This would only require you to walk across the street and down a block after work. Yvette is over in one of the long-term care facilities," he said, pointing east.

Sylvia leaned in. "We heard you have magic hands. That your talent is something special."

Will nodded in agreement. "Any day this month would be fine."

"We've been struggling to come up with a gift," Sylvia said. "But Yvette doesn't need anything money can buy." She looked down and played with the buckle of her purse. "My daughter is in a persistent vegetative state . . . a waking coma."

Monica blinked twice and shook her head. "For how long?"

"Twenty-three months," Will answered in an oddly cheerful voice, one that obviously attempted to candy-coat what he had just said, either out of kindness to the listener or indicative of a hardy optimism.

"Oh . . . I've heard of Yvette," Monica said. "Her physical therapist is Adam Bank, right?" As she spoke, she tapped the tip of her mechanical pencil against the papers on her desk until the lead broke off. She had to figure out a nice way to get out of this. Her specialty was in therapy for sports injuries—head-trauma recovery was as alien to her duties as welding. Besides, she was booked.

"Don't be intimidated." Sylvia smiled. "Adam's work with Yvette is intended to prevent atrophy and pressure sores, infections, all that. None of it is intended to be enjoyable or mentally relaxing. What we want from you is no different than what you do for any ordinary client. We want pampering: scented oils, soft music, the works—like a spa." She clasped her fingers together, bit her lower lip, and waited for an answer.

Was it terrible to want to get out of this? Monica tapped on the surface of her electronic organizer, pretending to be checking her schedule. Tap, tap, tap, bleep, bleep. "I'm sorry but I'm all booked," she repeated with finality. "I just don't have time for new clients."

When Monica looked up, Will leaned forward. His gaze locked hers so powerfully that she thought that her eyesight was being physically gripped. She fully expected him to go for the sales kill, to try to strong-arm her into agreeing to do something she clearly didn't want to do. She crossed her arms and pushed her spine against the back of her chair, reminded herself to stick to her guns. But what she saw in Will Lucero's face surprised her: he opened up some part of himself, offering Monica a clear view into his pain, a humble and disarming appeal to her sense of kindness.

When Monica managed to overcome her surprise at the strength of her own reaction and disentangle herself from that pleading look, she stared hard to the left, into the vortex of a moon-shaped stain in the carpet where she had overwatered a plant. She sighed. There was no way she could let them go empty-handed. She snapped her fingers. "You need someone from the Healing Touch," she said, reaching for her business-card collection. "I know someone who'd be *perfect*. He's booked into the next century, but I know he'd love to work with Yvette. I'll call him right now."

Will abruptly stood up, and for a second Monica thought he was throwing in the towel. Instead, he pointed over her shoulder, to the bookshelf that filled the wall behind her desk. "Those are some fancy seashells. Not the kind people normally gather on a seaside vacation."

He was pointing to the row of *Conus* shells displayed on a shelf. Each specimen was suspended by gem prongs atop a six-inch metal collector's display stick. Without turning around, Monica said, "They're cone shells, arranged in descending order by the potency of their toxin." She tapped her pen and looked out the window, still trying to figure out what to do.

"They're poisonous?"

"They have a reserve of venom, which they inject via a harpoon with a barbed tooth," Monica said as she turned around. She picked one up and handed it to Will. "You're holding the deadliest of the bunch, the Australian textile cone. The ones in the center are less potent—that's the tulip, striate, marble, and alphabet cones. The one on the end, the chestnut one with the spiraled band of blood-colored speckles, is called the cone of fury. It's a family heirloom. Supposedly, its venom had some really wonderful medicinal properties."

Sylvia leaned forward. "What kind of medicinal properties?"

"Chiefly nonopiate pain relief—meaning it's unlike morphine in that the body doesn't develop a resistance to its effects over time. Also, it doesn't cause the usual mental dullness. The cone of fury may have had the capability to stimulate damaged nerve cells to regenerate. The indigenous people of El Salvador claimed that it could cure dementia and reverse memory loss."

Monica shrugged. "Who knows if any of it is true—the *Conus furiosus* is extinct."

"Are you sure?" Sylvia said, leaning forward and squinting at the row of shells. "It rings a bell." She looked at Will. "Now where did I hear something about sea snail venom?"

"The *Conus magus,* or magician's cone, is being looked at by several biopharmaceutical companies," Monica said. "*Sixty Minutes* ran a story on it last year."

Sylvia snapped her fingers. "That's it. I saw it on TV."

Will sat back down and leaned back in his chair again, lacing his fingers against the back of his head. Apparently satisfied with all he needed to know about cone shells, he said, "Monica, we're here because Adam offered to give up his appointment with you if you would agree to massage Yvette."

Monica suddenly understood. They really wanted *her.*

"But why me?" Monica pleaded, looking from one to the other and placing one hand on her chest. "Massage therapy is a little side thing for me. I don't even do it for a living. I'm a physical therapist. Sports injuries, hip replacements. That kind of thing."

Will looked up to the ceiling, as if carefully selecting his choice of words. "We want you because Adam Bank is a walking encyclopedia when it comes to alternative methods of healing. His knowledge and intuition are razor sharp and we trust him immensely. Adam told us that your talent for massage is nothing short of extraordinary. And we happen to be in need of someone extraordinary."

Damn, Monica thought. She let out a deep breath, summoning the nerve to just say no. Will continued to push back on his chair, waiting. Just as Monica parted her lips to warn him that that chair had a weak leg, a look of utter surprise flashed across his face, as if he had heard a loud noise she had not. The bad leg must have given under his weight, because he tumbled back against the wall of the office cubicle. He cried out and his arm flailed back and he tried to grab on to something. His chair slid back and landed with a loud crash, while the woolly, five-foot cubicle partition collapsed behind him. Monica bolted up to help, but the desk blocked her. The metal hardware of the wall's edge clanked against the drawer handles of a file cabinet on its way down, and it all landed with a dusty thud.

Monica stood with her mouth open. "Are you okay?" The mother-in-law remained unfazed, her hands primly clutching her purse. "He's a klutz," she said. Heads began to pop over partitions to ask if everything was all right. Luckily, no one had been on the other side.

"I'm okay," Will said, accepting Monica's hand when she finally got to him. He was a big guy, well over six feet, muscular, probably two hundred pounds. He looked around the collapsed office partition, shook his head in disbelief, and began to laugh. Then, he bared his teeth at his mother-in-law, growling and pawing at the air with elbows drawn close to his chest in an imitation of what he must have meant to be Godzilla, while Sylvia defended herself with her purse.

After they all shared a good chuckle, Will and Monica got to work reassembling the modular wall. Monica thought about his wife, the famously unlucky Yvette Lucero. Her name had come up among the staff, and Monica recalled Adam's description of her: *A beautiful Puerto Rican woman flipped her vintage Mustang, went down a hill, no seat belt. According to Doc Bauer, there is diffuse damage to the cerebral cortex, possibly some midbrain damage too. No improvement in almost two years.*

When they had rehabilitated the partition, Sylvia put her small hand over Monica's. "So what day are you available, dear? I really hate to take Adam's appointment, but I will if it's all you have."

"Saturday the seventeenth," Monica said wearily, wondering, just for a second, if they hadn't choreographed the fall.

***

MONICA ARRIVED at the long-term care facility a few blocks south of Yale-New Haven Hospital. Mylar balloons with "Happy Birthday" messages hovered over Yvette Lucero like watchful ghosts. The room was fragrant with the scent of several flower arrangements placed along the base of a large window. Will and Sylvia were standing at opposite ends of the window, half-turned, like twin archangels guarding a gateway. Already Monica could tell, by their stiff posture, that their mood was altered from a week ago. Her colleague Adam Bank had explained that the family members of brain-injured patients are often on an emotional roller coaster, swinging between the extremes of willful optimism and complete despair. Surely the moody New England weather that evening didn't help—early-summer rain, gray skies, and fog.

Monica approached the bed. She was shocked to see Yvette Lucero's eyes wide-open and darting from side to side. Will must have been familiar with the expression he saw on Monica's face because he said, "The sleeping phase of her coma only lasted three weeks. You can imagine our joy when she opened her eyes." He took a deep breath and let it out slowly. "But nothing else has happened since."

Desperate to lighten the mood and create ambience for the massage, Monica chirped, "Hi there, Yvette," in a voice that sounded as if she were talking to a toddler, which she desperately regretted. She put her hands on her cheeks, feeling them grow warm. Her mind went blank. This was such a mistake.

Will reached over and tugged at one of Yvette's toes, then gently slapped the bottom of her socked foot. "Hey, baby, pay attention. This is Monica Winters. She's going to massage your old bones until you're nothing but a pile of happy, quivering jelly. Happy birthday." He lifted her calf off the bed and brought her foot up to his mouth. He closed his eyes and slowly kissed the arch of her foot. Still holding her foot, he turned his head and looked at Monica. "Make her feel really good, please."

She nodded. Yvette's eyes continued ping-ponging back and forth. Monica remained motionless, confused and afraid of sounding ignorant or hurting someone's feelings. Still, if she was going to spend the next hour touching this woman's body, she had to have some idea if someone was home behind those strange, darting eyes. "Why do her eyes . . . ?" Monica ventured cautiously, moving her index finger between her right and left eyes.

"No one really knows *why*," Sylvia piped in. "Just that it's typical of cortical damage." She stood at the foot of her daughter's bed and began to dart from one end of the bed to the other, trying to keep in the line of vision of her daughter's mechanical, pendulum-like gaze. Monica's earlier discomfort doubled. She looked at her watch, desperate to get the massage over with. "So," she said, "do you want me to massage her in bed or shall we move her to my table?"

"In bed," Will said.

Sylvia waved one hand dismissively. "We'll move her to your table so she can enjoy the full effect."

"Not a good idea," Will said, his voice hardening. "Remember that her seizures caused her to slide off an examining table."

As if she hadn't heard a word he said, Sylvia unlatched the top of Monica's massage table. "Did you carry this in all by yourself?" Without waiting for an answer, she moved to the doorway and called to a nurse. "Ellie? Can you help us lift Yvette onto this massage table?"

A corpulent nurse entered the room, and Monica could tell by her posture (head back, chest inflated, hands on her hips) that she was used to ordering people around. She ruled in Will's favor, grabbed Sylvia by one arm, and sat her down like a preschooler. She rolled Yvette onto her stomach as if she were nothing but a weightless cardboard cutout.

"What's that?" Monica whispered, pointing to the equipment next to the bed.

"The doctors put her on the ventilator now and then to keep the air passages clean since she doesn't cough," Ellie said, pointing to her own throat. "Coughing is how we clean out our lungs." She smiled broadly and bellowed, "You don't have to whisper. The last thing you need to worry about around here is waking someone up." Monica stepped away and looked out the window, pretending not to have heard.

By the time the nurse left, Will and Sylvia were bickering again, while Monica began to set up her work space. She pushed back Yvette's pajama top to survey her dorsal side. The knobs of her spine stood out like stepping-stones leading across a garden. Monica squirted lavender oil onto her palms and got to work. She noticed that her fingernails, polished in red geranium, looked garishly healthy next to Yvette's ashen skin.

Massaging a person who was vegetative, Monica decided, felt like sneaking into someone's home in their absence. This sensation of being an invader was silly, she knew, but still, it felt oddly criminal to touch a stranger who was powerless to refuse. Monica ran her fingers up Yvette Lucero's spine, checking its alignment, feeling for irregularities, noting the absence of fatty tissue, the strange topography of atrophied muscles and the intrusive presence of so many bones. She decided to begin with the neck. A hairless, six-inch scar ran up the side of Yvette's head, just above her left ear.

Monica shut her eyes. It was the simple key to her legendary talent. It forced her to rely purely on the other senses—the pattern of breathing, the depths and sharpness of the client's inhaling, all of it guided and informed. She clamped her eyes tighter still and tried to let this client's strange body lead the way. Later, Monica would recall that something about Yvette's back (was it the irregular breathing? The ashy skin that felt as if it might disintegrate into sand at any moment?) made her thoughts wander back to Negrarena. Alma had taught Monica to run to the beach after a volcanic tremor and dig the full length of her arms deep into the sand. Monica would wait, motionless for what seemed like hours, until she felt the distant collisions of the earth's seismic plates trembling their way up to the surface in timid, fleshy spasms. Real or imagined, she couldn't say. Probably just a ploy to keep a kid busy for a while, but Monica believed that her mother was teaching her to converse with nature, to learn to ungarble its secret language by attuning all of her senses and silencing her mind. Eventually, Monica figured out that the same idea applied to the landscape of the human body.

A few moments later, Monica noticed that Yvette's skin emitted a distinctive odor, like wet metal, probably a cocktail of anticonvulsants and amphetamines being sweated out of massage-warmed skin. Since Yvette's muscles were so soft, it startled Monica to find a knot. Her fingertips reversed and rolled over the spot again. There was a familiar, tube-shaped inflammation of muscle tension running along the left side of the spine. The pattern of tension was a classic result of stress— Monica had dubbed it the bride's bar because she had found it on countless clients who were freaked out by the stress of planning a wedding, although technically it wasn't limited to brides. The knot was always two to six inches long, along the upper part of the spine, fanning up toward the neck area, usually on the left regardless of whether the person was right- or left-handed. Monica dug deeply into the knot's center, imagining the blood flow melting the inflammation like salt dissolving the rubbery flesh of a slug. Discovering the bride's bar on Yvette blew Monica's theory that it was a classic sign of stress. After all, how could Yvette have stress? In this case it was more likely to be the way they'd positioned her in bed, the alignment of her neck and head. Still, it was unexpected.

Monica opened her eyes and squirted more oil into the palm of her hand. "Either Yvette is not happy about turning thirty," she said softly, "or she's planning on getting married."

"You can feel her stress, can't you?" Sylvia said suddenly. "She's working so hard to emerge." Sylvia had returned to staring out the window at the foggy, fading afternoon.

Will, who had also been pensive and distant, turned to look at his mother-in-law, leaned against the edge of the window, and crossed his arms. He didn't say anything for a moment, just stared at her profile for what seemed like a long time. Then he approached the bed, took his wife's hand, and kissed it. As if he read her mind, Will turned to Monica and said, "The two-year anniversary of Yvette's accident is coming up in six weeks." He announced it with such a somber voice that Monica knew that this amount of time had some significance that she was missing, unless it just represented a disappointing mile-marker.

Monica hammered the tense muscle with the fleshy bottom of her fist as if she were grinding peppercorns with a pestle. "Does two years mark something specific in terms of her progress or care?" she asked tentatively. She didn't mean to pry, but they seemed to want to talk about it.

Will nodded his head slowly, deliberately before he spoke. "Recovery from vegetative state more than a year after injury is highly unlikely. According to Dr. Bauer, she has a three to five percent chance of recovery."

"Ten percent chance of recovery," Sylvia interrupted. "Remember the result of that new study I told you about, Will? It's up to ten percent, they say."

Will continued patiently, "If she does recover, Yvette probably won't be able to resume activity as a social human being. She might have a vocabulary of ten words, maybe less, be wheelchair bound and dependent on others." He took a deep breath. "Years ago, she and I had a hypothetical conversation about this subject . . . back when it was something that happened to other people. Yvette told me that two years was the maximum she would want to be on life support." He stroked his wife's forehead with the backs of his fingers. "Two years."

There was a short sniff from Sylvia, who had still not turned toward them, but continued staring out the window. "A year goes by so fast, and then suddenly you're coming upon two years, and . . . it's your daughter. . . . I won't have them stop her feeding tube. I won't."

Suddenly, Monica wanted to dash across the room and embrace Sylvia, to pick up that frail and sad little bird of a woman and make everything better. But Sylvia was unreachable across a chasm of unbearable pain. Monica looked at Will and held his eyes in sympathy.

"Massage therapy has succeeded in arousing people to consciousness," Will said, sounding a bit more cheerful. "So you see, Monica, you're a part of the master plan."

Sylvia turned and said, "We've tried everything, Monica, and we'll try it twice, a million times. Western medicine, Chinese medicine, Santería, Haitian voodoo. I'm considering making a pilgrimage to Mexico, to the site of the apparition of the Virgin of Guadalupe, Queen of Miracles."

Will rolled his eyes at the last part. "Let's just say we keep our ears to the ground on the latest in medical treatments and therapy."

"I'm researching the cone venom treatments we talked about the other day," Sylvia said, her hands pressed together as if in prayer.

Monica shrugged. "Cone venom is being studied to control chronic pain. I don't know that it could help Yvette."

"You said that the Indians in El Salvador believed that the

substance reduced symptoms of dementia and regenerated damaged nerve cells, right?"

"Right, but it probably wasn't true. I mean, it's so unlikely that . . ." Monica stopped. Who the hell was she to pooh-pooh the idea? No one had proved it untrue. Perhaps the local *Indios* had stumbled upon something special after all. And maybe the *furiosus* had resurfaced—mollusks did that all the time. It's not as if she kept up with the research. "Why not?" Monica said, holding out her hands. "If something as humble as mold can give us penicillin, then rare sea snails might be able to do great things as well."

Sylvia winked. "Exactly."

After considering and rejecting about five different things to say, Monica said, "Yvette is lucky to have you both. I'm sure that she feels your love."

Will nodded and said, "I hope so." He looked at his watch, then walked over to Sylvia and put his arm around her. "Come, *suegra,* let's allow Monica to do her magic. We're distracting both of them with our chatter."

Monica squirted more oil and continued at the base of Yvette's spine, working her fingers in perfectly measured motions that recalled the regularity of knitting, giving the muscles supporting each vertebra a dose of soothing pressure and motion. She wondered if this massage was having any impact at all. Monica imagined Yvette as a deep-sea diver trapped below great depths of water, looking up, waiting to feel the vibration of a single, dry leaf touching down upon the surface far above.

Where exactly, in time and space, was the woman these two loved and remembered? Monica realized she would have enjoyed posing this question to Alma because it was exactly the kind of thing her mother had loved to pontificate about. Monica had always assumed that same certainty would eventually settle into her own bones with age, but so far it didn't look as if she would ever achieve that cocksure confidence, that gift of unshakable faith that life has an underlying structure and meaning. Twenty-seven found her full of doubt, and witnessing Yvette's bombed-out life made her want to scream at the unfairness of it all, at the frightening chaos of blind chance. Monica paused in her work a few minutes later, but only briefly, to turn on a CD that featured harps, flutes, and the sound of ocean waves. She closed her eyes again.

The last thing she could have imagined was that along the eerie path of this woman's body lay a trapdoor to the dark well of her own memory. Monica easily stepped through it, plunging unaware onto the black sand of Negrarena, back to what she had spent the last fifteen years trying to forget.

ALMA HAD BEEN Monica's first massage "client." That first massage happened on the occasion of Alma's self-pity over an argument she had had with Monica's father, or with Maximiliano, or with both—Monica wasn't sure. But Alma's sense of being wronged or misunderstood was clear and must have been what triggered her defiant impulse to indulge in her family's extraordinary wealth, to eke out beauty and drama from her resentment. She packed a bag, told Monica to hop into the passenger side of her clay-splattered vehicle, and drove to the coast.

Alma ordered the servants at Caracol to set up a queen-size, four-post, antique canopied bed—complete with white linens and overstuffed pillows—out on the beach. Abuela was not there to impede this request, so the servants could do nothing but comply, all six of them disassembling the frame and mahogany headboard and hefting it from a second-floor guest room onto the infernally hot sand outside on the beach.

A full, cool breeze was coming off the Pacific Ocean that afternoon. When the bed was set up, Alma and Monica put their bathing suits on and lolled in that improbable sumptuousness. Mother and daughter stretched out across starched white linen sheets as crisp as rice paper, their index fingers loosely hooked together. They gazed up at the billowing white gauze canopy as it filled and expelled the salty air, pulsing like the head of a giant jellyfish. The clinking of ice cubes preceded Francisca, who was Maximiliano's mother and had been the nanny of two generations of Borrero children, including Alma and Monica. Francisca stumbled through the stretch of soft sand to deliver a pitcher of freshly squeezed lemonade. She placed it on a delicate wooden table next to the bed, pushing down on the surface to dig the feet of the table deeper into the sand. While Alma drank her lemonade, Monica played with her mother's hair, raveling it into a loose braid, then unraveling it.

Alma put her glass down and rolled onto her stomach with her face toward Monica and closed her eyes. *"Dame masaje en la espalda,"* she said, suddenly arching her back and wiggling deeper into the feather mattress. "I have all this tension in my back."

Monica complied with her mother's request by imitating what she'd seen her father do—she pushed her fingers into Alma's back, kneading the shoulder blades. She stopped occasionally to pet the back of Alma's head so softly and lovingly that some of the strokes only brushed the air. She listened to the sound of the waves crashing and rolling to shore and noticed her mother's back rising and falling in perfect timing with the rhythm of each wave. Soon Monica's mind was still and she was aware of only a few small details of her surroundings, such as the clean smell of detergent exhaled by the gauzy cloth of the canopy and the incessant scratching of a farm mutt hiding under the shade of a cluster of beach scrub. Monica didn't know it at that moment, but she was the happiest she would be for another twenty years. Alma, now fast asleep, offered an occasional snore.

The scuttle of something small caught Monica's eye at the

far corner of the bed. She sat up. An electric-blue-and-red shore crab, commonly known as a *caballero,* or "gentleman," appeared from under the linens. The crab was about the size of Monica's hand and was regal in his medieval armor. He charged up the back of Alma's leg, leaving little white scratch marks on her tanned skin. Alma had taught Monica that if you stay perfectly still, few creatures will harm you. Confident that her mother would sleep through it, Monica watched with complete absorption, waiting to see what it would do.

Alma continued to breathe slowly, her head resting on the backs of her folded arms, oblivious to the nasty pincers dragging across her bare skin. The crab reached the small of Alma's back, ascended the stepladder of her spine. As he climbed over her bathing-suit strap, Monica observed the toothlike bumps on the claws, the chela. She searched her memory for the correct term for those toothlike bumps, wanting to be ready to report the anatomical details when her mother woke up. The crab eyed her with detached, floating orbs before he scaled Alma's loosely roped hair, then stopped and rested on the base of her neck. *The chela are denticulate,* Monica thought, suddenly remembering the correct term. The crab spread his spindly appendages across Alma's neck, scarlet rays radiating from a core of electric blue, wet and gleaming in the sun. Monica's heart skipped as her mother's eyes darted from side to side under lightly freckled lids, seen in profile. Alma mumbled softly in her sleep.

Perhaps this otherworldly place, this dreamlike moment, was too beautiful to remain unblemished, too pure not to tempt the outside world to intrude. It was as if this "gentleman"—a scavenger whose territory included the farmhands' latrine—had come to deposit the refuse of the outside world. The creature pressed itself against Alma's ear, and she knitted her eyebrows together as she listened to what it had to say. Disturbed, she cried out in her sleep.

"Max," she said in a breathy voice. There was a silence, as if to give time for a reply, and Monica had the sensation that she was overhearing one side of a telephone conversation. Suddenly Alma shuddered and said, "If I don't leave right now, your wife is going to kill us both." Her sun-swollen lips continued to move, speaking inaudibly, ending in a great, inconsolable sigh. After she spoke, the startled crab turned opaque, folded up his appendages, and scurried off, like an unlicensed peddler shooed away by police. Alma rolled over to one side, her back to Monica.

Monica slipped off the edge of the bed and stood on the hot sand, staring at the wall of her mother's back, which might as well have been made of concrete. One of the panels of the canopy broke loose of its tie and slid between them. Monica watched over her sleeping mother through the fog of rippling translucent cloth. Monica grabbed a handful of it and wept silently into the cloth, because now she knew for sure what was going on. She looked up toward the mountain where so many campesinos lived. It all moved closer, somehow. Somewhere beyond those hills was a wife, someone who would kill to protect what her mother was dreaming about at this very moment.

Monica understood that the knowledge she now possessed was dangerous. If she could just keep her mouth shut, if she stood very still, maybe no one would get hurt. The peril might pass, slip quietly out of the white linens and into someone else's bed. That is, if there could ever be another bed quite like this, in which a beautiful woman napped under a billowing cloud of silk gauze, unaware of the real clouds gathering in the distance. Or another place on earth like Negrarena, where secrets dribbled out like saliva, leaving no trace on the parched sand of its desolate shore.

*   *   *

BELOW THE PADS of Monica's hands surfaced a faint tremor, then a shudder. Monica opened her eyes, jolted out of the digression of her memory. Had she inadvertently spoken out loud? Was it her imagination, or had Yvette arched her back a bit? Monica was unsure if she had shuddered at the vividness of her own memory, or if she had just sensed the struggle of a woman trapped below the surface of her own being. Monica had the eerie feeling that the shudder had somehow been the response of an audience to her thoughts. *She doesn't respond to outside stimuli,* Adam had said. Yet, a rash of goose bumps had erupted across Yvette's arms.

Monica looked up at the clock: twenty more minutes. She called the nurse to flip Yvette over. She would finish up with the head, then the feet, and then she was out of there. Monica massaged the temples of that pale, bony face. Now the eyes were still and staring blankly into space. When she finished, Monica devoted a moment to praying for Yvette, asking for a miracle, or at the very least, for the peace and comfort her family would desperately need for whatever came next. Feeling a bit like the startled crab, she packed up her supplies, rushed her good-byes, and fled, comforted only by the certainty that she would never have to see any of them again.

"Kevin is really racking up those brownie points," Paige Norton said, as she looked out over the wood deck that wrapped around the back of Monica's two-bedroom cottage. Monica was making tuna fish sandwiches and could see her best friend through the cutout in the wall between the kitchen and the living room. She had been thinking about the work going on outside on her sundeck, the peeling gray paint to be replaced with natural stain. The day was perfect for working outside, seventy-two degrees and just a hint of a cloud cover. Monica, her father, her boyfriend, and Paige had spent the morning working side by side and enjoying the view of the water from her home in Milford.

Monica looked up when her friend spoke and noticed that Paige's straight, auburn hair blazed in the sunlight streaming in through the picture window. Even her eyelashes trapped the sunlight, crowning her pale blue eyes with tiny arches of light. Paige tapped at the glass with her fingernail. "By allowing Kevin to make improvements to your house, you're indirectly agreeing to marry him." Paige raised her eyebrows authoritatively.

Monica stopped scooping the tuna out of the can and stared

into the white porcelain sink and frowned. "What? By asking him to scrape some old paint?" As she spoke, Monica felt a sharp pain on her thumb. She looked down and saw a thick drop of blood plop into the sink, her thumb sliced by the edge of the tuna fish can. "Now look what you've done. I cut myself."

Paige shook her head and looked out toward the deck where the two men were working. "When a parent enjoys your boyfriend more than you do, things have the potential to get messy."

Monica nodded as she washed her wound. "No kidding. Kevin gets along with my dad way better than me."

Paige said, "Look at them. Even as they scrape paint, they're gabbing away like a pair of little girls with a new tea set." She pressed her lips together and shook her head. "It's time to shit or get off the pot, honey."

Monica wrapped a paper towel around her thumb without commenting. Paige came into the kitchen and helped herself to a glass of lemonade. "I was just thinking about that couple you told us about earlier, you know, the guy with the wife in the waking coma. Amazing how your life can be gone all of a sudden." She snapped her fingers. "In her case it's even sadder because she had a life. Unlike me."

Monica scowled at her. "How can you feel sorry for yourself and talk about Yvette Lucero in the same breath?"

"I didn't mean it like that," Paige said, fussily rearranging Monica's plastic sea-creatures refrigerator magnets with one hand, the glass of lemonade in the other. "It's just that finding love has been such a slow and painful process for me. This woman found the Holy Grail, then it was over. It makes me wonder if it's worth dragging myself through the endless charade of dating." Paige stared up at the popcorn ceiling for a moment, then seemed to catch herself drifting toward self-pity again, because she said, "It's just not fair that it was all taken away from her."

Monica nodded. "Indeed, she had a few of the blessings that have eluded us." She stopped, cocked her head. "*Has,* I guess, because she's alive. But not really. It's so strange."

Out of the corner of her eye, Monica saw Paige turn and look at her. "Speaking of elusive blessings . . . you still think about your mom a lot, Monica?"

"Every day."

"Would she have approved of Kevin?"

Monica rolled her eyes and smiled ironically. "Did I ever tell you how my mother evaluated a man?"

"*Noooo,*" Paige said, putting her hands on her hips. She had always had an insatiable appetite for stories about Alma's life, and she needled Monica to retell the stories over and over in excruciating detail. Sometime around the ninth grade, Monica had begun to embellish, then ultimately to make them up completely. But she had never told this one, since it wasn't really a story, but rather a seemingly inconsequential incident that she now realized indeed had consequences. "Well, one day," she began, "while my mom and I were standing in a crowd outside the airport in El Salvador, I overheard her chatting with a toothless peasant woman—a *campesina* with a big heavy basket of fruit on her head. Anyway, the woman was telling my mom that she was finally going to marry her man after nine years and eleven kids. At the time, my mom was so out of touch with simple people and, in her infinite wisdom, thought she'd give this woman some advice on how to determine the worthiness of a man. She said, 'Can he change the world? Deliver justice? Can he save what's precious? Can he bring exceptional beauty to the world, or at the very least, relief of pain? If the answer is no, then you should move on.' The poor peasant woman just looked away. She was depressed by those lofty standards."

"*I'm* depressed by those standards."

"I think that little speech got under my skin, Paige. It's what made me select physical therapy as a career. So the answer to your question is no. Kevin doesn't fit any of those measures. And here I am struggling with the idea of a future with him. Coincidence?"

" 'Relief of pain' . . . ," Paige repeated, her voice trailing off. "It's what she pursued. And Max was a doctor who was fighting for what he felt was justice for the poor of El Salvador. That's what she saw in him. She *admired* him."

"Admiration," Monica said, holding up a finger. "Maybe that's what's missing in my relationship. That feeling of looking up to him and saying, 'Wow.' "

After a moment during which neither spoke, Paige stepped behind Monica, who was still at the sink, and put her arm around her friend's shoulder. She must have been about to say something profound or sympathetic, but then she looked down and saw the enormous nest of paper towels that Monica had wadded around her thumb. "My God," Paige said, putting a hand over her throat. "I hope you saved the severed hand in a cooler. We'll have to reattach it after lunch."

"Oh, shut up," Monica said, smiling and placing her injured hand protectively under her armpit. "It was your fault. You hassled me about commitment."

Paige bumped her at the hip bone. "Out of the way," she ordered, and took the spoon out of Monica's other hand. "No one wants bloody tuna fish."

Monica happily scooted aside.

"In a twisted kind of way, you're lucky you don't have a mother's constant pressure to get married." Paige slipped into a perfect imitation of her mother's voice. "When are you going to get married and have kids? Girls over thirty expire like milk."

Monica laughed. "She said that?"

"Swear to God."

"Well, you sounded a lot like her when you were standing over by the window, putting the pressure on *me*."

"With you it's different. You have a great guy just waiting for you. I say go for it, get it over with."

"When I was a little girl, I dreamed of the day when I would step into a big white dress, look into my beloved's eyes, and . . . get it over with."

Paige wagged the wood spoon at Monica. "I know a dozen women who'd swallow up your sweet boy in a second."

Monica's thirtieth birthday was still three years away, but she was just beginning to understand that thirty meant she was supposed to participate in an age-specific crisis, a developmentally useless milestone like cutting wisdom teeth. And although she was firmly Alma's daughter in this sense—she refused to buy into the idea that she had to marry at all—she was beginning to feel the tug of something, the feeling that time was passing faster and faster, and she just wasn't running hard enough to keep up.

She heard the voices of the men, accompanied by the sound of the screen door opening and slamming shut. Kevin saw her and blew her a kiss. Monica looked at his paint-speckled boat shoes. How long would he wait? Monica wondered. She was stalling, and she had done a great job of convincing everyone, except Paige, apparently—that the decision to marry was hung up only on her solemn duty to do One Great Thing before settling into a cookie-cutter destiny of kids and retirement goals, minivans and dinner at the in-laws' every Sunday night. But what was that One Great Thing? She didn't know. Something life-defining, something unforgettable, something she would spend her old age telling and retelling to bored grandchildren. Something that could completely absorb her the way the sea had engrossed her as a little girl.

But there was the mortgage on a waterfront property to pay

and there were college loans to repay, plus her indecision over which of a dozen ideas to pursue in the first place. Of course, there were some couples, she had heard, who actually went out into the world and did the Big Thing together. But Kevin Mitchell didn't see the point of leaving U.S. soil, ever. In fact, Kevin, like his parents, believed the world began and ended on the Connecticut shore. When Monica had brought up the idea of traveling to Europe or even back to El Salvador, his response had been "Why? So we can get sick on the water and have our traveler's checks stolen by a pack of kids who haven't showered in a year?"

And there stood the impasse. He wasn't the least bit interested in any of Alma's measures of a well-lived life, he just wanted to be safe and comfortable and unchanged. That attitude had become more and more infuriating to Monica as her own desire for adventure grew. But Kevin was attentive, kind, and good-looking in a tousled, all-American kind of way. And here he was, all hot and sweaty, sacrificing a perfectly good golf day to scrape paint. Was she ungrateful to want a more adventurous, ambitious man?

Kevin headed for the bathroom while Bruce washed up in the kitchen sink. He looked at his daughter's hand. "Did you cut your whole hand off? I've seen turbans smaller than that."

Behind her, Paige chortled. Monica cupped her injured hand and shot back, "Did you finish scraping my porch or are you just here to get fed, old man?"

"I think we can finish up in about an hour," he said, peering over imaginary bifocals and examining her thumb. "Then we can start to stain. You'll be having your first Fourth of July party on that deck this year."

Paige brought out a stack of plates and set them on the farmhouse table. "If you have a party, you should invite that Will Lucero guy. I'd love to meet him," she said.

"I hardly know him," Monica said, opening a bag of potato chips. "Besides, the last thing I want is to get friendly with him. He might want me to massage his wife again."

"Well, I figure he's going to have to start dating sometime. That wife is never going to find all her marbles," she said, pointing to her temple.

"Paige, that's sick," Kevin yelled from the bathroom.

Bruce scrunched up his face at Paige. "You're scavenging the scene of an accident for *a husband*?"

Paige put her hands on her hips. "You have no idea how hard it is to find a nice guy. Most attractive, quality men tend to hang around other men that fit the same description. He might have a friend for me. It's just good networking on my part."

Kevin sat down next to Bruce and elbowed him. "She's right about quality bachelors sticking together," he said, pointing his thumb at himself and then at Bruce. "Look at us." Bruce nodded and opened his eyes wide, looking at Paige as if that indeed proved her point.

"What about you, Bruce?" Paige turned her wooden spoon upon him. "Why haven't you remarried? You're not getting any younger," she said, aiming the spoon at his thinning hairline. "You're approaching your expiration date."

Bruce looked at her as if he had no idea what she was talking about. "I'm not a bachelor. I'm a widower."

Paige frowned. "That's a piss-poor excuse. When are you going to marry that poor Marcy?"

Kevin fetched two beers and handed one to Bruce. "Paige, has anyone ever told you you're nosy?"

Paige slapped a scoop of tuna onto a slice of white bread and handed it to him. "Has anyone ever told you you're boring?"

"Has anyone—" Kevin began, but Bruce put a hand up to shush them.

"I'm not a fan of marriage. Once was enough for me, thank you."

"That's not very complimentary to Mom," Monica said from the kitchen. "Or to Marcy."

"Who said Marcy even wants to marry me?" Bruce nodded in agreement with himself and took a bite of his sandwich.

Monica, Kevin, and Paige all laughed. "Dad, she already picked out her dress and the invitations. I'd say she's open to the idea." Monica heard a car pull up into the driveway. "Speak of the devil . . ."

Bruce lowered his head, looked right, then left, collecting each of their gazes before saying, in a low voice, "Edgar Degas said, 'There is work, and there is love, and we have but one heart.' " He put a hand over his heart as if to pledge allegiance.

They heard a sound outside and were silent for a moment as they waited for Marcy to make her way in, all of them crunching potato chips at the same time. Suddenly Kevin looked at Monica and smiled. "I don't agree with Degas. Work is what you do to support love."

Monica reached over and squeezed his hand. She was struggling to find a response that wouldn't make him bolt out the door and return with an engagement ring when the front door squeaked open and Marcy stepped in, a canvas bag in each hand, with flowers from her garden sticking out of the tops.

"Yoo-hoo. It's me . . ." She looked at Bruce. "Hello, darling."

Bruce leaned toward Monica and, as if to stubbornly emphasize work's priority over love, whispered, "Would you give me that fellow's phone number, you know, the one with the wife who was in the accident." He pointed at his temple. "While I was scraping paint, I had an idea for an article on the subject of brain-injury recovery that I might want to pitch to an editor." Then he stood up and held his arms open to Marcy.

EVERY MAJOR EVENT of Bruce Winters's personal life was instigated—or inspired—by his career choices, especially the bad ones. A prize-winning article he penned in his college newspaper won him a job as a junior reporter at the *New Haven Register.* His work at the *Register* won him a job as a bottom-feeder at the *New York Times* at age twenty-seven. A year later, his editor, who also happened to be his girlfriend, convinced him to go with her to work in press relations for the U.S. State Department at the embassy of the tiny, virtually unheard of Republic of El Salvador, a career choice he bitterly regretted from the minute he accepted and even more so when they broke up six months later.

A week after the split, he was nursing his wounded ego and pondering the course of his derailed career when the U.S. ambassador hosted a party for the country's most powerful families. Uncomfortable in any situation that smacked of social networking, Bruce preferred to process raw facts into news copy. But his presence was required, and so he stood in the corner of the room, itchy in a shirt and tie and feeling sorry for himself indeed. He was trying to avoid eye contact with his ex-girlfriend and hopefully soon-to-be-ex boss, who was chatting up a Salvadoran military chief across the room. His ex was trying to get his attention so he could take over and she could float to the next VIP, but he was ignoring her, standing next to a large glass punch bowl, watching the crowd of beautifully dressed people smelling of expensive cologne. The men all nursed heavy-bottomed highballs of the finest Scotch whisky, some of them with a cigarette in the other hand, gesturing wildly and swapping political jokes. The women in the crowd lacked the homogeneity of those Salvadorans on the street whose stout stature and high cheekbones marked them as descendants of the indigenous Mayan races of Central America.

It was obvious that these women were either imported or of European origin. Bruce watched a set of redheaded twins, several lithe brunettes; and a blonde who kept smiling at him from behind the rim of a big, floppy hat. With fashionable platform shoes and slices of bright blue eye shadow, one could easily transpose her, or any of the guests, to a cocktail party in New York City or Chicago. Bruce was fancying himself the observant but detached amateur sociologist when he felt a tug at his sleeve. He turned and looked down at a beautiful girl whom he had not seen before, with slick, black hair pulled tight behind her ears, and eyes so dark he could clearly see himself reflected in their distorting, convex mirrors. She couldn't be a day older than seventeen. She smiled at him and boldly asked if he would like to dance.

Bruce hadn't even been aware that there was music, so engrossed was he in his thoughts and observations. He stood paralyzed, with a crystal mug of punch in one hand. He didn't understand how an upper-class girl in this country would dare ask a man—*a stranger*—to dance. It was unheard of, simply impossible, and there was a stack of cultural briefings on his desk to prove it. Yet there she stood, totally unself-conscious, as if she had merely asked him for the time. Of course it would be ungentlemanly not to accept, and so he felt put on the spot, vaguely angry, his ears burning with embarrassment. All the while his more primitive alarms were beginning to go off— louder, louder, as they detected that this was easily the most beautiful creature he had ever seen in his life.

Before he gave her an answer, she took the cup from his hands, turned just in time to place it on a waiter's tray, grabbed him by the shirtsleeve, and led him across the room. He could feel the blood whoosh to his face as he followed in sheer terror. He had had a few dance lessons, but he was far from confident and prepared, and he had always assumed that the choice of timing would be his. Stumbling stupidly across the room toward the dance floor, he wondered if his ex was watching, which offered him a slight triumph, although not nearly enough to make up for his fright.

As he followed the audacious girl, he was again shocked by her boldness when she turned and looked back at him, flashing the seductive smile of a mature woman. He wondered if this dance was going to get him thrown out the window by a jealous boyfriend or a protective father. But he followed her onto the dance floor, helpless as if he were on skates. He tried to relax, to focus on the beautiful music played by a trio of guitarists crooning old-world boleros. He was about to engage his cardboard arms with hers when she pivoted and parked him squarely into the arms of a plump girl who beamed at him as if she had been waiting for him her entire life. She giggled excitedly and said, *"Ay, gringuito chulo."* Cute little white boy. She then squeezed him tight, so tight that when he looked down, he saw a tear of sweat roll down her doughy neck, which was freckled with a rash of skin tags that clung to her like fleas.

It was 1967, and the beautiful girl wore a floor-length "maxidress," which swept the white marble tiles and trailed behind her. Dragged along with her skirt, like the tail on a comet, were the glances of those powerful men upon whose laps she had probably squirmed and giggled just a few years back. She turned and gave Bruce a wink of gratitude as she disappeared into a cloud of cigar smoke.

Alma Marina Borrero made an auspicious entrance into Bruce Winters's life, leaving him with an early dose of the mystery she would surround herself with years later. And yet this awkward moment with the chubby girl would later prove to be serendipitous. Her name was Claudia, and she would become a great friend and ally, securing rare interviews for him with the military upper echelon, which would result in several journalistic awards. And with this awkward waltz he began a new chapter of his life—the brief chapter in which he liked El Salvador, even dared love it, as he entertained himself with his shameless courtship of a girl who had just turned eighteen.

At first, it was like a joke. Sure, he was an educated, professional, good-looking guy. And it was true that being a gringo with green eyes held some charm and novelty in Salvadoran society. But still, he was a nobody to the upper class, and the Borreros were about as somebody as anybody could be in those parts. Adolfo and Magnolia Borrero weren't about to squander their only child on a man whose family they had never heard of, and who could contribute nothing more than exotic facial features. "We don't even know your family," Magnolia Borrero had told him through the speakerphone outside the gated wall of their home. "Go away."

"Not a problem," Bruce had said. He returned with a color photograph of his parents and two sisters huddled next to a waist-high bank of dirty snow. "There you go, Doña Magnolia," he spoke into the speaker as he shoved the picture under the electrified iron gate. "That's my family. May I come in and see your daughter now?"

Girls like Alma came with an unnamed price. As the old adage went, if you have to ask, you can't afford it. Bruce decided that his only currency was patience and persistence, and so he decided to stick it out at the embassy in El Salvador for the four years that Alma was in college in New York. During this time, he saw her only when she returned home for semester breaks and holidays. Bruce became a speck in Alma's overwhelmingly complex social life, but he figured a speck was better than nothing. Besides, he was no monk during that time—there were endless weekends at the beaches and excursions to Roatán, Antigua Guatemala, and Belize with his own widening circle of Salvadoran and expatriate friends. There were days that he didn't even think about Alma at all, and he was starting to think that maybe his decision to stay in El Salvador had nothing to do

with her. He was used to the place, had made more friends in the first nine months than he had made in his whole life in the United States.

He became fond of his self-image—an expatriate writer, but unlike his friends who corresponded for newspapers from the outside, he had a certain amount of control over how long he might get to stay.

And Magnolia Mármol de Borrero—La Doña—was starting to come around. She insisted that they only communicate in English, so that she could practice, because her English wasn't good. Bruce was impressed that a woman of her age and rank found no shame in her language errors. She told long-winded stories in broken English about her girlhood that Bruce didn't always understand, but he was smart enough to laugh when she laughed. She began to invite him and his friends to the house, playing the role of grande dame to the young Americans and local journalists he brought with him. Alma was gone so long that Bruce actually started to note some improvement in the Doña's English skills.

In the years that followed, Bruce's career as a journalist began to pick up again, with requests from Washington for briefings on the civil unrest bubbling up all around Central America, especially in Nicaragua and El Salvador. The communist ideology was gaining strength in the countryside, with its intellectual nucleus at the universities and, some said, in certain Catholic pulpits. Rumors were confirmed that money and arms were being smuggled in from the USSR, China, and Cuba in rickety boats that pulled up to the remotest Salvadoran beaches, or through the jungles of Honduras and Guatemala.

During one of his rare dates with Alma, Bruce asked Alma and Magnolia what they thought about the political climate in their country. Serving as chaperone from the tiny backseat of Bruce's beat-up orange VW Bug, Magnolia had been fanning herself with a magazine. As they passed a rash of shantytowns, she ignored his question. "Bruce, when are you going to get an air-conditioned car? I'm going to faint in this heat."

Alma was sitting in the passenger seat. She shrugged and said, "I've never paid attention to politics. But I suppose if a civil war breaks out, then I'll have to start."

"Do you think we'll have a civil war in El Salvador, Doña Magnolia?"

Magnolia had slammed the magazine against the roof of the car, apparently to kill an insect. Then, she rolled the magazine into a funnel and tipped its contents out the window. "Civil war? No," she said dismissively, and Bruce could see in his rear-view mirror that she had turned her gaze toward the rash of tinplate and cardboard shacks. She narrowed her eyes and said, "We're going to put an end to that communist nonsense. If things get rough, we have friends who can help."

"You mean the U.S.?"

But Doña Magnolia closed that door as quickly as she had opened it. With her comment, she had allowed him a tiny glimpse into the very private world of the country's ruling class. Bruce wondered if she was indeed referring to the United States—or to a secret paramilitary society whose mission was to eliminate suspected communists in a harsher and more efficient way than the government could manage.

That particular date had ended in the same fashion as the ten other "dates" before it: with a kiss on the hand for Magnolia and a peck on the cheek for Alma. Four years after he had met her, Bruce still hadn't kissed Alma on the lips. Whenever he called to ask for a date, Alma would accept with a caveat: "As long as you know that we're just friends, Bruce. Nothing more."

But Bruce wasn't discouraged. He figured the seduction would begin when she came home for good.

In 1972 Alma returned to El Salvador with dual bachelor's degrees in biology and philosophy. Her English was flawless, and she thought she might want to return to the States to earn a Ph.D. in marine biology. Alma said that unlike other women of her culture, she didn't "buy into" the rush toward marriage, and that she felt the need to do something significant before settling down.

But a month later, Adolfo Borrero, whose input had been dormant until this time, eyed his gold watch and declared that it was time for his daughter to get married. He made the announcement at dinner, during the soup course. Claudia and Bruce, who were the only guests that night, lifted their eyes from gold-rimmed bowls of crab bisque and turned to look at Alma. Alma held her soup spoon suspended midway between her bowl and her mouth for what seemed like an eternity. They waited, but she appeared to be stunned into immobility.

Adolfo turned to the guests. "I've decided that Alma should marry Augusto Prieto, the son of one of my business partners. Augusto is the heir to agricultural and textile interests throughout Mexico and Central America. The union of the two families would be . . ." His sentence trailed off and he nodded approvingly.

Magnolia said, "Adolfo, I thought we were going to talk to Alma in private about this."

Adolfo pointed his spoon in the direction of the guests. "Claudia is a friend of the family, so is Bruce. Alma trusts their opinions, that's why I'm telling them."

"But we should have talked to Alma first." Her voice had an edge of anger.

"Ladies," Adolfo bellowed, "I know what's best."

They were still waiting for Alma's reaction, but now she was looking past them, wide-eyed, out the window and into the yard. Then, she pinched the bridge of her nose and squeezed her eyes shut as if she were going to sneeze. She made a sound that Bruce thought was a sob, then a gasp that rose and exploded into peals of shoulder-shaking laughter.

Her parents sat stone-faced and waited for her to calm down. "What's so funny, Alma Marina?"

Alma pointed toward the window, and they all turned to look. It took a moment for all of them to recognize what Alma found so amusing. On the lawn, the gardener's dog—a mutt covered with horrid molten brown spots—was happily humping away at Magnolia's prize-winning standard poodle.

The Borreros jumped to their feet and ran out the door, screaming for the dogs to stop and calling to the servants for help. Alma clapped her hands and shouted, "Go, Fluffy, go!"

A few moments later, they watched as Magnolia's beloved Fluffy bared her teeth and snarled at her owners, which sent Alma into another round of stomach-holding laughter. It took three servants, ten minutes, and a bucket of cold water to separate the copulating canines. "They've been trying to breed Fluffy for *two* years," Alma gasped. "They bring these fancy-blooded males and Fluffy hates them all. She actually bit the last one." Alma wiped tears from her cheeks. "His name was Claude Arpège." Claudia let out a snort and the two of them giggled themselves silly.

When they finally calmed down, the two friends draped themselves like laundry across the dining room chairs. After a moment, Claudia's expression grew serious and she said, "Alma, your dad sounded serious about Augusto."

Alma rolled her eyes and looked at Bruce. "Can you imagine *me* married to Augusto Prieto? I've seen that boy get seasick on a pool raft, for God's sake."

"So what are you going to tell your parents?" Bruce asked. "Now that they've lost all hope for Fluffy and Claude Arpège."

There were more guffaws and knee slapping before Alma

answered the question. "I've managed to dodge a lifetime of that," she said, gesturing toward the empty table. "I'll dodge this bullet too. Trust me, I'm not marrying *Augusto*." She intoned the name with barely concealed contempt.

"I'll marry you if you need an escape," Bruce offered, trying to sound as if he were joking. "Did you know that I never, ever get seasick?"

Alma sat up. "Well, you should have told me that a long time ago," she said, patting his hand. "Level one is a man's seaworthiness."

Claudia asked, "What's level two?"

Alma turned her eternally wet, shiny eyes upon her friends. "Level two is a man's ability to change the world."

"An idealist?" Bruce asked. "I thought you didn't care for politics."

"No, I mean *change the world*. Deliver justice. Save the oceans. An artist who brings exceptional beauty to the world. A healer who can release us from pain."

They were silent for a moment, then Claudia noted, "I don't even *have* a level one. Just being asked out is my level one, two, and three."

Suddenly feeling small, Bruce said, "I guess I don't want to know what your level three is, Alma."

Alma smiled in a way that reminded him of the oversexed smirk she had given him on the day they met. "I keep level three a secret."

ALMA'S STRATEGY to avoid marriage was simple: she completely ignored Augusto and all of the other pedigreed suitors that her parents lined up. "At least I haven't bitten any of them yet," she joked, but Magnolia didn't find it a bit funny. It must have occurred to her that she had made a great error of judgment in sending an already willful daughter off to the famously permissive USA. Alma's obstinate nature had only hardened with exposure to ideas like feminism, a concept as useless in their world as the white, lace-up ice skates that Alma kept in storage.

Claudia had been the one to suggest to Magnolia that they give the gringo a second look. She had overheard Alma defending Bruce in his absence at a dinner party, snapping at the critic and declaring Bruce to be one of the most intelligent men she ever met. "Perhaps a union of intellect would be more durable than a more traditional bond," Claudia had counseled during an afternoon coffee when she was alone with Magnolia. "Alma," Claudia had delicately proposed, "is exotic among our tribe. Of the pool of suitable bachelors, none are evolved enough to endure her liberal ideas for long. Bruce Winters just might offer the right balance."

After months of secret deliberation, the Borreros agreed with Claudia that the American wasn't such a bad idea. Bruce knew he had arrived at the final leg of his journey when he got an invitation to visit the beach villa at Negrarena, which, la Doña added primly, would permit him to glimpse her daughter in a bathing suit. He wrote to his folks that day and suggested they apply for passports. Now all he had to do was win Alma's heart.

BRUCE LOVED THE WAY the wood soaked up the caramel-colored stain, as if the grain contained a thousand tiny mouths that sucked it up all at once. As he worked side by side with Kevin, he marveled at the way history repeated itself. In the young man next to him he saw the same patience, the same devotion to a singular cause, that he himself had displayed when he was Kevin's age. Monica was nowhere near as headstrong and enigmatic as her mother had been, not even in the same stratosphere. But Monica was cautious, and Bruce wondered if the estrangement she had witnessed between her parents gave her cause to fear intimacy.

Bruce was happy today. At this point in his life there were few people he would rather be with than this trio. Paige and Monica had been friends since Bruce and Monica had returned to the States in 1985, and he had always been grateful to her. Paige was bossy, nosy, and often crass, but she watched out for Monica's interest like an old mother.

He thought about what Paige had asked him, about getting remarried. It was a wonder she hadn't brought this up before. The kids were right: Marcy would marry him in an instant. He just didn't feel the urgency, that's all. He was waiting for the pull he'd felt with Alma, although in her case, it was a violent undertow, destiny yanking him by the feet and sucking him into a vortex of crushing waves. He didn't need that at this stage of his life—he wanted peace, love, friendship, and, of course, attraction. He and Marcy had all that, so what was it then? Just plain age? Perhaps he had gradually lost interest in himself, thinking that there was no undiscovered territory left in his heart.

Bruce looked at his daughter. Summer was when she looked most like her mother. Although the eyes were his, Alma and Monica shared the same coiled black hair, the olive skin sprinkled with freckles, and the same slim but hourglass figure. But there was a softness to Monica's face that she had got from neither Bruce nor Alma, a kindness and calm that she must have scavenged on her own somewhere. He wondered how much of it was her nature and strength, and how much was a matter of not remembering the things that must have hurt and shocked her as a child.

Their memories of their last days in El Salvador were to each one private, and he didn't feel he had the right to probe that space of her heart. Monica talked about her mother a lot, and she seemed to have been able to hold on to the happy memories. But Bruce was unsure if the bad stuff had just floated away, or if it lay dormant, waiting to upset her life at some unexpected time.

Tuesday was the only day of the week that Will Lucero wasn't a provider, a caregiver, a boss, or anything else but a man who sailed a boat. On Tuesdays he didn't visit his wife and he didn't go to work. He got out of bed at five and used the morning hours to catch up on bills and errands. He intended to get out of the house by eleven and head to the coast with a cooler and his dog, Chester.

He had given himself the gift of Tuesdays even before he had got married. It was the one day he got to change the station and tune into something altogether different from his everyday life: a language of wind, waves, fog, and tides. To Will, heaven could be found in the ruffle of canvas, in the tentative gasp of a sail as it inhales its life from the wind, the clink of a halyard's metal hardware against the mast, the *perthunk* of the anchor plunging into water. As it turned out, sailing was what had saved his sanity over the last two years.

It was almost nine and Will still hadn't been able to pull himself away from his chores—a broken garage door, an infestation of ants, a discrepancy on three of Yvette's medical bills, a sluggish kitchen sink—all of them addressed but none of them wholly crossed off his list. At ten—two hours later than he'd meant to work at home—he decided he'd given it his best and started gathering his gear. Chester was already whining and giving him worried, woeful looks. When Will pulled his red duffel bag out of the coat closet, Chester went to stand by the front door, trembling with excitement. Will checked the fridge. It was almost empty; he hadn't had any extra time to grocery shop. He packed a plastic container with his mother's leftover *bacalao* salad, cold codfish mashed together with boiled yucca, vinegar, and olive oil. He packed two beers, five nectarines, and a handful of half-desiccated cherries he found on the counter. He put the weather radio on and listened for an update. Outside, the day was cloudy and still, a far cry from the television's prediction of a sunny, breezy day. He couldn't find his boat shoes and his mood was turning sour because of the time. When the phone rang, Chester barked and ran in circles, protesting yet another delay.

It was his mother. "You're still there?"

"Nope. Not unless someone's dying."

"I know it's your precious sailing day. I was expecting to leave you a message. Anyway, we're with Yvette and your father wanted me to tell you that she made a sound." Will's mother spoke to someone else in the room, presumably his father, then said, "It sounded like a moan, or a mumble, we're not sure which."

"Okay, call me back when you decide. Gotta go, Mom."

"Wilfredo—" she began, but Will interrupted her.

"Until she squeezes someone's hand when asked a question, blinks once for no, twice for yes—something we can all agree is an attempt to communicate—we can't read into every sound she makes. We've been over this, Mom, please."

She sighed. "Your dad says she mumbled something when he put a handful of lilacs under her nose."

"Well, tell him I said not to do that. He could introduce something harmful into her respiratory system. A bug, bacteria, pollen, you know how frail she is." Will took a deep breath. "Anything else?"

"*Solo eso,*" she said, clearly annoyed.

"Thanks, Mom, I'll see you Sunday."

"*Bueno, mijo.* Did you eat the leftover bacalao?"

"I'm having it for lunch, thanks. Love you," he said, and hung up.

A few seconds later, it rang again. This time it was his chief project manager, who was overseeing the restoration of an old Victorian in Mystic, a bed-and-breakfast. Will searched for his boat shoes, a Windbreaker, and other miscellaneous provisions while answering questions about roofing materials. He sighed as he hung up the phone, exhausted. He raised his hand to the base of his neck, wishing he had someone to massage his tension. He thought about how relaxed Yvette's face had looked after her massage. Heck, he needed a massage more than Yvette. Yvette wasn't the one trying to keep a business together; fighting insurance companies, doctors, relatives, and collection agencies. He'd have to work *again* this weekend, and he was so, so tired. He wondered if he had any muscle relaxants left. He looked at the clock and started to feel sorry for himself all over again.

When the phone rang for a third time, he backed away from it, hands raised like a prisoner. The heel of his right foot stepped on something that gave a crunch, probably the death cry of his new polarized sunglasses. As the phone continued ringing, he tried to step backward, over the duffel bag, but lost his balance and slipped on the small throw rug underneath the other foot. He fell sideways, catching himself on the edge of the kitchen counter, but bumping his elbow along the way. He grimaced, while the phone continued to ring. What was it with his klutziness lately? Was his body forcing him to slow down by sabotaging his motor coordination? He knew he could only ignore it so long before he really hurt himself, so he got up, put his hands over his ears, and walked out of the kitchen, allowing the machine to pick up.

The machine beeped and a woman's voice came on the recorder. He felt an unexpected wave of pleasure when he heard her say her name, *Mónica,* which she pronounced the Spanish way, with a hard *o.* She wanted to know if he would consider talking to her father, who was a journalist and was interested in writing a survey of traumatic brain injury recovery for a big magazine. Will hurled himself across the room, careful not to slip again this time, and picked up the receiver. "Sure, I'll talk to your father," he said breathlessly. "I owe you one for fitting us into your schedule." He sucked in air, rubbing his elbow and twisting his arm around to look at the pink gouge.

"You hurt yourself getting to the phone," she said flatly.

He was silent for a few seconds before saying, "Is there a secret camera in my kitchen?"

She laughed. "You held your breath as you spoke, then sucked it in through your teeth. I know that sound well. I'm a physical therapist. It's my job to make people make that sound."

"An interesting contradiction is that you also give massages. Pain and pleasure. Hmm."

Monica laughed. "I never thought of it like that." She paused and let out a deep breath. "So when would be a good time for my dad to call you?"

"Not so fast, therapy girl. I want to get Yvette on your calendar again. She seemed so happy and relaxed after you left. Normally her wrists and ankles are all locked up, but after you left she was like a wet noodle."

"Massage drunk," Monica said. "It happens."

"Maybe I'd better get in line now. I could definitely use a shot of whatever you gave to Yvette."

"No."

"No?"

"I told you I can't take any more clients."

"That's okay. I'll be the first on your waiting list."

"I already have a waiting list."

"Well, then how about going sailing with me?" The words flew out of his mouth without his approval, before the idea had even been posted across the marquee of his brain.

"Now?"

"Yeah, why not?"

"Because it's a Tuesday and I have to work. But I'll take a rain check," she said brightly. "Where are you going?"

"I'm thinking of going to a place called Plum Island."

"Have you sailed to Plum Island before?"

"No, but it's a course I've been meaning to try."

"I don't recommend it, it can be frustrating. You'll spend the whole day tacking back and forth, just to sail a few miles. If you drop your anchor, it'll drag because the crosscurrents are strong at Plum Island, especially at the Gutt. If you're pressed for time, you might have a more pleasant day sail if you head up to Napatree Point. The winds are more favorable for a sail towards Watch Hill."

"You sail?" he said, astounded.

"Nah. But let's just say I know that old sea like a bruised woman knows her ex-husband."

"A very intriguing answer, Miss Winters. You'll have to expound over coffee at the hospital cafeteria sometime."

Monica laughed. "You'd have to drink about fifty cups to hear the whole story."

"Then I'll have to buy you dinner. A very slow dinner. How about eight courses of fondue?"

Shocked, he thought, *Jesus, did I just ask her out?*

But she seemed to take it all lightly because she just chuckled and said, "Maybe eight courses of fondue on a slow boat to

China." Then she quickly steered the conversation back to the reason for her call. Will agreed to talk to her father.

When he hung up, Will caught a glimpse of himself in the hall mirror. His cheeks were flushed. He'd have to be more careful. What if she'd taken him seriously? He looked down at his dog, shook his head in confusion, and walked out the door.

WILL HAD NAMED his twenty-six-foot Hunter after the small town in Puerto Rico where his father was born—Yegua Brava, which means "angry mare." His brother, Eddie, had encouraged him to translate the boat's name into English before having it painted in script on the transom of the boat. "All those rich country clubbers will say, 'There goes the neighborhood,' when they see your dinky sailboat with a Spanish name docked in their fancy marina."

But Will didn't share Eddie's distrust of non-Hispanic New Englanders. Will proudly flew the American and Puerto Rican flags on his boat alongside the nautical ensign. Besides, in his experience, boaters were a part of a subculture that transcends ethnic divisions. Many of them saw landlubbers as alien creatures. Beyond that was the separation between the "purists"—the sailboaters—and the "vulgar" powerboaters, whose mega-engines' consumption of gas was rivaled only by their owners' consumption of beer. All "real" sea folk were members of a sacred tribe, and sailors were special to one another. Might as well be related by spit and blood.

Will motored the *Yegua Brava* out of the Yankee Yacht Club in New London. The first few minutes were always stressful, without anyone to help him crew the boat out of the marina. He had already put a few dings into the *Yegua Brava,* but it was still worth the dose of solitude. As he sailed out into Fishers Island Sound, he could feel his blood pressure drop. He dropped anchor off the coast of Rhode Island, amused that

Monica had been right about the nautical conditions. He had received the exact advice from the dockhands at the marina and so changed his course.

After making sure that his anchor was secure, Will sat on the deck of his boat, eating his mother's chopped codfish and drinking the cold beer. He regretted that in his haste he had forgotten to bring doggie treats. Chester licked fussily at a slice of nectarine, pushing it around the boat's deck with his tongue without actually eating it. Will tossed a ball into the water and Chester flew off the side of the boat, legs splayed, landing in a belly flop and spraying Will with cold water. Chester paddled back to the boat, rubber ball in mouth. They spent the better part of an hour like that, just tossing the ball back and forth until Chester finally began to grow tired of it. Will pulled him back up on board, and Chester shook off salt water infused with doggie smell. Will tore off his soaked T-shirt and went below to rummage through his storage lockers for something else to wear.

In these few, carefree moments, his reality blindsided him with a cruelty and force that left him dazed and breathless. From between the pages of a damp, outdated navigational guide—which had attached itself like a barnacle to an old polo shirt—a yellow sticky note dropped at his feet: *Babe, I went to Dave's Shanty to get whole belly clams. Be back in fifteen. Love you, Y.*

Will braced himself and waited. He anticipated that the needle on some inner gauge would rise and tremble, measuring the level of the blow. It rose to three, four, fluttered around five. Then stopped. It had been almost two years now. The days of the mean eights, nines, and tens were gone. Maybe he had become desensitized. Maybe it represented the passing of time, the eventual abandonment of hope, the scarring of the wound. He suspected that what he was experiencing was the evolution of grief and rage to acceptance and sadness. He had spent two years mourning the loss of their life together—and was entering a time where he mourned not for them, but for her alone, for an entire life that spanned beyond the brevity of her married years.

He looked down at the note and instinctively brought it up to his nose and closed his eyes. If any fragment of that time had been trapped and pressed into the paper, it might transport him back to her, back to what still felt like home for him. He asked himself, as he had a thousand times before, what would have happened if he had interrupted the flow of events on that forgotten day she went to buy those clams, even in the smallest way. What if he had suggested that they skip the local fry shop and head home early instead? It might have averted the contact point of time and space that placed Yvette in the car almost two years ago. Maybe the ripples of alternative effect would have traveled around the world in time to nullify her impulse to drive fast, or even the decision of a simpleminded bird to push off the branch of a tree, to unfold its red wings and cross paths with Yvette's Mustang.

Will passed his index finger over the round, curly handwriting and looked over his shoulder, summoning the image of her on the unknown day she had written that note. It came to him, all of a sudden, her legs dropping down the rungs of the boat's ladder followed by the soft *tap-tap* of her boat shoes. The backs of her legs were splotched with several angry mosquito bites, and she had scratched a few of them raw. The rolled-up cuffs of her favorite stretch denim shorts appeared, then her narrow waist, her back, then her arms, one of them balancing two white Styrofoam boxes. He smelled the fried batter as the back of her head appeared; her short brown ponytail peeked out of the back hole of a pale pink baseball cap. He stepped forward to take the boxes from her.

The sticky note slipped out of his hand; its edge made a quiet *click* sound on the wood table. When he looked up, she had vanished, but he could still smell the coconut sunscreen that clung to her freckled arms as she turned to hand him the boxes. The *Yegua Brava* rocked him back and forth, and he felt dizzy. A sudden, brief wave of nausea rose in his throat. He gripped the edge of the table and sat down, resting his head on his folded arms, and listened to the water lap against the hull of the boat.

Yvette wasn't coming back. Although Sylvia brought him newspaper clippings of miraculous recoveries from around the world almost weekly, the facts were hard to ignore. He had already said good-bye to his wife, at least to the woman he had married six years ago. He knew that in the unlikely case that she did emerge from her vegetative state, she would never be the old Yvette. The old Yvette lived only in his memory, in the eruption of blue hydrangeas she had planted in the front yard, in the red Tootsie Pop wrappers he still found wedged between furniture cushions. He thought he had found the last of her notes months ago, so he was surprised and grateful, despite all his other feelings, to find this little note addressed to him. Surely this was the last one.

So much had happened since Yvette had slipped into her snowy silence. Lucero Restoration had grown; he had finished his MBA, finally. His sisters had three new kids between them. His black hair had become streaked with gray. They had crossed into a new millennium. Will's family and friends had gently suggested, about a year after the accident, that it was time to begin a new life, one that assumed the inevitable reality of Yvette's absence. What they meant by "beginning a new life," Will knew, included dating. Dating would be the ultimate acknowledgment that he wasn't a man whose wife was ill, but rather, that he was essentially a widower.

It was true that he had been attracted to a couple of women since the accident, and he admitted he wasn't immune to a pretty face. In fact, Monica Winters had lingered in his thoughts during his drive to the marina. But so many things, like the note, kept him tied to the limbo of caring for Yvette's body and comforting her mother, working to pay the bills and keep the rest of their support system afloat. In any case, he couldn't imagine crossing the chasm that led to a new place, to whatever lay beyond his hectic and lonely routine.

The note flapped and tumbled across the table. A gust of wind lifted it and blew it out the open hatch. Will leaped after it, stubbing a toe and grimacing as he climbed the ladder and stepped onto the deck. Chester's claws scratched across the deck of the boat as he chased the scrap of paper. It fluttered, then dropped, then flickered up again as if to tease him. It hovered just above Chester's nose for a second, brushed his forehead once, making the dog snap at the air in vain. It lifted and crossed over the side of the boat, floating, floating, until it crashed down like a kite, sliding sideways onto the surface of the water. Chester turned back to look at Will. The dog's muscles were tensed and he whined for permission to jump in after it. But Will came up behind him and grabbed his collar. "Let it go," he said, and pulled the dog back.

The last thing he did before packing up and heading back was to pull out his binoculars and scan the view of Watch Hill. He admired the proud, water-view Victorian homes dotting the village. He saw the circuslike tent of the old carousel, where he and Yvette had taken his nephews for afternoon rides. The figures of fathers and mothers and children and dogs bounced up and down and sideways across his vision. For the millionth time, he wished that he and Yvette had had a child.

"YOUR DAUGHTER HAS YOUR EYES," Will said to the tall, thin man sitting in the lobby of DiSantis Center. Bruce Winters and his daughter, Monica, had the same green irises rimmed by a pencil-thin black edge. But on Bruce Winters, those eyes looked weary and noble as a police dog's. On Monica, as Will recalled, the same eyes looked fresh as cut grass. As Will began to recount the story of his wife's accident, he searched for more traces of the pretty therapist in this tall, thin man with wide, Germanic angles to his chin, nose, and forehead. Monica, Will decided, must have gotten all her soft stuff from her mama.

Bruce Winters was well informed and crisply professional, and placed a small recording device between them while he scratched away at a notebook. After forty-five minutes, Will escorted him over to room M42. Eventually Sylvia appeared, as did Yvette's neurologist, Dr. Forest Bauer. The doctor, who was normally in a rush, paused to answer Bruce Winters's questions in great detail and, to Will's surprise, even invited Bruce to follow him on his rounds later on. Yvette, he explained, was currently scoring a five out of fifteen possible points on the Glasgow Coma Scale, which measures the ability to respond to commands or sensations of pain, along with scores for eye-opening and verbal abilities. An eight or below was generally considered to be "severe." Yvette had made no progress on the Glasgow since the accident. Rarely did a patient like Yvette remain under expensive, professional care for so long, the doctor explained. But Yvette had been absorbed into a variety of medical studies that helped defray the cost of her care and retesting.

After the doctor left, Bruce was left with Sylvia and Adam Bank, Yvette's physical therapist. By the time Will came back from the cafeteria with four cups of coffee, Sylvia had steered the conversation over to her favorite subject: miracle healings. Since the fact-gathering portion of the interview was over, Bruce put away his notebook and recorder and folded his arms across his chest. Sylvia confessed to calling a psychic, whose 1-900 number she had seen on a coma-recovery discussion board on the Internet. "This psychic said she was getting visions from a woman in a coma who is trying to communicate with her family from another plane of consciousness," she explained. "So I called."

"And how much did the crook charge to tell you a bunch of crap?" Will asked.

Sylvia waved one skinny finger, bent like a small hook. "Wilfredo, you have to have faith."

Will put his hand on his chest and said, "I do have faith. I have absolute faith in the willingness of some people to profit from human misfortune."

Bruce chuckled along with Will until Sylvia flashed them both a forbidding look.

Adam Bank said, "Oh, honey," and squeezed Sylvia's knee. "You're wasting your time with apparitions and saints who drip oil out of their little plastic orifices. Alternative medicine is the way to go."

Adam was a redheaded, balding, middle-aged man who looked more like a Midwestern farmer than a medical professional. He turned to Bruce. "Sylvia found a magazine article about the use of snail venom as a treatment for head injuries. Get this: Two years ago, a man got stung by a marine snail off the Pacific coast of Mexico. He lost feeling in his foot and had some trouble breathing, so he and his companion got in the car and headed to the hospital. On the way, the driver was so flustered that she crashed the car. The man was thrown out of the window and hit his head against a rock at a very high speed. But despite the severity of the damage to the skull, he didn't slip into a coma, have brain swelling, or suffer any loss of function. They suspect the snail venom was present at just the right moment and prevented cell death. They've just now begun to study the possible correlation."

Bruce, who had been slouching over a steaming cup of coffee, straightened. His eyes had begun to look a bit hooded after twenty minutes of politely listening to Sylvia go on about the miracles of the Virgin of Guadalupe. Now he opened his eyes wide and said, "That venom would have a very specific chemical structure to cross the blood–brain barrier without being injected directly into the spinal fluid. As far as I know, there's only one type of cone that can do that."

"Hey," Adam said, slapping his hand on the table, "the article said the same thing. You read it?"

"No," Bruce said, "I just happen to know that obscure fact. Don't ask," he said, putting his hand up.

Adam leaned forward and looked around him, checking to see if Dr. Bauer was around. When he saw that he wasn't, he leaned in close. "That's the kind of thing I would be looking at if I had a loved one in Yvette's condition," he whispered, making eye contact with Bruce, Will, and finally Sylvia. "There's still hope for Yvette. She has loss of cortical, maybe some subcortical functions, and it's obvious that conventional medicine has come to a dead halt." He motioned toward Yvette's bed.

Will slid into a chair, feeling the familiar wave of tiredness he always felt when the subject of "miracle" treatments came up. "It's nothing new." Will shook his head. "There are several new drugs being tested on humans that have already proven that they can arrest brain damage if they are dispensed immediately after the injury. The window of time is about twenty minutes, last I heard. These new drugs aren't going to do Yvette a lick of good at this point. That's why she hasn't qualified for any of those studies."

"Well, this one's totally different," Adam said. "They claim they can treat injuries that are years old."

Will shrugged. "And if they can prove it works, it'll take years before they begin to test it here in the U.S. and another decade for the FDA to approve it."

"That's why you would have to take her out of the country," Adam said. "Somewhere where they have softer rules for this sort of thing."

Will laughed. "Like hell. We're keeping her under Dr. Bauer's watchful eye."

"I don't know about *that,*" Sylvia declared. She stood up and went over to Yvette's bed and began fussing with a loose thread on the robe of the Virgin Mary lamp that stood on Yvette's night table.

Will stared quizzically at Sylvia. "What do you mean, 'I don't know about that'?"

Adam raised one palm and then the other. "Sylvia has been researching the venom treatment. They think we have a shot."

"Who's 'they'?" Will asked, knitting his brows at Sylvia, his voice sharp.

"The people at Clinica Caracol," Sylvia said.

"Clinica what?" Bruce said, cocking his head.

"Caracol. It means 'seashell' in Spanish," Sylvia said.

"I know what it means. Where is it?"

"El Salvador," Sylvia said. "Do you have a fax? I'll send you a copy of the article tonight."

Will interrupted, "Sylvia, you haven't mentioned anything about any experimental clinics."

"I'll give you both a copy," Sylvia replied.

Adam turned to Will. "She figured you'd balk. Besides, it's frightfully expensive to transport Yvette to El Salvador."

"El Salvador?" Will scoffed. "As in the *country?* Might as well be five billion bucks and the moon. Why are we even talking about this?"

"Because it's an exciting new treatment," Sylvia said, her eyes lighting up. "And I wouldn't have discovered it if it wasn't for your daughter, Bruce."

"My Monica?" Bruce said, pulling his chin back. "Why Monica?"

"She had those cone shells on display in her office," Sylvia said, "and she told us about some of the medicinal uses of their venom. I was intrigued."

Will left the conversation and walked to Yvette's bedside. Hope, in her case, was an exhausting and expensive business that never paid off. Theirs was a case of damage control. How to stop this tragedy from devouring the rest of their lives, the rest of their youth, energy, money? The lifetime treatment cost for Yvette was projected to be in the millions of dollars.

He looked up at a pewter cross that hung above the bed. On the bottom, in tiny print, it said MADE IN MEXICO. He felt the overwhelming desire to pull it off the wall. He imagined what it would feel like to sweep his forearm across the shelf above Yvette's bed; to clear it of the pitying stares of all those saints, the creepy glass eyes of the ceramic Virgin Mary, the dried-out Easter palms, the gaudy rosaries wrapped around a lampshade like Mardi Gras beads, all of it cheesy, all of it dusty and plastic and depressing.

Will collapsed over Yvette and sank his head into the crook between her head and her shoulder, shook his head slightly, and dug his nose into the little space behind her earlobe. She didn't even smell like the same person. Some medication, he couldn't remember exactly what, gave off that weird metallic smell. He told himself it was what had driven away his physical desire for her. He was still able to feel it a year or so ago, back when her flesh still smelled like the woman he loved, before the medication with the metal smell robbed him of even that detail. He pulled away, closed his eyes. He wound his fingers into hers instead. They were so white, so skinny, so cold. He half opened his eyes to look at them.

And that's when he saw it. Between his half-closed eyes he saw her lips move. Not a twitch, but lips deliberately mouthing something, wrapping themselves around each letter of a word, something like *wather* or perhaps *other*. He saw the tip of her tongue press against front teeth to pronounce the *th* sound, which seemed to him to be somewhat of a sophisticated sound to produce involuntarily.

His entire body prickled and he held his breath. He stared at her lips, pale and thin and dry. He ran a finger over them and whispered her name, his own lips bearing down on the soft cartilage of her ear. He suddenly became aware of the others, talking excitedly to each other at the other side of the room. He looked away just a second, just long enough to see that Bruce Winters looked mesmerized as he read the article out loud with Adam and Sylvia looking over his shoulder. Will turned back to Yvette, squeezed her hand once, staring at her lips, waiting for the slightest repetition of movement. He waited and waited, wondering and doubting if he had seen anything at all. He squeezed her hand in pulses, whispering, "Can you squeeze back?" over and over. He blew gently into her eye. Nothing.

He remembered his mother's words: *Your dad says she mumbled when he put a bunch of lilacs from his garden under her nose.* Will took a deep breath and decided to discreetly inform Dr. Bauer. The key was to avoid getting Sylvia all riled up over nothing. Will already knew what the doctor would say about Yvette's vocalization—something about spasms, vocal chords, air passages, sounds that seem like words, but aren't. Still, it was unnerving to witness those occasional gestures that seemed to contain meaning. Behind him, Bruce, Adam, and Sylvia were still deep in conversation about the clinic in El Salvador, which vaguely angered him and stirred his sense of territoriality. Will excused himself and went into the hall. His hands trembled as he dialed the numbers of the doctor's pager. It was the only outward sign that the armor that guarded his heart from false hope now bore an invisible, hairline crack.

At five thirty in the morning Monica had a Salvadoran breakfast ready for her father: coffee, eggs scrambled with onion and tomato, sweet ripe plantains, refried beans, and some authentic corn tortillas she'd bought from a Hispanic grocery in a not-quite-gentrified section of New Haven.

"A nutritionally ideal breakfast if you're going to spend twelve hours under the sun chopping sugarcane," Bruce said, as he dug into the basket of warm tortillas.

"I don't remember signing up to chop sugarcane," Monica said. "I thought we were going fishing."

"You'll need the protein in those eggs to pull up all those monster fish we're going to catch today."

Monica poured the coffee and sat down across from him. "Let's get back in by ten. There's a front coming in."

Bruce took a sip of the coffee and closed his eyes for a moment, allowing the steam of the mug to rise up along his face. He sat back, eyes still closed. "Now that's real Salvadoran coffee." Bruce smiled a little, lifted the mug, and took another whiff. "Reminds me of your grandmother. Doña Magnolia had her coffee brought out to her at two o'clock in the afternoon, every day."

Monica took a sniff, inviting memories of times past, but it only smelled like coffee. "I always regret that I never got to go to her funeral. It just seems wrong. I was her only grandchild, after all."

"I regret it as well," Bruce said, holding his chin up with the palm of his hand like a little boy. "The Borreros called to inform me of her death after she had been buried for a month. It's part of how they managed to cheat you out of your inheritance. Bastards."

"It's too early in the morning for that," Monica said, waving one hand. "All I'm saying is that I wish I was able to attend my mother's and my grandmother's funerals. Most people need ceremony to get a sense of closure. Otherwise, it's just like the person is away on a long trip or something."

Bruce chewed faster, driving his fork through the plantains with unnecessary force. "Alma's memorial service lasted less than fifteen minutes. We all knew that anything reeking of tradition would be an insult to her memory. If we had been able to recover her body, your grandmother and I would have cremated her and scattered her ashes at sea." He filled his lungs up and burped into his closed fist, then pointed at his plate. "This is all very authentic."

"I want to know where Mom's marker is. I need to know so I can lay you to rest next to her when you die."

Bruce choked on the last of his coffee, fumbled for some napkins, and covered his mouth as he coughed. He pounded his chest, and his eyes reddened. Finally, he cleared his throat and said in a strained voice, "I'll be with Ma and Pa in the East Hampton Cemetery, thank you very much. Besides, what would be the point? You'd be burying me all alone, because your mother's grave is empty."

"Hmm. Good point." Monica considered, rubbing her chin.

Bruce looked at his mug. "Did you poison my coffee or something? If you need cash, just ask, for God's sake, no need to murder me."

Monica looked hard to the left. "I guess I'm just looking for an excuse to go back to El Salvador. I know I say that every year, but I've been thinking that maybe it's time to actually do it."

"Oh, I get it. You're trying to give me a heart attack."

"Dad, the war's over. What's the big deal?"

He looked at her sideways. "I find it disturbing that you should be interested in traveling to El Salvador. That place was very bad to you, Monica."

"It wasn't personal," Monica said. "There was a civil war going on."

Bruce folded his arms and looked away. "I may be going to El Salvador in the next month."

Monica laughed, shook her head. "What are you talking about?"

"Research."

"What?" Monica tilted her head and pulled on her earlobe, as if she were trying to shake water out of her eardrum. "I'm sorry. I must have misunderstood. I thought I just heard you say you're going to the *bad* place. You know, the one I shouldn't be allowed to even think about."

"May be going. May be."

Accustomed to having to pry information out of her father, Monica took a few seconds to calculate the degree of delicacy required to get the full picture. She stood up and consolidated the food remains on both their plates. She strolled over to the sink, dumped the food, and briefly ran the garbage disposal. "So you're writing an article," she said. "Tell me more."

Bruce cleared his throat. "Well, I got a nibble from *Urban*

Science and the *Cutting Edge* on the brain-injury article I told you I was pursuing. But it wasn't until after I had ended the interview with the Lucero crew and we were sitting around gabbing that I realized that something far more interesting was going on. Yvette's mother is willing to give any kind of superstitious voodoo a chance. Did you see Yvette's hospital room? It's full of religious paraphernalia. What's interesting to me now is the extremes we go to when conventional medicine fails to deliver."

Monica blinked and turned to look at her father. "What does this have to do with El Salvador?"

Bruce pursed his lips and stared down at the table, as if trying to decide what to say, or what not to say. He took a deep breath and exhaled slowly, then looked up at her. "Sylvia found a clinic in El Salvador that promises to 'fix' her daughter."

Monica shook her head. "Fix?"

"The Salvadoran government doesn't consider this nature-based treatment a narcotic, so therefore it's not regulated. In theory, that means that if there's something out there that can help someone like Yvette, these folks can isolate the solution a lot faster than we can here. That's the sliver of hope." He paused and held up a finger. "Now here's the interesting part, Monica."

Monica bounced on her heels. "Tell me. You're driving me crazy," she said, forgetting her resolve to approach him gingerly.

"This clinic is using cone toxins to attempt to jolt the injured brain into regenerating new cells." He opened his eyes even wider. "Cone venom, Monica. *Cone venom*. The same damn snail juice your mother drowned over."

"Is it the *Conus furiosus*?" she whispered.

"Yep. And Sylvia found this program because of you." He pointed at Monica. "Said *you* gave her a minicourse on the miracles of cone venom the other day."

Monica dropped a handful of the silverware into the suds. She blinked several times and put her wet hands together, as if in prayer. "You've got to be shitting me."

She never swore, and so Bruce raised his eyebrows and gave her a half smile. "Nope," he said, as he poured himself more coffee. "I admit that fact has added a personal touch to my curiosity."

Monica had to blink several times before she could even speak. "How could you sit across from me and discuss the authenticity of these refried beans when you knew someone found the *Conus furiosus*? Are you from another planet or something?"

Bruce shrugged and looked away. "I wasn't sure if you wanted to know that you're causing huge arguments between Will and Sylvia."

"Where on God's earth did they find it?"

Bruce turned his back to her and walked toward the living room and the picture window that, at this early hour, only reflected back his own image. "Mexico. Apparently mollusks can be declared extinct for a half century, then pop up in droves somewhere."

"The *Conus gloriamaris*," Monica said, following him into the room. "Abuela paid thousands of dollars to have an officially extinct seashell in her collection; now you can get one for thirty bucks."

"The truth is, I don't know if it's really the *Conus furiosus,* but it sure sounds like it. They're very secretive about the source for this treatment. The woman I talked to on the phone down there claims that the treatment is a 'blend' of venoms."

"What, like cheap wine?"

"All she would say was that one of the cones in the 'blend' was considered extremely rare to extinct, but that a small colony of them was discovered on the Pacific coast, near Oaxaca. Someone was stung, and the subsequent effects imply that the substance was chemically able to break the blood–brain barrier."

"Sounds like the *furiosus* to me," Monica said. "So what do they claim they're going to do for Yvette? Restore dead brain cells?"

Bruce nodded. "They have her mother convinced that they can offer some level of improvement."

"That just seems so far-fetched."

"That's what I say, but they claim that they have advanced lucidity in some cases like Yvette's."

"What does Will say about it?"

"He thinks it's ludicrous and dangerous. So do the doctors."

"Poor Will. It can't be easy to manage Sylvia on top of everything else. He seems like a nice guy. Patient. Kind," Monica said, and looked away.

"He's a *hell* of a guy. I can't begin to tell you how impressed I am by him." Bruce took a few steps forward, put his hands squarely on Monica's shoulders. "But don't you go setting him up with Paige. Will is married, after all."

"I wasn't going to set them up. *Paige* is a handful."

Bruce turned to scoop up his UConn baseball hat. He put it on, checked his reflection in the mirror above the fireplace, and rubbed his morning stubble. "Ready?"

Monica nodded, willing to let the conversation go for a minute while she allowed her mind to race. She went into the kitchen to grab the thermos of coffee and an old sweatshirt, then walked down to the water. Long Island Sound was still, making the water look thick and metallic, like liquid mercury. Bruce had already pulled the rowboat out of the garage, and it rested on the tangle of seaweed and rocks beyond the seawall. They loaded bait, rods, and a tackle box. Bruce rowed the boat across the silent, ethereal surface of the water. The morning fog concealed the low, flat arm of Long Island across the water.

When they settled on a spot, Monica said, in a hushed voice so as not to scare away the fish, "I feel really bad if my comment triggered more tension between Sylvia and Will. God, it was just an offhand comment. Will was the one who noticed the cone collection on my office shelf and asked me about them."

Bruce shook his head and tossed his line. "You shouldn't feel responsible, you didn't know. But I think those two are in for a battle if Sylvia decides to pursue it."

Monica's shoulders slumped and she stared out at the water. Bruce glanced at her and said, "Oh, hell. I doubt she has that kind of cash anyway. We're talking big bucks to transport Yvette."

"Who has more of a right to make these types of decisions, a spouse or a parent?" Monica asked.

"In their case he does. Yvette would have had to have signed a legal document assigning Sylvia."

"Do you think there's a chance the venom treatment is a hoax?" Monica said, crinkling her nose as she wrapped a night crawler onto a fishhook. She held her hook out to Bruce for inspection. He nodded, and she cast her line.

"A hoax? Maybe. But not necessarily. An impulsive, irresponsible, unmonitored experiment is more like it," Bruce said. "But you might call me a pessimist or a skeptic for saying that. Who knows, Monica, maybe it's something brilliant and fantastic and we're all going to be surprised. But I doubt it." Something disturbed the glassy surface and he gave Monica the thumbs-up.

Monica thought, what if Alma's beloved sea snails could turn out to be medicinal after all? And what a joyous miracle if their venom could help Yvette. Monica thought about the day she had massaged her, remembering the weird sensation that someone was *in there*.

Out of the blue, Bruce declared, "The thing I admired about your mother, in retrospect, was her devotion to nature. She was an environmentalist in a country that as a whole was ruthlessly ambitious. It wasn't a popular point of view."

Monica didn't answer, and they were silent for a while. Perhaps suspecting what Monica was thinking, Bruce raised one eyebrow and switched the conversation back to where he was comfortable. "What's weird is that I haven't found any other information published on the *furiosus*. You'd think this would be big news even if its success was documented on rats. I need to dig deeper, I guess."

"Paige can help. You know she has access to all those expensive academic Web sites through work."

Bruce nodded and tugged on his line.

"So who's paying for the cost of your research, Dad?"

"There's a budget for this kind of thing."

Monica got her first nibble, then a pull, and she began to reel in whatever was on the end of her line. Bruce whooped as she pulled up a striped bass. He unhooked it for her and threw it in the cooler.

As usual, they had succeeded in circumventing mention of Alma's partner in the quest for the *Conus*. Years ago, even the most casual mention of Maximiliano Campos could bring on a silence and melancholy that lasted for days. But the morning's talk of El Salvador naturally made her thoughts return to the man who had ruined life as they knew it, and the idea of her father reentering that world made her a bit uneasy, as if Maximiliano were still alive and waiting to wreak more destruction. But Max was dead, after all, and as she herself had said, the twelve-year civil war was over, the peace accords signed back in 1992. If anything, a trip down memory lane might make the past appear less overbearing, as a house appears smaller when a child returns to it as an adult.

Monica was twelve when her father put her on a Pan Am flight destined for Hartford. Shell-shocked and motherless, she sank into a silent depression during that first, long, rainy spring at Grandma Winters's house. It wasn't until the season warmed into summer that the nightmares began. Perhaps it was the silence of the forest with its trees as tall as cathedrals that invited the confessions of her soul. It was the safety of a nowhere New England town that finally allowed her mind to unburden itself in the darkness of her bedroom.

She dreamed of children running and shouting as they were hunted by unseen shooters; people in ski masks, armored trucks flying by, shouting warnings, telling everyone to run. Always there were black dogs in the background, and the recurring image of a village procession, painted faces floating by, a wooden Virgin Mary as big as a department store mannequin, with bright pink cheeks, carried on a makeshift float. In the dream Alma's hand is slippery as a wet fish, and Monica loses her grip on her mother and is lost in the crowd. Alma disappears, but the hem of her yellow dress is still visible, a handful of it pinched between two bodies. Monica reaches for it, but in a moment, it too slips away. Monica wanders through the crowd, crying and calling for her mother. She passes street vendors selling ribbons of green mango soaking in salt and lime juice. She smiles when she comes upon a man peddling live chicks dyed green, pink, and sky blue. Alma is standing before the vendor, scolding him for cruelty to the chicks, many of which will absorb the coloring through their skin, poisoning them to death. The wind picks up and Alma evaporates; like the sawdust art on the sidewalks, she blows away, bright and colorful and fragmented into too many pieces to catch.

In the morning, the only evidence of Monica's nightmares was fatigue and sweat stains on the sheets.

"What was that sound?" Monica asked her father, wrenched from the memory of the dream.

"What was what?" Bruce said without turning away from his fishing.

"I thought I just heard the sound of tinfoil crinkling." She looked around her, at the water of Long Island Sound, and realized that she had imagined it. It must have been in the lap of the water against the little boat, the smell of raw fish that she associated with the sound of someone ripping and balling tinfoil, someone getting ready to cook over a campfire.

"How could you hear something onshore from this far away?" Bruce asked.

Monica shook her head. "It was just my imagination. I was daydreaming."

Bruce opened the cooler again and released the smell of raw fish. She wrinkled her nose. No, it wasn't the sound of tinfoil she heard. It was the crackle of a fire. It was another memory emerging from the farthest corners of her brain, prompted by the smell of fish and the ruminations about her mother. Then it came back to her, suddenly, like a short movie. One night, she and her mother had cleaned and gutted barracudas for guerrilla rebels.

MAXIMILIANO CAMPOS was nourishing a pack of students, faculty, and others associated with the Salvadoran revolution on a boatload of fish, and so everyone was calling him Jesus. "Fish for strength, fish for stealth," Max said, as he passed around plates of grilled barracuda and hot tortillas with lime and rock salt on the side.

Almost one hundred people were at this beach property, ten minutes by car down the coast from Negrarena. The property didn't exactly belong to Max; in fact, no one but Max knew the owner, but he had identified it to be a safe place, a remote and lonely stretch of land where the intellectual nucleus of the revolution could meet to fill their bellies, laugh, sing, and play guitar without danger. Since it was on the coast, they couldn't be cornered because there was always the option of escape by sea. El Trovador, as the property was named, had several acres of beachfront, with rustic outhouses and open-sided huts with roofs made of dried palm fronds. The entire kitchen consisted of a grill and a wide, flat griddle made of burned clay. On the beach, rowboats appeared, slow moving in the darkness of the approaching midnight. They were coming from Nicaragua and Honduras, through El Golfo de Fonseca, an inlet of water that fanned across all three countries.

"Tomorrow they are going to attack one of the foreign embassies downtown," Alma had casually said to Monica. "But most of these people aren't going to be directly involved. These are the thinkers, the political side. They don't do the dirty work."

"So are they good or bad?" Monica asked.

"They're good," Alma said, but tentatively. "At least, they have good intentions."

"Then why are they hiding?"

"Because they're communists, honey. If the National Guard finds out they're here, they'll come in and kill everyone."

Monica swallowed hard and dug her fingers into her mother's arm. "These people are all communists? As in *guerrilleros*?"

"Shh. Don't say that so loud."

"Are they going to kill us?" Monica pressed, switching into English.

"Shhh." Alma put her fingers over Monica's mouth and whispered. "Speak in Spanish. Don't *ever* let them know you speak English."

When she took her hand off Monica's mouth, Alma relaxed and said, in Spanish, "Of course not. They're Max's friends. . . . It's exciting just to *be* here, to see history unfold. But remember, our names are . . ." She pointed to herself and nodded her head, prompting Monica.

"You're Leticia Ramos. And I'm your daughter, Fernanda."

"And you go to the public school . . ."

"At Cantón El Farolito."

"Don't ever mention that you go to private school, okay? Or that your dad's an American or that he's a journalist. Put your arm around Max every once in a while. Pretend he's your father."

Repulsed at the thought, Monica turned and surveyed the group behind her. "Why are we here?"

"It's our civic duty."

"We already helped make the tortilla dough and cleaned all that disgusting fish. Can't we go now?"

Alma smiled and cupped Monica's face with her hands. "Not just yet. We have to help Max with one more thing. A wonderful, incredibly special thing. . . ." Alma put her arm around Monica's neck and pulled her toward the shadows, away from the crowd. They walked across a dark, sandy field full of the smoky smell of fish cooking. Monica wondered if someone would smell the fish and call the National Guard. She shivered. Why had her mother dragged her here? She had heard about these people from her grandmother, her father, their friends, kids from school. It seemed everyone she knew was against them except her mother. Monica tried hard to shake off her nerves and just trust her mother.

They came upon a tiny thatched-roof hut. Monica could hear someone sobbing inside, a wretched, painful sound, as if a girl were being tortured. She froze, but Alma pulled her along. "C'mon, it's okay."

A man was standing in the shadows. He took off his hat and pressed it against his chest as they passed. They stepped over a sleeping dog lying across the entrance and entered the hut. There was no furniture except for a hammock hanging empty across the room, a transistor radio on the floor, and a dirty blue-and-white Salvadoran flag, which hung on a crude pole nailed into one of the rafters. The room smelled of sweat and rubbing alcohol.

Maximiliano was kneeling on the packed-dirt floor, and the parts of his face that were not bearded gleamed with sweat. He was wearing khaki pants and a dirty, bloodstained white guayabera that reached down to his thighs like a lab coat. An old woman who was normally his cook was at his side. When he saw them come in, he looked up and smiled. "Are you sure *la princesa* can handle this?" he asked with not just a bit of sarcasm.

Alma nodded. "Monica has seen every type of animal birth at Negrarena. She's ready to graduate to humans."

Max said, "Come," and signaled with his finger to Monica. No one asked the patient.

Monica stood next to where Max was kneeling. On a straw mat lay a girl, two or three years older than Monica, at the most fifteen. Her black, straight hair was splayed all around her head like a fan. She was lying on her back, legs parted, an enormous belly weighing down her small frame.

"This is how life begins, Monica," Max said, pointing to the head that was beginning to crown. Monica craned her head and looked. She blinked, took in the wonder of that little, hairy head emerging. It wasn't so different from the livestock births, except the girl's cries were far more unnerving. The whole scene made Monica grit her teeth. Maximiliano pressed his fingers around the little head. Monica watched, fascinated but growing woozy. Alma stood over her shoulder for a moment, but was soon helping Max to shift and reposition the girl's hips and to soak up some of the blood.

The room began to spin a little, so Monica crawled to the girl's side. She talked to her, dabbed at the sweat on her forehead and neck with the hem of her skirt. The girl gave Monica her hand, which was hot and moist with sweat, and Monica took it, but turned her head away from the scene. She was trying to gain her footing over the swimmy feeling, all the while feeling some kind of elation in the look of gratitude in the girl's face. The girl continued squeezing Monica's hand, harder, until Monica wanted to cry out herself, but then the baby was out and the adults clapped and laughed and announced its male sex in unison: *"¡Es varón!"*

The adults were busy cleaning up the girl and the new baby, which had already found its lungs, when the girl turned to Monica and whispered in a hoarse, exhausted voice, "Do you want it?"

"Want what?" Monica asked.

"Mi angelito."

"You're giving your baby away?" Monica asked, stunned.

"My father said I have to get rid of it. We already have eleven kids in our house."

Monica looked into the girl's face, round and short, with the characteristic thick, straight eyelashes of El Salvador's indigenous people.

"You can feed him breast milk, can't you?" Monica said, thinking she had resolved the issue.

The girl smiled sadly. "For a while. And in six months he'll begin to need some real food."

"What about the baby's father?"

The girl looked away. *"No tiene."*

"No father? How could he have no father?"

"You know how it goes."

Monica didn't have the foggiest idea of "how it goes," but she nodded anyway, trying to understand something so beyond her. The girl raised her head and asked Alma and Maximiliano if either of them wanted the baby. "I can't take him," Alma said, "but don't worry, we'll help you find a good home for him."

Monica spoke in English this time so the others wouldn't understand. "Mom, I want the baby. I'll take care of it."

"This is a child, not a puppy," Alma said. The matron returned with a dishpan of water, and they cleaned the baby to screams that made them all pull in their heads like turtles.

Monica insisted that she could take care of him: she'd bathe him, feed him, teach him to read and write. But Alma shook her head no again and again. She and Max left the hut together with instructions for the matron to finish up. Max was going to clean up and get back to his guests. They let Monica stay with the girl. The girl's father was waiting outside to take the girl and her unwanted baby home.

Monica watched, cross-legged on the floor, as the matron showed the girl how to nurse the baby. Monica thought of the cattle, horses, pigs, and chickens at Negrarena, eating bushels of feed every day. Was it possible that anyone could be so poor that they couldn't afford to feed a little creature that weighed less than seven pounds?

"I'm Maria del Carmen. What's your name?" the girl asked.

Monica hesitated, not knowing if this girl was one of the communists on the beach. Outside, the girl's father called to her, and the girl replied that she needed just a moment more.

"*¿Sos comunista?*" Monica asked outright.

"I don't bother with that stuff," the girl answered.

Confident that the girl could be trusted, she whispered, "*Me llamo Mónica.*"

"*¿Mónica qué?*" The girl insisted on a last name.

Suddenly understanding the girl's boldness, she answered, "Winters Borrero."

"Oh, you're very rich then," Maria del Carmen said, brightening. She rocked the baby in her arms and smiled broadly at Monica. "God sent you to us."

When the matron went to fetch some aspirin, Maria del Carmen called her father over and whispered in his ear. The old man mumbled something to Monica that she didn't understand because he was toothless. He carried his exhausted daughter in his arms, and the two disappeared into the darkness of the fields beyond the beach.

When the matron returned, Monica was curled up on the

straw mat where the girl had been. The matron knelt beside the figure she thought was Maria del Carmen. Instead, she found Monica whispering to the infant. Monica had wrapped him in the Salvadoran flag for lack of a swaddling cloth, and the baby's little fingers curled around her index finger. She had unbuttoned her cotton shirt, and the baby happily suckled on the unopened buds of her tiny, pubescent breasts.

"YOU KNOW we can't keep that baby," Alma said. "It has to go to the orphanage."

"*He,*" Monica corrected. She sat at the kitchen table at Caracol, watching Francisca feed the baby powdered milk from a Raggedy Ann baby bottle that had been Monica's.

"Why not?" Monica insisted. "Everybody else has a brother or a sister. Why can't I?"

"Because, Monica Marina, we can't take care of him."

Monica stood up and leaned forward. She made her hand into a fist and banged on the table. "We have five maids, two gardeners; our family owns a dairy plant. We can afford this baby."

Francisca smiled and raised an eyebrow at Alma. "Maybe she's right, Niña Alma. Here I am, employed as a nanny but with no more babies to watch."

Alma closed her eyes and took a deep breath. "Yes, we have enough food. But babies need more than food. They need parents. They need someone to take responsibility day in and day out. We don't have anyone here who is willing to do that. And you're twelve years old, Monica, for God's sake."

Monica stared at her brown suede earth shoes, fuming. "You say you care about the poor of El Salvador, but you won't sacrifice to help one little baby. You just want to be liked by Max and his communist friends." She turned and ran out of the room, partly to keep herself from saying more, and partly to

avoid the consequences of such disrespect. She heard Alma calling after her, but she was hiding in the one place Álma would never look: her father's office. Monica sat at Bruce's typewriter and began to type a letter to the president of El Salvador, pleading with him to authorize the baby's adoption, even though she was only twelve. She had already named the baby Jimmy Bray, after a boy she had a crush on at the American School. She had fantasized that this was her offspring with the blond, blue-eyed expatriate boy from Alabama in her sixth-grade class. They'd only spoken once, when Monica asked, "Is this your library book?" Jimmy Bray nodded his shiny blond head and took the book from Monica. Not much of a relationship yet, but Monica considered it a good start.

The other part of her fantasy was that Jimmy Bray junior would be more like her brother, the child her dad could do "boy stuff" with, the child who could bring her family together. They *needed* a baby to glue them back together—and this baby desperately needed them.

But the next day little Jimmy Bray was gone.

When they saw Max at the San Salvador farmers' market the following Saturday, he was amused with the whole ordeal and had put his arm around Monica and tried to console her. He said she was a good girl, with a big heart, and that the baby was safe and they had found a nice family to take him in.

Monica wanted to see for herself, out of a deep distrust that was blossoming between her and her mother. But Alma refused to take her to see Jimmy Bray, out of punishment for her disrespect. The baby, Monica learned, had been "renamed" José Martín Castillo.

When Bruce returned from Nicaragua that Sunday night, his twelve-year-old had matured by years, already having assisted in a birth and, in her own mind, having endured a mother's loss of her baby. She sobbed into Bruce's shoulder and complained about her mother.

Later, Monica heard her parents arguing. Bruce didn't approve of the field trip. "A human birth, for God's sake? She's too young, Alma," he scolded. "You treat her like she's a mini-adult. You need to slow it down, shelter her innocence a bit longer." There was a pause and then he asked pointedly, "What were you doing with Maximiliano anyway?"

"Monica and I were at Negrarena when Maximiliano sent a *mozo* on horseback with word that he needed help with the birth. He was doing it as charity in a neighboring town, but needed an assistant. I couldn't leave Monica alone, so I went. The last thing anyone expected was that the family would take off and leave us with the infant."

Another long pause, and Bruce spoke again. "I think you've been spending way too much time with Max. I know he's your childhood friend and that you share an interest in science and medicine, but you're a married woman. It doesn't look good, and it's not healthy. Why don't you and Monica come with me on my next work trip instead?"

Alma made a face. "Too dangerous. There's a war going on out there."

As a last attempt, Bruce, whose voice was far deeper and more audible to Monica than Alma's, said, "It hurts me that you spend so much time with him. I'm asking you to stop."

There was a pause.

"Alma, look at me. I'm asking you to stop spending so much time with him and start investing your time and energy in your own marriage and family. Will you at least reconsider the idea of a baby? Monica is obviously desperate for a sibling."

Their bedroom door slammed shut. Monica heard her father's footsteps in the hall as he made his way back to his office.

In bed that night, Monica cried for the lost baby, for the mother and the grandfather who had walked away from their own flesh and blood, thinking the baby would be raised with the comforts and privileges of a prince. She felt a sudden confusion over Max, whom she had sworn to hate, but who was tending the wounds of the poor and delivering their unwanted babies. And more disturbingly, she felt the weakening of loyalty to her mother, who was keeping her from having a normal family with brothers and sisters like everyone else. Most disturbing of all was that her father wanted more children. She had always believed that they agreed on this issue.

A week later, over breakfast, Alma held up the newspaper for Monica. Monica recognized one of the men by his fuzzy hair, even though he had a bandanna covering his face. It was one of the young communists that had been at the beach that night, eating barracuda. He had recited a long poem by Rubén Darío for Monica.

"That guy is dead," Alma said. "And sixteen of his friends are missing. There was a government raid in Chalatenango."

Monica pushed the newspaper aside. "Are you in love with Max? I have to know."

They could hear Bruce moving around in the other room. The phone rang. He picked it up and began to speak to someone.

Alma stared at her. "Are you challenging me?"

Monica stared back. "You don't love my dad."

Alma looked down and began to chip away at her pearly nail polish. "I admire Max. I love the places he's going . . ." She stopped. "Yes, I love him. He's always been my friend. Since I was a kid. As for your dad . . ."

Monica looked away. "Are you going to leave him?"

Alma looked at Monica as if seeing her for the first time. When she spoke, it was more to herself than to Monica. "Shit, you're turning into me."

Alma leaned over and tried to hug her, but Monica took a step back. "I said, are you going to leave my dad?"

"Lower your voice." She leaned back, studied her daughter,

searching her face for the source of this new aggression. "No, I'm not leaving your father, Monica. And don't talk to me like that."

"Max is taken," Monica sneered. "He doesn't belong to you."

Alma turned pale; she sat back in her chair. "Who told you that?"

"I heard you say it in your sleep."

"SO WHY ARE YOU THINKING of going to El Salvador, Dad?" Monica asked as Bruce rowed the rowboat toward shore.

Bruce looked at her oddly. "What do you mean? I just told you. Cone venom."

"Nothing else?"

"I wouldn't mind looking up some old friends, taking a leisurely stroll down the bombed-out section of memory lane."

Monica nodded. "That's why I'm going with you."

"Why?"

"Same reason."

"There isn't anything there for you."

Monica lowered her sunglasses. "Do you have some illegitimate children down there you want to tell me about? Are you wanted by the law? Because I don't believe it's just about uncomfortable memories."

Bruce gave her an acid look. Monica looked out at the approaching shore. She spotted her narrow, two-story cottage with its double layer of decks facing the sea among the tightly packed crowd of beach homes. It was Bruce's future retirement home, and Monica paid the mortgage while she was living there. It surprised her that he had elected a house by the sea. She would have expected him to look for something buried deep in the forests, something more solitary and landlocked, like him.

"Dad," Monica said softly as their boat approached the shore, "do you remember that time Mom took me to watch a birth and the girl gave the baby to me?"

Bruce looked up from behind the rim of his hat. "Yeah."

"Why didn't we keep him?"

Bruce got out of the boat and tossed the cooler onto the seawall. He got a scaling knife out and began to gut the fish, tossing the fish parts into the water. He rinsed everything off with a garden hose from the neighbor's yard. "Your mother didn't want any more kids and I wasn't home nearly enough to take responsibility for an adopted child. Besides, look what a mess our family turned out to be. He's better off."

"What about what you wanted, Dad? Why was it always about what she wanted?"

"Parenting requires buy-in from both sides."

"Did you guys try counseling or anything like that?"

Bruce turned his head suddenly, as if the conversation had suddenly crossed a line into the distasteful. He took a deep breath and Monica understood that this was the last thing he was going to say on the subject. "We didn't need anyone to tell us what was wrong with us. We knew exactly what was wrong with us."

They packed their fish in freezer bags. "Fish for strength, fish for stealth," Monica intoned as she rearranged the frozen strawberries and chicken breasts to make room in her freezer.

On Thursday, Monica rushed home from work to freshen up and change into loose cotton clothing before her evening appointment. Her father had given Will Lucero his massage time slot as thanks for the interview. Monica had protested that he had no right to do that, but of course by then it was too late. "Besides," Bruce had said, "you owe him something for getting Sylvia all riled up about cone venom."

She opened her front door at ten minutes to six. *"Hola,"* Will said, bending down to kiss her politely on the cheek.

She pointed over her shoulder toward the interior of the house. "I'm ready for you," she said, her standard greeting suddenly sounding provocative. She bit her lip. As he passed, she noticed that he smelled freshly showered—of Ivory soap and clean cotton. His hair was still wet.

Will approached the large picture window in her living room that faced the water. He crossed his arms and said, "There's just something about the water . . . it's so peaceful."

Monica gave him a tour of the downstairs and the deck, but stopped short at the stairs leading up to the second floor. He complimented her taste in furnishings, the black-and-white photography in paper-thin black frames, hung in clusters throughout the house.

"You could paint this wall a bold color like indigo blue or black cherry," he said, making wide, sweeping motions in front of the cutout wall that separated the kitchen from the dining area. "Maybe with some light texturing. It would completely rebalance this room. You could pick up any of those three colors from the rug under your dining set. You have so much light in here." Monica folded her arms over her chest and stuck her lower lip out as she considered it. Will said, "I'm the finance guy at my family's company, but I watch the decorators. I'm always amazed what color on the walls can do to change a room and create a mood."

"I need something to offset the gloominess that sets in after October."

Will put a hand on his chin and looked around. "Then what you need is butter- or lemon-colored walls. Details in tangerine. Poppy. Fuchsia. You'll be so happy all the time, you won't be able to stand yourself."

Monica laughed and thought, *I like him*. She said, "This entire part of the country is plagued by too much gray, white, brown. Maybe we should all paint our houses in crazy colors like they do in the Bahamas. It would be so wonderfully defiant to have a watermelon-colored house."

"Especially in January, when there's three feet of snow on the ground."

Monica stepped into the kitchen. "Can I get you anything to drink before we get started?"

"Water is fine," he said, following her. He cleared his throat. "I had no idea you were a Latina. When your dad told me you were born and raised in Central America, I was floored. You're tall, slim; you have green eyes, no accent. I would have guessed you were Irish. You are definitely hard to place, ethnically speaking."

Monica smiled and hunched her shoulders, handing him a glass. "Really?"

"What did your mom look like?" He followed her out of the kitchen, and she walked over to a blond wood table that ran along the wall at the foot of the staircase. She grabbed an eight-and-a-half-by-eleven photo in a polished silver frame and handed it to Will.

"It's you," he said.

"No, it's my mother. You think it's me because she's squinting and you can't see her eyes that well."

They stood staring at Alma's photo for a moment. A shark tooth hung from Alma's neck, glowing bright in the sun like a tiny dagger. A thin blindfold of her long, coiled black hair was blowing over her laughing face. Will looked up at Monica, then back at the picture and back at Monica. "Amazing. The smile is exactly the same." He handed her the frame. "She's beautiful."

Monica thanked him, blushing at the reflected compliment, and had to spend a few extra seconds fussing over the items on the table so as not to have to turn and look at him right away.

"So are you ready?" she said cheerfully, looking at her watch. "Six o'clock on the nose. Would you prefer to be massaged out on the deck or here inside?"

Will craned his neck and looked outside, raised one eyebrow. "It's a bit muggy outside. How about right here? We still get the view."

Monica nodded. Her "soothing massage" CD was ready to go and her massage creams were warming in a pump bottle plugged into the wall. "Do you have boxers on under there?" she asked, pointing to his pants, blushing uncontrollably this time. "Or do you need to borrow a pair?"

Will smiled and said, "No, I'm all set. Where's the bathroom?"

She pointed to the half bath next to the entrance. He walked down the hall, bending down to scoop up a small duffel bag that Monica had not noticed before. She heard him banging his elbows against the walls of the small half bath. She remembered his fall in her office. Was he accident-prone? She was pondering this when he came out, bare-chested, with biker's shorts poking out of another pair of more loosely fitting athletic shorts. Monica was both impressed by his physique and relieved by his modesty. Some of her clients chose to wear nothing but a towel.

"I don't know if you're interested, but I have some extra faucet knobs I could give you for that half bath. They're the old-fashioned porcelain kind that are labeled HOT and COLD in black letters. I think they'd look nice with the antique white linen theme you have going on in there."

Monica patted the massage table. "Yes, I'd love them. Now, no more redecorating. Just lie down here and stare out at the water for me."

"I'm sorry, I hope I'm not being obnoxious."

"No, no. I just want you to forget your work and relax."

He lay down. Soon he was under the spell of her healing hands, and her fingers glided over the vastness of his freckled back. No thin sliver of neck tension here. This man had solid tension everywhere, the kind that came from rigorous physical activity combined with intense emotional stress. His oohs and aahs came quickly and spontaneously, especially when she flattened out the palm of her hand and pressed down on the muscle centers, radiating the heat of their inflammation. She accidentally brushed his lips with the yoke of one finger while she massaged his face. He opened his eyes and looked at her, smiled, then turned his head and closed his eyes again. She felt a spark of pleasure spiral its way down through her body, and it made her terribly uncomfortable.

Instead of trying to tune in to the language of her client's body—those little clues and patterns of the body that spoke so loudly—she made an effort to tune them out. She tried to focus on the skill of her own movements, to pace her breathing so that she wouldn't tire so fast. After all, deep-tissue massage on a muscular man took a great deal of strength. She couldn't help but notice the little bruises here and there, the way he recoiled slightly when she pressed them.

"Is someone beating you?" Monica asked. "I've counted five bruises already."

"Oh, it's just from working like an idiot. I'm so crazed all the time, rushing around and trying to do too many things. For the last two weeks I've been bumping into stuff, falling off chairs, tripping on rugs."

"This might hurt a little, but it helps distribute the blood that's pooled under there." She rubbed the bruises, then slapped them lightly. "They'll go away in two or three days. Is there anything you can drop to make life a little easier on yourself?" She put her hand flat on his back. "Don't answer that. It's just a question I pose to all my clients, something for you to consider. A tiny bit of restraint can save your neck, your back, your feet, you name it. Stress is so expensive in the end."

"That's why I sail on Tuesdays," he mumbled. "It's one big deep-brain-tissue massage. It gets the bad gunk out. Clears my head."

Monica squirted fresh massage cream into her hands while he continued, "But even with the antistress effects of sailing, I'm still sore around my neck, my shoulders, along my spine. Three of our guys called in sick on the same day this week, so I had to pitch in with the heavy lifting."

She rubbed up and down his spine. This was the part when

most people got quiet. But Will kept chatting away. "To answer your question, I don't know what I could drop. I can't work less, our business is only eight years old, and we have to be aggressive about building relationships with contractors and customers. I exercise; I visit Yvette and stay on top of all her health care. That's a full plate right there. Sometimes I think I should just sell the house in Durham and move closer to New Haven, but I love our house, I restored it myself." He sighed, a big hopeless exhaling.

"Is there any chance Yvette could be moved to a facility nearer to home?"

"She's at the closest facility already."

Will was silent for a moment, then said, "So what do you do to get your gunk out, Monica?"

Monica paused her massaging for just a few seconds before beginning again, taking a half step back to leverage more strength. "I fish with my dad. I volunteer at the Mystic Aquarium doing educational projects for kids. I take a ferry out to Martha's Vineyard and spend the weekend. Oh, and I hang out with my boyfriend."

"And what puts the gunk *into* your life?" he asked, his voice muffled by a towel Monica had stuffed under his neck.

"Mostly my boyfriend." She laughed, but her laugh sounded brittle even to herself. She felt something pass under her hand— a tensing, then releasing. He had been about to say something, then decided not to.

"But you know what?" she said, digging her fist around his deltoids. "You're here to relax, not to talk about problems."

"I'm relaxed just talking to you. But okay. I'll shut my trap."

Over the next fifteen minutes, Monica thought of three things she wanted to ask him, but bit her tongue. Will was finally silent, and although she was itching to learn more about him, the ideal environment for him to reap the full impact of her hard work was silence. Monica could tell that he was, as she called it, "gelling down." He was relaxing, releasing endorphins, a mild euphoria setting into his muscles. His thoughts were wandering freely. Soon he would start to feel sleepy.

Next, Monica got to work on his feet. She squirted warm cream on one hand and kneaded, rubbed, and pulled his toes so they made little snapping sounds. In a moment, she heard his heavy breathing; a few moments later, light snoring.

She always stopped at this stage, because what was the point of massaging someone who was asleep? She would let him sleep for twenty minutes, then wake him up and finish the massage. She moved about quietly, washed her hands, and went into the kitchen to get something to drink. Then, she stepped out to the deck, laced her fingers together, and did some quick stretches. She breathed in the muggy air, and even though it was sticky and uncomfortable, she decided to stay outside a few minutes.

She looked at her watch. Kevin wasn't due to take her out to dinner for another hour and a half. Plenty of time. Thursday and Saturday were their date nights, and Kevin was rigid about that because he watched his favorite TV shows on Mondays and Wednesdays. Tuesday and Friday nights he worked out at the gym and Monica gave massages at home.

When the twenty minutes were up, she stepped back into the house, relieved to return to the air-conditioning. Will was still asleep, facedown. She opened a wood armoire and searched for a livelier CD. She popped in a collection of flamenco ballads and lowered the volume. Her intention was to raise the volume slowly, so as not to startle him.

Monica heard a soft clicking sound behind her. She turned around to see Kevin, in shirt and tie, appear in the hallway, jacket tossed over one arm. In his other hand was his laptop computer bag. The hallway was carpeted, so he had not made any noise as he came in. Monica held her index finger up to her lips to hush him. But something caught his eye and he looked away for a second or two and did not see her. He stepped into the living room, his work shoes clicking on the hardwood floor as he said, in a loud, irritated voice, "Who the hell is parked in my spot?" As he spoke, he turned slightly to toss a handful of keys into a nearby ceramic bowl. The keys made a loud jangling noise.

Will's lids peeled open and he sat up, fists raised, muscles flexed, his face registering a wild confusion. Startled, Kevin jumped back, letting go of his computer bag to hold his hands out in front of him. The bag landed with a loud crash on his foot.

Monica sprang to Will's side and put her hand on his arm. "Easy, easy," she said. "I was massaging you and you fell asleep."

Will shook his head and dropped back onto the table, flopping one hand over his eyes.

"I'm *so* sorry," Monica said. "I didn't expect him for another hour or so." She shot Kevin a look. "Thanks, Kevin. All that work for nothing."

Will sat up again and leaned on one elbow. "Are you kidding? You were great."

At those last three words, Kevin turned and eyed Will's muscular upper body. A little frown line appeared between his eyebrows.

Will stepped off the massage table and offered his palm to Kevin. "Instincts, man. I didn't know where I was. I'm sorry." Kevin accepted the handshake, but his face was bright red.

"Is your foot all right?" Monica said, pointing to Kevin's foot. "That had to hurt."

"I'm fine," Kevin mumbled, motioning dismissively with his hand and limping up over to the stairs, where he took his shoe off and rubbed the toes inside his black sock.

After Will changed back into his clothes, Monica walked him out to his car. He gave her sixty dollars for the massage.

Monica refused the money and apologized three times, and each time he repeated that the fright hadn't ruined his massage and pressed the bills into her hand.

"I really like your dad," Will said, changing the subject. "We've met three times already. I imagine he told you he's considering going down to Clinica Caracol to do some nosing around."

"What did you say?" Monica stopped.

"He wants to write an article about brain—"

"I know that part. The name of the clinic is Caracol?"

"Yeah, the word for 'seashell' in Spanish."

"I know what it means," she said. "Caracol was the name of the beach house I grew up in. My dad didn't mention that detail."

"He said your mom was searching for a miracle snail up until the time she died. No wonder he's so interested."

Monica raised an eyebrow at Will. "Really? He talked to you about my mom?"

"Not really. I'll stop by to see you at the office one of these days. Yvette is vocalizing, moving a little, doing some things out of the blue. Dr. Bauer is retesting."

"That's great news."

Will shrugged. "The human body does a lot of things on a completely involuntary basis. Some activities can be misinterpreted as reactive when they're not. Yvette's 'crying' turned out to be the result of eye irritation. Some of the early signs that we saw—yawning and the opening and closing of the eyes—is a circadian rhythm directed in the brain stem and isn't one of the upper-cortex functions we're looking for. Same goes for the noises. They appear to be just noises, rather than attempts to communicate. The challenge is to determine if a specific activity is deliberate."

Monica blinked. "Sounds like a hell of a roller-coaster ride, Will."

Will opened the driver's door to his truck and leaned against the open door. He examined his key ring as he spoke. "After we passed the one-year mark, I chose not to let it be a roller-coaster ride. Call it logic, call it pessimism, call it a self-defense mechanism, call it by any name. When it comes to brain injury, time is your enemy. The longer you're out"—he pointed to his temple—"the slimmer your chances of coming back. Once a person's been vegetative for a year, the outcome has already shown itself. What is five percent improvement? Ten percent, twenty? What does it mean if a year from now Yvette can complete a toddler's puzzle? In ten years, she might be able to complete a slightly more difficult puzzle and say six words." His voice trailed off at the end of the last sentence, and his face flushed. The keys fell out of his hand and Monica bent down to retrieve them and handed them to him without looking into his eyes, which she wasn't brave enough to do.

"Then maybe this El Salvador thing is worth looking into, Will. If Yvette already has very little to lose in terms of mental ability . . . ," Monica offered, daring to catch a peek of his face. "If you say there's very little hope . . ."

Will looked up toward the tops of the sparse pine trees that separated the cottage from the neighbor's. "Trust me—nobody's taking Yvette to El Salvador. I think it's great to become educated on what's being tested, *maybe* considering participation in a very well-controlled study at a highly reputable institution like Yale. But we're not sending my Yvette to El Salvador to participate in some wild experiment. That's just irresponsible, doing something to appease ourselves rather than doing what's safest for her."

Suddenly, the tension in his face vanished, and he smiled while he was still looking up at the sky. "Hey, look, a full moon. That explains why I almost attacked your boyfriend."

Monica looked up, then hung her head. "I'd managed to forget the incident for a moment or two."

Will smiled weakly and leaned over and kissed her on the cheek. "Now I get to look forward to another massage."

She watched him get into his truck and pull out of her driveway. He stuck one arm out the window and waved. As he pulled away, Monica was surprised to see a golden retriever standing in the bed of the pickup. She waved back and the dog offered a few happy barks.

As her hand cupped the faintest pocket of wind coming off the water, it recalled the smooth grain of his skin across the palms of her hands. She looked up at the full, silver moon. Her awareness of it was like a tip, a bonus he had generously left behind. She tried to remember the first time she had ever touched Kevin's skin, and how it felt, but couldn't.

Monica thought about Yvette and felt ashamed that she felt attracted to Will. But it was no sin, as long as she didn't act on it or nurture it in any way. There was not a single good reason to contemplate this little crush longer than the full phase of the moon. Alma's mantra rang though her head:

Can he change the world? Deliver justice? Can he save what's precious? Can he bring exceptional beauty to the world, or at the very least, relief of pain? If the answer is no, then move on.

No, Will wasn't curing cancer, saving whales, or sentencing criminals. But he was restoring the historical properties of Connecticut, which perhaps counted as bringing exceptional beauty to the world. Still, it was a stretch, as it was for most mortals. As if love were a board game, she thought. You love a doctor, a judge, or an environmental biologist; you pass go and collect two hundred dollars. If you love a postman, a construction worker, or a man who owns a fruit stand . . . shame on you for squandering your love. Go directly to jail.

That night, Kevin and Monica spoke little over dinner. Kevin's mood was spoiled, and although he was normally not one to hold a grudge, the incident with Will really seemed to rattle him. During the drive home he said, "Besides your dad,

Adam, and me, I want you to consider having a clientele of females only. You know, for safety reasons."

"Don't be ridiculous," she said.

Despite the fact that they hadn't seen each other since the previous Sunday, Kevin dropped Monica off at her house without getting out of the car. He said he had a headache and an early morning meeting. She ran and got his laptop computer and handed it to him through the open window of his Honda. They kissed, but coolly. He drove away, and Monica went upstairs and went to bed. She lay awake, staring out at the gray horizon, at the glimmering water and the swollen moon. She had the first inkling that something about Kevin seemed to bring out her most independent and stubborn self, made her dig in her heels far more than she meant to. Most of the time, the passion of their arguments flared up into romantic ardor, and then they got to enjoy the making up. But not tonight. Tonight they were just frustrated with each other. Tonight she was glad he was gone.

MONICA FOUND THE ARTICLE she was looking for at the hospital library. She checked it out and made three copies. She sat in the break room at work, eating a ham sandwich between appointments. She finished reading the article, which was three pages long, while holding the sandwich up in the air without taking a single bite. The article, entitled "Natural-Born Healers," stated that BioSource, a British-owned biopharmaceutical start-up, was the financial sponsor of a clinical trial in Central America. One trial was to be held in San Salvador, while another separate trial was being held in an undisclosed rural area. Monica drew a question mark in red ink next to that sentence. The article went on to state that BioSource was synthetically mimicking a snail peptide (product prototype name: SDX-71) and hoped to offer the drug to the U.S. FDA and Europe within three years. BioSource claimed that, although there was no known substance that could reverse brain damage, SDX-71 had shown success in "energizing" stalled or extremely slow progress. The program's recruiter and company contact was listed as Leticia Ramos.

Monica's attention snapped back to the name. Her mother had used that name as an alias back in the days of the war. Did Alma know this Leticia Ramos? Had she been a friend? Or was it a coincidence, with Alma having picked the name at random?

As Monica sat and pondered the possible explanations for that old name to reappear, she felt an unexpected mix of emotions bubble up to the surface. Although nothing had yet been proven, she was proud that Alma's life quest had been the pursuit of something wonderful and healing. There was also sadness that her mother had died before achieving anything to that end. If SDX-71 turned out to be viable, the credit would go to someone else, although surely they had stood on the back of Alma's research. If only Alma hadn't complicated her life with Maximiliano.

Leticia Ramos. Monica underlined the name several times, slowly, so that the red ink bled onto the next line. She gnawed on the name like an oversize wad of chewing gum. A colleague, perhaps a mentor? El Salvador was a small place, and Leticia Ramos wasn't a common name. Monica was so curious that when she went back to her desk, she ignored her work and began researching the name and the subject of the venom trials. She scoured the Web sites of the academic organizations that had received credit in the article, but found nothing. Surely her father would find out everything there was to know after he interviewed the staff. Monica looked at her watch. Her hip-replacement client was due in twenty minutes. She closed the magazine and decided it was time to visit with Sylvia Montenegro, alone. Monica was clumsy and distracted through her next two appointments. At three, she picked up the phone and asked to be connected to Yvette Lucero's room.

"TELL ME ABOUT EL SALVADOR." Sylvia patted the space on the vinyl couch next to her. "I know very little about it. I just remember it was in the news around the time that President Reagan was in office." She unfolded an oversize, soft-cover book of world maps and spread it out on her lap. Her bony finger traced an outline of the small Central American country. "I see here it borders with Guatemala on the north and west, Honduras to the north and east. The Pacific Ocean to the south."

Monica peered over her shoulder at the map. "Twenty years ago, when I came to visit my relatives here in Connecticut for the summer, people around here would say, 'So, I hear you're from Ecuador. What's it like living right on the equator?'" Monica said, then laughed. "Anyway, the civil war did a lot to put it on the map in terms of the public's general sense of geography."

"As wars always do," Sylvia said, with a thicker accent than normal.

Monica used a pen she had clipped to the breast pocket of her suit jacket to point to the country's belly button, a star with a circle around it. "That's the capital city, San Salvador. The whole country is sitting right in the middle of a seismic zone. It has more than twenty volcanoes, some extinct, some active. See that lake? Lago de Coatepeque. It's sitting in the crater of a dead volcano. Nobody has been able to discern the depth at the center . . . like it's this orifice that leads to the earth's center."

Sylvia raised one eyebrow. "Is El Salvador still unsafe?"

Monica shrugged. "It recovered a great deal from its civil war and subsequent disasters, which included a huge earthquake. But I wouldn't know firsthand. I haven't been there in fifteen years."

"You should go, Monica. When was the last time you visited the land you came from? You have to return to your mama's lap." Sylvia patted her hands on her thighs, as if she were inviting a child or a small dog to dive in.

Monica rested her chin on her knuckles. "My mama wasn't really the lap type, Sylvia. Anyway, she's dead and my dad is estranged from her family. He hates them."

"Then it's your father's baggage, not yours. It's like my husband used to say, time waits for no one."

Monica sighed. "The wounds go pretty deep between them."

Sylvia turned and pointed to a framed photo next to Yvette's bed that Monica had not seen before, one of Will and Yvette on their wedding day. "I find that a lot of men close the door on the past more tightly than women. They turn away from the scary stuff, they keep their feelings locked up. Not us," she said, patting Monica on the leg. "We stare it down, don't we?"

Monica nodded. "Yes, we do."

"If you feel you have to go, then go. To hell with your father, he'll get over it when he sees that you're fine. He'll realize then that you didn't automatically inherit his old traumas. He'll probably be relieved."

"I don't *have* to go," Monica said. "I said I'd *like* to go. Under the right circumstances. In reality, it's always been something I just talked about, complained that I had no one to go with, no one to go see. Blah, blah, blah." She opened her eyes wide. "I'm not sure if I actually meant to follow through." She crossed her elbows over her chest and rubbed her arms, trying to iron out the gooseflesh that had erupted underneath the sleeves of her blue cotton blouse. "What about you? Are you feeling like you have to take Yvette?"

Sylvia raised a thin, penciled-in eyebrow and stated primly, "I'm feeling like I have to know everything there is to know about this treatment, especially the specifics they don't get into in the article."

Monica glanced at Yvette's bed, then back at Sylvia. "Did you know my dad's talking about going down there to research their claims?"

Sylvia stared at the tile floor for a moment, as if to arrange her thoughts. She nodded, then folded her hands over her lap. "I'm ahead of him. I've been corresponding with a woman named Leticia Ramos." She stopped speaking, looked around. She got up and closed the door to the room.

"Yes, Leticia Ramos," Monica practically shouted after Sylvia had pressed the door shut. "Who *is* she?"

"You can't breathe a word of this to Will," Sylvia said, pointing one finger up to the ceiling. "I won't tell you a thing unless you promise to keep this conversation a secret."

Monica drew an imaginary line across her lips. "But why are we keeping it from Will, Sylvia?"

Sylvia's sparkling eyes darkened and she balled her small hands into a fist. "Because he isn't a mother, that's why. He has no instincts, no intuition, and he won't get out of the way and let me help my child." She cupped her abdomen with both hands. She glanced back at the bed behind them. "She's my baby, dammit. She's a part of *me*."

Monica let out a breath, slowly. She stared at the floor in silence, deeply moved by the fiercely protective maternal presence. There ought to be more of that in the world, she thought. The world would be a better place if every mother felt like that. She held her right hand up. "Okay. I promise not to tell anyone. You have my word."

When she was satisfied, Sylvia put her hand on Monica's knee again and looked deeply into her eyes. "Out of twelve cases similar to Yvette's they have succeeded in facilitating an 'assisted recovery,' as they call it, in six cases. That's a phenomenal track record. *Phenomenal*. Anyway, the tough part is the cost: special air transportation is about ten thousand dollars. Plus the five thousand to the clinic."

Monica whistled.

"I have the money," Sylvia said softly.

"I thought it was a trial—a study. How can they charge five thousand dollars for a trial?"

"The fee is for room and board, ongoing daily care for twelve weeks, pharmaceuticals, physical therapy, on-site family accommodations, and unlimited local transportation. When you add it all up, you'll find it's actually dirt cheap compared to what all that would cost here in the States. The venom treatment itself is free of charge."

"Did they send you literature? A map or an address?"

"No, they just pick you up at the airport. I don't really know which end of the coast it's on. I just know it's on the beach."

". . . Did they mention a contract, an application, anything?"

"It's not a Club Med, Monica. It's top secret."

Monica made the most horrified expression she could come up with. "Sylvia, I wouldn't even talk to them unless they can produce some literature that spells out details."

"I'm not stupid." Then, in a softer voice, almost a whisper: "I was thinking of maybe going along with your dad."

"Now that's a *great* idea."

Monica took Sylvia's hands and leaned so close that she could see the pinhead-sized dots on the cushions of Sylvia's earlobes where earring holes had apparently closed up. Monica looked past her, at the toes of Yvette's pale yellow socks pointing inward on the bed and whispered, "Someone built that clinic and the treatment around my mom's work. I know it."

"Let's go then," Sylvia said, opening her eyes wide. "It's your duty to make sure your mother gets credit. Let them know you're aware of what they're doing. Who knows, they may want to ask you things about your mother and her work that weren't documented. You can stay at a nearby guesthouse for a few dollars a night."

Monica felt a current of excitement rush through her. Still, she refused to get completely swept up just yet. "What does Yvette's doctor say? Did you show him the article?"

Sylvia laughed bitterly and spoke in a deep voice, imitating Dr. Forest Bauer. " 'It's something to watch,' he says to me. What the hell does he think I've been doing for two years? *Watching.* Every little movement, every breath she takes." Sylvia shook her head and pointed at the door. Her face was contorted with inner conflict. "The FDA will approve importation of foreign pharmaceuticals if there is no other available treatment here in the U.S. . . . as long as you can get a U.S. doctor to oversee the treatment." She kept pointing at the door, shaking her head.

"But no one will," Monica said.

Sylvia hung her head. "No one will."

"Well, that's not a good sign. We have some of the best neurologists in the world here at Yale, Sylvia. If they don't think it's a good idea . . ." Monica began to feel the weight of responsibility for commenting on the cones in the first place.

Suddenly, Sylvia brightened and pulled a gold chain out from under the neck of her blouse. Attached to the chain was an antique locket, but bigger, like a small pillbox. "Look. I just got this from Rome. A real strand of Saint Anthony's hair. Four hundred dollars. A bargain if you think about what a relic it is. It's supposed to return lost things, people included."

Monica eyed the object with scrutiny. "Saint Anthony was completely bald from adolescence. Besides, it's Saint Joseph who's the patron of lost things."

Sylvia gasped and looked down at the locket. She turned it over slowly. Monica heard her whisper a word that sounded like "Cheat." She looked up at Monica, then back at the locket, shattered.

Monica tugged her arm and smiled. "Sylvia, I'm teasing. I don't know anything about saints."

Sylvia's shoulders slumped in mock relief and she held up the pendant. "Good, because I'm really counting on this to work."

When Monica left, an hour later, she had the direct phone number of the mysterious Leticia Ramos. Sylvia suggested that Monica stick around and say hello to Will, who was on his way, but Monica rushed off, saying she had a massage appointment. It was a lie, of course, and she blushed violently as she recalled the pleasure with which she had purged the anxiety from his spine, spooling the invisible threads of tension that had woven themselves around his bones. When he left, she had mentally unwound and examined them in secret. He was searching for something, it told her. Just like everyone else, he was searching for something he'd either lost or never had.

Bruce found what he was looking for in a box in the attic labeled ESCRITORIO — SALV. The labels on the boxes were in Spanish, which was only remarkable in that they were scribbled in his own handwriting. Years later, it tickled him there had been a time when a foreign language could wrestle down the English of his internal dialogue and become dominant enough for him to use it in household notations to himself. He remembered feeling proud the morning after his first dream in full Spanish sound track, a major milestone of life as an expatriate.

Bruce figured that most of the phone numbers and addresses in his dusty spiral-bound notepad, circa 1972, would still be good. Salvadorans seemed to maintain loose relations with past dwellings; there was always an elderly aunt or a nephew hanging around years later who could tell you where to find the owner.

The names written in faded ink were the dusty bones of a life and a time that had passed. For Bruce, it was as if time itself had been trapped between these pages, its vibrant wings pressed into limp, transparent sheets that crumbled the moment he exposed them to the pale sunlight of the attic. He wondered what would happen if he marched downstairs, picked up the telephone, and punched in one of those odd number sequences. He might dial into a twilight zone where kids born in the seventies were still toddlers, where his old pals were slim and had heads full of thick, black hair. He and Alma would be invited over for *gallo en chicha,* a native feast of rooster meat cooked to shreds in a delicious sweet, dark sauce that looked like oxidized blood.

His thumbnail split a section that was stuck together, and the pages parted to reveal the name Renato Reyes Fuentes. Bruce gasped a little, his hand unwittingly resting on his heart, an old sadness spilling out on the page like an overturned ink bottle. Twenty-two-year-old Renato, who had been born with a clubfoot, had been doing odd jobs for the Borreros since he was fifteen. What Bruce remembered so vividly about Renato was that he possessed an amazing optimism despite his crippling deformity. He lived his life among the hungry, the angry, the hopeless, and the dead, and the brightness of his spirit was as astonishing as a red poppy blooming in a field of snow. He maintained an almost naive sense of trust in the spirit of his countrymen to be reasonable, to see the path to peace through empathy and respect. His mother had once been on the domestic staff at the Borrero house, and she was a favorite of Alma's. When Renato visited his mother every Sunday in their hometown, Gotera, Alma always sent her cash and free-of-charge meds, courtesy of Dr. Max Campos. Gotera at that time was the hotbed of guerrilla-military confrontations. On one of those visits, Renato stepped out of his mother's humble, one-room house to visit a friend who lived a few blocks away. He was never heard from again. A month later, Bruce saw his photo on the corkboard at the Mothers of the Disappeared headquarters.

Eighteen years later, the irony still made Bruce's arms prickle. The idea that thousands of people could fall into a black hole, their end a mystery for all eternity, was haunting. Renato's family—which included a wife and a child—could only surmise what had happened. He had probably been shot by the National Guard, which targeted the "red" towns. The pea-brained military thugs, predatory and reasonable as a stampede of raptors, suspected all citizens, especially young men, of being *guerrilleros,* or at the very least sympathetic to the communist cause.

But it was just as possible that the rebel side had swallowed poor Renato. They might have killed him for refusing to join. His mother told Bruce that the guerrillas were charging monthly fees for their promise to protect local families from the military raids. Renato's mother had fallen behind on her premiums, the equivalent of twenty dollars a month. She confessed that for a time she had kept up her payments by selling the medications that Alma sent, despite needing them to treat her high blood pressure. The word on the street was that Renato's disappearance was a lesson to anyone who refused to pay.

Two months later, Alma had found a bed for the old lady at the main Borrero house in San Salvador, and even old Magnolia did her part by putting the other maids in charge of her care. But the old lady only outlived her son by a year. She died of a broken heart, which took the form of a deadly stroke.

Bruce flipped the page and scanned the rest of the list. Even though there were ten or so people Bruce would enjoy seeing again, only five remained actual friends after the erosion and corrosion of fifteen years. Out of those five, one had fallen victim to cancer, another was living in Spain, and two were journalists living somewhere in California. The only person he considered a true friend who was still living in El Salvador was Claudia Credo. He flipped through the book, looked under *C,* and found her name. The pages made crackling noises as he turned them. The dust of the attic was making him sneeze, so he decided to go downstairs, clutching the wire-bound notebook to his chest. He laid the relic on the coffee table and sat back, trying to remember the country code to dial.

Claudia Credo's loyalty was earnest and undeniable. She consistently went out of her way to include Bruce in her social circles even during periods when he himself wasn't investing much in their friendship. If he was cranky and unsociable, she said, "Oh, you've been working too hard, Bruce. You should get some rest." If he went months without returning her phone calls, she never mentioned it when they finally talked. It *had* crossed his mind that perhaps the source of her loyalty and patience was something other than pure friendship. After all, it had been Claudia who had targeted Bruce at that fateful embassy dance. She had used Alma as a decoy, never imagining the destiny she would unleash.

But time had shown Claudia to be the kind of person who spontaneously gave of herself to everyone around her. Over the years Bruce hadn't attributed her devotion to anything else but the easy familiarity that can spring up—often inexplicably—between two completely different people. Theirs was a friendship that could be unfrozen at the last sentence, like releasing the pause button on a home movie. He tracked her down at her parents' house.

"Gato, I can't believe it!" she cried, after the maid, who answered with a polite *"Buenas tardes,"* handed her the telephone. Bruce chuckled at recalling that Salvadorans assigned nicknames with the spontaneity and tenacity of fourth graders. He had often been struck by the insensitivity of these little handles. Take Claudia Credo, for example. Even her parents called her Santa Clau, a reference to her corpulence. Poor Renato was dubbed Llanta Pacha, "flat tire," for his limp. A guy who hid the stump of a missing hand by tucking it in his trouser pockets was called Yo Pago, meaning "I'll pay," since he appeared to be eternally digging for his wallet. Bruce always considered himself lucky that he got his benevolent nickname early (Gato because of his catlike green eyes). A British journalist had once pointed out that in El Salvador early nickname assignment protected you from a far more creative, accurate, and less flattering version later on.

The two friends settled into an easy chat. Claudia Credo told Bruce that she was still living with her parents, still not married, but had moved up professionally from working in the press office for the National Guard to working directly for the Office of the President. After they had filled each other in on the big stuff, Bruce asked her if she knew anything about the mysterious clinic. She did not. He told her what he had discovered the previous day: that venom trials were being held at Negrarena, at the Caracol villa. She was silent for a moment. "You know that property was abandoned for a long time after Magnolia died."

"Abandoned?" Bruce said, sitting back in his recliner. "After her nephews screwed Monica out of inheriting it?"

"They couldn't agree on what to do with it. While the family was busy squabbling—and this went on for years—the place filled up with squatters. The owners showed up one day and the Moroccan swimming pool had been drained and was full of fighting cocks and goats."

An image of the crystalline swimming pool with its hand-painted imported tiles flashed in his mind. "Wow." He drew in a great breath as he shifted in his chair. Just approaching the subject of his battles with the Borreros required taking his weight off his knees.

"So then someone must have bought it and cleaned it up."

"You know there's nothing I can't find out, Gato."

"I know that very well, my dear. That's one of the reasons I called."

He could actually hear the smile on her lips as she said, "I've decided I'm going to start exacting a price for my friendship, Gatito. I'll find out what you want—for a price."

"And what might that be?"

"That you come to see us," she said, her voice switching to a child's pleading cadence. "Everyone asks about you, everybody." She began to name their mutual friends by their nicknames: "Loco, La Seca, Feo, Dormilón, Cuto, Chele, El Fantasma, Pánico Británico, everybody."

"Really?"

"Just because you don't think about us doesn't mean we don't think about you. We wonder what's going on in your life. Like maybe El Gato finally gave up drinking crappy beer and switched to Scotch."

Bruce laughed, then heard someone speak in the background, and Claudia's voice seemed to turn away from the phone to respond.

"That's right, Mamá. The gringo who loved your sugar tamales."

Bruce smiled. "Tell your mom I said hello. . . . Anyway, Claudia, you don't have to try to convince me to go to El Salvador, I'm already planning a trip. I'm researching a magazine article. I'm interested in what's going on at Clinica Caracol."

"Bravo. I'll pick you up at the airport and you can stay with us. In the meantime, I'll get started on the nosing around." There was a pause, and she seemed to search for the right words before she spoke. "You know, Bruce, the spirit of your wife has replaced La Siguanaba as our most popular folkloric tale. I believe that's one of the reasons Caracol was empty for so long. One of the Borrero cousins got it in his mind that her spirit was haunting the place."

Bruce laughed bitterly. "For God's sake. I knew they were a pack of wolves, but I didn't think they were superstitious."

"Guilt manifests itself in funny ways," Claudia said. "The Borrero cousins knew that getting Magnolia to sign everything over to them wasn't what she would have wanted had she been of sound mind. By all rights, your daughter should be a very rich young woman."

Bruce crossed his arms, nudged the receiver into the crook of his neck. He looked out to the public golf course that stretched out from under his house like a lush green carpet. "Monica doesn't know the whole story about the family wars. I didn't want to contaminate her with my anger." He took a deep breath. "She's been saying she'd like to go with me to El Salvador, but I'm extremely uncomfortable with the idea."

"Monica is how old?"

"Twenty-seven."

"How time passes." Claudia whistled. "Wow. Twenty-seven."

"I don't want to alter anything in her peaceful life by unearthing the rotting past."

"Are you afraid she might blame you for what happened?"

"I wish I could be sure she would blame me. I'm far more worried that she might blame herself if she knew. She set the events into motion that ended in her mother's death. I think it would be tough to live with that."

He heard Claudia exhale, and for a moment there was only the eerie scratch of the long-distance line, hissing between them. "Then discourage her from coming. The subject of the Borreros is a gossip magnet down here. Everyone will be curious about her. She'll be like some long-lost princess."

"That's what I'm worried about."

"Well, whatever you decide, I have plenty of room for both of you. When are you arriving?"

"I'm waiting for the green light from my editor, is all. I'll know within the week."

"I'll start rounding up the old gang. I'm sure they'll want to see you."

"How about if you keep this to yourself for now? I don't

want the Borreros to get word that I'm around, especially if they have anything to do with this clinic. Besides, my editor could change his mind. *If* I go, I'll probably stay a week. Is that all right?"

"A week?" Claudia exclaimed. "A week? What can you do in a week? I'll never understand you gringos, always in such a rush."

"Okay, maybe a week and a day. We'll see. I have an open ticket." He sighed. "I owe you big-time, Claudia."

After he hung up, Bruce couldn't get up out of his big chair. Drained of energy, he reached over to an end table and pulled out his humidor. He selected a genuine Cuban, smuggled in via Canada by Kevin on a business trip. He put it in his mouth without lighting it. There were no matches in the humidor and he didn't have the energy to get up. He let the cigar sit between his lips, turning it in his mouth and tasting its dry sweetness in the loose bits that spilled onto his tongue. *Alma has replaced La Siguanaba as our most popular urban legend,* Claudia had said.

Bruce chuckled, but bitterly. He hadn't heard the word uttered in so long, the reference yielded the same eerie, evocative sensations as the old address book. Bruce had first learned about La Siguanaba, El Cipitío, El Cadejo, and other native Central American mythological characters in his culture and language training classes at the U.S. embassy.

La Siguanaba, legend has it, had once been a beautiful Mayan princess who had an affair with a young man who was far below her family rank. For her mistake, she was cursed with immortality and the unending search for her lost, illegitimate child in the loneliest paths of the countryside. Her spirit appears young, beautiful, and half-naked to men riding on horseback in desolate areas at night. The men agree to give her a lift, only to regret it when they turn to see that she is transformed into a disfigured hag. She slashes her victims' necks and backs with her teeth and claws and leaves them injured, horseless, and lost. Bruce recalled Alma telling him that most peasants still wholly believe the native legends. Upper- and middle-class people scoff at them, except occasionally, while walking alone through the countryside at night.

Had Alma been a bit like the cursed Siguanaba? Perhaps. But Alma didn't bite or scratch. She withdrew. She injured with her absence and unfaithfulness.

He was going to El Salvador. His indecisiveness with Monica and vagueness with Claudia was his way of staying in control. Earlier that day, his editor had given him the green light on the story. *It is exactly the kind of thing we are looking for,* she had said. *The timing is perfect. Go for it.*

He just had to figure out a way to convince Monica to drop the idea of going with him. After all, what you don't talk about for fifteen years isn't something that's going to be pleasant to examine under the harsh light of San Salvador's sun. Suddenly, a thought occurred to him that made the dry cigar fall out of his mouth and roll down his shirt to rest in the valley between his legs: Maybe she *did* talk about it. Maybe she talked about it with a shrink, with Paige, with Kevin, with her boss, her dentist, and the package deliveryman. Maybe she just didn't talk about it with *him*. What did that say about him, about their relationship? Who was the fragile one after all?

WHEN MONICA ARRIVED at her father's house that night, she released a torrent of questions that left him breathless. Monica was the daughter of a journalist, and so he shouldn't have been surprised that she knew how to do her homework. She had talked to Sylvia, to Adam Bank, she had called *Alternative Healing,* contacted the director of the clinic in El Salvador. She was more than curious now. She was agitated by how little she really knew about her family history and its players.

Why didn't you tell me the clinic was actually at Negrarena? Do the Borreros still own it? Who is Leticia Ramos? Who could have found the furiosus *and mined it into a business? What's the big deal about not wanting me to go to El Salvador, anyway?*

When he saw doubt rising like the morning's first light in her eyes, he stepped forward and wrapped his arms around all her questions in an attempt to contain them, but they spilled out like sand the more he tried to hold everything together. Even though Monica was fairly tall, she looked so small, so vulnerable all of a sudden. His paternal instincts bristled with the fear of what might be approaching.

I don't know any Leticia Ramos, he had told Monica. *It's a common name.* A lie. He knew exactly who she was. She was Maximiliano Campos's estranged wife. And when Monica finished sorting through the tangle of connections that trailed out from Yvette Lucero's veins, there would be more questions, of that Bruce was sure. Without a doubt, the clinic was somehow linked to the Borrero family. But who had pursued Alma's dream after all these years? Who, among those rapacious predators ruling above their kingdom of peasants, had the intelligence, patience, and scientific training to do it?

One day, Monica might put the pieces of the puzzle together. She might remember her tortured confession so many years ago, her plea that her father mend his crumbling marriage. Still out of her grasp was the realization that her decision to interfere in her parents' troubles had unleashed a series of explosive consequences: that her confession had enraged her powerful grandmother, whose vein-choked hand was kissed every day by a *coronel* in the military, and that Max had been hunted down like prey. Alma had been at his side until the last, winning her escape from a society she hated by diving into the frothy wings of her beloved sea.

* * *

MONICA WASN'T HAPPY that Bruce had invited Will Lucero and Sylvia Montenegro to her Fourth of July party. Her reaction took him completely by surprise. "I thought you liked them," he said, astounded. "Did something happen?"

Monica looked as if she wanted to reveal something, but chose not to. She and Paige were sitting on barstools in the kitchen, concocting a garlic-and-whisky glaze for the pork ribs. Bruce could see Paige watching Monica's face. Overwhelmed by thoughts of Alma and travel to El Salvador, he welcomed the lightness of the party preparations. He almost felt giddy at the sight of the sunshine on the water, the hanging baskets overflowing with red and pink geraniums and brand-new patio furniture on the wood deck.

"What's the big deal about inviting Sylvia and Will? We must have bought thirty pounds of meat. There's plenty of food."

"It's just not a good idea, trust me," Monica answered, and she and Paige looked at him as if the reason were so obvious that it might insult his intelligence if they actually said it.

"Of course it's not a good idea," he said, scratching his head and leaning on one hip. "Sylvia Montenegro is obviously the type who will bring a bagful of Tupperware and leave with all the leftovers." He held his hands out. They shook their heads. He peered at the popcorn ceiling, then snapped his fingers. "Oohh, Paige wants Will and he's unavailable?" he said, lowering his head, as if to avoid a flying object that might be hurled at him at any moment. The women snickered, and Bruce held up a third finger. "This is it for sure," he said, suddenly lowering his voice and growing serious. "Our Kevin is jealous?" He pointed over his shoulder, toward the front of the house, even though Kevin wasn't here.

Paige rocked her pinkie and thumb back and forth and said, "Getting warmer."

Bruce shrugged. "I give up then. Will and Sylvia are going to Will's parents' house for most of the day and they said they'd stop by on their way back. They won't stay long." He picked a handful of olive slices off the top of the Mexican dip. Paige slapped his hand away, but not before he managed to steal them, plus a jalapeño garnish, and pop it all into his mouth. "Will and Sylvia were having a really bad day yesterday. Turns out the funds to keep Yvette in the top-notch facility she's in are drying up in a few months. Sylvia was crying, Will was screaming on the phone at the insurance company and the state social worker," he said, throwing his hands up in the air. "So I invited them over so they could get their minds off their problems. *Problem,*" he corrected himself, holding up a finger. "They really only have one. And it's a big one."

He too had wondered if it was a good idea to invite Will and Sylvia, but only after he'd already blurted out an invitation. With them around, it was hard to contain the drip of information leaking from Sylvia's discovery, not to mention the excitement he and Sylvia shared. Bruce wanted the chance to pre-inspect that information for hidden razor blades, to predigest and carefully regurgitate it in tiny doses fit for his daughter's consumption.

As he headed to the neighbor's garage to carry the extra lawn furniture they were borrowing up to Monica's deck, he pondered the viability of the cone venom therapy. El Salvador had witnessed unimaginable human suffering, but it also contained threads of the deep spiritual continuity between man and nature, man and the sea, man and the pagan spirits trapped under the crumbled civilization of the Mayas. If Yvette was ever going to emerge from her state, it wasn't going to be in a hospital in New Haven. She'd already proved that. In the El Salvador he recalled, gravity was about the only law that couldn't be broken. Perhaps in this case, that could be an advantage. If life could end so easily in the explosion of gunfire, why not its opposite?

As the first guests began to arrive for her Independence Day party, Monica stood at the window of her second-story bedroom. She removed the window screens and leaned them against the wall. She unfurled her American flag, dropped the wood pole into its cup. She waited until she saw the four feet of nylon drop and drape down cleanly, its colors bright and regal, its pole cap directing the eye toward the cloudless sky.

Monica heard Paige down on the deck, summoning her to come down. She waved and held up one finger, signaling her to wait a moment. Monica walked across the room to the closet and opened it. From behind her ski gear and extra umbrellas, she unearthed a second flag, which she unrolled on the rug and smoothed with the palms of her hands. It was a faded housecoat blue, made of raw cotton, half the size of the American flag. The triangle-shaped crest at the center contained the image of a range of volcanoes, the ink having been stamped a few degrees outside its intended outline. The flag had a yellowed stain in the corner where the newborn Jimmy Bray had pooped for the first time in his life almost two decades ago. Monica drove the flag's metal pole through its cuff. She dropped the pole into a holder next to the American flag. The heavy cloth remained stiff and immobile, until the warm summer breeze managed to animate it to a tentative sway. The Salvadoran flag looked so humble and small next to the lush red, white, and blue nylon; like a disoriented brown pigeon touching down alongside a bald eagle.

Was it an indignity or a privilege, Monica wondered, for a nation's flag to serve as a diaper for one of its poorest citizens?

MONICA WOULD REMEMBER her Fourth of July party as one big blur, an evening that would mark the beginning of the second half of her life, the night the first domino fell. The afternoon began with her observation that entertaining large groups of people feels like an out-of-body experience, probably because attending to so many tasks forces abnormal shifts of one's attention every few minutes. She had to interrupt her conversation with a group from work to greet new arrivals from college. A few moments later she found herself frantically waving a dishrag at a screeching smoke alarm because Paige had forgotten to tend to a batch of chicken wings. There were introductions to be made, endless dashes to the kitchen, gifts of liquor to be refrigerated or served, crudités to be passed around, dips to be reheated, chip bowls to be refilled, music to be kept up, half-heard jokes to laugh at.

The guest list was a mixed bag of fellow UConn alumni, a sprinkle of friends from high school, a few from work, plus an unknown number of Kevin's and Paige's friends. At Kevin's sage advice, Monica had invited a range of neighbors three houses thick in each direction—to insure that the police wouldn't be visiting if the music got loud. Bruce and Kevin were partnering on the grill. Paige was tending bar.

"Today is your lucky day," Paige shouted to the guests already cramming the deck. "I'm going to treat you all to Paige Norton's Bitchin' Brew." She stirred a bowl of mysterious liquid. "But be warned—if you drink more than two, then plan on crawling home." She held up a red, white, and blue plastic tumbler. "Who's my first victim?"

"It's just a high-octane *mojito*," Monica said, as she passed around a tray of stuffed mushroom caps. "Paige got the recipe from a Cuban bartender she woke up with in Miami one morning. It's a Cuban staple, but she's succeeded in convincing many an unsuspecting gringo that she invented it."

Across the deck, a small crowd clustered around Paige's makeshift bar, and it wasn't long before she had them tipping the concoction of white rum, ice, seltzer, raw sugar, lime, and freshly crushed mint leaves. She added a few lethal splashes of tasteless, odorless, extrafine Siberian vodka—the secret seventh ingredient that allowed her, in her mind, to patent it as her own. Paige's Bitchin' Brew had a stealthy, mind-erasing effect, and soon the guests were congratulating Paige on the brilliance of her invention. Monica put her tray down and watched her old friend hold court. Paige winked and blew her a kiss from the limelight of her social throne. *She makes me more fun,* Monica thought. *Everyone should have a Paige in their life.*

THE AFTERNOON WAS HOT and sticky and the *mojitos* were icy and clean. Two hours later, no thanks to Paige and her potion, Monica suffered the shock of seeing her father make out with Marcy on the dance floor of her deck party. Paige was so drunk that she mistook Monica's grimace for a reaction to the booze. "There's a line to get into both of your bathrooms, Mon. Just puke in the petunias." She pointed at the neighbor's garden.

The party had gotten a bit out of control, with everyone bringing someone extra, who in turn brought an extra someone too; and although the "someones" were behaving, the "extras" were not. By eight, she could hear Kevin and his old frat buddies laughing and splashing just beyond the seawall, all of them nude. Monica was thankful that most of her neighbors were already too compromised to complain, especially after that game with the garden hose. She looked around and wondered if she wasn't too old to still be having the kind of parties where people wake up with regrets.

With the help of a friend, Monica walked around collecting dirty paper plates. She had committed a few party fouls of her own: she had a wood splinter lodged in the sole of her foot from dancing barefoot, and a huge bruise on her hip where she had smashed into the corner of a folding table while dancing to "Mambo Number 5."

Monica was relaxed now that everyone had eaten. She found herself scanning the crowd for a glimpse of Will. She looked at her watch. It was just past nine. She was drunk enough to let herself long for his presence, guilt being the burden of the sober. She wondered what his mouth tasted like, if he would be wild with desire after two years of nothing but stress and celibacy. She thought about his body, warm and slick with massage oil, and how she had fought so many mental images during that session. Rubbing his neck had made her want to take his earlobe in her mouth, to smell his skin up close . . .

She saw her father, one arm slung around Marcy, point upward. A hush spread through the crowd like a stadium wave, as the first fireworks crackled and webbed their light across the darkened sky.

NO ONE WOULD HAVE HEARD Bruce's mobile phone ring if Bruce hadn't forgotten it in the bathroom. Monica was on the toilet and had been enjoying the brief respite from the noise and chaos outside when the phone rang, startling her enough to clench up midstream.

Should she pick up? She hated the idea of talking on the phone with her shorts around her ankles. She unclenched, letting it ring a second time. But what if someone was lost and needed directions? It rang again.

"Hello?"

"Monica." Her name was pronounced with such utter relief that she knew right away something was wrong.

"Will?" she whispered, leaning forward to cover her lap with her elbows.

"Is Sylvia there? Has she called?"

"I don't think so, there's a ton of people here and it's very loud. Is everything okay?"

There was a silence, then the sound of a dog barking in the background. He exhaled loudly, and she could tell by its muffling that he ran his hand over his face. When he spoke, he sounded tired and far away. "I was at my parents' house all day. Sylvia arrived at Yvette's at ten this morning. She had them put Yvette in a wheelchair and said she was taking her for a walk to the park across the street like she usually does. It's after nine now, and they've been gone for eleven hours. We've looked everywhere, and I mean everywhere. I thought maybe by some remote chance she was at your party."

"With Yvette?" Monica had this flash vision of Yvette in her wheelchair out on the deck, her face frozen and her eyes roving as bodies swung and dipped all around her. Monica's heart prickled and she was jolted into sobriety. "No, she's definitely not here."

"Did she say anything to you about going to that clinic in El Salvador?"

Monica inhaled, much more loudly than she meant to. She hugged her knees and didn't answer. In a moment, Monica understood that her silence had already answered for her.

"I knew it," he said.

"Let's get my dad, Will. He'll know more. Hold on, I'm in

the middle of something here, hold on," she mumbled, placing the tiny, credit-card-sized telephone down next to the sink and yanking up her underwear and shorts. She put her hand on the receiver and wondered how she was going to flush the toilet without his knowing that he had caught her in the bathroom, and she grimaced at herself in the mirror. How to flush? Her fingers fumbled with the tie string at her waist as she rushed to get out of the bathroom. She reached for the mobile phone with a half-soapy hand, sending it flying over the edge. It disappeared into the basket of balled-up pink toilet tissue. Monica was about to go after it, but someone was knocking and she ran out, shouting to anyone in range not to use the bathroom yet. She scrambled out to the deck to unpry her father from Marcy's arms. Under normal circumstances, seeing her father suck face with anyone would have made her want to hide under a rock. But the discomfort flashed over her radar for a second and disappeared as her father turned to look at her with sleepy, moony eyes.

BRUCE AND WILL SAT at Monica's kitchen table at two in the morning on July fifth. Paige and Marcy were asleep, dueling snores on opposite couches in the living room. Kevin was sleeping upstairs on Monica's bed, wearing nothing but swimming trunks and someone's cowboy boots. An unidentified couple was wrapped up in a comforter on her bedroom floor next to the bed. Some of her college pals had cleaned up and skillfully consolidated the food and the guests into an ever-tightening circle. By the time the last guest had left, the party mess was contained to the center of the deck.

For the last hour and a half, Will had been on his mobile phone with various air ambulance companies, with his uncle, who was a New Haven cop, with hospital administrators and his parents. Somewhere amid the back-and-forth he discovered a new message from Sylvia, left over five hours ago but delivered by a slow satellite just minutes before.

She was in El Salvador, at Clínica Caracol. She had cashed out her retirement savings to enable the trip. She was sorry if he had suffered any worry and apologized for going against his wishes, but everything was okay, and he was welcome to join her as long as he promised he wouldn't interfere with Yvette's treatment. Yvette would start her treatments immediately after a day or two of testing.

"Maybe it'll work, Will," Monica said tentatively. "Maybe you and Yvette will end up on all the morning shows telling your story."

Will looked at her but didn't answer. His mouth was full, he was scarfing down a pile of charred hot dogs and cold baked beans. Bruce looked at Monica, leaned his head toward Will, and said, "Nerves."

Will shrugged, kept his head down, and kept eating.

"Retirement savings. God-dog," Bruce said, shaking his head. "Who does Sylvia think is going to pay for her care when she's old?" He pointed across the table at Will. "You, my friend, that's who." Bruce was cupping a mug of black coffee. Earlier, Monica had sent him upstairs to take a shower and wash off the sweat, smoke, salt water, spilled liquor, and lipstick. Now his wet silver hair was parted on the side and he had deep bags under his eyes. His olive-colored tropical-pattern shirt was spotted with barbecue sauce, but he was otherwise back to his old respectable self.

"Sylvia and I agreed that we would never make any decisions without a consensus, but technically, I have the final say. It's frightening that my wife, whose life is in my hands"—Will raised his palms and looked at them—"a woman for whom I have an awesome responsibility . . . can be whisked away to a foreign country without my consent. Or her doctor's." He banged his fist on the wood table. "How the hell did she do it?"

"It's kidnapping," a voice said from across the room. Paige looked at them and rubbed her eyes.

"Thanks for the contribution, Paige," Monica said. "Now go back to sleep."

"Anytime."

"She's right. It's kidnapping," Will said, staring hard at the table. "What Sylvia's done is illegal."

"Never mind that," Bruce said. "Remember that Sylvia feels the same weight of responsibility that you do."

"Sylvia carried Yvette in her womb for nine months," Monica said, her voice suddenly tense. She thumped her index finger against the table for emphasis. "It's a mother's duty to protect and care for her child. If she failed to help her child, then she'd be a lousy mother." She felt her face reddening. Marcy raised an eyebrow at Paige and they exchanged a sideways, knowing look.

"Well, I'm not going to sit here and just wait to hear how it goes," Will said, his tone softening. "So far, I haven't been able to find a flight to El Salvador until Friday—on the same flight as Bruce."

"Excuse me." Monica peered at her father and cocked her head. "Wasn't it just last week that you said you were thinking of *maybe* going at some point *maybe* next month? How is it that you already have an airline ticket?"

Bruce looked away. "I agreed to get bumped off a flight to L.A. once, and so I have an open ticket. I can use it whenever."

Monica narrowed her eyes at Bruce. Bruce shook his head and raised his hands. "Hey, I'm traveling for work."

"I *have* to go," she said. "So let's figure out a way for me to get a ticket in my hands."

"Why?" Bruce said. "Why do you think you have to go? This has nothing to do with you."

Monica stood up, her eyes filling with tears. "I told Sylvia about the *Conus furiosus* in the first place. That's what started this whole mess. And I *knew* she wanted to go down there soon, she swore me to secrecy. But she told me she was going to go with you, Dad. I don't know why she suddenly skipped over the whole research phase." Monica covered her chest by crossing her arms and collapsed back into a sofa. "I'm so sorry, Will."

Will shook his head. "Don't be. It's not your fault."

Monica looked up at Will, then at her father. "Sylvia trusts me. That's why I have to go."

Bruce's shoulders slumped and he exhaled and covered his face with his hands. "Not a good idea, Monica," he insisted.

"It's a great idea, and I have a ticket you can have," said another voice from the darkened side of the room. This time it was Marcy, and she was sitting upright, her face bright and sober as if she hadn't just been snoring away a hangover. "I think it's time both of you went back down there. I'm sick of living with Alma's ghost. . . ." She put up her hand. "No offense."

Bruce stared at Marcy, shocked. He opened his mouth, but Marcy spoke first. "I was on the same trip to L.A. with your dad, Monica. You can have my ticket."

Monica went over to Marcy and hugged her. She felt the crispiness of Marcy's gelled curls against her cheek.

"Thank you. That's incredibly nice of you."

"You're not offended are you, Monica? You know what I mean about your mom, right?"

"I know exactly what you mean, Marcy."

Marcy put her hand under Monica's chin. "Ain't nothin', darlin'," she said, then looked at Will, briefly pointing a finger. "Now you go easy on your mother-in-law, young man. Husbands come and go, but a mother is a mother for life."

Will sighed. "I know."

Bruce looked pale. He was staring at the floor, hands folded.

"You don't know what you're talking about Marcy," he said in a tight, hard voice. He stood and walked out of the room, only to return a few moments later.

"I just hope Sylvia purchased a two-way ticket on that expensive air ambulance," Paige said. "Otherwise, how are you going to get her home?"

Will ran his fingers through his hair and looked distraught.

Marcy took a deep breath. "This may sound sacrilegious to you, Will, but maybe you should have a little faith. Yvette hasn't made any progress in two years. What do you have to lose?"

"I was just saying that earlier," Monica said.

"I say go for it," Marcy said. "Give it a chance."

Will cupped his head in his hands. "I'm tired and my head is killing me."

Monica went to the kitchen and returned with aspirin and a glass of water for Will. He was sitting on a barstool, and he blinked his eyes a few times, hard and quick, and she could see a cloud of fatigue pass over his face. He tossed the aspirin into his mouth and took the water from her. "Thanks," he said, and gave her a look of complete exhaustion, then closed his eyes for a moment. When he opened them, he said, "Stop looking at me like that, Monica. You didn't kidnap my wife. Sylvia did."

"I should have told you what I knew."

"Yes, you should have."

"We'll bring her home, Will. You can count on it."

"I am," he said, and stood up.

Monica and Will walked Bruce and Marcy out. After they pulled out of the driveway, Will and Monica were alone in the darkness. Despite their exhaustion and the sense of crisis, she could feel the electricity between them buzzing softly in the thick, phosphorus-scented air. She looked up at the moon. It was still full if you looked quick. She could feel the body heat radiating off Will's skin; a faint trace of his cologne triggered the image she had been replaying over and over all night, of her palms massaging his back. Her head felt swimmy again as her mind's eye shifted back and forth from memory to present.

"I think Yvette is trying to emerge," she said, and felt a chill ride up her arms. She rubbed up and down her biceps. "I felt something when I massaged her, Will. I felt *life*."

She could feel his eyes straining in the dark to see her face. "You did?"

"Haven't you?" she asked softly.

"She's been making some noises, but . . ." His voice trailed off.

"You might find hope," she suggested timidly. "In El Salvador."

"You're starting to sound like Sylvia." He tilted his head up and looked at the sky. "I know that centuries of science and medicine have a thing or two to say about it." He placed his hand over his heart and bent forward slightly. "Sylvia thinks she's the only one who has intuition. But I have a brain and a heart, and they're both telling me that Yvette is not going to recover. Not as the old Yvette, not even as a fraction of herself. She'll never speak or look up at the sky and say, 'Wow, what a pretty moon.' I've already made peace with that. And I don't want to add any more damage to her condition."

Monica looked down and kicked at some dirt with the edge of her flip-flops. "It's a long shot, huh?"

"Like trying to sink a golf ball from here to a hole in Boston." He stepped in closer and put his hands on her shoulders. "Get ready. I have a feeling this is going to be a hell of a fight."

His skin was warm and fragrant, and she froze with the overwhelming temptation to touch him, to press her fingers into the hard wall of his waist. She nodded but didn't hug him back. Her arms hung wooden at her side.

"I'm glad you're coming," he said. "Your history with the

place is going to help." He turned and looked down the road, where Bruce's Lincoln had disappeared. He leaned down, kissed her politely on the forehead, turned around, and walked to his truck. As he opened the door, he stopped and pointed up at a window of her house. "Kick those monkeys out and get some rest. You'll need it."

Monica cocked her head to the side and raised an eyebrow. His truck turned the corner and left a fading comet tail of red light in the darkness. She heard a noise from above. She looked up and saw someone's figure standing in the window frame.

"Need some rest for what?" It was Kevin, slurring his words.

"We're going to El Salvador," Monica said calmly. Someone spoke to him from inside the room, and Monica saw Kevin step back from the window and turn his head. Kevin had been working a lot of hours over the past week, and she had the feeling he'd only been half listening when she had explained the progression of events prior to tonight. She wasn't about to explain it all now.

She found a beach blanket in the trunk of her car and took it to a hammock she had set up between two trees in the small strip of yard next to her house. She hopped in and looked out to the water and the lights of Long Island. She could hear Kevin inside the house, searching for her; Paige's protest at being woken up, then the crunch of his footsteps on the gravel of the driveway. Kevin didn't know that Monica had found a nook under a tree for a hammock. Veiled from view behind the skirts of an elm tree, Monica rocked herself, impervious to his calling. He went back upstairs. She listened to the agitated murmurs upstairs until they quieted down and the house went dark and silent.

The Connecticut coast was quiet, placid, foggy, civilized; a world away from the pounding waves that smashed the ancient volcanic boulders of Negrarena. She had always known that there was an immense difference between this crowded, domesticated seashore and the majestic ocean of her childhood. She imagined that the difference in character of those two bodies of water was like the difference between contentment and awe.

part TWO

No one noticed that Yvette Lucero mashed her jaw as the needle injected a tiny amount of clear fluid into her spine. Had anyone noticed, it would have counted as a pain response and would have represented a bump of two whole points on her Glasgow Coma Score. The pain was cold, dazzling, and pure as a plunge into ice water. She felt a stunting and weighty rage. But the pain passed as quickly as it began, followed by a blinding deluge of snow that pattered on the roof of her brain and pulled her down into the emptiness of sleep.

Yvette squeezed through a hatch that led to unconsciousness — three levels below sleep — and hunkered down to weather the storm. She got back to the daily task of digging her way out of her prison with fingernails that were beginning to turn the bruised color of denim. No one knew that she was here. She sensed that the outside world had set sail without her, and she was alone on this island, with no way to get home. She could only feel and smell the existence of an external world. And she could think, of course. The outside world had changed, she was sure of it. The air smelled unfamiliar — like wood varnish, seaweed, and coffee. She could feel the shifting tide of the sea nearby in the movement of air, tasted it on the spongy fibers of her tongue every time she took a breath.

She had also been working on the reconstruction of the past. Her mind did the backbreaking work of a chain gang with its incessant digging. She had a few tattered fragments of her life, three bright strips of living material that didn't fit together or suggest anything useful. The first was an image of the yellow chiffon sleeves of an anemone, waving through the thick and distorting glass of a public aquarium tank. The second was an image of a man's leg, muscled and flexing back and forth with the effort of lifting something. And finally, there was the memory of standing in a magnificent rose garden. In this frame, a man holds a camera. The sun behind him is bright and all she can see is the outline of his figure. She is about to tell him that it's not a good angle, that she's going to look overexposed and squinting, when he shouts, "Smile!"

Flash!

As always, those three strips of footage were stilled and mounted against the gray cinder-block walls of her mind, loud and bright as graffiti on a subway wall. But this time, something was different. She blinked with disbelief.

Yvette was standing before an explosion of new, living, moving strips of imagery. She didn't know which to look at first, with all of them moving at the same time, in different directions, skateboarding across her vision faster than she could study them. She had the impression that she was looking through the eyepiece of a pair of binoculars, peering out at a distant shore from the bouncing position of a boat. She was excited and happy and devoured the explosion of colors and shapes. She got to work trying to group them together, comparing them to each other like the pieces of a jigsaw puzzle, keeping some, rejecting others. She was elated to find that each memory contained irrefutable evidence of her own existence in the world.

Bruce, Monica, and Will arrived in El Salvador three full days after Sylvia's departure, due to the unavailability of seats on flights headed into San Salvador. They eventually picked up separate connections, Will and Bruce through Miami and Monica through Atlanta. His old friend Claudia Credo came through on her offer and ended up making two separate runs out to the airport on the same day to scoop all the travelers.

They were to spend the first night with Claudia and her parents in San Salvador. Within an hour of her arrival, the phone rang for Monica. It was Kevin. He was jealous of Will, he admitted, and equally hurt that Will was now "in" with Bruce. Not that Kevin wanted to be included in the trip—he just didn't want Will near Monica. "Give me a break," Monica said. "He's here because of his *wife*."

"Time can tear down anything," Kevin warned.

"If two years hasn't done it, then two weeks certainly won't."

"How can a man love someone who can't talk, laugh, have

sex, or cook a meal? He can't even get yelled at for leaving his clothes on the floor. Nothing. Nada."

Outside, it was beginning to get dark. A small, lime-green parakeet landed on the sill of her window, scratched at something, and flew away. Monica said, "Kevin, you should see her. The unfairness of it makes you want to drop to your knees and scream."

She heard him take a deep breath. "I bet." But he persisted with his rivalry. "Will must see you as a possible escape."

Annoyed at the conversation, Monica said, "Maybe he already has someone on the side. What do we know? It's none of our business, anyway."

"Be very careful, Monica."

Monica felt her face get hot with embarrassment at the thought that someone might overhear this conversation—it presumed so much. She felt vain just entertaining the concept that Will might have felt the same flicker of attraction as she did, which at the moment seemed horribly crass even to her secret self. Was she that transparent?

"Point taken, Kevin. I'll be home in two weeks. You've been so busy lately, you won't even miss me."

"Monica," he said, in a long, drawn-out breath that made Monica anxious to get off the phone. "I wasn't expecting someone like Will to come along or for you to run off to El Salvador, but it did force me to stop and appreciate what I've got. I haven't been putting in a lot of effort lately. I'm sorry about that."

"Please, no need to apologize. You helped me with the new deck and you do all kinds of nice stuff for me." Between yawns, she added, "What we're looking at is called territoriality. Sociology 101. Remember?"

"It's called love. I miss you."

She looked up at the old-fashioned alarm clock on the night

table. "It's eleven o'clock here, sweetie. One in the morning your time. I'm exhausted. I'll call you when I have some news."

In bed ten minutes later, Monica realized that she had not told him that she loved him too. Its significance hunkered in the darkness long after she had hung up the phone. Monica kicked off the sheets and stared up at the blades of the ceiling fan, her arms extended at her sides as she waited for the sweet refuge of sleep.

CLAUDIA CREDO estimated that Kevin's four phone calls would cost him close to two hundred dollars if he didn't have a special international calling plan. *"Mil seiscientos colones!"* Claudia's elderly mother gasped, quickly computing the exchange rate and placing four bony fingers over her stretched lips. "He must really love you," she said with a nod of approval, then went back to rocking herself to sleep in her chair.

Claudia shuffled her houseguests into the dining room, which had been set up with a linen tablecloth and casual china. Will slung one hand over Monica's back and squeezed her shoulder. "Bruce, what do you think of this guy Kevin for your daughter? Do you see him as your future son-in-law?"

Monica turned and frowned at Will. "He made a bad first impression, I know."

Will raised one eyebrow. "The second impression wasn't so great either. I really could have lived without seeing his bare ass out on the seawall."

"He had too much to drink, like everyone else."

Will just smiled, tilting his head and holding one hand out, encouraging her to continue defending.

"Sit," Claudia said, pulling out chairs. In the courtyard just outside the window, a huge, chesty parrot prattled incessantly, calling out for someone named Chabela, who turned out to be a housekeeper who had died over ten years ago. "It gives us the creeps at night," Mama Mercedes confessed.

The housekeeper rushed about, setting down plates of steaming eggs, tortillas, refried beans, and Mama Mercedes's sweet tamales. "Adelfa," Claudia reprimanded. "I told you to serve the orange juice first."

Bruce praised Mama Mercedes's tamales ad nauseam, and they all enjoyed making the old lady's ancient eyes sparkle with pride. She rang a small silver bell that sat on the table. When the maid failed to appear, she got up and shuffled off, complaining how hard it was to find a good *muchacha* these days.

By the time they'd sat down to eat, Monica had forgotten that Will had pressed Bruce about Kevin. But ten minutes later, Bruce extracted a prune pit from his mouth and placed it on the side of his plate and turned to Will. "To answer your question, Will, I think Kevin is a very nice fellow. In fact, I consider him a friend. But I don't think Monica lets Kevin drive," he said, his hands gripping an imaginary steering wheel. He turned to his daughter. "Kevin has zero influence over what direction you take."

Monica frowned. "Is that what you think love is? A drive down the parkway?"

"I think you could do better, Monica," Will said, his voice dropping into a more serious tone. "You are . . ." He held his hand out flat, as if he were presenting her to an audience of strangers. "You're beautiful. You're a smart, professional woman with grace and talent, and Kevin may indeed be 'nice,' but he's not as impressive a man as you are a woman." He folded his arms over his chest and looked at Bruce. "There. I said it. Not another word or I might get my ass kicked by a pack of naked ex-frat-boys when we get home." He covered his mouth and looked at Claudia and Monica. "Oops. Pardon my French."

Claudia shook her head, indicating she didn't understand the expression.

Monica felt a wave of sadness over the futility of her relationship with Kevin. They were right, it wasn't *it*, and she had known it all along. The morning had dawned on the realization that she didn't love Kevin. But still, she had grown to care about him a great deal, and they knew each other so well; saying good-bye seemed like such a waste. Her eyelids pressed out two thin, hot tears and she hunched one shoulder to catch them with the fabric of her blouse.

"I'm sorry," Will said, "I hit a nerve."

Claudia got up and put her arms around Monica's shoulders. "You'll work it out."

"*Gracias,*" Will said at the same time, accepting a glass of orange juice from the maid's tray. He took a sip, closed his eyes, and moaned a little. "Oh . . . fresh squeezed." When he opened his eyes, he looked at Monica. Sympathy crossed his face. "Keep it in perspective, Monica. I'd give anything to be back where you are."

"And where's that?" Monica asked, using her cloth napkin to dab at the corners of her eyes.

"The time in your life where the future is still up to you."

WHEN CLAUDIA'S DRIVER pulled into the circular driveway of Clinica Caracol, Monica could feel Bruce, Will, and Claudia searching her face for a reaction. She bulged her eyes out and said, "What?" She had to admit it did feel odd, but not overwhelmingly so. In fact, what she was beginning to feel was a giddy sense of happiness at approaching Negrarena, still the mother of all beaches. Even though she lived near the sea in Connecticut, the feeling of approaching the coast in El Salvador was far more perceptible, since the contrast between land

and sea was so much more pronounced. Its presence called upon all the senses. First, the sudden thickening of the air, followed by quick glimpses of blue that appeared between the surrounding mountains, the feeling of descending into an expanse of magic. Then the soothing sound, the smell of salt and fish. Will said, "My God, it's gorgeous."

They drove up to the great gates of Villa Caracol and the driver honked his horn. A man came out and took their information and let them in. The exterior of the sprawling beach villa was the same as Monica remembered, only it had been freshly painted a warm, sunrise pink with terra-cotta brown detailing. The row of coconut palms still lined the entrance and led to an old marble fountain upon which a mermaid blew into a conch shell. The trees and lush, flowering shrubbery that Monica remembered had been cut down. The driver parked the van under the carport, turned around, and looked at Claudia, waiting for his instructions. "Hang around, Santos," she said. "We'll be about two hours."

Monica kept her head down as they stepped from the bright sunshine into the deep shade of the foyer. She welcomed the familiar cool air, like stepping into a library or a museum on a hot summer day. The ancient smells of the thick stone walls blasted her with a rush of memories, and she looked around with wonder at the vaulted ceilings and large, Italian terrazzo tiles. All of it was somewhat smaller than she remembered, but it still made for an impressive entrance. Monica closed her eyes and filled her lungs with the fragrance of time, the antique furniture and tobacco and coffee, all of it laced with undertones of sea smells. Tears sprang up in her eyes for the second time that day. She felt a smile spread across her lips as she imagined Abuelo smoking his pipe and reading the morning paper. She remembered him sitting in a huge, Mexican wood chair, under the sun beaming through an arched window with pink and indigo blue stained-glass edges. She opened her eyes and the scene evaporated into what was now the lobby of a medical clinic.

Abuela's heavy, baroque wood-and-glass display cabinet now housed a collection of seashells from all over the world. The other monstrous dark-wood armoires and overwrought chairs had been replaced by shiny glass cases, illuminated from within. Monica rushed up to them and pressed her hands against the glass until the edges rattled in their tracks. Each specimen was labeled with both its common and scientific name, its country of origin, its discoverer, and the year it was discovered. They were grouped by species—cowries, scallops, murexes, limpets, slit shells, lightning whelks, cones. At the center of the room was the star—a single cone shell in its own case, polished to a high, beige, blood-speckled gloss.

"The molluskan hall of fame," Bruce mumbled in Claudia's ear.

Claudia nodded and said, "They're beautiful. I never paid much notice to seashells. I had no idea there were so many varieties."

"This doesn't even come close," Monica whispered breathlessly. "She had more than this."

"Who?"

"Mami. This is her collection." Monica said, smiling hugely. She could feel herself tremble with excitement. "They're so . . . beautiful. I'd forgotten . . . to see so many of them together. . . . They're like works of art."

Bruce said, "You can't possibly say with certainty that she owned these specific shells."

"Yes, I can," Monica said, speaking quickly now, authority strengthening her voice. "The fingerprint of a collector is in the choices she makes in what to collect. The *furiosus* species," she said, tapping the glass with her fingernail, "was registered over a century ago, and this particular specimen was collected by my great-grandfather." She took a few steps along the front of the case. "That *Conus gloriamaris* was a birthday gift to my mom from Abuela. It's the one I told you she spent thousands of dollars for back in the 1960s."

"Alma kept her shells in smelly boxes in a room at her parents' house," Bruce said to Will and Claudia. "This is all news to me."

"Abuela must have created this display after Mom died," Monica said, "because I remember Mom kept them in smelly boxes too." The mention of the odor of rotting snail flesh released a brief recollection of her mother's clever use of black ants to eat the carcass of the dead snail lodged inside a difficult-to-clean shell interior.

"Have you added any new ones?" Monica asked the receptionist as she approached them and greeted them in Spanish. The young woman shook her head, but said that she had been charged with ordering more from a catalog. She rolled her eyes and said, "I've been putting it off. Like I know anything about buying shells."

Monica almost jumped out of her shoes. "I can help," she said, sounding more like an excited child than she meant to. The woman looked at her as if she were the biggest nerd ever born, then recomposed herself and asked who they were. She got their names and returned with the office manager—a tiny, rotund matron named Soledad Mayo. They all rushed to the center of the room and began speaking at once, Bruce and Monica in Spanish and Will in English.

Soledad held up a hand, then folded her arms behind her back, as if to force her own body language to appear friendly. She spoke to them in heavily accented English. "La Señora Sylvia told me that you would be arriving, Señor Lucero. We are here to serve you and honor your wishes, whatever they might be, and would like you to feel comfortable with whatever treatment you elect for your wife," she said, all the while giving Will a cautious sideways look. "All we ask, before we take you to see

her, is to consider our treatment before making your final decision."

"I did make a final decision, and it was to keep her in the States," Will said, his voice echoing off the tile floor. "My mother-in-law betrayed my wishes and the doctor's recommendations. I'm here to take my wife home."

The woman looked at the other three for support and, not finding it, turned back to Will with large kohl-rimmed eyes. "La Señora Sylvia told us that her financial and medical platform of support is being gradually withdrawn because Yvette has made little progress since her accident."

"That's not the point," Will said, raising his voice, his face turning bright red.

Bruce put a hand on his shoulder. "Take it easy, man. Let's take the tour, become informed, then we'll get Yvette out of here," he said, winking at Soledad and pulling a notepad and a pen out of his hip pocket. "I'm the reporter who spoke to you on behalf of *Urban Science*."

Soledad's face brightened, then clouded, as she shifted her eyes to Will. "Oh, yes, Mr. Winters. I . . . didn't know you were together."

"Originally we weren't, but then Sylvia . . ." Bruce's voice trailed off and he pointed toward the door. "It's a long story."

Nothing in the ensuing rooms reminded Monica of her ancestral beach home. The vaulted ceilings had been dropped with acoustical ceiling tile; it could be an outpatient facility anywhere. The staff moved about their business, looking up with occasional curiosity, but otherwise, the labs, administrative offices, and conference rooms were both professional and unremarkable. Monica kept glancing at Bruce, trying to read his face as he sized up the new construction against what he remembered of the old floor plan.

"Who owns this property?" Monica asked Soledad.

"This property is privately owned by a family and is on loan to the venture. Caracol was completely decrepit and abandoned for a long time. It all came together when Dr. Mendez secured funding from a British company named BioSource to study the effects of cone shell venom on humans."

"Back in the States, we begin with mice," Will barked.

Soledad closed her eyes as she spoke. "This treatment is beyond that point."

"How did the Borreros get involved?" Bruce asked, putting his hands on his hips.

The woman looked surprised that he knew the name. "The Borreros have a long history of expertise with mollusks. It began with Reinaldo Mármol, a doctor who used the venom of a local cone species as an anesthetic upon the request of Indians who distrusted Western medicine. His daughter, Magnolia Mármol, was a collector of rare and beautiful seashells. She married the wealthy industrialist Adolfo Borrero. Their daughter, Alma Borrero, was the one who took that interest to the level of passion. She collected most of the specimens you saw in the lobby."

Monica almost burst out with triumph, but managed to restrain herself and settled for clearing her throat and giving her father a quick glance. He pretended not to notice, underlining what he had told her back home—that he didn't want the staff to know their connection to the family. He claimed that it could compromise his access to information. Fortunately for him, so far they had only run into the clinic's staff, none of whom would recognize them or link them to Alma.

Soledad continued, "The *Conus furiosus* variety that was used so successfully by Dr. Reinaldo Mármol in his medical practice disappeared from sight for a half century. It was his granddaughter who inspired the search for the elusive species by her family members, friends, and local entrepreneurs who saw it as an opportunity to re-create it synthetically—in a lab—

and manufacture it primarily as a far superior substitute for morphine."

"Really?" Monica said playfully. "That's just remarkable. So what happened next?"

"Alma died tragically before she ever found the cone. A few reappeared two and a half years ago, in Mexico, El Salvador, then Guatemala, and they seem to be coming back strong in Panamic waters near Costa Rica."

"So who grabbed the brass ring?" Bruce asked, and Monica knew him well enough to know that her father was straining to appear cool and only mildly interested. Soledad looked down at her own ring finger, confused.

"It's an expression," Bruce said. "Who created this clinic? Who made it a reality?"

"Oh," she said. "Mostly a woman by the name of Dr. Mendez."

"And who is Leticia Ramos?" Monica pressed. "I know she's the one that Sylvia spoke with initially."

"She's a friend of the Borrero family. She doesn't get involved with the day-to-day of this clinic. We report the results to the trials committee in San Salvador via phone conference and e-mail because Negrarena is such a remote location. But most of the emphasis is on the chronic-pain trials. The brain-trauma application is brand-new."

"You might have a better chance of winning Mr. Lucero's confidence if we can meet the wizard," Monica said. "We want to make sure we're not dealing with a tiny man and a dog behind a curtain."

The woman laughed politely, making it clear that once again she didn't understand the expression, but grasped the underlying meaning. "Fair enough, I'll see what I can do. I have no idea if Dr. Mendez and Ms. Ramos are even in the country, but I can call when we get back to the office."

"I want to see my wife," Will said. "Is that the door to the infirmary?"

"One last thing, Señor Lucero." Soledad held up a finger. "There's the presentation."

Will's face grew white and he pointed a finger at Soledad, then at himself. "I don't like the way you're imposing your priorities above mine. My right to see my wife stands above your right to show me your propaganda."

Soledad pursed her lips and glared at him. "I'm just following procedure, señor."

"Is it procedure for your clinic to prey on desperate people? Is it procedure to encourage them to cash in their life's savings? Is it procedure to facilitate kidnapping?"

Soledad didn't say anything, but her eyes roamed over Monica's and Will's faces in search of validation once more. Finding none, she turned and said, "Follow me."

WHEN SYLVIA SAW the Winterses walking behind her son-in-law, her face brightened as she stood to hug them. She was dressed in a short-sleeved, crisp apricot linen suit with matching sandals and smelled of Jean Naté. Claudia clutched Sylvia's hands like an old friend's and said, "I'm Claudia, a friend of Bruce and Monica. At your service."

Monica watched from behind Bruce's shoulder as Will bent down over Yvette's bed. He scrutinized her for damage, resting the palm of his hand on her forehead for a few seconds, then pulled back her eyelids to inspect the whites of her eyes. She was hooked up to some kind of monitor, and he leaned forward to examine the various digital displays, apparently familiar with each one. When he was satisfied, he kissed his wife on the lips and whispered something into her ear.

Monica experienced a perverse sense of jealousy followed by an immediate sense of relief that her growing attraction to him was just her silly little secret. This served as a firm and much-needed reminder that Will Lucero still belonged to this motionless, silent woman. When Monica had massaged Will, his stress and loneliness were as unmistakable to her touch as rocks hidden in a bowl of thick, corded dough. And yet, still he remained a devoted and faithful husband. Monica instantly recognized the paradox of her admiration. There was no impending ethical dilemma. She was completely safe because Will would step into an unflattering light if he ever abandoned his heroic post. His devotion to Yvette was the battery power of his beauty, and her attraction to him would always remain a blessedly secret, entirely temporary, full-moon crush. Nothing more.

DURING THE VISIT, Monica detected a false, tense cheeriness in Sylvia's voice that was unsettling. "Monica," she said, stroking her arm in a way that reminded Monica of a school nurse, "the physical therapist quit, and they don't have anyone to massage the patients." She clasped her hands together. "Do you think you could massage my Yvette, just once, dear, could you?"

"She didn't come here to work, Sylvia," Will said, his voice flat and cold. "It's totally inappropriate for you to ask."

Monica surprised herself by deciding then and there that she would have to ignore her previous discomfort with the idea. This was an entirely new landscape, and encouraging peace between Will and Sylvia had suddenly become top priority. "It would be my pleasure, Sylvia."

Soledad stepped forward, still trying to give her presentation. "At Clinica Caracol, we consider massage and sensory stimulation to be the sacred partner to the drug therapy. We will have a physical therapist available in a few days. I apologize."

Claudia stood over Yvette's bed and put one limp hand in hers. "I'm going to call you La Bella Durmiente, because you look like you belong in a Bavarian fairy tale." She looked up at the five other people in the room clustered around the bed. "Did anyone check this princess for a poisoned apple lodged in her throat?"

Sylvia chuckled appreciatively, then shook her head sadly. "My Yvette. She was so pretty."

Monica cringed inside, believing in her heart that Yvette had somehow heard and understood that comment from her mother, spoken in the past tense. "You're still very beautiful, Yvette," Monica said, a strange mix of guilt and protectiveness braiding themselves inside her stomach as she placed one hand on Yvette's. She looked up at Claudia. "The poison apple was Blanca Nieves. Snow White."

"We're going to go to the beach now," Bruce said, pulling Claudia and Monica toward the door. He made a face, a not-so-subtle hint that it was time to leave Will and his mother-in-law alone to face each other in their battle for control over Yvette's fate.

MONICA, BRUCE, and Claudia Credo walked around the back of the clinic to Negrarena beach. On the way, they noticed that the Moroccan-tile swimming pool had been restored to its former glory. A light breeze ruffled its surface, and it sparkled, empty and inviting in the afternoon heat. They passed through the old gates that separated the property from the beach, and Monica had a flash vision of Alma's slender arms pushing the gates open, then slowly turning to look behind her, as if expecting someone to call her back from the doorstep of her paradise.

The image of Alma was marred by the presence of a newly added cement platform, apparently a sunning area, with a special ramp for wheelchair access. Monica put her hands on her hips and mumbled, "What's the point of a sunning deck if the patients here are all in a coma? I don't get it."

. "I guess they figure that no one here has an excuse for pale legs," Bruce said, pointing to one of his pasty shins.

After a few moments on Negrarena, Monica could no longer restrain her joy. When the first monster wave rose up and crashed over the shore, Monica felt a surge of electricity, her inner fluids rising to mimic the motion of the water, diving, tumbling, and spraying her insides with a salty thrill that made her kick off her shoes and sprint across the beach. The infernally hot black sand made her hop and she had to turn around and run back to get her sandals. She opened her arms wide as she ran to meet the ocean, and she had the delirious sensation that the waves *remembered* her. They leaped up onto her, licking her legs and drawing her in until she dropped to her knees and let the cool, bubbly water run over her thighs, soaking her sundress. A larger wave rumbled toward her and she decided to go ahead and get good and soaked. The undertow of the wave wrapped itself around the back of her waist and pulled her toward itself like a determined lover.

She pushed her fingers through black, viscous sand that felt like facial mud. She smeared it on her face, imagining that it looked like war paint, and when the next wave came, she leaned over it and washed it off. When she passed the tips of her fingers over her face, her skin felt smooth as a river rock.

Farther down along the stretch of beach Monica could see the distant figure of a woman, strolling in the company of a dog. She was walking away from them, poking at the tide pools with a stick. She reminded her of Alma. Monica looked up, beyond the woman's path, and saw a crop of houses that had sprung up where there was once only trees and scrub.

When Monica turned around, Bruce and Claudia were enveloped in the cocoon of their own conversation, chatting happily. Monica suddenly wished she and Bruce were alone. She wanted to share with him a small gift of memory she had found in the sand.

Alma had taught Monica to press her arms deep into the wet, black sand in the minutes after a volcanic temblor in order to feel the life pulse of the earth, to hear the secret and distant undulations of its great beating heart. She wanted to tell Bruce, because she had not done so back then, and she had a feeling that he still didn't understand what magic it was to let Alma lead the way, how the natural world became powerful and amazing through her eyes.

AFTER ANOTHER HOUR with Sylvia, Soledad, and the doctor on duty, Will agreed to give them exactly one week to show some kind of evidence of improvement.

". . . Which of course is impossible," Bruce said to Monica and Claudia. "He figures he's appeasing Sylvia, but Sylvia's strategy is to use the week to work on him to give it more time."

After the three came out of the room, Will looked drained. He glanced at Monica, shook his head, and said, "She won't hand over the air ambulance information to transport Yvette back home. I could take legal measures, but that would just take more time, so I'm caving in and giving it a week." He rubbed his eyes, and Monica noticed they were rimmed with red from a lack of sleep. He ran his hands through his hair and it made his hair stick straight up on top, making him look strikingly younger, like a disheveled teenager. "I just hope I'm wrong about this place," he said in a soft voice, almost a whisper.

Outside, Claudia's driver was waiting to take her back to San Salvador; he'd been waiting for four hours now. Claudia had taken the day off from work and had to get back to the city. "Who's coming with me and who's staying?"

Sylvia already had accommodations at the clinic, and the rest of the party decided to stay at a rustic guesthouse a half mile down the road. Soledad agreed to send a driver to get them in the morning. She'd tracked down the mysterious Leticia Ramos, who would meet with them in the afternoon. Monica was growing more and more excited.

Bruce, Will, and Claudia were wrapping up their affairs in the front office, and Bruce was jotting down some notes for his article, when Monica wandered out to the lobby to get another look at the shells.

She always marveled at the individuality and artistry manifested by the shells' architects. One could understand why they would go to such great lengths to construct such beautiful dwellings: naked, they were wretchedly unattractive. They were also helpless. The creature inside a Chilean murex, for example, constructed tall, elaborate spires with the intention of making his fortress look impenetrable to his predators. In the process, his craftsmanship achieved the grace and excellence of a tiny Renaissance cathedral, completely contradicting the measure of his intelligence. In the background of the display was a backlit silk screen printed with script text, a section of French poet Paul Valéry's essay about nature and seashells:

Nature has preserved her cautious methods, the inflection in which she envelops her changes of pace, direction, or physiological function. She knows how to finish a plant, how to open nostrils, a mouth, a vulva, how to create a setting for an eyeball; she thinks suddenly of the seashell when she has to unfold the pavilion of an ear, which she seems to fashion the more intricately as the species is more alert.

On the way to the door, Monica saw the specimen catalogs, obviously dumped on top of the coffee table by the receptionist. She sat down on a wood-and-rattan sofa and leafed through a catalog from a showcase-specimen dealership in Brussels peddling everything from bizarre and prehistoric insects trapped in petrified beds of primordial mud, to a Neanderthal tibia, and of course shells, recent and fossilized.

The receptionist came into the room and said, "You can take them with you if you like, I only need the current issue to place an order. I've never seen anyone even glance at them, never mind get as excited as you. They just gather dust. I have a few more in the back if you want them. We get new shell price lists every few months."

Monica smiled and thanked her. "I forgot to bring reading material for the slow moments of this trip."

"What could possibly be more boring than reading specimen catalogs?" the young woman said. "Maybe your *posada* will have a television. There's a really good *novela* on at eight. *Amor Salvaje*." She opened her eyes wide. "Tonight we find out if the heroine is pregnant by the hacienda foreman or the effeminate husband she can't stand."

Monica raised one eyebrow. "I can tell you who the father is without watching a single episode."

"You don't know what you're missing," the woman said, stepping into a room behind the reception area. She emerged minutes later with eight more specimen catalogs.

THAT NIGHT, Bruce went to bed at nine thirty and Will and Monica sat on two dirty chairs inside a tiny general store named Tienda La Lunita. The innkeeper at the *posada* had warned that it was not prudent for "elegant-looking people," as she had called them, to wander around the village alone and at night. The store was only two blocks away. "Get what you need and come right back," she said, wagging a finger. *"Peligroso."*

"Elegante?" Will repeated in a delayed echo, looking down at his khaki cargo pants and sale-bin T-shirt.

Monica shrugged. She hooked her thumbs on the shoulder straps of her short overalls, suddenly feeling as if she had to speak in a Southern drawl. "What she meant was, y'all don't look like you're from these parts."

"Oh . . . ," Will said, and looked down again, this time at his rubber and Velcro sandals. He wiggled his toes. "Thank God we're not."

"My dad would kill us both if he knew we went wandering around this Podunk village at night in a quest for beer." She held up the brown bottle of the local brew, Pilsener. "Cheers."

Will held up his bottle and they clinked the bottoms. "I'm glad your dad went to bed. This is kind of cool, just hanging out with you," he said, catching her eye.

Monica held up her bottle to his again, tilted her head to the side, and smiled widely. "To a new friendship, then." She tipped the bottle back and took two long gulps of beer so that she wouldn't have to look at him right away.

"I feel like I'm in the third world, but in a good way," Will said. "That's a new concept to me, mind you. Sure it's rustic, and we saw a lot of shanties and poor people on the way, but there's something special about Negrarena. I can't put my finger on it, it's like there's something in the air."

"Maybe you just needed a change of scenery."

Will raised one eyebrow. "Could be. I'm so relaxed right now I don't know what to do with myself." He wiggled his arms and his shoulders around, rotated his head. "My neck is sore, though."

Monica held up a hand. "Don't look at me. I'm on vacation."

Will signaled to the shopkeeper with two fingers to bring more beer. Monica sat back in her chair and looked around the store at all the food products she hadn't seen in years. There was something about this night—her senses were sharper, her eyes keener. Maybe it was the thick beach smells, the shadows of night, just being in El Salvador, all of it so, so intoxicating. Will was right about this place. Her whole body felt effervescent.

When Monica looked up, she was stunned to see that Will was watching her, his head cocked to the side a bit. A faint smile passed over his lips. His dark eyes were buttery, intense, and unflinching, and without a word he handed his admiration over like a parcel, warm and squirming on her lap. By the time she recognized it, she had been staring back at him for a long time, reading his face, until she understood what they had just exchanged. She could almost hear the groaning shift of weight, the settling into place of something newly created.

She tore her eyes away. She put her hand up to her forehead to try to cover her eyes. The skin on her face and neck was burning. "Maybe we should get back," she said, looking around.

"Oh, come on, just a little longer. I'm enjoying the crowd," he said, gesturing toward the empty room behind him. "And I know for sure that you're not anxious to get back to that decrepit guesthouse with the shore crabs staring up at you in the shower."

Monica smiled, amused by his reference to the creatures that populated her childhood. "I guess you met the *caballeros. Gentlemen*—isn't that a funny name for crab? I used to know their Latin name. Anyway, I told you it was rustic out here."

Will opened his eyes wide. "I used to define *rustic* as camping on a beach in Rhode Island, where a distant relative to the *caballero* is served with drawn butter and a side of onion rings."

Monica chuckled and began to peel the gold-edged ace-of-hearts label off her beer bottle. There was a moment of silence between them, and she could tell Will was looking at her again. "I remember watching a *caballero* crawl on my mother's back when she was asleep on the beach," Monica said cautiously. "She mumbled in her sleep and it scared the crab away. I'll never forget it. She revealed something I wasn't supposed to know."

Will leaned forward. "What?"

Monica took a deep breath and exhaled slowly, trying to decide whether she should share. She sipped her beer and looked at his face. Even though it was half-lit, she still glimpsed a confidence and maturity that she wasn't accustomed to seeing in men under fifty: that paternally driven instinct to protect, to identify problems at the root and fix them.

Monica picked up a napkin and began to fold it into ever smaller triangles before she spoke. "My mother confirmed my suspicion that she was having an affair with a married man. It was the saddest moment of my life, next to the day my father told me she had drowned."

"How old were you?"

"Twelve."

"That's a lot for a kid to deal with. Supposedly, most kids feel responsible for their parents' marriages."

"Exactly." Monica nodded. "And I don't know why, but my father is vague about anything having to do with my mother, her death, our life here." She gestured behind her, in the direction of the beach. "Marcy told me that she got blasted by my dad for giving me the airline ticket. They had a big blowout over it. But when I ask him point-blank what the big deal is, he just brushes me off." She tossed the napkin back into the center of the table, then watched it, the way you toss a stick into a bonfire and wait for it to burn. She narrowed her eyes. "I've come to the conclusion that he's afraid I'm going to find something out about my mother that will hurt me." She looked up at Will. "But what could be worse than her affair?"

Will drew his eyes down to the dusty tiles of the floor. "Something about her death?"

Monica shrugged, looked up to the exposed wood beams of the room.

"I think this conversation calls for cigars," Will said. "Will you indulge me? We're going to be here awhile."

"Where are you going to get a cigar?"

Will held up a finger and summoned the shopkeeper, and a few minutes later she produced two dried-out Dominican cigars, which she said she kept in stock for one of the doctors at the clinic who came by infrequently. She chopped off the ends and handed the cigars over with a book of matches. Will lit both cigars in his mouth and handed one to Monica. When she took the cigar into her mouth, the moisture he'd left behind on the tip felt like an unintentionally intimate exchange. She closed her eyes as the smoke rolled back toward her face.

"Okay," he said, settling back in his chair. He took a puff of his cigar, tilted his head back, and blew upward. "Take me back to the days just before she disappeared, to the first domino that knocked everything else down. Start with what you had for breakfast that morning." He pointed the cigar at her. "And I bet you still remember that detail."

Monica closed her eyes against the screen of smoke that rose from her own mouth. She thought it was interesting that her family's past was somehow becoming a part of Will's present.

On a damp morning in June of 1985, Bruce was in his study, furiously tapping away at his electric typewriter. He was a correspondent for the Associated Press then, and he was covering the Zona Rosa massacre: thirteen people, including four U.S. marines, were gunned down in cold blood in San Salvador's lively strip of upscale eateries and bars. The photos strewn about Bruce's desk showed bloodied corpses lying at the foot of a sidewalk café. Someone had covered the victims' faces with linen restaurant napkins. On the phone a few minutes later, Monica heard her father shout, "Of course the shooters weren't real *militares;* they were communists in stolen military uniforms."

Monica stared at her mushy Cap'n Crunch cereal, unable to eat. She knew it wasn't the right time to talk to her dad about her mother and Max, but seeing the color photos sitting on his desk had triggered something, a realization of what Max and his friends were a part of. All the talk of fairness for the poor and equality among citizens didn't add up to those horrifying photos: the old lady who had been selling roses just minutes before the shooting now lay dead next to the man who had been waiting for his chauffeur. Each victim had sprayed the sidewalk with the same red blood. What more proof did anyone need of equality?

Everyone was so anesthetized from all the violence. In fact, Monica was sure that the witnesses who had spilled out of the Mexican restaurant across the street had eventually gone back to stuff themselves with chimichangas and margaritas. But Monica's own numbness had just worn off at the sight of those crime-scene photos. She felt dirty from exposure; from knowing people who believed that the importance of their beliefs stood above the right of others to be alive. If her mother's philosophy was true about the ocean claiming that which was unclean and making it pure, then El Salvador was due for a flood of biblical proportions. Downtown, thirteen people were dead. It wouldn't be long before something terrible happened, and Alma was right in the middle of it.

At school that week, some of Monica's friends had expressed shock that Monica's parents didn't employ armed bodyguards like all of the other affluent families. "Your mother *es una loca,*" someone had said in the Spanglish that was the official language of the American School. "She's going to get *secuestrada* by *guerrilleros.*" It had become fashionable among teenagers at the American School to brag that their parents were rich enough to be worth kidnapping. "I'd be embarrassed if I were you," a classmate advised Monica. "I'd worry people might think we couldn't afford bodyguards."

If they only knew that Mami and I once gutted fish for one hundred *guerrilleros,* Monica thought.

The answer to the family troubles came to her from the back of the box of Cap'n Crunch cereal, with its offer of temporary tattoos with three proofs of purchase. It was the cereal her grandmother Winters always got for her when she visited her home in Connecticut. Grandmother Winters had two extra bedrooms, a perfect place to start a new life. Monica decided right then and there that they had to get out of El Salvador. It was time to flee.

Monica went back into her father's study and approached his desk just as he pulled a page out of the typewriter. "There," he said. "I have to run to the office to wire this. You want to go for a ride?"

They got into his red Toyota pickup. He drew the lap belt over her legs and snapped it in place. When they pulled out of the driveway, with him still jabbering about the massacre, Monica interrupted him and said, "Dad, we have to move to Connecticut."

The somberness of her voice made him take his eyes off the road. He shifted gears, drove slower down the steep hills of the Escalón neighborhood. "What's going on?" he said, glancing briefly at the road, then back at his daughter, a look of deep concern already visible on his face. Monica was silent as she fought the grip that was taking hold at the back of her throat.

He said, "Is it something going on at school?"

She shook her head.

"A boy?" he said almost hopefully. Again she shook her head.

"I don't want you and Mom to get a divorce, and I'm afraid something bad might happen to Mom," she blurted.

"Did your mom say she wants to divorce me?"

"No," she said, pulling at the threads on her skirt.

"Then don't worry about it. Your mom and I are fine."

"No, you aren't," she said, staring out the window as they passed block upon block of homes hidden behind twelve-foot brick walls topped with garlands of electrified razor wire, some of them with armed guards standing out front. Others were protected more subtly, from castlelike turrets hidden among the leaves of almond trees overlooking the street.

Then it came, like hot vomit erupting from some secret,

contained place inside her: "Mom is with Maximiliano, Dad. Mom is *with* Maximiliano," she repeated, hoping he understood.

Bruce exhaled loudly, beeped his horn at somebody, and stepped on the gas. They approached the edge of the property of a mysterious, overgrown mansion of crazy construction—an Italian Renaissance palazzo from the north face, a red-and-white Chinese palace on the south. Bruce pulled the truck into a strip of driveway just before the mansion's grand gates. He turned off the engine. The sun dropped through the windshield with the oppressive weight of a wool blanket. A skinny, black dog appeared and sat beside Bruce's door, sniffing at the air.

"Are you sure about what you're saying, Monica?" He sounded angry.

Monica looked down at her sandals. She began to cry, now that she had spoken of it. She looked up at her father. "They take me on trips with them," she said, covering her face with her hands, hoping he wouldn't need for her to go into detail. After a while, she turned to look at him.

He was staring straight ahead, and for a moment Monica wondered if he had even heard her. He bit down on his lip, hard. Sweat beaded up among the blond hairs on his forearm. The tip of his nose reddened and his eyes became glassy. If there were any tears, he managed to blink them away. "God" is all he said. Outside, the skinny, black dog began to scratch at his door, then came around and started whining and scratching on Monica's side.

"We have to get out of here, Dad. Max's wife is following Mom and me around." Monica felt a wave rise deep in her entrails. She opened the door of the truck, leaned out, and threw up a yellow pool of liquefied Cap'n Crunch cereal. Almost immediately, the dog leaped forward and happily lapped it up.

*　*　*

"MY FATHER DELIVERED his news story, and then took me home," Monica told Will. "He locked himself in his room for a few hours while I just freaked out. I thought he was mad at me. When he came out, he was drunk. It was the one and only time in my childhood I saw him like that. He was finally able to hug me and tell me that I had done the right thing. I made him promise he wouldn't tell a soul about my confession."

"The part I don't understand," Will said, "is what your mother saw in the communists." He bent down to pet a mangy, skinny, black dog that had wandered into the store and looked at them with hungry, haunted eyes.

"Be careful with that dog," Monica said. "I'm sure that he hasn't been immunized." She continued, "Max was the son of our family nanny, Francisca, who cared for both my mother and me as children. Mami and Max had crushes on each other during their entire childhood, but of course, a courtship was strictly forbidden. Eventually, it became an unfulfilled Romeo and Juliet thing. By the time my mother felt strong enough to defy our family's social code, she was already married to my father, and Maximiliano was *adjuntado* to someone in a common-law marriage. Obviously, he never spoke of her, and I only caught a quick glimpse of her once, in a supermarket. My mom called her 'the witch.' I was afraid of her, but I felt sorry for her too."

"I wonder," Will said, "if they had just left them alone if they wouldn't have eventually grown apart and lost interest in each other, especially being from different worlds. It's the lure of forbidden fruit. . . . And how did the pauper of our story get to be a medical doctor?"

Monica shrugged. "First of all, he went to some semi-accredited program in El Salvador, which issues medical degrees in less time than it takes to get a bachelor's degree in the States. My grandfather paid for it—less an altruistic gesture than a move to gain power and influence over Max. He must have had a sense that Max already had my mother hooked, and Abuelo wanted to put an end to it. Although the degree couldn't buy him a fancy practice in San Salvador, it allowed him to hang a shingle outside his door, write prescriptions, and practice general medicine as a humble country doctor. Eventually, he dedicated his medical training almost exclusively to aiding the revolutionaries. Not exactly what my grandfather had in mind."

"*Ya vamos a cerrar, señorita,*" the shopkeeper warned. Monica negotiated another fifteen minutes, so she could finish the story.

"Anyway, after my confession, my mother called to tell me that the *Conus* she had gone to see was probably not a *furiosus,* but that she thought it was worth examining. She had placed it in a dishpan of seawater and had intended to take it back to the university lab. She was unsure when that might be because Max had asked for her help with some campesinos who needed medical attention. They were headed for El Trovador, a coastal farm not far from Negrarena. She asked me to cover for her by telling my father that she had gone to Guatemala for a few days. I told him the truth instead. Eventually, our anger was replaced by worry."

"Was your grandmother alive?"

"Yeah. But I begged my dad not to tell her what was going on. I wanted to keep it between us, because I feared an over-the-top reaction from Abuela."

Will reached across the table and took her hand, squeezed it. "I'm so sorry all this happened."

Monica nodded and gently pulled her hand away.

Will looked down, crushed the butt of his cigar into a plastic ashtray on the table.

"Finish your story," he said, glancing up at a clock on the wall. "She's going to kick us out in five."

"There's not that much more to tell. I got to stay home from school for weeks on end. I stayed with my grandmother at the beach house. I guess we were both in a sort of personal seclusion, trying to deal with what was happening. She was always surrounded by people, always so formidable, so in control. But in the weeks after my mom went missing, Abuela doped herself up with tranquilizers and slept most of the day. Eventually, my dad told me that I should prepare myself for the probability that my mother might never come back. She didn't. A witness said they saw her thrashing far out, and so all we could conclude is that she drowned. By fall I was enrolled in junior high in Connecticut."

"What about Grandma Borrero?"

"Abuela? She came to visit us in Connecticut a few times, but my dad didn't want us to return to El Salvador. She died eight years ago."

"And so who got all your family's money?" Will asked.

Monica made a face at him and, looking around, said, "Shh. Remember where you are."

Will clamped a hand over his mouth. Monica lowered her voice too. "The short answer is Jorge, who is my great-uncle. Jorge was the only living Borrero brother by then. In her last will and testament, my grandmother left everything to my mother, assuming that my mother would eventually pass it down to me. Seven years after her disappearance, Tío Jorge had my mother legally declared dead. By then my grandmother had developed Alzheimer's disease and was unable to make any adjustments to her will. Somehow, Tío Jorge got every last penny."

Will said, "It sounds like your grandmother didn't really believe your mother was dead or she would have revised the will to include you."

Monica slapped the tabletop with one hand. "That's what

everyone said, that she was in denial." She paused, looking off into the distance. "But I saw her mourning. It was no show."

"She may have mourned the death of the relationship rather than the person."

"My dad's theory is that as the executor of Abuela's estate, Jorge was able to manipulate the legal process in his favor." Her eyes drifted up to the wall clock. "That's my story and our time is up." She stood, and Will paid the woman. They stepped out into the dimly lit street and headed back to the guesthouse.

In the street, they kept an eye out for danger, and Monica asked that they walk on the side of the street that was most il-luminated. Will slipped his hands into his pockets, then brought his feet together and stopped.

"What?"

He looked around, crossed his arms in front of him, and stared down at the packed-dirt road. "Hmmm."

She waited, and he shifted his position, tugging at his lower lip, before he turned to her and said, "Have you ever wondered if . . . your dad . . ." He let the sentence trail off.

Monica tilted her head. "If my dad reported Max's where-abouts to the *militares* in a jealous fit?"

Will shrugged. "Did it ever cross your mind?"

"Of course it did, years later. But I honestly don't think he did. He loved my mother, and he knew that it was dangerous for her to be near Max. I know in my heart that he would never send harm her way, he just wouldn't."

As she finished speaking, she felt a pair of eyes boring into her back. Her heart skipped a beat and she jumped back when she saw the black figure that was shadowing them, eyes shining in the pale light of the moon.

A second later, she laughed and put her hand over her heart when she saw that it was the dog from the restaurant. "Oh, that's bad luck."

"What's bad luck?" Will said, just as he saw the same

shadow and jumped and put his arms protectively around her shoulder.

"El Cadejo is following us."

"You know this dog?"

"No, it's a local legend. If a small black dog follows you, it just might be the dreaded Cadejo. He's part of a collection of local folklore—there's a crazy woman named La Siguanaba who kills men near rivers, and she has a son who's a Freddy Krueger type." Monica looked up at the barrel-tile roofs of the small buildings, at the chipped plaster exposing brown adobe bricks beneath. She scratched her head, trying to remember. "There's also a phantom wagon, just like the rickshaw in that Kipling story. El Cadejo announces tragedy—or delivers it, I can't remember which."

Will took a step toward the dog. "Shoo! Go home, mutt."

"Shoo?" Monica said, rolling her eyes. "He doesn't know *shoo,* Will. He doesn't speak English."

Will tried kicking one foot in the air, and the dog bowed his head but didn't budge. "How do you shoo a dog in Spanish, then?"

Monica picked up a pebble, held it up to the light. "You throw a small rock at him, then you say *shit* without the *i*. Like this: Shhht." She stomped her foot and tossed the rock at the dog, which he caught in his mouth, sampled, then let drop on the sidewalk.

Will punched his fist through the air. "Wow, you really showed him."

"*Chuchos* are tough. They're not scared of anything but hunger." She put her hands on her hips. "If this dog is the legendary Cadejo, he has demonic powers. He might beat us home by crawling up the front of that building and appearing on the other side, just like a lizard."

Will went through his pockets. "I wish I had something to give him, I feel sorry for him."

They hurried through the darkened streets, and when they passed through the entrance of the inn, Will grabbed Monica's shoulder, turned her around, and said, "Hey."

Monica felt a sudden panic that he might kiss her, just by the way he said "Hey." She stared down at his rubber sandals, tilted her head, pushing an ear toward him with her face still turned away. "Hmm?"

"I hope you weren't offended by what I suggested about your dad. . . . I was playing at being an amateur detective, but I feel badly about saying it. This is your life, for God's sake, not a whodunit novel. It was a stupid thing to say, and I apologize."

Monica looked up and smiled, relieved. "I told you, I'd thought of that possibility myself. It didn't happen that way, I'm sure of that. But it's a perfectly logical conclusion."

The innkeeper was awake and nervous and fussed at them like a mother for being out so late despite her warning. Monica thanked her for her concern and wished her a good night. Monica stepped toward Will and gave him what was supposed to be a quick hug and said, "Night." But he kept her locked in and pulled her closer to him, one arm around the small of her waist, the other around her shoulders.

"I'm glad you told me that story," he said. "I feel like I've known you for a long time."

And when he let her go, the look on his face was open and flushed and serious and made Monica dizzy. How easy it would be to bring her face a little closer to his. Just an inch or two closer and they could change the course of their budding friendship forever. It was the longest journey a chin could ever make. What unknowable danger might lurk if she were to let herself look up at him with eyes that howled the truth about her full-moon crush?

"Next time," she said, pointing a finger into the center of his chest, "it'll be your turn. We'll get cigars and you can tell me a long story about your life with Yvette."

As a cold shower, it worked. He stepped back, nodded his head, smiled briefly. "Good night, Monica Winters Borrero," he said. "See you in the morning."

Monica turned and walked down the hall toward her room. She could feel his gaze descending her dorsal side like fingers reading the braille of her backbone. She heard his fading footsteps as he disappeared down another hallway.

In her room, she went to the window. She cranked the metal handle that opened the glass jalousies. Outside, the same black dog from the store was watching her from the street, its tongue hanging out, its eerie eyes shiny and flat as metal coins. He gave Monica the creeps, so she pulled the curtains closed, not wanting to think more about the mythical Cadejo, precursor to misfortune.

Yvette Lucero remembered being on a sailboat that was motoring out of a channel. It was an overcast day, a bit chilly. Red and white buoys dotted the gray water. A large sign stated there was to be NO WAKE. She read the sign out loud, several times, and wondered if this meant that she should abandon hope. Still, it was a channel, and that in itself invited possibilities.

Her husband was standing at the helm, tan and handsome. He blew her a kiss and the sunlight caught on the gold band around his finger. An orange dog was moving excitedly about the deck. Yvette shivered in the damp air, looked down at her arms, and saw they were covered in gooseflesh. She rubbed herself once and got up and moved across the boat, stepped onto the ladder, and went down to look for a sweatshirt, scratching some bug bites on the backs of her legs. Her mother was sitting in the galley. She looked up and tried to hide something but it was too late, Yvette had already glimpsed a section of knitted pale green and yellow yarn in her lap. Her mother was knitting a baby blanket. Yvette wagged a finger at her and her mother smiled guiltily and pretended to be interested in the newspaper that was lying on the table. "You promised no baby pressure, remember?"

Yvette felt kinship without emotion for these two people, something like the pleasant but detached curiosity one might feel upon viewing old films of long-dead relatives whom you never met. The thrill was in discovering that a fresh strip of visual footage had been added to the meager inventory, a brand-new, never-been-seen episode appearing upon a screen that had been in a numbing and continuous loop for as long as she could remember.

She felt a needle drive into her spine again. The sailing memory bubble collapsed into a noisy fizz, and she scrambled to compact herself before the avalanche of mental snow buried her in its suffocating blue.

This time, as her anger began to rise with the pain, she wondered if there would be more gifts of memory waiting. She would consider this a fair trade. As the pain cascaded toward her, she curled up into herself. She folded into a child who shriveled into a fetus, then an embryo the size of a peppercorn, who decomposed into a zygote, then nothing but coiled strings of DNA and a tail.

She discovered that the less of her there was, the less they could hurt.

The crow of a rooster woke Will Lucero long before dawn. The rooster's crow alarmed a dog and triggered a competition of howls and cock-a-doodles that continued for hours. He wedged his head between two pillows but it was futile to pursue sleep with all the racket outside. By the time the sun began to illuminate the edges of the dusty window curtains of his rented room, he had been awake for two hours, and yet he wasn't at all irritated. As his feet stepped down on the cool tile floor, he had the sensation that he was waking up to a different world from the one he had gone to sleep in the night before. Sometime during the night, he had woken up and attached words to the absurdly premature feelings that had taken hold of him over the last week.

I'm falling in love.

When the four words came to him, they zipped into his room like a line of fireflies, buzzing and snapping with eerie luminescence. Their arrival left him stunned and unable to do anything but repeat them over and over, watching their secret display of fire and magic.

It was the closest thing to the mighty "thunderbolt" he remembered reading about in *The Godfather*—Michael Corleone sees Apollonia for the first time on a trip to Sicily, and in a sudden, blinding flash he is transformed into a man who is so in love he can't even remember his own name. Not exactly the same thing here, Will thought. He'd first walked into Monica's office in late May, so he'd known her for over a month now. Still, he recognized the truth in the fiction. It really does shoot you out in another dimension. The proof was that he found it amusing and even slightly charming to be woken up by cocky farm animals two hours before dawn.

He stared at his face in the mirror as he brushed his teeth, then rinsed his mouth with bottled water. This new state of heart didn't feel at all disloyal to Yvette. For some time now he had begun to imagine that Yvette's soul was already in the next place, waiting for him. He believed it was Yvette who had sent him this gift because she could see that his time on earth would be long.

He looked up at the bare clay tiles of the ceiling. "Yvette," he mouthed. "Thank you, baby."

Sylvia wouldn't see it that way, of course, but he decided not to worry, there was no need to act on anything at this point. For now, he just wanted to enjoy the feeling of being totally smitten, like slipping into a warm bath on a cold winter's day.

He stepped into his rubber flip-flops, took his shaver, shaving foam, soap box, and towel and headed down the hall to the shared shower. Inside, there was no electricity, and the only light came through in beams of sunshine blasting through the perforations in the decorative brick that butted up to the ceiling. The shower had a single knob and a single temperature— freezing cold. He remembered the innkeeper's suggestion that he shower in the afternoon, because her method of warming frigid well water consisted of piping it into a large outdoor cistern that was painted black in order to absorb the sun's heat during the day. But he was a creature of habit, and so he stuck one shin into the spray and grimaced as he forced himself to step into its stream. Goose bumps sprang up on his arms and chest. He almost cried out as the needles bounced off his chest, and he soaped himself up in record-breaking speed.

As he showered, he wondered if Monica had thought about him as she laid her head on her pillow the night before. He felt himself grow warm down below at the recollection of holding her for a brief moment the night before. He impressed himself with his body's healthy reaction to the memory, considering that he was standing in a cascade of ice water.

As he dried himself with a towel, the warm, salt-heavy air lifted the chill. A cloud passed over his breezy morning humor when he thought of the difficulty that this new beginning might face: Monica was not comfortable with his circumstances; she had made that clear last night. Still, he understood that he had entered a space of possibilities. Existence in this intoxicating space was usually the privilege of the very young—where some aspect of the future can still be impacted by boldness, imagination, and luck.

THE *POSADA,* GUESTHOUSE, was built in a square, in the tradition of the old Spanish colonial style, with an overgrown courtyard at its center. On the inside, each room along the edges of the square opened directly to a hall lined with wicker chairs and rockers in various states of disrepair. Will found Bruce sitting in the hallway, drinking his coffee and talking to an old man. They both faced the garden, which was alive with the strange clicks, chirps, and calls of tropical birds, frogs, and insects.

There were few guests at the *posada.* In the dining room Will got a cup of coffee and a slice of flat, sweet, delicious breakfast bread rolled in sesame seeds. He pondered the day ahead: more meetings with the Caracol staff. He had to call in to work. He had left at the height of the Mystic Victorian project, and even though his father and brother had told him not to worry, he had serious concerns about their juggling the finances in his absence.

Despite his concerns about Yvette and the clinic, the trip was an unexpected mental vacation. He liked El Salvador, at least he was impressed with the natural beauty he had seen on the trip down from the capital—the looming volcanoes, the lush mountains, and the dark, desolate virginity of Negrarena. He was surprised that the capital itself was so hypercommercialized. His only point of reference was Puerto Rico, since he had never been anywhere else in Latin America. Despite Puerto Rico being part of the United States, the two places were similar in the blocky, concrete constructions of the middle class, the iron bars over the windows, the walls and gates and thick foliage that waved in the tropical air. But even the wealthiest Puerto Ricans didn't necessarily have the live-in servants that were commonly employed by middle-class Salvadorans. "Even the maids here have maids," Bruce had said. "You can get a live-in to work full-time, six days a week, for about a hundred and twenty dollars a month. I pay almost that much in Connecticut just to have my house cleaned once."

The part Will was not prepared for was the shocking, highly visible poverty—children running around naked, little huts made of adobe and sticks, or the occasional rash of shacks made out of tinplate and cartons. There were barefoot men peddling enormous bundles of coal or wood, which they carried on their shoulders like Atlas bearing the weight of the world. And despite the billboards advertising American brands, the place had a certain rawness—a feeling that its origins were closer to the surface, less diluted by the outside world, more cleanly contained. Perhaps the inability of the largest part of the population to afford imports kept the culture a bit unspoiled.

Will sat down on a rocker with his coffee and warm, fragrant bread next to Bruce and the old man. The old man, who hailed from Venezuela, had a white mustache that didn't match his thick, black eyebrows. He said that his grandson was at Caracol, but had not responded to treatment. He claimed he had seen two patients get up and walk out with their relatives. He pointed a finger at Will's face, got really close, and said, in Spanish, "Your wife could emerge. Get ready."

"Ready?"

The man nodded. "She won't be the same person, though, you know that?" He pressed his thumb between his index and middle finger, as if lowering the plunger of a needle. "The venom is to brain stupor"—he pointed to his head—"like a jumper cable to a dead car battery."

"A battery has to be in a certain state to accept the charge," Will replied.

"Exactly," the man said. "That's the unknown factor—does this person have any capacity left? And then, what's it going to look like when that brain receives the charge? One of the patients left Caracol a raving lunatic, strapped to a wheelchair up to the neck. By coming here you're greatly increasing the chances of an emergence but abandoning the gentleness of a slow, natural awakening. The person is altered by the jump forward in their capacity to be conscious."

Will's recall of Monica's words outside her house in Connecticut coincided with her appearance in the hallway. *I felt something when I massaged her, Will. I felt life.* He felt a little current wash through his body, and he wondered if it was obvious because he noticed Bruce looking at him oddly. Will stood up as she approached and the two older men followed suit.

"Did you all hear the rooster and the dog making all that racket this morning?" Monica said. She was wearing a marigold sundress, fitted on top and falling loose almost to her ankles, with a white seashell necklace around her neck. Her hair was twisted behind her head, and a few coils of it had escaped and curled at the base of her neck. She wore no makeup except for a soft wash of lip gloss. The scent of acetone followed her, and the nails on her fingers and toes were a shiny, wet, pale pink. Her eyes seemed a bit darker today, green and speckled like the skin on an avocado. He laced his fingers behind his head and dared to take in a long, thirsty look at her while her father looked directly at him. Monica was the most refreshing sight he had ever laid eyes on, clean and simple and beautiful. Her presence implied coolness and sensual joy: a glimpse of cascading water on a hot, stifling day.

The older men groaned at the mention of the noisy animals, and the old man said he had searched for a machete to slice off the rooster's head, but had had no luck because it was too dark to find anything. Monica laughed and kissed her father lightly on the cheek. She looked up. "And you, my friend?" she said to Will.

"I woke up a new man today," he said. "C'mon. I'll show you where they keep the coffee." As she followed him into the dining room, he wondered if indeed it was her gaze that he felt run up and down his body, lingering somewhere in the middle—or if it was just his own memory of watching her last night, mixed with a bit of wishful thinking.

To conjure last night's sense of intimacy and camaraderie, Will thought he'd pick up the conversation at the point they had left off. "What about Maximiliano's wife?" he whispered to Monica as a servant woman put yet another wheel of cheese bread upon the dining room table.

Monica looked at him, startled. "What about her?"

"You said he had a wife. What ever happened to her?"

"Can we talk about her after I've had my coffee? Tell me how Yvette is doing."

Will poured himself another cup of coffee and took a sip, then handed her a clean set of silverware. "And what makes you think I want to discuss Yvette's imprisonment before I've had *my* morning coffee?"

She clinked her empty mug against his. "That's your second cup." He noticed that she carefully examined the inside of her mug, then took a napkin and wiped it before she let him pour her coffee.

"Why'd you do that?"

"Bug parts," she said. "Welcome to the jungle."

BRUCE AND WILL headed to Caracol at eight, but Monica chose to lounge around the guesthouse during the morning hours. A driver would come get her around eleven. She felt relieved to have some time to herself after the excitement of the last few days.

Monica was grateful for her own restraint the night before and resolved to try to avoid being alone with Will. She thought about Yvette, tried to imagine what her life with Will had been like. Had they been happy? Monica didn't know for sure, but her guess was that they had been happy in a normal, if not extraordinary, way. Sylvia had shown her some snapshots she kept around to try to help Yvette remember her own life. Monica could see that Yvette had indeed been pretty, and that she had been social. There were even a few pictures of old boyfriends. "Will understands," Sylvia had said. "Showing her these pictures can help her reconstruct her past." But one photo in the pile had made Sylvia frown, one of Yvette holding hands with a tall, dark-haired hunter who was dangling a dead pheasant in the other hand. Sylvia had scratched at the surface of the photo and said, "Now why would she want to remember you?" And she returned the photo to the pile.

Monica thought it would be a privilege to witness Yvette's unlikely recovery, to witness impossibility melting into miracle, to watch the emptiness of grief flush and engorge with relief, gratitude, awe, and love. It would be a gift to all, a sign that God is neither cruel nor passive, that He was at least willing to meet man halfway. Being smitten with Will made her understand what beauty and light this girl would return to. It would allow her to cheer in a louder voice. Will was Yvette's to keep, and Monica did not want to covet what was intended for another—especially someone as helpless as Yvette.

Monica sat in one of the rocking chairs and listened to the birds in the courtyard while she glanced at one of the local newspapers. She made a mental note to call in to work, call Paige, Marcy, and Kevin. She was about to get up to inquire about using a public phone when she remembered the shell catalogs. She felt like having more coffee, so she went to get the catalogs out of her room and sat back in the rocking chair, lazily leafing through the last of the pages she hadn't yet seen, pausing at length only when she ran across mollusk discoveries and interviews with marine biologists.

What caught her eye about the *Hexaplex bulbosa,* or swollen murex, was that it had been discovered in Costa Rica. Most of the new discoveries were in Indo-Pacific waters; Central American discoveries were rarer. This shell had rose-colored bands and was unusually inflated through the body, with a long foot and large spines with jagged edges. She studied it for a moment and scanned the text below, which was written in a print that was tediously small. She was about to turn the page when a word snagged her attention like a protruding nail. By now she had already turned the page, and she flipped back, wondering if she hadn't just imagined it. If the page had been stuck, she would have moved on. But, no, there it was, at the end of the paragraph. The name of the discoverer.

"Borrero."

Monica shook her head. What were the chances? And in Central America.

Scientific protocol did not include listing the person's first name, so the book offered no more information. Had one of her estranged cousins been inspired by her mother's collection at Caracol? It was certainly possible. But to actually discover a new species of mollusk was the work of a careerist. If Bruce insisted they be secretive about their family ties—well, she would just have to research it on her own. It wasn't that hard to do, considering she had been planning on calling Paige, researcher extraordinaire. Paige did fund-raising research for UConn's development office, and she had access to a universe of members-only commercial and academic journals, databases, and archives. Monica looked at the picture of the shell again. It had been found in a researchers' expedition off the Panamic coast of Costa Rica, in 1999.

Borrero.

She skipped the extra cup of coffee and ran to find a phone.

LETICIA RAMOS looked vaguely familiar to Monica. She was in her fifties—short, squat, with graying hair pulled back into a bun. When she smiled, she flashed a row of lab-coat-white teeth as perfect as piano keys, which were striking against her dark skin. Bruce and Will were sitting in the two chairs across from her desk. Bruce had just finished interviewing her. Monica sensed tension in the room as she stood at the doorway. "May I come in?" she asked.

Will stood and offered her his chair, and Monica accepted it while a passing staff member brought in another, then returned with a tray of small china coffee cups for everyone. "I hope I'm not interrupting," Monica said. "It sounded like you were finishing up."

"We were," Leticia said eagerly. Will flashed Monica a look that suggested the contrary. He forced the conversation to return to issues of regulation and accountability, and Monica, who sat observing in silence, noticed that half-moons of moisture had sprung up under Leticia Ramos's armpits. Monica studied the face. She had seen her before. But where? She was connected to the Borreros in some way—not by blood, of that she was sure. Was she related by marriage? Was she a step? An ex?

"Whenever you're ready," a voice said out in the hall.

The men stood. "This is my daughter, Dr. Fernanda Mendez," Leticia said. "She is the brain behind this clinic."

So there *was* a real Fernanda behind the old pseudonym. Monica turned and looked behind her. It took less than a second for her to figure out who these women were. Fernanda was about her own age and looked very much like Leticia, except for one thing: the unforgettable, pumpkin-colored eyes of Maximiliano Campos.

Monica stood and held out her hand. "Hi, I'm Monica, his daughter," she said, pointing at Bruce. "You look familiar to me," Monica dared. "Did you by chance go to grade school in a little town called El Farolito?"

The woman smiled, baring a row of tiny, coffee-stained teeth that were too small for her mouth. "As a matter of fact I did live in El Farolito," she said, and paused, waiting for Monica.

"I lived with my aunt for a short time, and I was enrolled in school at El Farolito for a few months," Monica lied. "I was quiet, you wouldn't remember me, but I never forget a face." Monica didn't dare look at her father, lest she invite reckless denial.

"Who was your teacher, do you remember?" Fernanda asked.

"Oh, gosh, I don't remember."

"Well, then, we'll have to get reacquainted while you're here," Fernanda said. "We can talk about the good old days." She rolled her eyes at the last part, then paused, cocking her head. "I'm surprised I don't remember you. El Farolito is a poor town in the middle of nowhere. Someone like you, with those green eyes, would have stood out."

Monica chuckled dryly but didn't reply. Bruce flashed her a look of warning, got up, and headed toward the door.

"How are you two related to the Borreros?" Will asked casually, slipping his hands into his pockets and delivering Monica's shoe an almost imperceptible, conspiratorial kick.

Fernanda's chest and voice rose with pride. "My grandmother was the nanny of several Borrero children, including Alma Borrero. And when Magnolia Borrero was old, my grandmother took care of her."

". . . Grandmother on her father's side," Leticia clarified.

"Yes, and Doña Magnolia Borrero left my grandmother a nice sum of money that paid for my medical school. So my mother and I have close ties to the family. I originally learned about the potential of cone venom from my father," Fernanda said, hands on her hips, orange eyes suddenly bright. "The Borreros already had this history with seashell collecting, and they had the facility, the capital, and the interest to pursue a cone venom study. It's a marriage made in heaven."

"And speaking of marriage . . . ," her mother said in a sing-song voice, smiling brightly. Monica couldn't help but think that it was a damn shame Fernanda hadn't inherited those fabulous teeth.

Fernanda waved at her mother in a dismissive, embarrassed way, but Leticia persisted. "Fernanda is engaged to one of Doña Borrero's nephews," she said proudly. "He's a chemist."

"Congratulations," they all said, and Fernanda nodded her head modestly.

Monica suddenly noticed the three-carat engagement ring on Fernanda's short, stubby finger. By American standards it was huge, but by Salvadoran standards it belonged in a museum.

"So interesting" was all Monica could manage. "And is your grandmother still alive?"

"Barely," Fernanda said. "She works at the Borr-Lac dairy plant, not too far from here. She's so old she hardly does any real work, but she hates being idle. The Borreros keep her on the payroll because she's a family relic."

Suddenly, Fernanda slapped her hands together, signaling that chitchat time was over and she had more important things to do. "So, Mr. Winters, Mr. Lucero—what are we going to talk about today?"

"I want to talk about competence," Will said, clapping his hands together in mockery of the bossy way she had clapped her own. "I want you to convince me that you know what you're doing."

Fernanda pursed her lips and nodded. She pointed down the hall. "My office is down the hall to your right"—she motioned to Will—"please." They all shuffled out into the hall. Will and Bruce stepped into the office and Fernanda followed them in and closed the door.

Monica and Leticia Ramos were left alone in the hall. Leticia turned to Monica slowly, her head turned to the side, as if someone far away had just called her name. She blinked twice, then smiled oddly, a cold smile with only the teeth. She said, "Nice to meet you . . . Monica . . . Winters." And in that slow and astonished pronunciation Monica understood, without a question, that the woman who had once been Maximiliano Campos's common-law wife had just now figured out exactly who Monica was.

THE MEETING had left Monica giddy. She wondered if Bruce had figured out the connection to Max or if he was truly as distracted with his vigorous note-taking as he appeared. Leticia Ramos, the only staff member at Caracol who would remember Alma when she was alive, had picked up on the mother-daughter resemblance. Surely she would tell someone and it would get back to the Borrero uncles, the ones who'd cut Monica out of the will. But so what? After Bruce walked out of the doctor's office, he would have all the raw material he needed for his story. The two of them would go home in a few days anyway. Besides, she wasn't here to take a piece of their empire or to discredit the program. If anything, they all had one thing in common: everyone wanted the venom program to work.

Monica sighed. Maybe, just maybe, the whole money saga had two sides; maybe there had been some miscommunication somewhere along the way. But it seemed like wishful thinking, since according to Bruce, they had essentially erased her from the family. No, the Borreros would undoubtedly be threatened by their presence. She decided against telling Bruce about her moment with Leticia. He would only get more nervous than he already was.

So the old nanny Francisca was still around, Monica thought with a mix of nostalgia and delight. Francisca had been so worn-out by raising hellions like Alma, Max, and several other Borrero urchins that by the time she got to taking care of quiet little Monica, she had been a loving but tired grandmotherly figure. Monica thought she would definitely like to pay her a visit.

Monica headed toward the lobby and looked at her watch. Three o'clock. By now Paige would have spent her lunch break scouring for information on the Costa Rican shell. Monica guessed the registrant of the shell would turn out to be Fernanda's fiancé, the chemist. Which cousin was he? Monica wondered. The doctor had not said his name. Monica took inventory of her Borrero second cousins—not much more than a blurry memory of a crop of scruffy schoolboys: Rodolfo? No—too young. Alejandro? Marco, maybe. She wondered what had changed in their prideful code of behavior to allow him to marry so far down socially. Perhaps it was just a matter of history repeating itself—perhaps this cousin was the rebel du jour, and Fernanda was the new Max.

Looking into Fernanda's all-too-familiar eyes had made Monica's head feel swimmy with the sensation of peering into the past. She had the feeling that she was rushing toward something, like being on a ride at an amusement park; she was no longer certain of where she stood in the context of things from one minute to the next.

There was a public phone in the lobby of Caracol, across from the seashell displays. Monica looked at her watch and dug her calling card out of her purse.

"PAIGE NORTON, Development Research."

"Monica."

"Hello? Hello? Hello?"

"Hello? Paige can you hear me?"

"Monica? I can barely hear you."

"Now?"

"Yeah, hi there. Hey, I'm running to a meeting, so I can't talk for more than a sec, but the good news is I found it. The shell was registered with the Conchologists of America in 1999 to someone named Alma Borrero, who also happens to be a current member of the COA, with the membership dues paid up right through next month."

Monica chewed on her bottom lip.

"Are you there?"

"Yeah."

"Since this doesn't make any sense, I called the COA. As it turns out, this Alma Borrero penned an article that will appear in the next issue of their magazine, describing the adverse effects of biopharmaceutical conotoxins on the human nervous system. They sent me an abstract—something about the treatment causing extreme aggression in trial studies on mice."

Monica was sitting on a padded bench near the pay phone. She was playing with the plastic calling card, flipping it over and over as she listened. She pressed the edges of the card until they left a white line on the yolks of her thumb and index finger. Pressing even harder, she whispered, "There isn't anyone else in the Borrero family named Alma. No adults anyway."

"A married name then," Paige said. "How about someone using it as a pseudonym? Or perhaps it's just someone unrelated to you. . . . Is Borrero a common name? Like Lopez and Martinez?"

"Not at all," Monica said, curling her bare feet under her marigold dress.

"I gotta go, love. But I'll work late tonight and research the name itself. I'm curious to see what other traces are out there on this person."

Monica hung up and went to sit down on one of the sofas in the lobby. She pulled the specimen catalog out of her day bag. She spread it open on her lap and went to the page she had dog-eared, to the *Hexaplex bulbosa*. The plain little shell was suddenly a little calcified box of secrets. She sat for a moment, trying to clear her mind, figure out the strange riddle, and calm her creeping nerves. On top of everything else, Paige had hit upon controversy over the use of cone toxins on humans, a discovery even her father had failed to make—or mention.

Despite the warm air, a shiver ran up Monica's arms. She felt the presence of a thousand seashells, curled around the axis of their own mysterious past and glowing in the soft light of the display cases across the lobby. She tilted her head and heard the first stirring of something, or someone, approaching; like wind rustling through trees in the distance. *No one ever found her body.*

The specimen catalog slid off her lap and landed upside

down on the tile floor. Monica didn't pick it up, but rather remained perfectly still, her spine straight. Her green eyes blinked at the glass cases in disbelief, as if all those pale pink lips had suddenly abandoned their calcified state and had curled themselves around those words before returning to their silence and mystery. She remained that way for a long time, until Will appeared, sat down beside her, took her hand in his, and asked her if something was wrong.

MONICA HAD AGREED to massage Yvette and three other patients at five o'clock that evening. Since her mind was racing, she welcomed the opportunity to occupy her hands. She believed in doing the most difficult thing first, so she chose to begin with Yvette.

Yvette's eyes had ceased their former ping-ponging, but her hands kept up a strange, almost constant motion of combing or digging. Her skin seemed to have turned a yellowish hue, and her lips were chapped and stiff. Will dipped a washcloth in a cup of water and moistened her lips. Monica volunteered her favorite stick of lip balm, which she later threw out in the bathroom trash, as if it were contaminated with Yvette's decay and ill fate.

"Can I help with the massage?" Will asked, trying to still one of Yvette's unnervingly busy hands.

"Sure," Monica said. "Crank the foot lift on the bed up about a foot." After he had elevated his wife's legs, Will cupped his wife's small feet in his hands, just as he had on the day of that first massage.

Will said, "Look at those hands. They won't stop digging. How can I get her to relax?"

"We can both massage her hands. It's a very nice feeling to have both hands or both feet rubbed simultaneously." Monica pointed to the night table. "Grab some lotion."

It worked, because Yvette's hands stilled almost immediately. Soon, Monica's mind drifted back to the conversation with Fernanda Mendez and what Paige had said on the phone. Monica was tugging at Yvette's pinkie finger when Will said, "Relax, honey," and for a moment, Monica thought that he had been speaking to her. When she recognized her error, she felt her stomach recoil. As if she could read what was going through Monica's head, Yvette abruptly withdrew her hand from Monica and slowly turned her head toward Will.

Will fixed his eyes on something behind Monica. Monica turned and saw an electric fan on top of a dresser, oscillating soundlessly into the space above them. Monica turned back to Will and said, "I know what you're thinking, and, no, it wasn't the cold air. Will, I think she turned away from *me*."

Will shook his head. "If she could do that, then she could get up out of that bed and make a ham sandwich. You're tired, Monica, I can see it in your eyes. Why don't you get some sleep?"

Monica shook her head and rubbed her eyes. "I have three other customers. Now get out of my way." Will sat down in a chair across the room and opened up a newspaper. After a while, he wandered out of the room.

Almost as soon as he left, Yvette's fingers recommenced their roaming and digging. Monica was massaging one of Yvette's quadriceps, lost in thought again, when a thin, paper-white hand locked onto her wrist, then squeezed hard. Monica reacted as if she had been burned: she cried out and yanked her arm away. She rubbed her wrist, searching Yvette's face for a sign of life. There was nothing. Her brown eyes were as vacant as a doll's.

Monica was so unnerved that she cut the massage short. Eluding Will, she packed up her tools and told the nurse on duty that she wasn't feeling well, and that she would conduct the balance of the massages over the next two days. She found the driver and went back to the guesthouse, tumbling quickly into an empty, dreamless sleep.

"LET'S GO to the little store again," Will said as he stood outside Monica's door at the guesthouse two hours later. "I want a beer."

"I'll pass." Monica opened the door a bit. "I had to drag myself here from the infirmary. Maybe my dad would like to go."

"I don't enjoy his company quite as much as yours."

Monica shrugged. "It's time to settle in. Watch some TV."

"There's no TV in the rooms, only that minuscule black-and-white one in the dining room, and there's already five women glued to it watching the stupid *novela*."

"So what do you want from me? A coloring book and some crayons?"

He looked at his watch. "It's eight o'clock. What am I supposed to do for two hours?"

"Start a journal." Monica covered her mouth and yawned. "Or would you prefer to study one of the specimen catalogs?"

He grabbed her by the wrist. "Put your shoes on, you're coming with me."

"Excuse me?"

"You're the one that's actually from this boring place. If you're not going to take me dancing, then the least you can do is buy me a cold beer."

She took a deep breath and gave him a look that she hoped communicated all the reasons they shouldn't be alone together. It didn't work because he just kept looking at her, eyebrows raised in anticipation.

"Okay, one beer." She looked at her watch and pretended to

yawn. "Hopefully your life's story won't take more than an hour."

MONICA FIGURED THAT if she could keep control of the conversation, then she could keep the evening pleasant and free from uncomfortable and compromising moments. "So where did you meet Yvette?" Monica began. "Did I hear Sylvia say that she worked for you?"

Will took a swig of beer and settled back into his chair in a way that some men do when they're about to tell a long story. "I was nineteen," he began. "I dropped out of the engineering department at UConn and took a job as a department manager at a large store. Yvette worked for me part-time. She was starting her freshman year at a local community college, and when we started dating, she hounded me about going back to school. It worked, and I was back at UConn the next semester, this time in the business program. My parents went wild—she was smart, pretty, polite, and a good influence on me. That she was of Puerto Rican descent was a *huge* cherry on top."

"Do you think that matters?" Monica asked.

"To some degree. It does make things smoother if you know what's expected of you, culturally speaking."

"And when did you decide to get married? Was it love at first sight?"

Will laughed. "You sound like the chorus from *Grease*."

"'Tell me more, tell me more,'" Monica sang.

"I need a cigar first," Will said, and stood up. "Care to join me?"

Monica shook her head. "Not tonight."

When he was seated again with the last of the store's dried-up cigars, he got back into the long-story position and drew in a good long puff.

"So how did you know that Yvette was the one?" Monica asked.

He looked up, slowly. Monica knew by his expression, before he even spoke, that he was about to confess something. He looked off to the side for a moment, blew out his smoke, and said, "The crazy thing is I almost backed out of the wedding."

IT WAS WINTER, and Will had gone to visit a buddy who had the flu and was stuck in his dorm at the UConn campus. The friend was the type who would die before seeking medical help, and his girlfriend had broken up with him a few days before. Will was worried about him and so trekked up to campus after a snowstorm, on treacherous, icy roads. The afternoon was gloomy and dark, and he struggled through snowdrifts and footpaths in construction boots, his toes wooden with cold. When he got to the dorm, his friend's room was empty. Will walked around, checking the bathroom and asking for him, but no one knew where he was. A half hour later, Will was about to give up. On his way out, he happened to glance out the window of the dormitory's main hallway, to the open field on the back side of the building. He stopped when he saw his friend's figure standing out in a foot and a half of snow, recognizable by the bumblebee-colored ski jacket. The friend had just finished digging a giant heart shape in the snow. Inside the heart he had written, in letters as big as a person, "I love you, Alison," and was looking up, occasionally throwing snowballs at an upper-story window. Apparently, his gesture was being ignored by the ungrateful Alison. An hour later, Will succeeded in dragging his lovesick friend to the infirmary, but what ailed him was far more serious than the threat of the flu.

Later that night, Will dreamed of the heart carved in the snow. In his dream, he was filling in the heart with words for

Yvette. He was trying to spell out *Te amo,* "I love you" in Spanish, but the letters kept rearranging themselves to spell out a far less flattering sentiment: *Me ato*—"I tie myself down."

Will woke up with a weight of uncertainty on his chest, wondering for the first time if what he felt for Yvette was anything less than real love. Maybe, just maybe, what he took for love was no more than contentment and comfort. Worried, he skipped work and took a ferry out to Block Island, where his brother, Eddie, was spending the weekend with his wife. Will found them at their cottage and told them what had happened. Clenching his fists, Will lamented that he'd never risk pneumonia for Yvette. "Maybe love *should* make you do crazy stuff like that."

Eddie and his wife had assured him that his friend's antics were more about getting attention than demonstrating mature love. By the end of the weekend they had him convinced that his friend's gesture wasn't passion, but rather, immaturity. A year later, Will and Yvette were married.

MONICA THOUGHT he had finished his story, but he surprised her by pulling his chair closer to her and continuing, "About a year after our wedding, I went into business with my father and Eddie. It made sense to delay having kids for a while. After five years, I told Yvette that I was ready, that she could go off the pill whenever she wanted."

For some reason she didn't quite understand, Monica felt the need to look away.

"Yvette had a friend who had almost died in childbirth, and so she was extremely intimidated by the whole idea." Will hung his head for a moment. "I tell you, Monica—I wish we had had a child, because then I would have a part of her." He didn't look at her as he said it, but Monica could tell by his quick blinking that his eyes had become moist for a brief moment.

"God, I'm sorry," she mumbled. And she couldn't think of another thing to say, so she waved to the shopkeeper. "Please. I need another beer."

AT MIDNIGHT, when the store closed, they were still talking. Monica had shared every last detail of the day: that Leticia knew who she was, her conversation with Paige, the specimen book, the hints of controversy surrounding conotoxin treatment that Paige had found, her confusion about Alma's name being out there in the world. Monica told him that she had decided to visit with Francisca, the former Borrero nanny. Francisca, Maximiliano Campos's mother, had been a kind and loving caretaker to both Monica and Alma for decades. Francisca was also Dr. Fernanda Mendez's grandmother and might be able to provide information no one else would.

Will said, "Yvette has testing tomorrow morning, and they want Sylvia and me out of the way. The Caracol drivers said they'd take me anywhere I want for a fee. Let's sleep in tomorrow morning, then go to Borr-Lac around ten."

When the trip was settled, the questions outlined, the theories discussed, they sat in satisfied silence for a moment. Will looked out the door, toward the star-filled sky. He smiled. "She knows what she's doing."

Monica looked at him, confused.

"Yvette. She plotted out this whole thing, this convoluted road with its little trail of bread crumbs leading us to this remote, unlikely place," he said, still looking out at the sky. He pointed up. "That's where the real Yvette is, you know."

Monica looked up to where he was pointing, as if she might indeed see a young woman's figure floating over the Salvadoran coastline.

"There's a reason for everything, Monica, and I have a feeling we're about to find out why we're here." Then, he put down his beer and gave her a charged look, but unlike her earlier attempt, his was dead accurate in communicating meaning. She understood that what was happening under the surface was deeper than attraction, perhaps even beyond admiration.

How had this happened? Who was supposed to watch the milk so it didn't boil over? She thought she had been vigilant.

Monica looked away and coolly said, "Kevin and I decided we're going to host a party for you and Yvette." She crushed a mosquito between her hands and smiled. "After Yvette's interview on *Oprah*." Then, she pretended to yawn again, trying to be more convincing this time. She laced her fingers and stretched. "Time to go back. I'm tired."

On the way home, she told Will that she was grateful to have found a true friend in him. She made sure she repeated the word *friend* three times, and when they said good-night, she just waved.

In her bed that night, exhausted beyond reason, Monica couldn't sleep. On top of the maelstrom of emotions she was feeling at being "home," there was Will, and their disturbing drift toward intimacy. That cold and unnerving wrist grip from Yvette had served as a stern reminder of exactly whom he still belonged to.

Monica wanted to go to see Francisca Campos alone, but Will insisted she should have someone with her. Sylvia was idle that morning, and so Monica was worried that it would be rude and inappropriate to exclude her from any excursions. Will said it was not a problem; he had overheard someone talking about a religious festival going on in a nearby village, charmingly named El Delirio—the Spanish word for "euphoria." Will had instructed Monica to invite Sylvia, but to be sure to mention that the streets of El Delirio were cobblestone. "She has bad knees," he said. "She'd never go."

Feeling a bit sneaky yet excited about seeking out her old nanny, Monica had done as Will instructed. She described to Sylvia what one could typically expect from a Salvadoran village festival: "Folkloric dance, marimba music, sawdust art on the concrete of the central plaza, and the effigy of an unheard-of saint, usually made up with far too much rouge, paraded through the streets."

"You kids go," Sylvia said, rubbing her knees. "And don't

forget to pray to the unheard-of saint for our Yvette." She smiled sheepishly and held out her hands. "You never know."

Monica felt a pang of guilt, but reminded herself that at the core of this trip was their intention to know more about the clinic and Yvette's treatment.

Bruce was working on his laptop in an empty office of the clinic, so Monica and Will slipped past the lobby and jumped into a van with a driver who would take them to the Borr-Lac plant and back for the equivalent of three dollars.

AT THE LOBBY OF BORR-LAC, Monica asked to speak with Francisca Campos. A floor supervisor gave them hairnets to wear and walked them through the dairy plant that Monica's great-grandfather and his two brothers had built in 1918.

Monica laughed heartily at the sight of Will in a hairnet, which made his ears stick out.

"It's not your best look either, cafeteria lady."

The milk was transported in clear plastic tubing from vat to vat, great mammarian ducts that nourished the whole country. The smell of fresh cow milk—musky and thick—made tears spring up in Monica's eyes. The scent took her back to a morning when Abuelo had taken her to watch the cows being milked, back before the fancy machines. She remembered the workers loading trucks with aluminum tanks that were still warm with the animals' body heat. Now, everything had changed—the facility was modern and immaculate, even air-conditioned.

"Francisca's very old now," the supervisor warned as Will and Monica followed her along a wall made of air-packed cheese bricks. "I normally don't just let people in like this, but she has a hard time walking all this way. She's such a relic that *los jefes* let her work here no matter what. She can't produce much, because she has cataracts, but she doesn't want to retire. Here she is. . . . Doña Francisca, you have visitors."

Francisca had shriveled into a raisin of an old lady. She had a sprout of gray hair growing on her chin. She pursed her lips as she searched their faces and began to struggle out of her chair. "Please stay seated," Monica said, kneeling before her. "Do you remember me? I was a little girl when you took care of me."

Francisca moved her lips and mumbled. She shook her desiccated head no.

"*Soy Mónica. La hija de la Niña Alma.*"

Her eyes grew enormous. "*Dios mío,*" she said, putting her hand on her heart "So it's true that you're back."

"You know these people?" the supervisor asked.

"*Claro que sí,*" Francisca answered, as if it were the stupidest question in the world. She smiled and put her arms out. "*Mi niña.* I didn't recognize you all grown up. Is this your husband? *Que guapo.*"

They hugged, and Monica was horrified when Francisca kept referring to Will as her husband, despite both of them insisting that they were just "*amigos.*" Even worse, she called everyone round and introduced Monica as the "rightful heiress" of Borr-Lac.

Monica looked over at Will, who was quiet, but staying close, taking it all in. They met every last worker in soft cheeses and tried to explain where Connecticut was, which elicited blank looks until she told them that it was near "*Nuevajork.*" Eventually, she asked to be left alone with Francisca. She hugged the old lady again and told her how much it meant to her to see her again. "You were like a mother to me," Monica said, her voice full of emotion. "Now that my grandmother and mother are gone, and we don't speak to the Borreros, you're the only mother figure I have left. I've missed you."

The old lady pulled at Monica's hands until Monica sat down next to her. She pressed her hands together and closed her eyes. Even though her words were mumbled, Monica could tell by their rhythm that she was saying a Hail Mary. "*Virgen santa, purísima, ilumíname el camino.*" The old woman sat in silent prayer for some time, and not knowing what else to do, Monica scratched at a scab from a mosquito bite on the back of her elbow. Will wandered away for a sampling of freshly made sour cream.

When Francisca opened her ancient eyes, she took Monica's hand and said, "You want to know about your mama. That's why you're here."

Monica looked up to the ceiling, thinking, *So there is a truth to be known.* "Yes," she whispered, then shouted it, because she knew the woman had not heard her. "Tell me."

Francisca nodded. "The Holy Mother has given me permission to speak." The old lady reached into the neck of her flower-print polyester dress and pulled a tissue out from somewhere inside. She dabbed at her upper lip, at the corners of her old, milky eyes. "*Cielito,*" the old lady began, using an endearment from Monica's childhood. "I agree with the Virgin, I think it's time." She gnawed her gums and stared into her tissue, then gripped Monica's hand with surprising strength. "By now you probably know your mother didn't die, right?" Her eyes were suddenly bright. "She survived that terrible incident at El Trovador, where the military killed my Maximiliano. She came to see me before she left for Honduras, because she wanted to tell me how my son died, why, and who did it."

Monica seemed to float above the scene, watching her own face framed in the elastic of that ridiculous hairnet, the half-moons of sweat at the pits of her blouse. She even saw Will come up behind her, and before he kneeled before her, she knew that his face was registering his realization that something monumental was happening, that her heart was undergoing, at this very moment, a molecular reconfiguration.

"Your mama comes to see me sometimes when she's on a research project, living on a big ugly ship that collects samples of things." Francisca sniffed and dabbed at herself some more.

"She was traumatized when my Maximiliano and the others died," she said, pointing a bony finger at her own temple. "I tried to convince her that running away was a mistake, that she would regret it, but she wouldn't listen."

Will asked, "Are you okay?"

She nodded but was seized by an uncontrollable, feverish shivering. "My mother must really hate me," she said, knowing that she sounded like a child, that the word *hate* was a quicker, easier term than what was required. Still, whatever it was, abandonment was just as lonely and boundless and sickening. That her mother was alive was a concept in the realm of the surreal, like the discovery that water is imaginary or that death is purely optional. After that, nothing can make sense anymore.

"She doesn't hate you," Francisca said, and for a second Monica didn't know what she was talking about, so far had she journeyed mentally from her own words. "I don't understand it either," Francisca rasped. "But by now Alma ought to be ready to give you an explanation. She's lived long enough to regret the consequences of her decision."

"Where is she?" Monica whispered, looking around, as if Alma might step out from behind a six-foot vat of curdled milk fat.

"Where a person is physically matters less than where a person is here." Francisca pointed to her heart. "You have to be ready to travel a great emotional distance for her. But she is not far. Physically."

"Is she mentally ill or something?" Monica asked.

"No, nothing like that. It's just that she's one of those people who are very good at looking forward, not back. Most of us around here aren't like that. Some see her as cold for that reason."

"I wasn't expecting any of this," Monica said, shaking her head in disbelief, one hand over her mouth.

Francisca looked distressed. "You didn't know she was alive?

I thought you came here because you knew and wanted to find out where she is."

Monica said, "I didn't know, Francisca. I've always felt that some things didn't add up, but I didn't imagine that she was alive. Where is she now?"

Francisca's eyes clouded and she mashed her gums. She said wearily, "Your mother is trying to shut down my granddaughter's clinic. The whole thing is a great distress for me. I don't want to get caught in the middle. I love them both."

It dawned on Monica that whether the old lady was conscious of it or not, she had an underlying motivation to blow Alma's cover. For most people, blood ties still ranked above loyalty to employers and benefactors; even if those boundaries had become blurred over time.

"So she's here in El Salvador?"

"She's on a research ship, out at sea, on this side of Central America. They come into a port every week for supplies, at a small station owned by the university's new marine school."

So they're still close, Monica thought. How else would an illiterate, elderly woman know that the national university has a new marine school—or that Alma's on a research ship versus any other sort of ship?

Will cleared his throat and spoke. "We're in El Salvador because my wife is being treated at Clinica Caracol. . . . Do you know why Alma wants to shut it down?" Will spoke in coarse, "Newyorican" Spanish.

Francisca shrugged. "She says the studies of *veneno* are too immature, that it shouldn't be used on people." Suddenly, she brightened and said, "Fernanda is marrying your cousin Marco. They're in business together."

Ignoring the last comment, Will said, "Alma thinks the cone venom treatment is dangerous? My God, my wife has another treatment scheduled in two days."

The old lady shook her head and squinted one eye. "I wonder if Alma isn't just jealous. She always wanted to find those cones."

They all looked at each other for a moment.

"She has a point," Monica mumbled in English to Will, who looked pale with worry.

Francisca took a deep breath and exhaled, her old breath stinking of all the years she had swallowed. "Marco is a Borrero, and in El Salvador, you know that what a Borrero wants, a Borrero gets. That hasn't changed. And in El Salvador, Alma is a dead Borrero. She doesn't exist. She would have to *choose* to exist."

Monica said, "So why did you think I knew?"

Francisca smiled. "Because you're her daughter, and you're smart. I knew you'd figure it out eventually. Years ago, I told Alma that if you ever came looking for her, I'd tell you everything I know." She pointed up. "I just had to check with the Virgin to make sure it was the right thing."

"So why did she do this, Francisca, why?"

Francisca shook her old head, and the floppy skin underneath her chin continued to vibrate even when she'd stilled her head. "That part is for her to tell, *Cielito*."

"Where is the marine station, and how do I find out when the ship comes in?" Monica asked.

"What day is it?"

"Monday."

"It comes in on Wednesday," she replied. "At noon."

IN THE BACKSEAT of the van, Monica dropped her head over the edge of the seat, her hands folded over her stomach, her eyes shut tight. Will slid into the bench seat next to her. He lifted her head and positioned it on his shoulder. He spread his fingers across her forehead, as if to check for a fever. Again, he asked if she was all right. As the driver pulled onto the road that would take them back to the clinic, Monica repeated the old woman's words: *Your mother came to see me before she left for Honduras.* She turned to Will and said, "What the hell am I supposed to do with that?"

Will shook his head, eyes wide. He looked out the glass of the van's window, toward the hulking presence of a volcano in the distance. "The way I see it, there's only one thing you can do, Monica. Find your mother . . . and ask her yourself."

This stupid bug must think I'm deaf, Yvette thought. *They don't have mosquitoes like this in Connecticut. Where the hell am I, anyway?* The insect drove its stinger into her neck. What followed was a maddening itch, a tickle so intense that it made her wish she could scratch it with a rake. The prickles peaked into a maddening crescendo; torture only a hair away from an explosion of relief; her only obstacle was her inability to scratch herself.

Yvette knew her mother was in the room by her scent. Was Sylvia the only person left on the planet who still wore Jean Naté? Yvette concentrated on trying to lift her hand to swat the vampiric pest that was still circling for a second go at it. Something is happening, she thought. I can wiggle my fingers and toes.

In the distance, she heard the ocean; the waves of high tide were savage, violent, and unfamiliar. The sound was far enough away to distract her, if only for a second, from the infuriating itch of her skin. She knew that someone would be back to stick another needle in her spine. Now, she willingly submitted to the delirium in exchange for the rewards of the clarity and alertness that consistently followed. Among the last batch of memories she had found the key that connected her to the outside world. She had found the treasure among a pile of useless recollections. It was horrible and shocking footage to watch, but it was the last segment of her life before this. She recognized that this memory was the key that would release her from imprisonment.

I WONDER IF he recognized my car, Yvette thought for the third time as she headed home in her Mustang. The sun was strong and the air smelled like farm manure and wildflowers, but this time she wasn't enjoying the ride nearly as much as she had on the way downtown. She gripped the spongy surface of the steering wheel as she tore down Cider Mill Lane, past an ancient red barn on its green cushion of summer grass. A triangular yellow sign warned of a dangerous curve ahead. She tapped on the brake a little. "Cruel Summer" was playing on the radio and she turned it up as loud as the volume dial would go, thinking it was the perfect song to complement her mood. The car curved with the stone wall that wrapped around a pasture of Holsteins. It wasn't so bad. She sped up again.

Up ahead, Yvette glimpsed a male cardinal sitting on a wood fence. He stood out like a droplet of blood against the lush dark green of the woods behind him. As the car got closer, the bird dove across the road. The instant his tiny claws pushed off the wood fence, Yvette's reflexes computed the speed and distance between her windshield and the bird. Her foot jumped to the brake pedal.

The tire skidded across a patch of sand, while the rear of the car fishtailed in the opposite direction. A second later, the front of the car swung in the direction of the bird. There was a dull thud, and a spray of blood and red feathers appeared across the windshield. Yvette cried out in disgust. Her left foot instinctively jumped to aid her right foot in stopping the car. When she tried to pump the brake with both feet, she recognized a second too late that it was the accelerator. The car lurched forward and climbed over an embankment. Then the car hit something from the front, and she was thrown across the seat. Within that instant of shock, she realized, with complete horror, that she had been so distracted that she had failed to use her seat belt.

All was dark. Water began to creep up her nostrils—or was it blood dripping down? She didn't know. She tried to call someone's name, but it was useless, she couldn't remember whom to call or where she had been headed. She was slipping, drowning, or fainting.

How long ago had that accident happened? Yvette wondered. How long had she been fighting to regain her memory? It didn't matter now, really, because she was almost on the other side. She'd find out more details later, when she arrived.

JUST AS THE CARDINAL'S red wings had sent her into darkness, the mosquito's paper wings were transporting her back to a world of smells and sounds. Why had she been in such a rush? This was the piece that was still missing, and she was curious to find out. She had a sense that she had been upset, or that she had been fleeing. So when the needle slid between her vertebrae, she scrambled to coil up and simplify, as she had done before. It was becoming increasingly difficult, so bloated and bulked up was she with recovered memory.

Yvette decided that it was time to prepare herself for the inevitable ejection to the outside. She looked around at the dungeon that had been her home. She signed her name in the dirt with her torn nails. She had no idea what the date, hour, or year was, so she just wrote "Cruel Summer" next to her name. Maybe someone else would find it and know that there was hope for escape. In the meantime, she got down to the immediate business of forgetting that she'd ever been here.

THAT NIGHT, a storm rolled over the coast. The water was clenched in tense clouds that roiled like the intestines of a huge animal. When the first clap of thunder rattled through everyone's bones, Yvette wrapped her arms around herself, curled up, and began to shake. Will was standing by the door talking to a nurse. He walked up to the bed, and it was as if she had spoken, had said, *Come to bed, honey. Hold me, I'm frightened.*

At first he only took her hand and leaned in, whispering that everything was okay. She thrashed her neck as if to say, *No, it's not.* Will climbed into bed next to her and took her in his arms. "It's okay, honey. It's just thunder." The next boom actually made her jump and Will held her tighter.

A woman entered the room and Will hastened to get out of the bed. He explained that thunder had always frightened his wife. There was the medical talk about the impossibility of Yvette responding to the sound of thunder, but that the reverberation could activate her primal instincts.

"Monica," Yvette heard Will say. "Monica," and "Monica" and "Monica." He said the name with a mix of intimacy and urgency, as if he were speaking to someone who owed him the answer to an important question.

Yvette clenched her teeth until her jaw hurt and her teeth wiggled in their soft pink rows. Will would be so surprised when she burst from this mental paralysis that kept her from moving or speaking or keeping the events of her life in the right order. Right now, she couldn't tell if Will had been lying next to her a few minutes ago or if she was remembering something that happened in the distant past. Still, she was floating just below the surface, looking up. The world looked distorted and

swirled, as if she were looking at it through a wall of glimmering, wet glass.

SEEING WILL COMFORT YVETTE made Monica want to run screaming into the storm and be cleansed once and for all of her unholy desire. She felt dirty, and for the second time that she could remember, she experienced an odd combination of sadness and relief that things weren't going to work out. She chastised herself for forgetting that the heart is an unreliable guide—its advice will always be in favor of love. *Love him,* it urged. *But not so much that you can't give him back.*

As she stood at a window watching the storm over Negrarena, Monica decided that if she couldn't help falling in love with Will during their Salvadoran journey, she could certainly put a stop to it all when they got home. In the meantime, she promised herself that she would never sleep with Will in a moment of weakness. She remembered Yvette's bony grip on her wrist, and it made her shudder. She had told no one about that incident, and she never would. After all, Yvette was a severely brain-damaged woman incapable of communication. Monica had heard over and over about all the meaningless, involuntary actions that were typical of her condition. What had rattled Monica was not Yvette's grip, but the feedback that it elicited from her own conscience.

Bruce was standing in the lobby of Caracol when he heard a van pull up to the carport. He walked over to a stained-glass window and looked out, sighing with relief at the sight of his daughter. Sylvia told him that they had gone to a village festival, but Bruce didn't like the idea of those two running around El Salvador unescorted, for a variety of reasons, only one of which was safety. Will could barely take his eyes off Monica, and she had been uncharacteristically guarded lately. As much as he liked and perhaps even admired Will Lucero, he didn't want to see his daughter ensnared in a dead-end relationship with him. Perhaps, as a father, he was jumping the gun by worrying about the possibility of romance between those two, but he figured it was his parental right. Will's load of emotional and financial baggage was simply unacceptable.

Bruce looked at his watch. The two had been gone for four hours. Not such a long time, really, but he knew that one could change the course of one's life in less than five minutes. He frowned as they walked in.

"Hi, Daddy," Monica said, looking surprised to see him as

she walked in the entrance of the lobby. (When was the last time she had called him "Daddy"?) "Sorry I didn't catch you before I left—we just had to get out of here," Monica said, cinching her fingers around her neck. "Will's gonna ask Sylvia to get ready for dinner. The driver will take us somewhere to eat, then he'll drop us off at the guesthouse and return Sylvia back here. Sound okay with you?"

Bruce nodded, his mood lightening at the mention of food. "I'm tired of *pupusas* every night. I heard there's a nice little seafood place down the way."

"Back in about twenty," Will called out as he disappeared in the direction of the infirmary.

Bruce turned to his daughter and said, "So where was this festival?"

Monica gave him a long look, took his arm, and tugged, leading him outside. "We have to talk," she whispered. "Let's go out on the beach."

They flung their shoes onto the empty sunning patio and headed out to the wide, empty strip of beach. Bruce felt a tightening in his diaphragm, so he took a deep breath to dislodge his tension. He tipped his head from side to side, making an audible crunching sound as he tried to loosen the tightness around his neck. "I'm due for a neck massage," he said, looking for an excuse to delay a discussion that for some reason he was already instinctively dreading. "You've been neglecting your old man."

"Then sit," she said.

The words hadn't left her mouth before Bruce plopped himself down on the sand and took his shirt off, bowing his head forward in anticipation of a massage. As Monica began to rub his neck, he marveled, as he always did, at her talent for such a thing. She truly had a gift for healing. It felt as if she were plucking tightly strung strips of muscle, like guitar chords—

there was pain, release, then a music-like rush of blood flooding the soreness. Pain, release, rush. Pain, release, rush. Ah, she was an artist.

"I'm so glad I sent you to college to study therapy," he mumbled. "Well worth it."

Ten minutes later, when she had relaxed the fierce grip that his sore muscles had on his withering skeleton, she said, "Now lie flat on the sand." He obeyed. She sat down next to him, her legs folded. She faced the water. He was waiting for some kind of bonus scalp or shoulder massage. After a moment, he looked up and saw that her eyes were closed.

"Is that it?"

"Yeah, that's it."

"So what did you want to tell me?"

Monica opened her eyes. She pursed her lips and looked down at her hands for a moment before she spoke. "I didn't go to a festival today, Dad. I visited Francisca Campos." She took a deep breath and said, softly, "Mom's not dead." She opened her eyes and looked at him. They stared at each other for a moment. "Did you know this?"

He looked away, not having a clue what words should be coming out of his mouth. He was glad to be lying down. "No," he said finally. "I know no such thing."

"I asked Paige to do some research on a seashell discovery, an uninteresting little murex found off the coast of Costa Rica last year. The discoverer was listed as 'Borrero.' Paige followed the trail of professional memberships and found an Alma Borrero, born in 1949, now a marine biologist working for the University of Costa Rica. Francisca just confirmed it, Mom's alive."

He sat up and said, "That's ridiculous," even as the idea was already settling into his bones, fizzing up like a hard, white tablet plunked into his bloodstream. Alma had told him, the first time he'd ever been to Negrarena, that she both loathed and craved her parents' moneyed world. She had said that she wished she could start anew somewhere else, somewhere where she wasn't a Borrero and where she wasn't expected to be someone she wasn't and would never be. And if Francisca said Alma was alive, then it was true.

"Dad, you never buried a body."

He took a deep breath. "I don't even know what to say, Monica. All I can say is that I need proof. Besides, why would she . . . ?" His voice trailed off, the sentence severed by the weight of the questions bearing down. He pulled himself up and sat next to Monica, keeping his eyes focused on one house in the distance, with its giant slanted roof. A bird, brown with a white breast, landed a few feet away on the sand and looked at them as if fascinated by their conversation.

Monica said, "If you made her go away, let's say by reporting her and Max to the *militares* . . ." She turned and looked at him, and it took him a moment to understand that this was in fact a question. He felt a sickness rising in his stomach, a tiny spot, shiny and round like a black olive, gleaming and burning in the sponginess of his entrails.

He didn't have a chance to process his answer. She dove upon him in a fierce embrace, a gesture so sudden and unexpected that she knocked him off-balance and he had to put an arm out to support his torso. He opened his arms—the great, broken wings of a raven, flimsy shields of armor that encircled his daughter's shoulders. "I didn't turn them into the *militares*, Monica," he said. "That would have been murder."

Monica dug at the sand with a finger. "Then she just left us?" She looked at him, and he saw that her eyes were filling with tears, begging him to come up with a plausible excuse for her mother.

"If it's true she's alive, then, yes, Monica, she just left us."

The bird cawed as if in response and continued to watch them. "She didn't love us, then," Monica whispered.

Bruce grabbed her shoulder and looked into the eyes that were so like his own. "She loved *you*."

"Not enough," Monica said, pretending to smile. She wiped her tears and hopped onto her feet, folding her arms at her chest. Will appeared in the distance. "We're over here," she shouted, then turned to Bruce. "Will knows. And now he has a stake in finding Mom because Francisca told us that Mom is trying to shut down Caracol." She pointed behind her, toward the building. "I'm starting to think that everyone in that clinic is in danger."

THE RESTAURANT was up on a second story, built on stilts over an inlet of water. It was rustic, with wood picnic tables and benches. Beefy, torpid black flies circled the colorful plastic baskets of food left behind at another table. The sole decoration was a hand-painted map of El Salvador on the far wall.

Will, Monica, and Bruce picked at their grilled red snapper. Will draped a paper napkin over his fish head because, he said, he couldn't "perform surgery with the patient staring back." Sylvia, on the other hand, ate with the delicate, methodical appetite of a cat, pulling up the spine structure like the separator in a metal ice-cube tray.

"Two patients were aroused out of their comas in the last week," Sylvia announced cheerfully. "One of them is a questionable success—a young woman who was already reacting to music and voices when she was admitted. But the other was out cold for a year."

"How did the treatment go this morning?" Bruce asked.

"Incredible," Sylvia said, smiling and opening her eyes wide. "Yvette's Glasgow score has gone up two points."

Will put down his fork and cleared his throat. "We're suspending the treatments and starting the arrangements to take her home. I have reason to believe—"

"We're not suspending anything," Sylvia said, chuckling falsely. "I'm not going to listen to rumors. The treatment is working." She thumped her index finger down on the table. "Working, working, working."

"A man staying at the inn told us one patient woke up a raving lunatic," Will said, his face bright red. "Is that what you want? To trade one altered state for another? Better to let her body continue to reconstruct itself naturally. That place is really beginning to scare me."

"We heard some bad things about it today," Monica said, looking at Sylvia. "Maybe it's prudent to hold off until we know more."

"And how long do you think I can afford to stay here?" Sylvia snapped back. "I have bills stacking up back home. It's now or never." She put down her fork and looked at Will defiantly. "I'm not backing down."

Will closed his eyes and looked away, apparently counting silently. After ten seconds he turned and looked at his mother-in-law. "Sylvia, it's not your decision to make."

Bruce and Monica shared a worried look.

"I have the airline tickets," Sylvia said softly. "Unless you have five thousand dollars in your pocket . . ."

"We're gambling with Yvette's health," Will said. "Dr. Mendez is playing with people's lives. If the enterprise fails, there are no consequences, no accountability. The patients die or go crazy, oh, well. Dr. Mendez doesn't have to worry about being sued in this country because she's not doing anything illegal. And no consequences means the freedom and ability to take high medical risks for high rewards."

Sylvia slurped her bottled water, avoiding Will's gaze.

There was a moment when no one spoke, and Monica guessed they were all too emotionally exhausted to argue anymore. "Did they hire a new therapist yet?" Monica asked, trying to redirect the conversation.

"Not yet, darling," Sylvia said, patting Monica's hand. "God will repay you for your hard work. They don't need to be massaged every day. Every other day is fine. And if you're really tired, you can massage just Yvette." Sylvia quickly glanced at Will, or rather, at his neck, and said, "Yvette knows when you're in the room. Maybe you should spend the nights with her at Caracol. I can go stay at the guesthouse with Monica. Will, you can take my bed." In a low voice she said, "I'm sure Yvette would appreciate some attention from her husband." And with that, she cut the head off her red snapper and got back to eating its delicate white flesh.

Bruce looked at Will, who was staring unhappily out at the water, looking trapped.

Without looking up, Sylvia said, "So shall we make the swap tonight?"

Monica stole a glance at Will for a second, then she quickly returned to the task of stirring her Cola Champán with a straw, as if cream soda needed to be stirred.

"Maybe tomorrow night," he mumbled.

"It's a great idea, Sylvia," Bruce said, suddenly recognizing the benefits of her plan. "I don't know why we didn't think of it before."

AFTER DINNER, Monica sat with her father in the hallway facing the courtyard. "Leticia," Monica said, "was Maximiliano's wife. Did you pick up on that?"

"No," Bruce said, suddenly arresting the agitated rocking of his chair on the long corridor of the guesthouse. "I never met Maximiliano's wife."

Monica put her hand out. "Weren't you listening? Dr. Mendez said her grandmother was the nanny—that's Francisca."

"I didn't make the connection."

Monica shook her head. "You're an award-winning journalist. You're either lying or the old German's coming to get you."

"What old German?"

"Alzheimer."

Bruce eyed his daughter. "Okay, Nancy Drew, then why do mother and soon-to-be-married daughter have different surnames?"

Monica shrugged. "Dunno. Marriages. Lack of marriages. Divorces. Death. Take your pick."

Bruce stopped rocking. "Would you consider *not* going to find out about your mother?" He leaned over and crunched a beetle with his shoe, then kicked it away.

"Do you honestly think that's a fair thing to ask? Put yourself in my shoes."

He took a deep breath, raised his fingers to his mouth, and began to pull gently on his lower lip. "Then I guess there's something you should know."

Finally, Monica thought. *Cough it up.*

He took a deep breath and said, "The day you told me about your mother and Max," he said, looking out to the garden, "I was angry and confused to say the least. . . . So . . . I did tell one person of Alma and Max's whereabouts that day."

Monica turned, looked at his profile. "Who?"

He took a deep breath and exhaled, "Doña Magnolia."

"You told Abuela," Monica said flatly, sitting back. "That pretty much explains the rest."

"I always wondered if she got word out to her friends in the high military as to where Max could be found."

"Of course she did, Dad," Monica said. "She was hell-bent on breaking them up. She was furious at both of them."

Bruce folded his hands on his lap. "You were right about one thing out on the beach today, Monica. I was very jealous

and very angry. So I lashed back by informing the most powerful person I knew."

"Abuela."

"Abuela," he repeated softly. "I figured she wouldn't do anything to hurt Alma, just punish her somehow, put an end to her
disgusting behavior."

"Francisca said several others died with Max," Monica said.
"What really happened at El Trovador, Dad, what?"

"I don't know. I have a headache." Bruce put his hand over
his eyes. "I don't even know what to think anymore."

"Are you coming with me to meet her boat?" Monica asked.
"We'd have to stay a few more days."

He let his hand drop to his lap. "I don't want to go, but I
don't want you to go alone. I'll think about it overnight."

She nodded, then looked up to see Will coming down the
hall. She waved without smiling. It was no surprise to either of
them that he was defying Sylvia's earlier proclamation that they
would swap quarters.

"You're getting a little too close to him," Bruce said in a low
voice. The words rolled into a forced smile as Will approached.
He was freshly showered, but Monica could see sweat was already beading up along his upper lip and his forehead.

"What's your take on what happened today at the factory,
Will?" Bruce said. The question surprised Monica, since Bruce
normally avoided the subject of Alma at all costs. Perhaps her
father was experiencing his own version of hot and cold when
it came to Will.

Will shook his head, was about to say something, then
paused and sat down next to Bruce. "I have to admit, Bruce, I
encouraged Monica to pursue her suspicions for my own selfish
purposes. I hope you understand that I'm very, very worried
about Yvette. If it's true that your wife knows something about
the treatments at Caracol . . ." He wrinkled his brow. "Wife?
Ex-wife?"

"Wife," Monica said. "Technically, they're still married."

"I have a certificate that says she's missing and presumed dead." Bruce shook his head. "That makes her my ex." He rubbed his razor stubble and pulled at an imaginary beard. "As for Yvette and the treatment, I don't blame you for taking a hard look at the program. You two are one step ahead of my own research; I would have stumbled upon Alma's publications on the subject eventually. I just don't know how I would have handled it."

Will sat forward, folded his hands together, elbows resting on his knees. "And she just left one day," Will said, as if Monica and Bruce were hearing the story for the first time. "She divorced her own kid," he whispered, shaking his head. "An intelligent, beautiful woman from a powerful family, who could hire ten full-time nannies if she wanted . . . and yet she walked away from everything. I don't get it."

Monica looked down at her hands, at the fingers that were once small and pudgy and fragrant with innocence, hands that had become strong and competent with the skill of healing. She turned them over and looked at her narrow fingernail beds, painted pale pink like seashells. Her hands folded onto one another, tenderly and without being willed, as if they were comforting one another.

Monica wondered, what kind of woman could walk away from the same arms that reached out to her every morning from inside the crib? And how could she bear to see her twelve-year-old wave good-bye for the last time from a bedroom window? When she felt her eyes well up, Monica took a deep breath, then cleared her throat and straightened up. She gave Bruce and Will a fake smile and looked at her watch. "It's nine o'clock. Anyone feel like taking a walk to the little store with me? I need a shot of something strong."

*   *   *

"AGUARDIENTE," Monica pronounced, as she held up a capful of Tíc Táck, El Salvador's national brand of moonshine, "is made out of fermented sugarcane. The campesinos buy it because it packs a punch and is cheaper than dirt."

Bruce had accompanied Monica and Will to the store to buy the liquor, complaining all the way that decent people didn't drink moonshine. "We're in the middle of nowhere," Monica said. "If you want me to drink something classy, then show me a place within a hundred miles where I can buy a nice bottle of chardonnay. I need something to take the edge off."

"Given the day's occurrences and the fact that there's nothing but moonshine in this little town, I'd say moonshine is perfect," Will said. "Now do we drink it straight up, on the rocks, or with Coke?"

Bruce made a face but held out his plastic cup. "On the rocks I suppose," he said. By eleven, after several shots of Tíc Táck, his face was in his hands. He had meant to stay up as long as Monica and Will wanted, mostly to prevent them from being alone together. But by eleven thirty he couldn't stand it and went to bed. He left them sitting at a small, round cement picnic table at the center of the courtyard, surrounded by moonlight and palm fronds and stinking of insect repellent and moonshine.

Will took another shot of *aguardiente,* coughed, and said, "It sure tastes horrible, but I feel like my grandma just wrapped me in a warm blanket."

Monica traced a line from her neck to her belly. "You can feel it burning its way down. . . . Hand me that bottle, will you? I'll have another one."

Will moved the bottle away, placed it behind him on the ground. "I think a massage is a far more healthy sleep aid," he said, taking away the plastic tumbler in her hand and placing it on the table. He stood up, walked around the table, and sat on the bench next to her. "Turn around," he said, pointing at the foliage. Before she could move, he grabbed her shoulders and spun her around on the bench. He pushed his thumbs into her shoulder blades and began rubbing. Even with the shots of moonshine in her, she was still so tense he could barely get his fingers into the crook of her neck. "Relax," he said. "Take your own advice and let it go."

"Easy for you to say. Your mom is probably home baking cookies right now."

He laughed, then got to work rubbing out the knots, noticing a long bar of tension running up along her spine. She pulled away when he pressed his thumbs along it. He worked in silence for a while, then, he dropped his hands onto his lap. His ears were buzzing with the pounding rush of blood as he explored the geography of the bones and muscles along her back. "Monica," he whispered, allowing his lips to graze the velvet of her earlobe. "It's taking all my strength not to turn you around and kiss you."

Monica twisted at the waist to look up at him. Will suspended his breathing, hoping that she was offering her mouth to him. But what he saw in her eyes was a tired melancholy. "We couldn't do that to Yvette," she said, and looked away.

He dropped his forehead to her shoulders for a second. He wanted to tell her that he was sure that their meeting was no coincidence. But it seemed a bit much for now, so he just breathed quietly and leaned against Monica, listening to the crackle of insects in the darkness.

"I can wish, can't I?" Will whispered, and leaned in to see her profile. He pushed away a stray coil of her hair.

"It's all we can do, Will."

He slid his face into the crook of her neck and inhaled deeply, as if to drink in any words she might have left unspoken. Then, he parted his lips and ran the tip of his tongue along a small patch of her neck, tasting the salt on her warm skin. He found the pulse of her jugular, thumping softly beneath his mouth. He delighted in its quickening. Monica drew in air, but didn't move.

"I won't kiss you then," he whispered, as he dug his face deep into her hair. His hands encircled her waist. When his fingers met in the middle, he laced them together and pulled her toward him. Then, despite his best intentions, he sat forward just a little, just enough to let her know that his body was in love with her too.

ON WEDNESDAY, they left the guesthouse by nine in the morning. A phone call from Bruce to San Salvador had brought Claudia Credo tearing across the country to accompany them to the marine station to await the research vessel. Bruce, Claudia, and Will sat in the first row of the passenger van, while Monica curled up in the back. She had slept little all night, but her eyes finally fell shut as the morning sun warmed the backseat of the passenger van. Sleeping wasn't so easy since she was sliding around on the vinyl seat as the driver sped up and slowed down, avoiding oxcarts and stalled cows. Will complained and ordered the driver to slow down. "I don't want to die on a dusty country road in El Salvador," Will said. "No offense." The driver just laughed and kept driving, slowing down for a few minutes before getting back to his erratic driving.

Monica's mouth was cottony, her eyes stung, and she had a dull ache in her head. Claudia chatted excitedly in the front seat. "There was a rumor that Alma was around. And it's not such a strange thing in El Salvador, people disappearing in the chaos, then reappearing after the war."

"I bet," Will said.

"I hope that Alma's research can enlighten your decisions," Claudia said to Will, making the sign of the cross and pressing her hands together. "It's great that someone is working to discredit any enterprises that may be reckless."

"Sylvia and I have been arguing nonstop on this whole trip," Will said. "I feel really bad about our rift, but I've been distrustful of this clinic all along, and she—she's so dogged in her pursuit. I've already made up my mind to take more forceful measures. I really need to find out what company helped transport Yvette down here. Then I can see if I can work something out. At least in the States I'd have the law on my side."

"I can help you," Claudia said. "Let's think about this." She held up a finger. "Over hot coffee." She had apparently packed a thermos, and Monica heard her pouring it into Styrofoam cups, the smell of it making her nauseated as she lay in the backseat. Just as she was about to doze off, she heard Claudia say, "Remind me to tell Monica that her boyfriend has been calling my house nonstop this week, looking for her. I told him he's welcome to stay at my house if he wants to come. But first, he has to produce a nice little engagement ring." She laughed and Monica strained to hear who responded, but no one did.

Monica realized, with complete amazement, that she had forgotten to call Kevin in several days. She recalled the moment that had passed between her and Will the night before. She kept circling her mind to see if it was still there, her skin bursting with gooseflesh at the memory of his warm breath on her neck. This is what she had been missing all her life—the feeling that every moment together was a little nugget of happiness, something worth trapping in a capsule of memory, worth replaying over and over behind the surface of her eyelids. The fact that they had no future together didn't make it any less of a gift. She could enjoy his presence in her life; but she knew that they had to bear the consequences of that unfulfillable attachment. Otherwise, she'd be exactly like her mother. Monica knew firsthand what it was like to be burned by the fires that others built to keep themselves warm at night.

But what to do about that sexual pull that rushed and ebbed as predictably as the tides? Now she and Will had begun to lean on each other for moral support as their pursuits became more and more entangled. Was it possible that it was love she was dealing with here? The idea that she would have to sever something that was already pulsing with the lifeblood of the soul was terrifying. And the strange landscape didn't help matters: El Salvador was a place where anything could happen—powerful men were recycled into mangoes and girls gave their babies away; sea creatures injected healing, and dead people reappeared like magic. The germination of love was an insignificant miracle by comparison.

Lying in the backseat, Monica pulled a handful of fabric from Claudia's day bag over her eyes to block out the sun. It helped her headache a bit. She wondered what kind of marriage Will and Yvette would be able to patch together if Yvette emerged from her state. If Will was falling in love, he might be less eager to begin the hard climb toward a future with his damaged wife. What if the harm was already done? She suddenly recalled a riff from an old bolero that Abuelo used to play on his guitar:

> *Si negaras mi presencia en tu vivir*
> *bastaría con abrazarte y conversar*
> *tanta vida yo te di*
> *que por fuerza tienes ya*
> *sabor a mí*

She agreed with the song. The sensory recall of love is permanent. We are transformed by the taste of our own longing, and once savored, that same intimacy brands itself into the heart. *Sabor a mí,* she thought. *I have made my mark on you, Will.*

Now her thoughts swung back to her mother, then again to Will and Yvette and back to her mother, in nauseating circles. She contemplated how strange it was that the future was a place in which her mother was alive. She wondered what people do when a loved one is released after a lengthy prison sentence. A wave of nerves took over with the realization that she would see her resurrected mother in a few hours. What would she say to her? All night she had rehearsed: casual, like running into an old friend; angry and outraged; relieved and eager to forgive. Or should she just stand before her mother and wait to hear and feel and say whatever came?

Will announced that he too was going to take a nap, and Monica, her eyes still covered, heard him lay down on the bench seat in front of her. After a few minutes, something brushed Monica's skin, and she removed the makeshift blindfold and saw Will's hand appear behind the seat. His fist was closed, as if he were offering something, or asking her to guess what was inside. Monica reached over and pried his fingers open, but there was nothing inside. It was a trick: he pushed his fingers between hers. He rubbed the back of her hand with his thumb, the rest of him unseen to her. His wedding ring was gone, and Monica stared at the pale band of skin around his finger. She let go of his hand at the first chance and rolled over. She heard him shift and sit up, felt his eyes on her back. She squeezed her eyes tight and didn't answer when he spoke her name.

An hour later, at noon, the driver announced that they'd arrived.

The Carmelite nuns were chanting at Yvette's bedside when the birth canal of clarity finally spit her out into the world. *Santa María, Madre de Dios, ruega por nosotros pecadores ahora y en la hora de nuestra muerte, amén.* Their harmony and repetition was trancelike. When the skin peeled back from Yvette's vision, she was staring into the backs of their coarse brown cotton habits. Her vision was foggy, her eyes dry and flattened, as if someone had been pressing on her eyeballs for a long time. At first, she didn't recognize the skinny sticks at her sides as being her own arms. Across the room, her mother was praying with the nuns over someone else's bed, a string of small pearls dangling from her hands as she repeated the words with them.

"Am I back?" she tried to ask, but no one heard her, because they were shuffling to another part of the room. She cleared her throat and rolled her eyes to the opposite side of the room, but it was curtained off and she couldn't see.

"Something bad happened in this place," Yvette said in a dry, hoarse voice. "I can hear it in the exhaustion of the sea."

Her mother slowly turned her face toward her. Sylvia floated down the center aisle, her head cocked to one side. She stopped at the foot of Yvette's bed.

"I love you, Mama," Yvette said.

Sylvia's disbelief lasted the length of two slow blinks. Then, her face flooded with emotion.

part THREE

Mateo Jesus Peralta was loading boxes onto a hand truck when Bruce and Monica walked up the ramp to the marine station. The half-blind, redheaded fisherman didn't recognize Monica Winters all grown up, but she remembered him from the days of cone-shell hunting with her mother and so called him by name. He told her that the research vessel *Alta Mar* had already arrived for a special project having to do with a local elementary school. Claudia and Will waited inside the small, barren marine station, sitting on molded plastic chairs and sipping grape sodas they didn't really want. They waved and wished father and daughter good luck as the two walked on without them to a sandy stretch, where a crowd of schoolchildren were gathered around several people wearing black dive suits.

It wasn't hard to spot Alma. She was the only woman. She was surrounded by children, kneeling over a blow-up swimming pool, her palms covered with baby sea turtles, like potato chips with legs. She was demonstrating something to the smallest of her audience, a dark brown little boy with crutches and a stump for a leg. Bruce and Monica slipped into the small gathering of teachers and colleagues. Monica peered into the crowd, shielded by a tall man standing in front of her.

Alma's voice returned to Monica like a rush of warm foam. She could still hear the sea in its subtle, effervescent popping. Alma had a diving mask pulled up onto her forehead and was barefoot, red toenails gleaming in the charcoal-colored sand, and she flipped one of the baby turtles over to point to some anatomical part on the turtle's underside.

Monica drew in her breath slowly, quietly. She doubted that she would ever understand the woman who was standing before her, a woman who could engross herself in the wiggling of baby turtles, oblivious to the adult daughter who stood watching her across a distance of fifteen years.

Alma returned the turtle to its upright position and looked up, first at the faces of the people standing in front, then beyond them. Monica instinctively darted sideways and hid behind the tall man. Her heart punched at her rib cage.

A hand went up. "Excuse me, *Dr. Borrero,*" a familiar voice said, loud and booming like the voice of a stage actor. "If cats have nine lives, how many do sea creatures have?" Everyone turned to look. In sudden horror, Monica realized that it was her father speaking. Alma was motionless—a stunned fish playing dead, trying to blend into the environment. Slowly, she looked down and began dropping the turtles into the pan of water, one by one, each making a soft splashing noise.

"*Sólo una,*" she said simply. Just one.

"Well, it appears that you, Dr. Borrero, have more than one," he said. "Like a cat."

The crowd was silent, not because they understood what was going on, but rather, because a tall, green-eyed man had just shouted something in a foreign language. They gawked unashamedly. Alma stood up and took a step forward, toward Bruce.

"Bruce Winters," Alma said. "You found me."

A little girl ran into Alma's arms, butted her head right into Alma's abdomen like a football player. Alma teetered and put her hands over the little, dark, curly head. Monica, still hiding, saw herself at seven, back when her mother's body was a trampoline that would always catch her and bounce her back to the world unharmed. Monica imagined that she was that child. Alma must have sensed it, because when she looked up from the curly head, it was to look directly at Monica, still peeking from behind a tall man.

"Monica?" she asked.

Monica bit her lip and stepped out from behind the man. They stood there, mother and daughter, looking at each other, blinking, each waiting to see what the other would do. The crowd lost interest and resumed its chatter. Finally, Alma said, "Come closer." Without answering, Monica stepped forward and dove into her mother's arms, hating herself even as she breathed deep and squeezed, gulping the scent that made tears spring up in her eyes, made her close them against the pain that flooded through her and filled her with rage.

Alma let go first. "I'm so happy to see you," she said delicately, fearfully, as if she were speaking to a three-hundred-pound Bengal tiger. She took a deep breath and looked up at Bruce. The line of eye contact between them spit and zapped with dangerous electricity. Correctly assuming their intention, she said, "Let's go someplace where we can talk."

ALMA TOOK THEM to a small park area, a mini-zoo nearby where someone was rehabilitating tropical animals in large, fenced pens. There was a sitting area, and she sat down first, taking off her diving mask and daintily placing it in her lap like a pillbox hat. The long, dark coils of her youth had been sheared to a pixie cut and were streaked with gray. Her eyes were lightly marked by years spent in the sun, and Monica noticed that her accent had thickened—but otherwise she looked the same. Monica sat next to her and Bruce sat across from them. Monica made a steeple with her index fingers and pressed them against her mouth as she stared down at the ground.

"Well," Bruce said brusquely, pulling up his pants at the knee. "We're here to confirm with our own eyes that you are indeed alive and well and living without us by your own free will."

Alma said, "You sound like an old-time sheriff."

"Dead or alive, Alma," he said, pointing at Monica's shoulder, his voice icy. "You have no idea what you put her through. No idea."

Suddenly, Monica felt a wave of panic: she was afraid that he would antagonize Alma before they had their answer, or worse, that in her reply, she would break his heart all over again.

Alma squinted at him, looked down for a moment, apparently planning her words. She took a deep breath. "Where would you like me to begin?" Alma said, her tone matching his. "There's so much to tell."

"Wherever you think it began, Mom," Monica piped in. "I'm twenty-seven now. Whatever it is, I can handle it. I promise you both I can handle it." She looked from one parent to the other. "Let's get it all out on the table. All of it." She calmed herself down by breathing deeply, then gave her mother an abbreviated version of what had led them from Yvette Lucero's hospital room to El Salvador, then to Francisca and ultimately to meet Alma's ship.

After she heard the story, Alma bit her lip and folded her hands before her. She closed her eyes for a second. "This is difficult to talk about," she said. Behind her, a spider monkey banged on the fencing of his pen, grimacing and crying out, exposing his perversely pink gums and white, white teeth. He reminded Monica of Leticia. A tear of perspiration streaked down Bruce's temple, and he sat rigid, his eyes obscured behind dark sunglasses.

"It began when Mateo Jesus was a fisherman at the port of La Libertad." Alma pointed toward the station where they had seen the half-blind fisherman. "It was that last weekend before . . . everything got out of control. That last day, he sent word that he had pulled up a variety of cone shell that he had never seen before."

DOÑA MAGNOLIA MÁRMOL DE BORRERO paced the floor of her bedroom, throwing handfuls of her dirty laundry at her daughter as she shouted. "I hear people whispering behind our backs, Alma. 'Can you believe Magnolia's daughter is involved with that dirty *comunista*?' Oh, what a delicious tidbit."

"We're partners in a humanitarian project," Alma replied, catching a stiff, nude-colored girdle and letting it drop to the marble floor. "And besides, none of the gossips at your 'society' tea parties contribute a damn thing that's worth the oxygen they consume."

"The hell with what *they* do. You're involved with Maximiliano and I know it, and you know it, and everyone knows it, including the government. It's obscene, Alma Marina. It's morally wrong and it's dangerous."

Alma picked up her mother's silky slips, conical brassieres, underwear, and dirty washcloths and tossed them on the mattress of the four-post bed. "When we find the *furiosus*, I won't have reason to find myself alone with Max anymore. When I decide to cut off contact, it will be for me." She cupped a spot above her heart. "Not for Monica, not for you, or Bruce or your criminal friends in the high military or any of those hypocrites you care so much about." She shouted the word *hypocrites*, then resumed her calm tone. "I hate it here, you know that? I hate my life in El Salvador. I hate my boring marriage, I hate the shallowness, the fixation on materialism, the greed, and all the while, the campesinos have nothing to eat."

"Maximiliano has turned you into someone I don't know," Magnolia said, her hands on her hips. "Did you know that those filthy communists slaughtered one hundred and sixty head of prime cattle and twelve calves at Hacienda del Bosque last night? The Montenegros lost seven million colones."

Alma could see a blue vein had plumped up in her mother's throat. "Maximiliano is a doctor, Mother. He heals humans, he doesn't kill cows, so don't blame it on him."

Magnolia pointed her finger at her daughter. "Don't you dare tell me that you agree with his politics. If this country falls to communism, we're all going to burn in hell, because that's what communism is, Alma, it's a prison with no windows. Our warden will be some, some *demonio peludo,* some hairy beast who doesn't shower or believe in God."

"I haven't showered in two days, come to think of it," Alma said, raising her elbow over her head and sniffing loudly. "I must be communist."

"Do you enjoy mortifying me?"

"Do you enjoy yoking me like a beast?" Alma shouted back.

"Forget about the cone shell. Go home. Be a mother. Be a wife. Be a decent woman for God's sake."

Alma turned her back to her mother. "Mateo Jesus said this one is special. I'm going to see it."

"Fine, I'll go with you tomorrow morning. I know more about local mollusks than anyone else in this entire country besides you. We'll be back in San Salvador by afternoon."

"I'm not fifteen, Mother."

Magnolia pointed at Alma's face again. "Because you're going to meet Maximiliano, aren't you? You godless little whore." She spat a bit as she said it.

Something inside Alma snapped. Some basic outrage that had nothing to do with Maximiliano, or the country's war, but rather, was part of a lifelong war fought with words, needles of varying size that provoked them both into a constant state of inflammation. Alma grabbed the bundle of laundry off the bed and threw it at her mother. She groaned with the force she put behind it. Then she turned and ran, leaving Magnolia hurling obscenities and insults from the center of a pile of laundry stinking of stale French perfume.

In less than five seconds, Alma was flying down the grand staircase of her parents' home, heading toward her car. The affair was going to have to cool off, Alma knew, at least until she and Max each decided once and for all either to cut things off with their spouses or say good-bye. She loved Max with all her heart, but the quest for the *furiosus* had deteriorated into a sad excuse for adultery, and for now, they both felt a sense of duty and obligation to their families. Besides, Max's wife, Leticia, was stalking her, slashing the tires on her car and following her and Monica around from store to store at Metrocentro. Just a week ago, Leticia had thrown a sack of *cebada* flour at her in the supermarket, showering her with pink dust, a spectacle for all to see. No, her mother didn't know the half of it. And now Leticia was after the cone shell too, trying to beat her to the finish line, thinking that the slimy little trophy would win her Max's love. It was sick, she knew. But it was just her life, and what a small sacrifice it was if she could find the cone, copy the venom, mass-produce it, and offer it to anyone who was in chronic pain. They had also talked about selling it at a premium on the world market, then using the profit to create schools or housing or orphanages or to buy up farmland and parcel it out to the humblest peasants. If their unlikely alliance could culminate in the realization of a single dream, then perhaps the princess and the pauper could snap the social codes like paper shackles and make some good things happen in El Salvador. And then what could anyone say? Max and Alma. Making love. Making medicine. Making their lives count.

Alma and Maximiliano had agreed to meet at the fishermen's wharf at La Libertad to take a look at the new cone. She had made up a story to appease Bruce, who was caught up in reporting the Zona Rosa killings. She and Max had quarreled about this when Alma complained that the violence at Zona Rosa, perpetrated by a communist sect similar to Max's, had been shameful and pointless. Max had argued that the "imperialist gringos" needed to "lose a few appendages" before they would understand that it was time to back off and go home.

Normally, Alma would grant Monica the opportunity to be present at every sighting of a suspected *Conus furiosus*. But the situation with Leticia was getting explosive. As Alma packed her overnight bag, she tried to push away her anger and focused on the possibility that this cone might be the right one. She had a cleaned, polished *furiosus* shell in her collection, but a live one would look very different, with the outside still hooded with the protective skin of the periostracum. Mateo Jesus was a sharp and reliable fisherman who knew his sea creatures. Since he didn't have access to a telephone, he had sent word to Alma via an employee of his local Borr-Lac distributor.

THE WHARF AT LA LIBERTAD was extremely busy on a Saturday morning, lined with crudely built fishing boats tied up to the sides of the pier. Alma looked around but didn't see Max, so she strolled along the pier, drinking in the pungent scent of the sea. The array of marine produce was dazzling: flattened, dried, and salted stingrays strung on a rope like freshly washed laundry, nurse sharks stacked on top of each other in barrels, barracuda laid out like French baguettes, baring sinister teeth. She scolded the vendors who were selling soft-boiled sea turtle eggs, a popular snack at the seaside bars and resorts. Some of the stands offered raw, inky shellfish marinated in lime juice, red onion, and cilantro, and of course, cold Pilseners.

At a trinket booth, Alma bought a necklace with a shark tooth hooked on string for Monica, exactly like the one Alma always wore around her neck. It infuriated Magnolia to see her daughter sport a shark tooth the size of an arrowhead from a gold choker that had been intended to display a sapphire-and-diamond-encrusted cross. *It's who I am,* Alma thought.

Alma asked around for Mateo Jesus and found him at the end of the pier, selling shrimp and octopus. He nodded at her, then pulled up a cracked, red dishpan and dropped it on top of his iced-shrimp display. Inside, a three-inch-long cone shell sat half-submerged in dark gray sand and water. He handed her a set of metal tongs and she used them to turn the creature over. The frilly foot of the gastropod swirled like live, angry dough, and a harpoon shot out so quickly she had to look up at Mateo Jesus to confirm that she had indeed seen something.

"Cuidado," Mateo Jesus warned. "I know you respect these creatures, but be very careful with this one. I've never seen anything like it."

"I will be," Alma said. "This little guy looks lethal. It's very similar to the *furiosus,* Mateo Jesus, but it's completely solid. The *furiosus* invariably has at least a sprinkle of red toward the top. But it could be an abnormality, so I'll take him anyway. I'll send him over to the university. We can extract his venom for testing and keep him alive in a tank." She reached into her bag and handed Mateo Jesus fifty colones. He shrugged at her in a way that made her reach into her purse and pull out another ten.

"I'll keep looking, Niña Alma."

"Just remember, don't show anything to anyone else unless you call me first."

"Understood."

Alma walked down the pier with the pan held between both hands, water sloshing from side to side. She saw Max in the parking lot and he helped her put the pan in her Land Rover, on the floor of the front passenger side, half-tucked underneath the seat, with rags snaked around it to keep it from sliding around. He kissed her and said, "I'm needed at El Trovador again. I can use your help for an hour or two."

Alma remembered Magnolia's rage, and worried what her mother might do. Still, she was sure her mother would not tell Bruce, nor would she know where to find her after they left the wharf. "I'll call home and leave instructions with the maid. I'll tell Monica what to tell Bruce, and where I really am, in case of an emergency."

"I still don't think it's such a good idea to trust a kid with that kind of information. In fact, I feel sorry for her. Why do you have to be so open with her? It makes me uncomfortable. She knows exactly what's going on."

"She can handle it, Max. Besides, I don't want my daughter to grow up thinking that everyone else lives like a Borrero. Because of the exposure, she has developed empathy, sensitivity, wisdom, maturity. She's not a brat like I was at her age. You saw how she wanted to adopt that baby, how she accused me of being an insensitive rich hypocrite. I had to discipline her because of the disrespectful way she spoke to me, but all the while I was thinking, 'Bravo, Monica. You're standing up for what you believe.'"

Alma found a public phone and told her daughter that she was heading to El Trovador to help Max tend to some peasants. She instructed Monica to tell her father that she had decided to make an unexpected trip to Guatemala, and that she'd be back Monday morning. She felt guilty about teaching Monica to lie, so instead, she focused her thoughts on the finish line. The *furiosus* was still out there.

LATER THAT DAY, when they arrived at Hacienda El Trova-dor, there was no one, which was strange, because normally a couple of people guarded the entrance. "Who are we expect-ing?" Alma asked, wondering what, if anything, she could do to help Max prepare for his patients. She had helped him many times before, and so she knew what to expect. Soon, the bleed-ing and the sick would arrive smelling faintly of fruit, from the truckload of fresh sugarcane, oranges, or lemons they had hid-den beneath to slip by a military checkpoint.

An hour passed before they heard a truck in the distance, saw the boiling cloud of dust as it passed through the open gate and sped toward the beach house. Max and Alma waved and ran to meet the truck.

When the truck was a little more than a hundred yards away, Maximiliano suddenly slammed his hand across Alma's chest, almost knocking her down. "Run," he shouted, his voice filled with terror. *"Militares."*

She spun around and followed him, sprinting and sinking in the soft ground that was half-dirt, half-sand, her body flood-ing with adrenaline. She ran until her lungs felt as if they were going to explode and her legs were wood, in a sheer, blind panic, with the truck gaining ground behind them. To be caught here would mean she was a sympathizer, an aider and abettor, and the military didn't take this kindly.

Slightly ahead of her, Max continued running toward the sea, and when she looked up, she suddenly understood what he had in mind. She saw a small motorboat, remembering that it had been used to smuggle in arms from Nicaragua the night before. Escape by sea, she thought. Perfect.

And that's when Max broke away and ran ahead. She

thought him clever to push ahead to get the engine started, and he did. Alma rejoiced at the sound of the engine roaring to life. Thank God, she thought.

Then, the boat spit up white water and tore away.

And he left her.

Alma jumped up and down on the shore, screaming his name. She might have jumped in after him, but he was crouched down, not looking back, which paralyzed her with shock. She looked behind her. The soldiers stopped the truck and jumped out.

She couldn't believe he'd left her. Did he think she'd be all right on shore because, like it or not, she was really one of them? Or was he ultimately just another coward trying to save his own skin?

She raised her arms when she saw that she was cornered. One of the men grabbed her while the others ran into the water and shot at the boat with a weapon that looked like a portable rocket launcher. The sound rocked her, and she fell to her knees. An explosion followed, fiery pieces glowing on top of the water, dark smoke rising like a volcanic eruption. Only a flat, main section of the hull remained on the surface of the water, a smoking raft floating away.

She screamed and tumbled to her knees. She covered her face with her hands and imagined that she could splice time so that this moment would never have happened. She might rewind to a few hours before, and tell him, *No, let's not go to El Trovador, tell your patients to meet us at your home instead.* Something, anything but this. Max dead? She peeked at the smoldering raft floating away in the current, heading in the direction of Negrarena.

The four soldiers laughed and cheered, complimenting the shooter with a string of obscenities. One of the soldiers held up a finger and hushed the others. In the distance, the sound of another truck. They cocked their heads to listen, then smiled at each other and nodded their heads. "More *comunista* vermin," one of them said. "Lopez, you secure the woman in her car. Chucho, you'll drive the truck when we're done," the leader said, and they crouched down and clutched their weapons as they headed toward the house.

The chaperone soldier made her get inside the passenger side of her Land Rover. *"Te gustaba el comunista?"* he asked, licking his lips. Alma noted he used the familiar *tu* instead of the formal and respectful *usted* that every civil servant who knew his place would use to address a member of the country's oligarchy.

She could tell him who she was—but, no, she thought bitterly, she couldn't use her family name to get out of this situation. She could never live with herself if she said, *Do you know who you're talking to?*

As if he had read her mind, the soldier said, "Your mother told *el general* that Maximiliano Campos was here at El Trovador."

"My mother sent you after me?"

"Not after you," he said, pointing at the water. "Him."

Alma covered her face and began to weep. But her sobs ebbed almost as soon as they'd begun. The soldier was looking at her, narrowing his eyes in voyeuristic pleasure at her display of emotion. She couldn't cry in front of him. She stared straight ahead, ignoring his greasy stare.

Monica. Monica was the only one who knew where she really was, or who knew the exact location of Hacienda El Trovador. Monica must have finally blown the whistle. She had told either Bruce or Magnolia or both of them or one had told the other, it didn't matter. Maximiliano was dead because of it. Max, whom she'd known all her life, a boy who had grown up beside her, climbing trees, collecting bugs, and riding horses at Negrarena. A man who just twenty-four hours ago had woken her up from a lazy afternoon nap by dragging the tail feather of a quetzal across her belly. Max, her Max, speeding away, leaving her in the hands of the enemy. What had gone through his mind at that moment? Had he figured that she was bulletproof because of her last name? Did he still think of her as one of them? Perhaps it had come down to pure survival instinct. The latter was the only explanation she could live with, and so it was the one she chose.

With Max dead, Alma now felt completely and utterly alone in the world. She could trust no one in her family, not even her own child. Alma understood that she too had done more than her share of betraying, but she had always expected that an enormous good would come of it, eventually. What a mistake.

She looked out the window of the truck. In the distance, the soldiers were lining up the peasants who had just arrived in a truck full of sugarcane, which included two young boys and a pregnant woman. "No," she lamented, and turned away, because she knew what was going to happen next. She balled her hands into fists and paid homage to the last slice of time that those six people would be alive in this world. She began to shake, digging her nails into her skin as she pressed her fists together tighter and tighter, until the nails broke through the skin of her palms.

Time seemed to pass slowly, although it was probably less than five minutes before she heard the sound of the rifle shots. The sound traveled cleanly to a chamber within her mind that swelled open to contain them. The six echoes were swallowed and quarantined in a cold, anesthetized place that would allow her to keep them separate from all other memories. This would allow her to store them safely, until she had the courage, years later, to open the box and peer in.

Inside the Land Rover, the soldier next to her placed his hand on her knee, leering at her, exposing a row of decaying teeth. He was too stupid and arrogant to care whose daughter

she was. Alma looked down. Peeking out from under her seat was the edge of the red dishpan. As the soldier leaned over to grab her breast, she reached down with the hand closest to the door and grabbed the cone between her index finger and her thumb, holding the base away from her hand. The soldier had a lurid half-smile on his face as he mashed at her breast. She turned and leaned into him, placing the creature as gently as she could on his lap.

The snail felt its way around the strange new environment of army-issue cotton. It took exactly four seconds for the soldier to cry out. He stiffened his limbs, raising his pelvis up so it crashed into the steering wheel. His hand flew to his crotch, where he picked up the innocuous-looking shell, examined it, confused, not connecting it with the coldness that was already spreading up his abdomen. Alma remembered hearing that the sting of some cones mimicked the sensation of flesh being ripped away from the grip of dry ice.

Alma tore off her sandals and leaped out of the car. She bolted across the sand, not looking back, and headed in the direction of the beach. She knew enough about the paralyzing effects of that venom to know that the soldier would be too shocked and numb to do anything, much less fire a gun. Behind her, the other soldiers saw her run. They shouted at her and fired their guns in warning. She ran across the desolate beach, then over a stretch of rocks that ripped up the soles of her feet. When she stepped into the surf, she felt the searing pain of the salt entering open flesh. She dove into the water, pumping her arms and kicking her feet up with every last bit of energy she had, propelling herself forward, deeper and deeper into the restless waters. Only a few yards out she could already tell that the currents were exactly what she had hoped for. She filled her lungs with air and dove under, calculating her every motion to take advantage of the water's drag, keeping in mind the direction that she had seen the flaming boat drift. She dove down deep, eyes open, and saw the shots being fired into the water around her. A foot away, a beefy parrot fish exploded into bits.

A great undertow swept her deep and far across the gloomy landscape of black sand and swaying aquatic plants. Just as she felt she was going to pass out, the water spit her up long enough for her to fill her lungs again, then pulled her down again. The current carried her like that—up and down, concealing her yet letting her breathe, like a needle that dips into cloth and rises, stitching its way across a great distance.

SHE RODE THE CURRENT all the way to Negrarena. The gate was locked, since her mother was in San Salvador. She scaled the wall, cutting up her legs and elbows on the razor wire, and dropped, bleeding and exhausted, into a den of rottweilers. They greeted her with whimpers and licks, all of them offspring of a puppy she had brought back with her from college.

She snuck into Caracol undetected. The caretakers lived in the front part of the hacienda, but it was such a large property, and Alma succeeded in quickly hushing the well-trained dogs with belly rubs and baby talk. She limped over to the villa and retrieved a hidden spare key. She spent the evening alone, in one of the back guest rooms, nursing her cuts with trembling fingers. She curled up into a ball and contemplated the truth she had always known: that the ocean claims that which is sick and no longer functional. She now fit that description, and yet the sea had concealed her, carried her on the magic carpet of its currents, unharmed by sharks or rocks or jellyfish, then gently spit her back to safety. The sea had handed her a rare second chance at life, and she had not missed its significance. She would always be a daughter of privilege, she could see that now. Even the ocean made an exception for Alma Borrero. The only thing left for her to do was to give herself over to it completely, an act of gratitude and worship.

Before dawn the next morning, she let herself out of Caracol, with a pocketful of spare cash she kept locked in one of the closets. She walked to the nearby town, stopped in front of Tienda La Lunita to wait for the early bus, wearing a big sugarcane cutter's hat to shroud her face.

Forty minutes later, she was rapping on Francisca Campos's bedroom window in her hometown. Alma told her the whole story, minus the detail of Magnolia's involvement. The two women wept together, and Francisca offered Alma an even more comforting explanation for his abandonment: that he presumed she would be safer alone than with him. And he had been right—after all, if she had been on the boat with him, she would have died too. Two hours after leaving Francisca, Alma was at a guerrilla camp, where she found some of Max's friends. They helped her sneak into Honduras. The next day she placed a phone call to one of the newspapers, *La Prensa Gráfica,* and said, "I witnessed four soldiers murder six peasants, Maximiliano Campos, and Alma Borrero Winters at El Trovador, one hundred kilometers east of La Libertad. I wish to remain anonymous."

"THE MONTHS THAT FOLLOWED were a blur," Alma told Monica and Bruce. "I discovered that I'm not communist or socialist, that I am in fact quite apolitical without Maximiliano to fuel my interest. I knew I had to get back to the only thing that was really mine—the sea."

Bruce stared up into an almond tree, listening, unnaturally still and unblinking. "The press was all over it," he said without looking down. "I was sick with grief, and on top of that, everyone knew I was the cuckold."

Alma looked at him, almost apologetically, then looked at

Monica. "I had squirreled away some money in an account in Miami, a good sum my father had left me. No one knew about it, and that's how I funded my escape. It's sad and ironic. . . ." She shook her head. "I went back to school. I got a Ph.D. in marine science. I began to do research on the effects of thermo-volcanic changes on the environment of mollusks, and I've been doing research all over the globe—Hawaii, Puerto Rico, Brazil, California, Mexico, the Philippines. At one point during a graduate project, I was at Woods Hole Oceanographic Institution on Cape Cod."

"You never thought to come see us?" Monica asked.

Alma smiled crookedly, then looked at her daughter. "I was in the audience when you were in *Carousel* in the tenth grade. I saw you graduate from high school, my dear."

Monica drew in her breath, and a little gasp of wonder escaped from her lips as she rolled up her eyes and searched her visual memory—in vain, of course—for confirmation. She frowned. "You did that for yourself, Mom. It did nothing for me. I didn't know you were there."

Monica turned to her father, narrowing her eyes a bit. "Mom was at my high school play, publishing, and teaching, and you had *no idea* that she was alive all this time?"

Bruce shook his head and turned his gaze on Alma. "There was a war going on, and in 1985 El Salvador, people weren't trackable like they are in the States. . . ." He scratched his head, looked down, then up again at Alma. "What is your citizenship?"

"I am a citizen of Costa Rica. It was important to me, at the time that I left El Salvador, to cut all ties. I surrendered my Salvadoran citizenship, and thanks to some old connections, I secured a university job in Costa Rica."

"So why didn't you change your name?"

"I did. It was Alma Winters, and I reverted to Alma Borrero."

"An ironic choice, no?"

"Not at all. I wanted to be myself before I lost control of my life. I counted on the fact that once everyone thought I was dead, no one would be looking for me. Years later, I went ahead and published articles in my real name because my field is extremely obscure. I knew that even my mother, a shell collector, would never read a science journal about mollusks." Alma smiled weakly. "Besides, I'm a marine biologist and my given name is Alma Marina. Soul of the Sea. How could I give *that* up?"

Bruce nodded, then cupped his chin with one hand. "You still haven't answered the question of why . . ."

Now Alma stood, looking down at Bruce, and she spoke more softly; they could tell she was struggling to face the core of truth. "When the shock and grief wore off, all that was left was disgust at myself and a loss of hope for being able to pull off the dream without Max, without the *furiosus,* for that matter. I sank into a deep depression." She looked off to the distance. "No one believed the soldiers' story about me running off into the water, everyone thought they killed me along with Max. I heard there was a search, initiated by my mother."

"Even Claudia didn't believe the soldiers," Bruce said. "But we settled on drowning as the cause of death."

Alma nodded her head. "Two of the people who were murdered at El Trovador were under the age of twelve. Another victim was a girl I knew named Maria del Carmen. Remember her, Monica? We had delivered her baby at El Trovador a few years before. She was pregnant again, and they killed her, just like that."

Monica blinked in disbelief. "They killed Jimmy Bray's mother?"

Alma nodded. "Makes you sick, doesn't it? Such a senseless waste. I was beside myself with rage at my mother for unleashing something she couldn't control. My guess is that when she placed that call, she thought they'd put Max in prison, rough him up, and stop us from tainting the family name. But those thugs weren't capable of keeping it reasonable. What I saw was four men becoming giddy with bloodlust after they blew Max away."

Bruce let out a great breath and shook his head. "And do you feel you were responsible in any way for these events, Alma?"

"Of course I do, Bruce. That was the hardest part of all. It's why I left my family," Alma said, looking at Monica. "Because I was driven to punish my mother and exile myself to keep from doing any more harm to anyone."

Monica sat with that for a moment, running her mind's fingers over the surface of her mother's words, searching for the rough edges of an excuse. For now, it all rang true emotionally, but she would give herself time to evaluate it, to let it all sink in. Monica spoke the truth that lay before her: "I told Dad the location of the hacienda, Dad told Abuela, and Abuela made the phone call that put it all in motion. All of us have blood on our hands." Monica looked at her father, then down at her own hands, as if indeed she expected to find them to be coated and dripping with red. "I guess this is what you've been protecting me from all these years, Dad."

"Except I believed that we caused your mother's death," he said, looking as if he was about to cry. "I didn't want you to live with that guilt, as I had. Imagine . . . ," he whispered, shook his head a little, and let the sentence trail off as he looked away from them.

Monica looked at Alma and said, "I don't understand how you could walk away from me. That's the one part that defies my understanding. When the dust settled, you were alive and could have stayed at Caracol for as long as you needed. You could have come home. You could have divorced Dad, and we could have all moved on, in separate directions if that's what you wanted. But instead you vanished from *my* life. Help me with that part, Mami."

Alma turned to look at her, stared at her wide-eyed, her eyes gleaming with memory. "I felt that I didn't deserve you, and that you would be better off in the sole care of your father. I don't have any other answer than that, Monica. I wanted to sever all ties with my former life. A life of research and study was the only anesthesia I knew. I had always wanted to find a painkiller from the sea and I found it—in the achievements of my students, in scholarly journals, on dives, under microscopes, and aboard a research vessel. After a while, the decision to let everyone back home believe I was dead became a way of life, and it became harder and harder to undo. Two years later, I had essentially become someone new."

Monica nodded to acknowledge that she had heard. Thick, hot tears spilled down her face. "You're the most selfish person I've ever known," she said, waiting for the shocked look to rise in her mother's face, but it didn't. Alma just looked at her with eyes that were hungry for anything Monica had to say, so Monica tried harder to shake her. "You figured your role of scientist was so much more important than the simple job of being a mother to one child." Monica held up a finger. "One quiet girl who didn't take up much room or eat much or ask for anything but love. You didn't even bother to say good-bye. Your heart belongs entirely to something that will never love you back."

Alma stared into her own hands and nodded her head. "I disagree with the last part. The sea does love me back. But, Monica, all I can say is that I thrive on my work—I buried myself in it—although I admit there are days that I can't keep it all from seeping in. On those days, I lock the door and take a little blue pill that dulls the ache of my regrets. I had always told myself that I'd contact you when you became an adult, but when I

THE HEIRESS OF WATER

thought about it over the last few years, it seemed like such an intrusion, such a shock, I figured you would never forgive me. And yet, here we are. You found me, you did all the work."

"And here we are," Monica echoed.

Alma sat down next to Monica again and grabbed Monica's hand, squeezing it until her own knuckles turned white. "You can't imagine how happy I am that you found me, Monica. I'm still as marooned as ever, somewhere out at sea. I've never found my way home, I've never learned to trust anyone. I never remarried. I never had any more kids. But I would like to have something on land worth coming home for."

Monica looked into her mother's eyes then, looked at her as an adult for the first time. She didn't intend to judge, at least not in that moment—but rather to understand her mother from the perspective of a woman, a grown woman who was now entangled in her own morally dubious relationship. In those dark, terribly familiar eyes she saw Alma's shame at using Monica, at asking her own child to lie to her father, at failing to shield her from lust, from disaster, from pain and war and death. Perhaps she had been right to go away, Monica thought. She was indeed unfit.

Monica stood. "If you really want peace, Mom, then begin with Dad," she said, remembering Marcy's words on the Fourth of July about Alma's ghost. The entire family needed this exorcism, this purging of the past, and Monica knew that her father had been the one most haunted. Monica briefly grabbed her father's hand and said, "This man spent the last fifteen years thinking that he killed the woman he loved."

Now Alma was looking at her husband, her eyes heavy, her lips pressed together. With as much delicacy as she could muster, Monica said, "You let Dad and Abuela both live with that awful burden, Mom. It's time for you two to talk about that. If my father can forgive you, Mother, then I can." Monica turned and bear-hugged her father at the shoulders. She could see sweat beaded up on his scalp and his skin looked pale. "I'll be up at the station with Claudia and Will. Call to me when you're ready." She got up and walked away, leaving her parents alone for the first time in fifteen years, the tension between them broiling in the thick, salt-laden air.

BRUCE LEANED FORWARD. He pointed at his own heart. "She's right—you could have saved us a lot of trouble by just asking me for a divorce."

Alma had her arms folded in front of her, a defensive position. "You just didn't do that back then, in Salvadoran society. It wasn't even an option."

"Bullshit. You weren't a convent novice. You were a selfish coward."

"I blamed you and my mother. I wanted something far worse than a divorce."

"Ah, now we're getting to the truth." Bruce scratched his scalp and cocked his head to the side. "I understand punishment. I wanted to punish you for cheating. But I wasn't going to take it out on Monica."

Alma pointed her finger at him. "I didn't take it out on Monica, I spared her. That's how I saw it at the time. You were a good father, and I was a bad mother. After I felt strong enough to resume my life and recognize my mistakes, I no longer had any right to her. Am I wrong?"

Bruce raised an eyebrow. "No, you're absolutely right. And I am the better parent. Take just now, for instance. All these years I've been trying to shield her from the knowledge that what she told me that day triggered your death, and you just blurt it all out."

Alma shook her head. "But I'm not dead."

"But others did die."

"Putting everything on the table is the best thing. She's almost thirty, for God's sake."

Bruce exhaled slowly. Alma gripped the edge of the bench with both hands and said, "I'm so sorry I ruined your life, Bruce. I never loved you, you know that. I should have been braver, I should have defied my parents and just followed my heart from the beginning." She made a cutting motion with her hand. "I don't expect you to forgive me. But I do want to say I'm sorry for my actions, because I am."

He stood. "Feel sorry for yourself. You've ruined every chance life gave you to be loved."

She looked down at her toes, pushed the sand about. When she looked up, he saw himself reflected in those impossibly dark eyes. Eyes were supposed to be the mirror of the soul, he thought. They weren't supposed to reflect back your own image. He remembered suddenly that there had always been something terribly lonely about loving Alma, and that was it. You only saw yourself reflected back, you never got a glimpse of what was inside. She pulled at his wrist and said, "Don't go."

He sat. "Why?"

"Because," she said, lifting her fringed eyelids to reveal those black-mirrored irises with no pupil, no center, no heart of vision.

But she was right, there was more to say. He looked into her face, taking in the eternally swollen lips, the double accent marks of her eyebrows, the high swell of her cheekbones, and for a moment, he spoke to the face, not to the woman. "I accept responsibility for getting caught up in your beauty. I *chose* you despite the fact that you told me over and over you didn't want to marry me or have my child. I saw you and Maximiliano together that first weekend your mother invited me to the beach and I chose to ignore it. When your father sent Max away to keep you apart, I seized the chance. That's my contribution to the baggage than ended up on Monica's lap. All I ask of you now is that you make sure that Monica never knows that you didn't want to have her."

Alma winced, remembering the pain of that failed attempt at an abortion. "That was destiny. That child was meant to live." She nodded her head and looked away. "I'll do whatever you say, Bruce. I feel as if life is granting me another chance, if only to seize the peace that honesty can bring."

Bruce pursed his lips and nodded. "Good."

They sat in silence for a moment, then Bruce said, "I have some things to ask of you if you're serious about starting a clean slate."

Alma just raised an eyebrow and looked at him.

Bruce said, "First, you're going to have to come out from under your rock. We're going to get a good lawyer and you're going to strip the Borreros of everything that belonged to your parents." He held his hand up just as she began to protest. "I don't care if it's uncomfortable for you. I don't care what your feelings about money are these days. You're going to force your relatives, and the law, to recognize Monica as the rightful heir to whatever is left of her grandparents' assets, which by now have tripled. You can start there."

Alma opened her mouth, then closed it, then opened it again, then closed it. She held her chin up. "What else?"

"And then you're going to sit down with Claudia Credo"— he pointed toward the marine station—"and tell her everything you know about cone-venom-based drugs and that clinic. Let the health department know who you are and why you're here and what concerns you have with what's going on at Clinica Caracol."

Alma bit her lip and finally nodded. "Okay."

"And no disappearing act. Alma, you had better be reliable and available for this."

She put up her hands. "I promise."

He raised his chin and squinted at her. "I was married to you for thirteen years. I don't trust you."

"Technically, you still are."

He frowned. "Well, I guess that's the third thing. I'm going to need a divorce."

Alma nodded and stood. She picked up the dried seed of an almond fruit and tossed it at the spider monkey. "It'll be my gift to you, Bruce."

Bruce kicked at the sand. "I won't be seeing much of you again, but Monica is an adult and I'm not going to interfere with whatever she decides to do. You're on your own with her, Alma."

"If I do these three things . . ." Her voice trailed off.

Bruce nodded. "Then she'll forgive you."

To keep his hands busy and calm his increasingly frazzled nerves, Will began to play with the baby sea turtles. He was encouraging a wrestling match between the two most aggressive ones. While everyone else kneeled on the sand and played with the tiny creatures, Claudia sat with Alma on a cement bench nearby. Alma said, "As I moved from guerrilla camp to camp, I discovered that the poor and the idealistic can be just as arrogant and dishonest as the rich. I came to realize that my ancestors worked hard to obtain their money. They were intelligent, focused people who didn't exploit anyone, and they deserved what they accrued."

"But your parents, if not your ancestors, were a bit of the elitist stereotype, no?" Claudia asked.

"My parents were the third generation, and that's when the fruit starts to rot," Alma said. "My parents didn't exploit the workers on our properties—at least not by local standards—but they were cold in their hearts, so removed were they from the humility of the poor. And as the sea carried me that day, I remembered exactly what drove Max to fight against the status quo. Everything came down to a memory, the story of which he retold many times. On the day of my seventh birthday party, he stood in line behind the other kids waiting for his turn at an enormous yellow piñata shaped like an airplane. Several kids took a turn at whacking it, and still nobody could break it open. Max grew more and more excited as his turn approached. When someone finally passed the club to him, my mother stepped forward and said, in front of everyone, 'These games aren't for you, Maxito. Go get a garbage bag from the kitchen and help your mother pick up all this trash.'

"I never forgot the humiliation and frustration in his face," Alma said. "Turns out that the expression on his face foreshadowed the feelings of an entire nation." She folded her arms and shook her head. "I never understood how you could work for the military, Claudia."

Claudia shrugged. "Some of us need jobs, Alma. I didn't have a trust fund waiting for me in Miami."

Alma bowed her head, conceding the point. "We each make our decisions based on what we need at the moment, don't we?"

"That we do." Claudia slid her sunglasses over her eyes and folded her hands together. She looked at Monica and smiled. "So, Monica?"

Monica looked at all of them self-consciously. "So Claudia?"

"So is everything resolved between you two?"

Monica shook her head at the boldness and indiscretion of the question. While she really wanted to say something cutting, she knew it was a cultural quirk and was completely unintentional. She searched to find more gentle words. Alma seemed to sink into her own shoulders. "I feel more in control of my past, and therefore my life, Claudia."

"A very diplomatic answer, Monica," Claudia persisted. "But is she forgiven?"

Even Will looked uncomfortable. He put the turtles down

and pretended to be interested in something he saw in the sand. Monica blanched with anger and chose to remain mute. Everyone fell silent. Bruce coughed. Will cracked his knuckles and Claudia's stomach rumbled.

Finally, Monica pointed at the pen of baby turtles. "Where is the mother?"

"Somewhere at sea, of course," Alma answered.

ALMA LISTENED to Will's story in silence until he came to the part about Yvette's treatment. "She's in danger," Alma said gravely. "That's why I'm here. A man was stung by a cone snail while we were traveling in Mexico, what you read about in *Alternative Healing*. The extent of his injuries makes it obvious that the cone venom prevented the 'cascade of chemicals' that typically causes as much injury as the blow itself. Also, there wasn't the normal amount of intracranial pressure damage that follows. I was very excited because someone was smart enough to save the cone, but it wasn't the *furiosus*, it was the *exelmaris*, which is very similar. I began to inject mice with the *exelmaris* venom, but their behavior became bizarre. The synthetic cone toxin Fernanda is using is not based on the *furiosus*, although I know they are fond of hinting that it is. It's a copy of the *exelmaris* venom, the same one I used to immobilize that soldier fifteen years ago."

"They call it *furiosus*-based in the article," Will said.

"That's either a lie, or if we choose to interpret the motivation more kindly—sheer ignorance. In fact, that claim is what tipped me off. The *Conus exelmaris* is similar to the *furiosus* in a lot of ways. But unlike the *furiosus*, the *exelmaris* produces a variety of adverse effects that can linger on indefinitely. Its ability to stimulate the brain is generally acknowledged, but not at all understood."

"It produces aggression?" Will asked.

Alma held up her hand and began to count off her fingers. "Tunnel vision, hallucinations, delirium, paranoia, suicide, and self-mutilation." She held up the other hand. "Another characteristic is that it is much slower to cross the blood-brain barrier than the *furiosus.*"

"How do you know that a mouse is paranoid?" Bruce asked.

"And how does a mouse commit suicide?" Claudia piped in.

"We know the risks to humans because my team interviewed the spouses or parents of some of the patients who checked out of Caracol," Alma replied. "Two committed suicide, one is suspected. As for the treatment that Dr. Fernanda Mendez is offering, the trials are so preliminary that we don't know what the long-term neurological effects are, but even the short term is looking very bad. I do know, from my research"—she placed a hand on her heart—"that it's best if you get her off SDX-71 immediately. Wait until the substance is reengineered."

"So who wrote the article in *Alternative Healing*?" Claudia asked.

"Probably someone on the Borrero payroll," Alma said.

"Do the Borreros and Dr. Mendez know you're hanging around El Salvador?" Claudia asked.

"I think that only Francisca knows. I'm looking for a contact at the health department. I'm preparing a case against its use. But I was having trouble doing it quietly, without giving them the opportunity to switch data, shred documents, et cetera. Plus I wasn't planning on having to deal with the whole issue of my identity."

"I can do it," Claudia said. "I work for the president." Alma nodded appreciatively and Bruce clapped his hands together.

"I'm going to declare an all-out war with my mother-in-law," Will said. "I've already contacted the U.S. embassy for legal support to get Yvette home. I discovered the name of the air transport company, but they don't want to honor the leg home without Sylvia's approval, since she's the one who paid for the round-trip. It's almost five thousand dollars each leg."

"Hold on, Will," Alma said, holding up a hand. "I want to make it clear that in spite of all the risks I just told you about, SDX-71 does have the potential to stimulate certain people to emerge from stupor. Five patients already have."

"Yeah, but what good is it if she just wakes up to suffer all the more?" Will said. "I question the wisdom of waking up someone who doesn't want to wake up. That's my basic problem with this whole thing."

They all looked at each other, a sudden, unspoken feeling of dread spreading among them. Alma said, "Get them to suspend the injections today, Will. While you handle the logistics of your trip home, I'm going to need someone to record specific medical data on Yvette for a period of twenty-four hours. I also need someone to photocopy her medical stats." She looked at Bruce. "Do you think you could pull it off? You can say it's research for your article."

Bruce considered it, then nodded. "I'll do what I can."

"I'll help," Monica piped in. "But I think they've figured out who we are."

Will shook his head, looked down at the sand. "I'm so glad we found you, Alma. I'm grateful for all of you," he said, suddenly making eye contact with all of them, his voice full of emotion. "I can't imagine dealing with this alone."

Ironically, Will's distress over Yvette's situation was providing Monica with a welcome delay in the long and painful process that lay ahead—of absorbing, understanding, judging, and ultimately choosing how she would feel about her mother. She was just beginning to get her heart and mind around the enormity of what had happened in the last few days. But now Will's mission was top priority, and it had quickly forced them to shift their focus to the far more urgent matter of protecting Yvette. Monica could tell, by the dramatic shift in tone of her parents' voices, that they felt the same way. "I don't mean to take away your hope, Will," Alma said. "Depending on the severity of her injuries, the treatment stands a chance of working."

"For how long?" Will asked. ". . . If she were to 'emerge?' "

"That's the part we don't know. People come in and out of this paranoid state and my lab rats are still affected after a long period. It's like an LSD trip that won't end. There isn't any detox treatment we know of, not yet anyway. It shouldn't be used on humans until we can control it on animals. For Fernanda, Leticia, and Marco to candy-coat the risks, in my opinion, is criminal."

Will was pacing. "Would you be willing to repeat everything you just said to my mother-in-law? I want her to hear this. It's why I'm here and not with my wife right now." He glanced at Monica, but she didn't know how to interpret the look he sent her way. "I don't want to have to rip Yvette out of Sylvia's arms and search the suitcases for the air ambulance contract, but I will, as a last resort. Alma, you're my last hope at changing her mind."

"Why don't we bring Sylvia to the *posada* tonight and have her meet Alma?" Bruce suggested.

"I like the idea of appealing to her in this way," Monica said. "She's a smart lady with good instincts. I think she'll pull back on her own if she hears what my mother has to say."

"Alma, would you be willing to talk to Sylvia?" Bruce said.

"Of course," Alma said, but it sounded more like a question, and she looked at her daughter for the answer, as did everyone else. Suddenly Monica understood that it all came down to whether she would allow Alma into their circle, if she was willing to give her wayward mother an opportunity to redeem herself. Monica remembered Will's arms encircling her own waist the night before, and Yvette, so still and tragic, with yellow, parched lips and no future.

"Mom," Monica said, "can you meet us there tonight?"

*　*　*

THE DRIVER dropped Monica, Alma, and Claudia off at the guesthouse. Will insisted on walking Monica to her room. He rushed her into her room and closed the door behind them, not caring who saw. As she parted her lips to protest, he whispered, "Shhh. It's okay," and embraced her tightly. "Are you okay?" he said into her ear. "You look dazed."

She nodded, and when she looked up, he saw dark circles under her eyes. "I just need to sleep for a while."

"Okay. I know." He pulled her to him again and said, "Thank you for asking your mother to come here. I have a feeling that this is all happening a bit too fast, so I thank you from the bottom of my heart." Monica looked up at him, and her chin began to tremble, and it wasn't long before her whole face broke up, and she began to cry. He sat with her on the edge of the bed, not saying anything, just holding her head on his shoulder. He didn't get up when he saw the door handle turn and the door swing open, nor when he saw Bruce's troubled expression as he stood in the doorway watching them.

A few minutes later, Monica kicked them both out, and in the hallway they heard the door lock slide into place behind them. Will asked Bruce to return with him to Caracol to persuade Sylvia to meet with Alma that night. "It works out perfectly," Bruce said. "Remember that you will be sleeping with your wife at the clinic from now on. Sylvia will be coming back here tonight to sleep in your room."

AN HOUR LATER, in the car, Will turned to Bruce and said, "I think you all handled the situation so well. It was really uncomfortable there for a while, with Claudia trying to force Monica into declaring a truce with Alma."

Bruce nodded. "The moral of the story, my friend, is that a

couple must decide early on who's going to mind the home fires."

"But real love is worth pursuing. And what you were pursuing back then wasn't real love. It was infatuation. Right?"

Bruce exhaled and looked out the window. "Love requires having the vision to look beyond today, beyond a pretty face, beyond the rush you get from the chase. It means walking away if she's not good for you, or if you're not good for *her*." He sighed and shook his head. "I should have run screaming the day I met Alma Borrero."

"Hindsight," Will said, hunching his shoulders.

"You know what I've come to believe, Will? That most women seek stability and love, just like you'd expect. But what they *really*, secretly want is a someone who inspires them to risk everything."

"Don't we all?"

Bruce considered this for a moment and said, "Yeah. I guess so."

"And it can happen that someone loves you right back," Will said, joining his two index fingers together.

"It's still not that simple," Bruce said gruffly, holding Will's eyes for a moment before going back to staring out the window.

Will resented, pitied, and respected Bruce's point of view all at the same time. This was a man who only knew failure in love, and whose lone success in the wars of the heart was to protect his child. It was what he did best.

WILL WOULD ALWAYS REMEMBER his arrival at Caracol as the most surreal moment of his life. He would remember the crowd gathered at Yvette's bed. The jubilance in Sylvia's voice, the chatter and the tiny brown nuns gathered like munchkins from *The Wizard of Oz* around Yvette's bed. They parted for him as he walked into the room. Sylvia prattled on about how miraculous

God was and what heroes the staff had proven to be. Yvette was propped up on pillows, and as Will stepped before her bed, he couldn't believe what he was seeing: her eyes fixed on him and followed him as he moved along the side of her bed.

Everyone turned and looked at him, and he felt the weight of dozens of brown velvet eyes fall upon him, along with their sudden hush. "Yvette?" he said softly, as if she might possibly be someone else. He took one of her skinny hands. "Yvette?"

"She spoke earlier," Sylvia said from the opposite side of the bed, tickling the underside of her daughter's chin like a baby's. "Say something, honey. Look, your husband is here."

"Where was I going?" she asked.

"You're okay now, Yvette," Will replied in a hoarse voice.

"Why was I in such a rush?" She wiggled about, and Will saw that she was restrained by arm straps.

Although he felt joy, he felt a sick bloating in his stomach, a lifting and puffing up of its contents, but he didn't understand why. Something about her eyes seemed so unnatural. "Is she okay? Is there any . . . damage?"

"Damage? Of course there's damage," Sylvia said absently. "She was in a car accident."

"Yvette, do you remember our dog, Chester?" Will said, grasping at some comforting memory of their past. "Do you remember the time we entered him in the Newport dog show and he won a ribbon?"

Yvette rolled her eyes up and smiled. "Yes," she said. Then, the smile suddenly disappeared and she squinted at him. "Tell the ocean to leave me alone." He tried to embrace her but she stiffened, and he got a whiff of the ever-present metallic perfume.

"She keeps complaining about the sound of the waves outside," Sylvia said, smoothing her daughter's hair. "Isn't that odd? Most people find the sound of water soothing."

"Shut up," Yvette spat. "Can't you see I'm in danger?"

"In danger of what, baby?" Will pleaded.

"The waves know my name," she said, and looked away. "They know too much."

Will looked at Sylvia and said, "Let's step into the hall for a moment. Something was tugging at him, something that wasn't allowing him to completely rejoice at what appeared to be a miracle.

In the hallway, Sylvia asked, astonished, "Aren't you happy?"

"Of course," he said. "I just want her thoroughly examined."

"At least she's here," Sylvia said, pointing at her temple. "We can work on the rest later."

Maybe she was right, Will thought. Maybe the rest of her was going to be okay. The strange hostility might just be an initial stage, some kind of reentry shock. Sylvia shuffled back into the room because they could both hear that Yvette had just insulted one of the nuns. "Back in a moment," she said.

Will went in search of Dr. Mendez. She was finishing up with another patient, and so he headed back to Yvette's room. He ducked into the chapel for the first time, dropping to his knees on the kneeler and pressing his palms together in prayer and supplication. He simply gave thanks for Yvette's emergence and asked for the strength to handle whatever was to come.

In the silence of the chapel, Will tried to remember if he ever did know where Yvette had been headed on the day of her accident, and why she had been in such a rush. Nothing came to him, and eventually he gave up, figuring that it was irrelevant. He was happy that, at the very least, she had been set free from her terrible limbo. As worried as he was about what Alma had said, he still felt a great softening toward Dr. Mendez and her staff. Maybe the old nanny's suggestion was right on the mark—maybe Alma was trashing the program out of envy.

His thoughts drifted over to Monica. In the last forty-eight hours, his feelings for her seemed to have grown exponentially, expanding across his heart to unwieldy proportions, filling him with hope, strength, and dread at losing her. He was sure of himself in this area, he didn't feel guilt or regret. His marriage to Yvette had been irrevocably altered by the accident, and even though she had recovered some of her faculties, she would never be the same. He had already lived for two years of his life without her, and because of it he wasn't the same person either. He looked down at his left hand, flattened against his right palm. Circling the fourth finger was a band of pale skin where his ring had been. It seemed to glow in the dim light of the chapel.

He felt both fear and a great sweep of relief when the decision came to him: he would sell the house and his prized sailboat to finance whatever was needed for Yvette's subsequent therapy. He would give up Tuesdays and work seven days a week. He would enable a new beginning for Yvette: his own version of the tunneled heart carved in the snow, *Me ato* returning to *Te amo,* at last, duty returning to love, even if it was an entirely different kind of love this time around.

Then, a question presented itself as if it had been spoken by the varnished wood figure of Jesus hanging from the cross before him. What if Yvette's spirit hadn't been released as he'd believed all along? What if her wifely love for him remained intact within her new consciousness? Will squeezed his eyes shut and pinched the bridge of his nose with his thumb and index finger.

Will felt Bruce's heavy hand on his back, and Will was surprised to see the man kneel down next to him, bow his head, close his eyes, and put his hands together in prayer. "I've never put much stock in religion," Bruce whispered out of the side of his mouth. "But today I'm willing to give it a try."

AN HOUR LATER, Yvette was unreactive again. Will ordered the staff to suspend any other treatments, and Sylvia flew into a tirade about her maternal rights. Bruce managed to convince her to come with him to the *posada* to meet Alma, but Will was so angry he had to ride in a separate car. *This is it,* he decided. *To hell with Sylvia.*

A mere two and a half hours had passed since Will had arrived at Caracol. Monica had slept for an hour and later claimed to have fallen into a precipitous slumber that had restored her with some of the energy needed to make it through the day. In the time before the men arrived, the two women had been alone and had begun the long and emotionally exhaustive climb, piecing together the shattered tableau of their lives. So difficult was that first hour alone together that they immediately welcomed the interruption of Will, Bruce, and Sylvia's arrival. Will summoned Claudia, who had been watching the soap opera in the kitchen with the innkeeper, and asked the three women to sit down.

No one expected the news they brought. Claudia's mouth was frozen in the shape of an *o,* and Alma alternated between nodding and shaking her head. Monica sprang to her feet and hugged Sylvia, and then Will, even her father. "I told you prayer works," she said to her father, and everyone unfroze and shared two more rounds of hugs and cheers for Will and Sylvia. "Down deep I must have been a bit skeptical myself," Sylvia confessed.

After a moment, the mood darkened when Will told them that Yvette had slipped back into stupor in only an hour. Alma pulled Sylvia aside and got down to business. Sylvia listened to Alma's warnings, interrupting her to defend the treatment on each point. "I don't care if she has a completely different personality," Sylvia said, smiling. "My love for Yvette is unconditional. She can be whoever she wants to be, and I still want her here with me—alive, awake, able to speak and respond. I'm determined now more than ever to leave her under their care."

"No, we're not," Will said, his fists clenched at his side. "I draw the line here, Sylvia. We're taking her home within forty-eight hours. The entire Neurology Department at Yale is on alert and is anxious to examine her the minute we arrive back in New Haven."

"You'll take her over my dead body," Sylvia said.

"Fine, then we'll pick out your coffin in the morning," Will said. "I'm not screwing around here, Sylvia, she's going home."

Alma put her arm around Sylvia. "Sylvia, we're going to shut Fernanda down. Her supposed sponsor, BioSource of London, is completely phony, invented for credibility. The Borreros *are* BioSource, and the cover will allow them to slink away with the family name unscathed if need be. You got your awakening, now go home. Yvette should be monitored constantly while she's conscious, and she will be again, have no doubt. But she is a danger to herself, especially immediately after a dose. Three of the ten patients who have been through this program appear to have committed suicide."

Monica asked, looking around the room, "Who's with Yvette now?"

"A nurse," Sylvia said. "They were going to take her out to the sunning deck so she could get some sunlight before the sun goes down. They said she needs to produce some vitamin D."

SO THIS IS IT, Monica thought, as she watched Will pace the floor, his face alive with plans to rescue his wife. *I'm finally in love with someone. Really, really in love. Unfortunately, my only reward is to know that it's possible. But I have to fulfill my promise to myself. So in secret, loving sadness, I give him back to you, Yvette.*

Yvette watched the nurse fill the syringe with clear liquid from a small brown glass bottle. The lumbar punctures still hurt, and Yvette blinked back tears as the nurse plunged the needle into her spine.

When she had finished, the woman put Yvette into a wheelchair. Yvette marveled at the concept of mobility; of seeing something other than the same high, closed window with frosted glass from the position of her bed. The woman rolled her out of the room without saying where she was taking her. Yvette saw that other people were lying about in beds, some with eyes open, others with eyes closed, but all of them silent and still.

The nurse took her beyond a set of gates, across a stretch of hard-packed sand, and parked her chair on a wide patio facing the sea. Now she could see a dark beach, strange and desolate as a surrealist painting. The sound of the waves was as soothing as a heartbeat, and she closed her eyes to better listen. The nurse was called away by someone a distance behind them. A few moments passed, and Yvette felt her soul rushed with the drumming of water folding upon itself, of sheets of white foam being stretched and pulled back and elongated until the waves were spread clear and thin as hot glass.

Tch-ch-cht.

Yvette opened her eyes but saw no one. She was having difficulty seeing. Everything appeared as if she were looking through a tube of rolled-up paper.

Tch-ch-cht.

She rotated her neck left and right. Her muscles were still too weak with atrophy to lift her head and get a good look at the source of the sound. Suddenly, the range of her conical vision filled with the face of a small girl. She had a basket balanced on her head. She was spectacularly beautiful, with caramel skin and big, honey-colored eyes: an angel in a dirty and ripped dress. The girl dropped her basket and tiptoed toward Yvette, looking to the left and the right before she smiled.

The little girl reached into her basket and plucked out a tiny chick, absurdly dyed cotton-candy pink, and placed it on Yvette's lap. Yvette looked at the chick's tiny, shiny eyes, its upturned beak, and willed her hand to move across her lap and stroke it. Its fur was so soft that Yvette could hardly believe it. The little girl stepped closer and spilled a handful of feed onto Yvette's lap, and Yvette watched as the chick picked it up in his beak, tilted his head back, and swallowed the tiny pellets. She felt the delicate weight of the bird moving about on her thighs. Yvette began to laugh with the delight of a child, marveling at the sensory proof that she was very much alive. The little girl laughed with her and looked extremely pleased. "You can keep it," she said in Spanish.

Suddenly, Yvette had an overwhelming desire to pull this child into her lap and comb her sun-split hair, teach her to read and write, and love her forever. Yvette looked down at the chick on her lap. It was finishing the last of the corn pellets. "It's time, Yvette," the little girl said in Spanish.

As the bird scooped the last yellow seed, Yvette suddenly remembered why she had been in such a hurry the day of the accident; why she had been so preoccupied that she'd forgot to put on her seat belt. The memory broke loose; and as it rained its details down upon her, it took her breath away.

On that last morning, she had just dropped off the dry cleaning when she saw him. She exited the laundromat, stepped onto the sidewalk, and headed toward the post office, digging through her bag to make sure she had brought the stack of envelopes to be mailed. And there he was, getting out of a car across the street. Yvette froze. She wasn't surprised to feel the old familiar coldness rise in her stomach, she knew it would always be there. Five years had passed since she had last seen him, and yet, it was as if someone had spliced time. Even from across the street, his presence still felt intimate and familiar. He was a bit heavier, but otherwise he looked the same. She had heard that he lived in Arizona now. Yvette felt a slight tremble begin in the bones of her hands, her knees, her teeth. She took a deep breath and tried to pull herself together.

Across the street, he took a step back and opened the rear passenger door of his blue sedan. He leaned into the car, and when he emerged, there was an infant clinging to his chest. A slender woman, whose face was hidden behind sunglasses and a hat, stepped out of the other side of the car and took the baby while he fed coins into the parking meter. Then, he took his wife's hand and they headed toward the Olympia diner.

Yvette stepped back into the laundromat and watched them from behind the safety of the glass storefront. She remembered the date—the exact time, actually—that he'd come to her apartment and told her that it was over between them. After he left (she could still hear the hushed sound of his footsteps on the hallway carpet), she lay awake most of the night, curled up into a ball, shaking violently at the prospect of the approaching morning. After she finally fell asleep, just before dawn, her exhausted body began to sweat, and when she woke up, her pajamas and sheets were completely soaked. He had left her the way an amputated limb leaves the body. There would always be phantom pain for him. Always.

When she had had a few minutes to compose herself, she headed toward her car, forgoing all her morning errands. She slipped into the seat of her Mustang, wondering if he had recognized it parked across the street. As she headed back home, driving fast felt healing and defiant. She had not felt that it was a betrayal of Will to experience this old hurt again. She loved Will in a healthy, trusting way. The love she knew before Will had been a reckless thrill ride to the edge of the universe, a blast that would continue its cascade into empty space as long as she was alive to remember it.

She thought, *He's someone's husband now. A father.* A yellow highway sign warned of a dangerous curve and fifteen-mile-per-hour speed limit.

The chick jumped up excitedly on her lap and Yvette shook her head. What a relief to be free of that terrible bondage, she thought. She remembered that the days after her loss had been even worse than the time spent in limbo.

Her thoughts turned to Will. The unexpected knowledge that he had not been her heart's first choice made her love him even more. Years ago, her own ability to love had been restored by Will's translucent and unspoiled heart, and whether he knew it or not, his loyal old soul would eventually sabotage him. Will would belong to his wife as long as her heart was beating. For better or worse.

And then there was her mother, her biggest worry. By the blinding brilliance of Yvette's brief lucidity, she could see that her recovery was a temporary gift. Eventually, the darkness would descend again and Sylvia would suffer even more. Yvette had struggled so long to arrive at a higher place, to escape the caverns of darkness. She just couldn't return—not for Will, not even for her mother. She was tired, so tired. To stay alive meant a life without dancing, without laughter, without cooking or children or shopping or swimming or sailing. To rot in a bed and wait years for the relief that was being offered to her right now.

The sea wanted an answer, so Yvette got down to the grim math of adding up the reasons she wanted to live, and subtracting the reasons she wanted to die. She had been listening to the call of the sea for days now, and she understood its organic language for the first time in her life. It had a pulse, like a great organ, and it whooshed through the world, energizing, cleansing, communicating, creating. It was frightening and terribly comforting all at the same time. The night before, it had invited her to die.

She felt the familiar snowiness begin to take hold, like a cloud interrupting her reception. She didn't want this anymore, this being snowed under. She shouted, "No more!" The sound of the waves grew louder. The chick, still pecking at her lap, startled and flapped its wings. It jumped out of her lap and onto the ceramic tile floor of the patio and began to run.

Yvette watched as the chick ran away, toward the sea, its toothpick legs racing toward the restless expanse, with no idea where it was going or what it was running from. A wave rose and rushed the chick. She waited but didn't see its head pop up out of the water, and she suddenly understood what she was supposed to do. She remembered seeing the sign in the marina channel that warned NO WAKE. As her heart quickened, she understood that there was a force in the world that had a claim on everything, and that it would take back what was sick and no longer functional and make it clean and whole again.

Finally, a pink dot appeared on the water's surface, then disappeared again, into the tumble of the sea. The reach of each wave thinned into foamy fingers pointing at the land, then directly at her. She was needed elsewhere, it told her. This time, she would not be sidelined in limbo. She would become a part of something immense and mysterious, and she would live again. Upon that beautiful and calming promise Yvette rested her decision: she would go.

Almost immediately, Yvette heard the instructions—explained to her in the strange language of those great liquid heartbeats. She reached down and unlatched the catch on her wheelchair. *"Empújame hacia el mar,"* she said to the little girl, who was waiting at her side. The girl obeyed and gave the wheelchair a strong push. The chair rolled across the tiles, then halted at the point where the sand became dry and loose. The water was still at least fifty feet away. Yvette took the girl's hand and waited.

The water advanced, waves groping blindly for something lost. A single swell broke from the turbulent swirls and rushed forward, stretching farther inland than any other wave ever had. It tore across the vast beach and flooded past the iron gates of Caracol. Salt water contaminated the crystalline Moroccan pool, leaving a brackish mess of seaweed and a carpet of black sand right up to the floor tiles of the entrance. The noise was heard inside, but only by the brain-injured. In the infirmary, toes wiggled, eyelashes fluttered, and smiles of relief spread across ash-white faces.

The sea opened its great yawning mouth and inhaled Yvette. She gave herself willingly, joyfully. Her frail consciousness was replaced by wonder and light, and she burst with the euphoria of death. She dove into the cool expanse and saw, with un-bounded relief and joy, that He was indeed the sovereign of all molecules, the timeless prophet of mercy, order, and hope.

The staff at Clínica Caracol stated that Yvette's death was caused by a pulmonary infection, a common risk of prolonged convalescence. Although Yvette had been taken outside for fifteen minutes of sun exposure, the tide had been high and the waves violent, and so the nurse had returned her to her bed and turned on a television program about hurricanes. Yvette had opened her eyes and spoken once that evening, about ten minutes before the estimated time of death. The nurse reported that Yvette had asked to be pushed "closer to the sea," which she had said in Spanish. The nurse took it to mean that Yvette was interested in the TV show and wanted a better view, so she had adjusted the bed back upward, then pulled the overhead television closer to Yvette's bed. The nurse said that she had heard another patient make a strange sound and left Yvette to go check. There had been a full moon, and for some unknown reason it seemed to trigger restlessness in the patients. A few minutes later, when the nurse returned to Yvette, she saw a single strand of saliva running down the side of her mouth and a peaceful smile on her face.

* * *

THE NIGHT AFTER Yvette's death was spent trying to comfort the bereaved. Claudia took charge of facilitating all the logistics and transportation for everyone, including Yvette's body, which would be taken back home for burial. "The health minister and the president will hear about this tomorrow morning," Claudia promised. "Dr. Mendez and the Borrero investors will be held accountable." Then she bowed her head at the futility, because nothing anyone could do would bring Yvette back.

By 6 a.m., the rooster was crowing again, making it impossible to sleep. Monica threw on shorts and a T-shirt and went to find some coffee. In the hall, she turned and looked out to the street and shivered at the memory of the black dog staring back at her. Just as the legend went, the presence of a black dog had indeed forecast heartbreak.

A half hour later, there was a knock on her door. It was Will. She let him in without a word and held him as he shivered in her arms. "I thought I'd already said good-bye to her," he whispered hoarsely after a while. "This is so hard. It's like we had her by the collar as she dangled off the edge of a cliff." He held his arm out rigidly, gripping something invisible with his fingers. "And we let her fall."

Monica pulled back. "Now hold on. She didn't die from the treatment. She died because her body was under the stress of convalescence and recovery. You didn't *let* her do anything. You, Sylvia, modern medicine, and the clinic kept her hanging on to this world longer than nature would have her stay. God claimed her, Will. Even He couldn't stand seeing her suffer anymore."

"She sent you, you know," Will said, examining Monica's fingers. "And no one is going to convince me otherwise."

"You think so?" Monica said, her eyes opening wide.

"She had a really big heart."

She looked up at him. "It's possible."

He looked at her, and she detected a flicker of lightness in his face for a split second, before the tension returned to his eyes. He pushed himself away from her and stood up.

"I want to pick you up at the airport," he said. "When you get back."

"You'll have your hands full for quite a while, Will."

"I'll make time." He took a deep breath, lifted his chin, and forced a smile. "And you . . . you need to be with your mom for a few more days. Alone."

"It's uncomfortable."

"Do it."

"I am."

They embraced for a long time, but he didn't kiss her. When he left the room, Monica felt a rush of love for him, followed by a nauseating wave of sadness. She fell back on the bed. She understood from his body language that he was gone, in spirit anyway, for a long, long time. While encircled by his sorrowful arms, Monica had had a flashback of the previous day's images: a vacant hospital bed, barren walls, empty vials in the garbage, a monitor with the power cord coiled up. A life, gone.

Will was headed for purgatory, that great sanitarium for mourning hearts.

TWELVE HOURS LATER, everyone had left except Monica. She planned to stay another week with Alma, who made good on her promises by running back and forth from attorneys' offices to public records offices, trying to dodge the swell of interest in her return. Just explaining the whole thing to the bewildered estate attorney took hours. Monica told no one of her intention to meet with her great-uncle Jorge before leaving El Salvador. First, there was something terribly important that Alma and Monica had to do together.

They headed back to the coast for a day and rented a boat in the protected waters of the Golfo de Fonseca. On the floor of the boat were ten crowns of white roses. Six of the crowns represented the campesinos that had been killed on that terrible day. One of the crowns was for Maximiliano Campos, one was for Yvette Lucero, the last two were for Magnolia and Adolfo Borrero. Monica tossed them out like life buoys, each one landing with a soft slap on the gentle waters. Alma's eulogy consisted of only a few words:

"We live because the ocean lives. It is the beginning and end of all things on Earth, and especially us, who are born from water and, in death, return to salt."

Almost immediately, the wind picked up and the wreaths began to drift and turn like wheels carting an invisible weight across the vast expanse of the sea. They spun toward the glimmering place where the sun blurs the horizon, beyond sight, beyond sound, beyond knowledge, or pain or sadness or regret.

"Participate again," Monica heard Alma say. Monica blew kiss after kiss and waved good-bye. As always, she had far less certainty than her mother about life after death. But she was encouraged nonetheless that if Abuela's Christian version of heaven was not awaiting, then at least there was Alma's version, an afterlife in which there were no limits and no waste.

Francisca punched her gnarled fingers into the number pad outside the executive offices at Borr-Lac. "He's only here on Tuesday afternoons," she said. "Down the hall, to the left." She pointed to a clock in the hallway. "He's having his weekly meeting with Fernanda right now. Good luck."

Monica brushed past the secretary and entered her great-uncle Jorge's office. Dr. Fernanda Mendez turned and fixed her orange eyes on Monica. "We were expecting you," she said, and it made Monica doubt that this was truly the spontaneous visit she thought it was. The doctor waved at the secretary. "It's okay, Mirta. Close the door."

Jorge Borrero, younger brother to Adolfo by fourteen years, was sitting behind a vast, empty field of polished mahogany. Now that he had reached his senior years, there was a striking resemblance between the brothers. He stood up, looked at his niece, but didn't say anything. Monica, determined to give blood bonds a fighting chance, brushed past Fernanda and kissed her great-uncle's cheek, pressing her fingers gently into the crisp edges of his dress shirt. He smelled faintly of aftershave and cumin, and his thick, short gray hair was slicked back with hair pomade. She looked into his eyes for a moment, allowing him to take her in too. *"Tienes unos ojos muy bellos,"* he said, pointing at his own eyes. *"Te los regaló tu papá."*

She thanked him for the compliment and turned to look down at his desk, which had been her grandfather's. Oddly, the only items on it were a telephone and a letter opener with an ivory handle. She ran her finger over the beveled edge. "Abuelo bought this in Morocco," she said, smiling broadly. "He bought it from a beautiful Gypsy who turned out to be a transvestite. *Se acuerda, Tío?"*

A cloud seemed to pass over Uncle Jorge's face at the mention of his older brother. He nodded and said, "I remember. Please sit," gesturing across his desk to the chair next to Fernanda.

In the few seconds that it took Monica to walk around the ornately carved desk, a sack of memories burst across her vision, and several long-forgotten moments rushed past her in a stampede. The last image in this unexpected, joyful stream of memory was of herself at seven, kicking off her sandals and hopping on top of that same desk. She loved to pretend to be a monkey, grunting and picking imaginary fleas out of her grandfather's silver hair while he shook with laughter at their secret game. She shook her head. "I'm sorry," she said, putting one hand over her heart. "You look so much like my grandfather now that I'm a bit taken aback." She turned and looked at Fernanda, whose gaze had been on Monica every second since she'd entered the room.

"If you don't mind, Dr. Mendez," Monica said, "I'd like to visit with my uncle alone."

"This is *my* meeting time," Fernanda said, pointing to a clock on the wall.

Monica glanced up at her uncle but he didn't say anything.

She spoke calmly. "My uncle and I haven't seen each other in fifteen years, can't you delay your business?"

Fernanda folded her hands together. "Yes, Jorge and I can finish our usual business another time," she said, and remained seated.

Uncle Jorge looked over at his daughter-in-law-to-be. "Fernanda is in charge of the clinic, Monica. She'd like to hear what you have to say."

"I'm not here to talk about the clinic, I'm here to talk about family matters, Tío."

"I am part of the family now," Fernanda insisted. "A very big part."

"Please leave us alone," Monica persisted. "I promise that it doesn't concern you."

Fernanda flexed her jaw, pressed her hands together, then swept her eyes back up to Monica. She patted the seat next to her. "Sit," she commanded.

Time to change tactics, Monica thought, so she slid her bottom onto the edge of her uncle's desk. Now a full foot above both of them, she folded her arms in front of her the way she had seen women do on the covers of business magazines.

"Like I said, I'm not here to discuss your clinic. I'm here to talk to my uncle about more personal matters. *Alone.*"

Fernanda narrowed her eyes. "Who the hell do you think you are?"

"You know exactly who I am, Doctor. And if you're confused about *your* role, then let me remind you that you are not yet a member of this family. You are a paid employee, and I, a Borrero, am asking you nicely to leave me alone with my uncle."

Fernanda threw her head back and laughed. "You're a Borrero in name only. You have *zero* power." She cupped the shape of an *o* with her fist.

"Then what I have to say shouldn't matter."

Fernanda stood up, pointed at Monica, and leaned over the patriarch's desk. "She's here to raid the family treasures and our clinic." Fernanda turned her head long enough to flash Monica a murderous glare. "That affects me personally," she said, burying the tips of her fingers into the letters embroidered across the breast of her lab coat.

"Then let's make an appointment to fight about it another time, Fernanda," Monica said coolly. "At the risk of sounding like a broken record—what I'm here to discuss is none of your business."

The uncle broke his eye contact with Fernanda and nodded at Monica. "I'm going to grant my niece her wish, Fernanda."

When the office door slammed behind Fernanda, Monica sighed in relief. "I wouldn't expect anything else from Maximiliano's daughter."

The uncle raised a hand. "That's in the past."

Monica looked down at her pink toes for a moment, then said, "Actually, it's not, Tío. Would you be surprised to know that my mother isn't dead?"

"I already know about your mother."

Monica leaned over the desk, propping herself up on her arms, just as Fernanda had a few minutes before. "How long have you known this?"

"Years. Even fish will talk if you pay them enough." He laughed the only laugh Monica would ever hear from him.

"When were you going to tell me? Are my dad and I the only morons in the world who didn't know this?"

He cast his eyes down for a moment before saying, "No one outside the family knows, except Francisca and Fernanda. Francisca is the only one who knew all along. I personally figured it out five years after Alma disappeared." He shrugged. "It was Alma's wish to be forgotten. I wasn't going to interfere."

Monica held back her urge to say, *Of course not. You wanted her to remain missing for the seven years it took to declare her dead in*

order to keep her money. But she bit her tongue. Her goal was to gain an impression of where this man's heart was, as free as possible from her parents' emotional filters. Was he the rat her father made him out to be? Since there was little time to waste, she decided that she had to go on the offense to disarm her uncle of his legendary frostiness and speak to his heart.

Monica dragged one of the chairs next to her uncle's, and without flinching, she sat, leaned forward, and took his old, manicured hand in hers. Jorge stared down at his hands in disbelief, as if she had just snapped him into a set of handcuffs. Monica instinctively understood that Jorge Borrero had been raised a gentleman. As long as she held those hands hostage, she literally held on to the truth. She took a deep breath, looked into his familiar old eyes, and began:

"In the years after my mother disappeared, you and the other family members just let me drift away. I had been through this traumatic event and yet there were no letters, no invitations, no word sent that you wanted me to remain a part of the larger family. I know you think I'm here to talk about money, and you're not entirely wrong. But for me, what's at the heart of everything else is this." Monica felt her voice tremble, and it made her angry to sound so vulnerable. She took a deep breath. "I'm here to ask you why you allowed the divisiveness, Tío Jorge. *You.*" Monica squeezed both of his hands hard to accentuate her point. "*You* were in a position to bring unity to the family. *You* are the patriarch. Everyone follows your lead. But you pushed me out even farther. I want you to look me in the eye and tell me your side of the story."

Now instinct overcame the uncle's fine breeding and he tried to pull his entire body away, but Monica gripped his hands harder. By his wriggling and his facial expression Monica could see that the hand-holding and close proximity made the old man uncomfortable beyond the experience of his eighty-two years. "It's now or never, Tío. Everything else goes from here."

She slid her hands up to his wrists, sliding her thumbs up so that the yolks of her fingers nestled directly over his pulse. It was an old trick—it's almost impossible to lie to someone who is taking your pulse.

Jorge began to perspire. He was tongue-tied for a second or two, before he straightened up and said, "Your mother has been nothing but trouble for this family."

Monica shook her head and laughed bitterly. "You think you're telling me something new?"

Silence. He dropped his head.

Monica tugged at his hands. She had arrived at the core of her visit with one simple and direct question: "Did you value my grandparents' money more than me? Yes or no."

"It's not that simple."

"Yes or no."

"Adolfo left a lot of debt!" he burst out. "He almost ran us into the ground."

"I don't believe it, but I'll grant it for now. That still leaves my grandmother's family money. She had inherited even more than Abuelo had earned in his life."

Jorge finally managed to yank his hands away and push himself back in his chair. "You want my story? *Bien,* I'll tell you what you want to know." He stood up and turned his back to her, facing a large window that overlooked Borr-Lac's operations. "After Alma left, Magnolia began to show signs of dementia. I could see the loneliness and sadness that she endured at losing her daughter, son-in-law, and granddaughter all at once." He turned at the waist only, a surprisingly sprite movement for an old crow. "I was running Borr-Lac alone, and I saw to it that your grandmother was cared for. You and your father were nowhere to be found." He turned his back again.

"I was twelve!" Monica cried. "What could I do?" She refused to accept his back, so she walked up and stood in front of him, blocking the view out the window.

"Magnolia died in *my* arms." He said the word *my* slowly. By the furtive casting down of the eyes, Monica detected the presence of something hidden. She recalled the way he had practically winced when she had mentioned his resemblance to her grandfather. *Holy cow,* Monica thought, *was Jorge in love with my grandmother?*

"Tío, I'd give anything to have been present for her when she died. I loved my grandmother very much, and I appreciate that you took care of her when she needed it. I'm also sure that you understand that I was too young at the time to be accountable for anything. But the fact remains that I am Adolfo and Magnolia's granddaughter, and you know very well that they adored me." Monica's voice rose, and tears sprang up in her eyes as she pronounced the last sentence. She dared to point to the center of her uncle's chest. "Your role in their life does not entitle you to keep everything that belonged to them."

Jorge took a step back, bumping into his leather chair. "Magnolia left everything to your mother. Your mother desired to be considered dead, and after seven years, she was. As the executor of her estate, I reinvested the money into the family business, including the clinic. Everything is as it should be, Monica." He pointed to the factory floor. "That money was earned here and here it will stay."

Now Monica's tears were flowing freely. She dried her cheeks by rubbing them against each shoulder, like a child. She stood tall and said, "Yesterday, my mother asked forgiveness for abandoning me. I'm standing here waiting for you to do the same."

Jorge pulled his eyes away. Again he looked past Monica back down at the activity below. "And your price is monetary?"

"Don't worry about the price. Just say you're sorry. And *mean* it."

He frowned and looked away.

After a moment of waiting, which seemed to last a thousand

years, Monica stepped away. She slapped her hand on his desk and said, "*Bien.* My grandparents' money has done enough harm in the world. That's going to have to change."

He nodded, finally breathing easy in the familiar, combative atmosphere he had expected. He almost sounded cheerful. "Like Fernanda said, we were expecting this from you. My lawyers are ready, Monica. Go ahead and just try to touch our money."

Despite her anger, Monica felt a string of sadness for this end. Bruce and Alma had been right, these people were unworthy. Still, she had seen that little trace of humanity at the mention of her grandmother—a little nugget of emotion, a pearl of love lost in a field of greed. It was all she needed. She could move on without the Borreros now.

Alma and Claudia took Monica to the San Salvador airport. "My guess is that it'll be a good six months before you have to come back," Claudia said. "We found the original will, before the family had Magnolia rewrite it. You could end up with one-third of Borr-Lac, the house in San Salvador, and Caracol. As for Fernanda and Marco, they both had their professional licenses revoked. That's the best we can expect, given their contacts and the network of muscle behind the family. The best possible scenario is getting the venom-trial family members back here to give testimony. I'd just advise you to be careful. Stay as far away from the Borreros as possible. You never know what they'd do to hold on to their money."

Monica said, "Will wants to help you shut them down at all cost. He said he'd fly back ten times if need be."

"Who's picking you up at the airport?" Alma asked.

"My friend Paige," Monica said, then, in a soft, chaste voice, "and Will."

"Not Kevin?" Claudia said.

"Kevin and I broke up a few days ago," Monica said. "He

got asked out by our city mayor's daughter, a girl he knew from grade school. He said he was calling to give me a chance to stop him from going out with her. But I didn't. I threw that fish back into the water, as they say."

"But why?" Claudia said. "Why would you let a perfectly good man slip away?"

Monica smiled. "Kevin . . . Kevin was born in Milford and Kevin will die in Milford. He's very involved in town politics. In fact, a long time ago, he told me he'd like to be mayor of Milford, so whether he knows it or not, this is the girl he's going to marry. I took it as a sign."

"You're okay then?" Alma said.

"Yeah."

"And Will?" Claudia said, giving Monica a sideways look.

"I'm sure we'll be friends for life" is all Monica would volunteer for now. She turned to her mother. "Mom, do you remember your credo on how to judge a man?"

Alma squinted. "What credo?"

"You said that as women we should only choose men who can change the world, deliver justice, save what's precious, bring exceptional beauty to the world, or at the very least, deliver it of pain."

Alma shook her head. "*I* said that? Really? . . . No wonder I'm still alone." The flight attendant announced the seating groups. "Christmas break," she said, grabbing Monica by the elbows. "Think about it. I know you would love Costa Rica."

Monica felt a flood of relief as she walked down the Jetway and onto the aircraft that would transport her back home to Connecticut. She looked over her shoulder and saw the two women waving good-bye. She felt so emotionally raw that she longed to go home, to be alone for a few days to go grocery shopping, do her laundry, clean out the freezer—to examine the last few weeks' events from the safe perch of distance and solitude. Up in the air, Monica stared out the tiny window of the airplane. Below, the quilt of farms and the musculature of El Salvador's mountains and volcanoes pulled away from her vision and evaporated into mist.

Monica would tell Paige and Will, on the ride home, that she hadn't forgiven her mother yet, nor did she completely trust her. But she admitted that she had begun to feel something akin to peace after the ceremony on the boat. "She looked so sad when she tossed the flowers in her mother's name," Monica said. "I saw a level of pain and regret in her face that made me turn away, like I was invading her privacy. Later, I thought, 'Good, it *should* hurt. We used to be a family.'"

NOW THAT THE FOG of mystery that had surrounded Alma's disappearance was cleared, Monica felt that it was her duty to correct all the mistakes of the past as best she could. Alma had rejected the role of heiress, and she obviously had no regrets. But Monica had so many loving memories of her grandparents and her childhood (an idyllic time she thought of as "BA"— "before the affair") that she didn't share the same repulsion toward inheriting her grandparents' property. Monica knew in her heart that her grandparents had never intended to disinherit their only granddaughter. They would gladly have skipped a generation and given it all to Monica had they foreseen the events that would follow Abuela's death.

The living Borreros were a formidable legal opponent—but between Bruce, Alma, and Claudia there was an impressive arsenal of contacts and long-buried friendships in high places that could possibly level the battlefield. Monica was back home, putting away her folded laundry, when she started to plan what she would do with all that money.

Monica wanted to convert the land around Negrarena into a preserve. She wanted to re-create her paradise so that other children could experience it as she had. She wanted to travel back and forth as she pleased between her two worlds, Connecticut and El Salvador. To have a baby someday. To roam the beach and teach her child to identify sea creatures, to pass on the secrets that those seashells were still whispering in her ear.

Perhaps Negrarena's destiny was locked in the past, in the mire of mistakes and betrayals of the Borrero family. Perhaps it was no coincidence that her maternal great-grandfather had been a doctor and that she was a physical therapist. Maybe her destiny as the abandoned child was a cleansing of the family greed, a purification of the past into a future of simplicity—a return to the old values of land and sea, of family, community, and healing.

Several days after she arrived back in Connecticut, Monica put on a swimsuit and sat on the rock wall just outside her cottage, facing Long Island Sound. The sound of nearby voices made her turn her head. Her neighbors were on their patio preparing to barbecue. They waved and shouted, lifting their glasses to her. Monica waved but declined their invitation to join them. She turned back to the water. Her heart was heavy.

Since Monica had chosen to remain in El Salvador for an extra week, she had missed Yvette's burial. Two days after returning to Connecticut, Monica had cut an armful of blue hydrangeas from her garden, got in her car, and followed Sylvia's directions to the cemetery until she found the landmark she was looking for. She got out of her car and walked up a grassy, sloping hill. A short distance away, at the bottom of the slope, she saw Will. His back was to her, and he was seated on a white folding chair across from Yvette's marker. His head was bowed in grief or prayer, and Monica couldn't tell if his shoulders were shaking or if it was just the wind rippling across the light fabric of his shirt. Her first instinct was to comfort him; to shout his name and run down the hill to embrace him. Instead, she put the flowers down in the middle of the path and took a step back. She quietly slipped into her car and went home.

The gray water lapped at the edge of the rock wall and Monica dipped in a foot, then the other, and slipped off the wall into the knee-high water. She winced. Even in summer, the Sound was so much colder than Negrarena. The breeze sweeping over the water carried the scent of fresh seaweed, and Monica imagined the motion of their strands as they swayed in the liquid wind below. Once her feet no longer touched bottom, she filled her lungs, dropped her head, and kicked down into the dim silence. She immediately sensed the presence of a million mollusks gurgling and burrowing deeper into their hideaways just below the surface of the sand.

I'm becoming one of them, she thought, recalling the generational chain of shell seekers—Alma, Abuela, and the great-grandfather who had studied the still-at-large *furiosus.* Back in El Salvador, Alma had told Monica that her research into the family tree had yielded even more ancestral connections to the sea, and especially to seashells. "Our bones are coated with mother-of-pearl," Alma had said. "Our aquatic intelligence is just the delay of our evolution, a mutant inability to forget our lives as lower forms."

Monica had laughed and said, "Where *do* you get these ideas?" But she'd cast her eyes to one side because it also sounded perfectly true.

Underwater, Monica opened her eyes, feeling the sharp sting of salt. She swam near the rocky bottom, following its gentle downward slope. She looked up at the wall of light floating above her. She saw the shape of a single maple leaf touch down on the surface. Monica was suddenly struck with a sense of déjà vu—coupled with the certainty that what she was looking at somehow held an echo of Yvette Lucero's life, and even more so when she swam up toward the leaf and it hastened its drift away from her reach.

When Monica's foot touched bottom again, she lifted her face up to the sun, filling her aching lungs with the damp summer air. *How strange and inexplicable,* she thought, *for a human being to understand the language of water.* And there, in the lack-luster gray chop of the Connecticut shore, Monica received her inheritance—or perhaps just now fully recognized the rarity and wonder of that gift. In the curling symmetry of the waves all around her, she deciphered a kind of handwriting in motion. It told of the sea's precision, of its unbroken circling of the world, of its solemn duty to clean, kill, and create. She was astonished that her mother had been right about so many things. Now Monica saw the obvious parallel between the sea and the life span of a soul: it paraded across the horizon in a hurried and glimmering journey with no beginning and no end.

bonusPAGES

SANDRA RODRIGUEZ BARRON was born in Puerto Rico and grew up in El Salvador and Connecticut. She holds an MFA in creative writing from Florida International University, and now lives in Connecticut with her husband and young son. This is her first novel.

READING GROUP GUIDE 3

QUESTIONS FOR DISCUSSION

1. Seashells are ever present in this novel. How are these objects a controlling metaphor in the story? Are there any similarities between the nature of seashells and the nature of any of the characters?

2. Monica is said to have an unusual talent for massage that is based on a razor-sharp tactile intuition. How does this characteristic relate to, lead to, and perhaps foreshadow the unusual talent that she discovers in the end?

3. Will Lucero and his mother-in-law both love and care for Yvette, yet are constantly at odds about the decisions relating to her care. Were your sympathies weighted with one character more than the other?

4. Will Lucero is torn between his loyalty to his wife and the hopelessness of her medical condition. At what point do you think the spouse of a mentally incapacitated person can move on emotionally to love another person?

5. The object of Alma's quest, the *Conus furiosus*, is never found in the span of the story. Do you think the pursuit of something that could potentially do so much good is worth a lifetime of sacrifice, even if it is never found?

6. Monica falls in love with Will first because of his physical appeal, then his humanity, then the intimacy of their situation as they struggle together in El Salvador.
Did you feel conflicting loyalties toward Monica and Yvette?

7. Do you think that the subconscious can influence the body during a traumatic event or illness? Did the cone venom treatment ultimately free Yvette or did it kill her?

8. Monica was herself a victim of adultery. When she reports her mother's errant behavior to her father, she unwittingly sets off a chain of events that cause a tragedy. Was Bruce Winters wise in hiding that fact from Monica all these years?

9. The sea is as much a character in this novel as are the people. Have you ever lived in a place where nature affects the routines, work, emotional, or spiritual nature of the humans who live nearby? How does Monica's description of her life in Connecticut set up the contrast to the mystical aura of Negrarena?

10. Throughout the novel there is a tension between opposites: Catholicism versus the spiritual nature of the sea, traditional medicine versus experimentation, wealth versus poverty, marriage versus adultery, anger versus forgiveness. Do you think that Monica has managed to strike a balance between these forces by the end of the story?

11. Monica is ultimately rewarded with three gifts that she did not initially seek: love, money, and a rare spiritual/intellectual inheritance. Do you think that Monica is better equipped than her mother to handle these gifts?

12. Do you think that Monica and Will might eventually get together—or will Monica's newfound gifts set her on a new, solo path? Is Will a good match for her, given who she becomes at the end of the story?

13. Do you think that Monica will follow in her mother's footsteps in any way?

A CONVERSATION WITH SANDRA RODRIGUEZ BARRON

As a writer, what interests you in a novel?

A novel allows you to get to know characters in the most intimate way, to hear their private thoughts, to witness their joys, fears, shames. Unless you're eavesdropping, reading a novel is the only time you get to know what other people talk about behind closed doors. It provides a way to view another mind and, therefore, another world.

Is there a part of you in Monica Winters?

I would have a lot of biographical facts in common with Monica, and we have a similar temperament. If she were real we would be great friends, but the events of her adult life are very unlike mine, as is our family life.

Who or what does Alma Borrero represent?

Alma Borrero is highly flawed, especially as a wife and a mother, but I admire her for having the guts to reject cultural expectations that she finds to be personally inappropriate. I haven't always been gutsy in this way, especially when I was younger. I find that Latin American culture can be especially inflexible in its expectations about what a woman should do with her time, how she should look, and how she should behave. There is the emphasis on physical beauty and a general lack of appreciation of depth or intellect in young women. Alma isn't remotely interested in beauty, wealth, society, or even being a wife and mother—all the standard feminine values. Alma is constantly going against the grain of what's expected of her, and that can be exhausting if you're doing it all your life. The tragedy of her family life is the consequence of a single moment of weakness in which she compromised with her parents and married a man she didn't love. Her otherwise stubborn nature represents a kind of feminine ideal to me, and I admire that unflinching focus on her life's passion. I find her fascinating.

What kind of research did you have to do to write Heiress of Water?

I had to research a lot of the details of El Salvador's civil war. Since I was Monica's age at the time, my perspective on those events was that of a child, and so I had to go back to books and old newspapers to process it with an adult mind. Marine science and head trauma were subjects that I had to research extensively, and in addition to consulting books and academic and professional journals, I did some field research by consulting with experts in both subjects.

There was this one perfect, sunny day when I got in my car and drove out to Sanibel Island to visit a shell museum, to speak with mollusk scholars, and view their vaults full of cones from around the world. In the quaint downtown area, I found shell boutiques that catered to serious collectors, where rare seashells were displayed (and priced) like jewels. After I'd gathered more information on shells than I could ever use in twenty novels, I drove around the island and combed the beach for its famously abundant seashells, gathering a few souvenirs to remind me of this lovely day. I was utterly smitten with Sanibel's natural beauty. I imagined that Alma and Monica would one day meet here for a vacation. They'd be in heaven.

What compelled you to write so lovingly about seashells and the sea?

One of the fondest memories I have of growing up in El Salvador is of combing remote, virginal black sand beaches for seashells. Every once in a while, I'd find something that looked like it was designed by Dr. Seuss, whimsical and inviting to the imagination. Back then, it never occurred to me to buy a book that classified them, I was just happy to clean them and take them home and enjoy their strange beauty. It wasn't until I started writing about those recollections that I saw the opportunity to give those memories structure by adding a scientific perspective. As I began to research mollusks and seashells in general, I discovered that there is an entire subculture of people who are obsessed with seashells, collectors who attend conferences and pay thousands of dollars for the rarest ones. Although I am not a collector myself, I could empathize with this passion, so I let the research guide my imagination. Later, when I stumbled upon the real-life research that is being done on the medicinal potential of cone venom, I was further captivated.

As for the sea, I have lived near a shore all my life: in El Salvador, in Connecticut, and I lived in Miami for ten years. I lived in one of those high-rise apartments with a floor-to-ceiling view of Biscayne Bay, and I always enjoyed watching sailboats as they seemed almost to parade across my living room. I took sailing lessons out of a marina in Coconut Grove. In Connecticut, I also went boating and sailing with relatives and friends, and I have always derived a very calm, spiritual feeling from being near water. But there is something about El Salvador's remote beaches that is intensely spiritual and artistically inspiring to me—maybe it's the nature, the solitude, the irony of violence that happened in the land beyond. I have no doubt that the psychology of color plays a role—a crowded beach of powder-white sand is festive, but a deserted beach of black, volcanic sand calls to mind richer and darker moods. Since my parents live in El Salvador, I am still able to maintain a connection with those places that so captivated me as a child. Negrarena is a fictional place, loosely based on a place called Playa El Cuco on the eastern shore.

Why did you choose to write about someone who is in a persistent vegetative state?

The subject of unconsciousness surged up during the process of mining my own life for material. When I was eleven, my brother contracted a virus that left him in a coma for two weeks. I have never been in a coma, thank heaven, but I have fainted at least a half dozen times, and each time, I experience this sensory rush, a loud ringing in my ears and flashing lights in my vision, it's very scary, and I always think that I'm dying. A few years ago, I compiled a huge amount of research on the subject out of pure curiosity. From fainting and my brother's coma, my interest began to include even more serious conditions. Eventually, I realized that there are many elements in this area that still remain a mystery to science, and anything we don't know can be claimed by imagination. The scenes inside Yvette's head were some of the wildest writing I've ever done. I related it to my own scary fainting experiences, where being "kicked out" of consciousness is much like being incarcerated, a claustrophobic cell from which I would desperately want to escape.